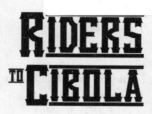

"With two Golden Spur Awards, Norman Zollinger has already established himself as a master."
—Tony Hillerman

"A strong, affecting novel, full of the taste and fragrance of the Southwest."
—Richard Bradford
author of *Red Sky at Morning*

"The raw beauty of New Mexico is the setting of this fine novel . . . which presents a family saga inter-woven with a man's struggle to exist in two cultures."
—Rudolfo Anaya
author of *Bless Me, Ultima*

"Norman Zollinger is a modern master of historical fiction."
—Win Blevins
author of *St-*

"Few write as knowledgeably and a~
Norman Zollinger!"

Forge books by Norman Zollinger

Not of War Only
Riders to Cibola

RIDERS TO CIBOLA

NORMAN ZOLLINGER

THE OVERLOOK PRESS
NEW YORK

This edition published in the United States in 2009 by

The Overlook Press, Peter Mayer Publishers, Inc.
141 Wooster Street
New York, NY 10012

Cataloging-in-Publication Data is available from the Library of Congress

Printed in the United States of America

1 3 5 7 9 8 6 4 2
ISBN 978-1-59020-289-0

For Gerrie

"Granted that they did not find the riches of which they had been told, they found a place in which to search for them, and the beginning of a good country to settle in."

—Pedro De Castañeda de Najera
Relación de la Jornada de Cíbola, 1543

INTRODUCTION

SEEN FROM THE AIR BY ONE UNFAMILIAR WITH HIGH DESERT LANDSCAPES—
as Norman Zollinger was the first time he saw it—the Tularosa
Basin must look surrealistic. Geologists call it a rift—a place
where the earth's crust sank thousands of feet, forcing mountains
upward on both sides. Now, eons later, erosion has smoothed
the mountains, partially filling the basin, and volcanic action
has produced new mountain ranges inside the rift. Parts of the
basin are covered with deep layers of lava—like a rough sea of
black ink somehow frozen at mid-storm. Parts of it are covered
by mile after mile of white gypsum dunes—the glittering dry bed
of an ancient lake. Looking down on this from a plane, one sees
an immense, empty landscape in which blacks and whites verge
into a dozen shades of blue and gray. Green, the color of fertility,
of humidity, and of money, is there only if you look high up the
mountain slopes. It's not a hospitable landscape. The scale is
too large for human comfort. It makes most people feel vaguely
uneasy, threatened, out of control.

Zollinger saw it first from the nose of an AT-11 bombing
trainer. He was stationed at the nearby Roswell Army Air Force
base, a boy from the green fields and treelined streets of Downers
Grove, Illinois. He was learning to be a bombardier. The Army
was using one of the basin's many empty places as a bombing
range. Writing about it forty years later, he recalled the stunning
effect of his first look at the basin—the space, the emptiness,
the startling contrast between the midnight black of the lava
malpais and the white of the dunes. He remembered how he
was "haunted by the notion of something fascinating lying
beyond the low piñon-studded hills we could see from Roswell,

something brooding under the haze which hinted of lofty peaks farther west . . . 'something lost beyond the ranges, something hidden, go and find it,' as Kipling put it."

After the war eight years passed before he returned to the Tularosa Basin. He came with his wife to visit one of her friends—the daughter of the owner of Indian Tank Ranch, which is on the edge of the lava flow country we call malpais. They reached the ranch house in the middle of the night after the long drive down from Albuquerque, which culminates in a jolting, jarring fifteen-minute ride over the track from the highway. At sunrise the next morning Zollinger saw the basin at ground level for the first time.

"There it all was, through the south bedroom window," Zollinger wrote in a subsequent essay. "To the east, still a threatening black against the morning sun, was big Carrizo Peak. My eyes started there and made the circuit. Indian Divide, the high gap between the Capitans and the Sacramentos, was half-hidden under a bank of clouds, giving no sign of the road that snaked across it on its way to Roswell. Sharply pointed Nogal Peak jabbed the sky a little farther south. And to the right, but a score of miles more distant, the twin domes of Sierra Blanca, the 12,000-foot monarch of the range, peered over the ridge line of the nearest mountains. From there the land made a breathtaking drop into an inverted parabola, rising sharply against the San Andres Mountains and the lower, rounded Oscuras in the immediate southwest. It was empty land, hard land, land I knew at a glance was probably cruel at times. And it was beautiful. My love affair with the Tularosa began that morning. I got a sweet ache in my throat that brilliant morning I could never swallow away completely even if I wanted to.

"Small wonder, now that I look back, that when I decided to become a storyteller, it was the Basin I chose to set my stories in. There were, of course, practical reasons for doing this. The land itself would be my principal character. Keeping my invented people at work on the vast, strange stage would lend my work a unity I lacked skill to achieve in any other way."

Those of us who list *Riders to Cibola* among the premier novels of realism and those judges who selected it for the Golden

Spur Award as the best novel of Western America of its year disagree with Zollinger's self-deprecating attitude about his skill. But the harsh and beautiful landscape of the basin is indeed a principal force moving it. It effects the action. More important, it has affected the characters. These people have indeed been invented in Zollinger's imagination, but that imagination was stimulated by the flesh-and-blood occupants of the Tularosa rift—by its ranchers, country lawyers, hired hands, and handy-men, and by the women who share, through love or by choice, this high, dry, empty place. They tend to be a little conservative, a little traditional, these Tularosa Basin people. There is honor in this novel, and courage, and endurance, as well as love.

Riders to Cibola was brought out by the Museum of New Mexico Press, a tiny appendage of the state museum system that published scholarly and scientific works. It had never dealt with fiction. There was no promotion budget and not much distribution. But word of mouth did its work. Readers told their friends. Zollinger's first novel became New Mexico's number one bestseller. It set an all-time record—which I doubt will ever be broken—for months on the bestseller list. Among those of us who know the basin and its people, time now has made *Riders to Cibola* a classic of our literature.

—Tony Hillerman
Albuquerque, New Mexico
July 1988

ORIGENES

Ramos, Chihuahua, 1900

TEN-YEAR-OLD IGNACIO ORTIZ LOOKED ACROSS THE CARVED DESK to where the troubled face of Padre Julian was bathed in the flickering yellow light of the oil lamp. The deep furrows which scored the old priest's face were beginning to soften, and the stern passionless mask which had greeted the boy when Brother Ramírez hauled him bodily into the study was sagging into sorrow and confusion. Ignacio had squirmed and twisted with all his might while in the grasp of the brother; once released he stood quietly and respectfully in front of the desk. As much as he hated everything else about the mission orphanage, his affection for the good padre was so great he could do nothing else.

It will be like the other times I ran away, Ignacio thought. There will be the talk—which will solve nothing—and then the whipping. He glanced to the corner where the long cane leaned, wondering how many times its length had flashed across his thin back. Well, it would hurt much less this time. The frail old cleric's arm had weakened pitifully in the three years Ignacio remembered, and he suspected the heart and will to punish were almost gone as well. The good man now suffered more than *he* did in these sessions. The next time he ran he must plan more carefully and spare Padre Julian this pain.

The padre laced his fingers across his chest and stared up into the shadows while Ignacio waited. For five minutes there wasn't a sound except for an occasional sigh from behind the desk.

"I am sorry, padre," Ignacio said, finally.

The priest nodded. "I know, Ignacio." He stood up and walked around the desk and placed his hands on the boy's shoulders. "Did you remember anything this time, Ignacio?"

"No, padre. Nothing. It was the same," Ignacio said. He drew a breath, and then asked again, as he always did, "Padre, will *you* tell me—now?"

The priest looked stricken. *Verdad*, the boy thought, nothing has changed, but I *must* try—once more.

"*Por favor,* padre." He knew his tone was flat and without fervor, compared to the pleas he had made so many times before. "Who am I, padre? Where did I come from? Why am I here?"

The aged priest slowly shook his head. "I cannot tell you, my son. Even if I did, you wouldn't really *know*. It would be like telling you about a stranger."

"But, padre"—he certainly could plead on this point—"it would still be better than the way I am!"

"No, Ignacio." The gentle voice did little to ease the agony of being defeated yet again, and as the expected words came once more, the boy made a vow that this time would be the last.

"No, my son. You must pull the past out of its dark corner by yourself—but with God's help. Pray, Ignacio, pray. Pray hard!"

Dios! Didn't Padre Julian know how many prayers he had offered up these past three years? Hadn't he seen him often enough on his knees in front of the Blessed Virgin? Didn't he know he had never passed a *camposanto* on the rocky hills around the mission without bending his back?

None of the prayers had worked, none had brought the faintest glimmer. The past, his past, remained as securely locked away as it was the day the old woman walked him up the hill to the mission. That was so long ago, he could scarcely remember her now, though it was the old woman he looked for when he ran away. He never told the padre or the brothers about her, nor had he told them of the only other clue he had—the dream.

It always took the same form, and he had dreamed it so often now he could see it clearly in the middle of the brightest day: the dim familiar figures in front of the wall; himself running toward them with his arms outstretched; the moment of recognition almost there—and then the wall growing whiter, becoming incandescent, blinding him, the wall alone, higher, thicker, more impenetrable by far than the massive adobe one around the mission.

"I *have* prayed, padre," was all he said.

"*Bueno*, Ignacio." The priest took his hands from Ignacio's shoulders and walked to where the cane leaned in the corner, "And now, my son, your punishment."

Ignacio was right. He hardly felt the blows. As they fell, one after another, each one softer than the one before, he made his final plan.

He had gone east to the great sea once in his searching flights, twice to the south, and once west into the Sierra Madres. Each time they had found him and brought him back. This time—and it must be soon—he would go in the last untried direction.

There was a river in the north, a great one, so he had heard. It was unlikely the brothers would follow him beyond its banks. He would cross that river, and see if something was hidden there to help him.

1

Chupadera County, New Mexico Territory, 1905

"FIFTEEN DOLLARS A MONTH, WITH ROOM AND BOARD, OF COURSE," THE big man said to the slim Mexican boy riding beside him. "Your own place, too, Ignacio—just a shack, but your own."

They rode on for ten more yards before the boy answered. He didn't look at his companion, but kept his eyes fixed on the three riders ahead of them.

"You know, *señor*," he said at last, only the earnestness of his voice making it rise above the sound of hoofs striking hard earth, "I have never worked cows on a ranch. Horses I know a little, *sí*—and I have gone with the trail herds like we did this week—but ranching, *quién sabe*?"

"How old are you, laddie?"

Ignacio drew in his breath sharply, hoping the man hadn't noticed. *Por qué?* Why did even simple questions about him always bring this tight feeling to his chest?

"I—I am not certain, *señor*," he said, adding quickly, "Fifteen—*sí*, I think fifteen."

"No matter." The big man's chuckle was the same warm rumble he remembered from the ride up, before they delivered the cows at the railhead. "You're dead sure young enough to learn. By the time you're twenty you'll be a top hand—a real vaquero."

Ignacio was silent again. He hoped this señor he already liked so much would not think him rude that he didn't reply to everything at once. If the rancher on the big horse felt that way, his face gave no sign of it. Instead, the older man hurried into more words of his own. It almost seemed as if he wanted to save the boy the embarrassment of speaking before he was ready—as if he understood the confusion and uncertainty the offer of the job had brought.

"Both my brother Angus and Mr. Terry up there"—the man raised a huge arm and pointed at the group ahead of them—"sure admired your work in the stock pens yesterday, and on the way up with the herd. You move that old bag of bones you're on like she was a filly. Now, I sure don't want to press you, Ignacio. Think it over. We've a fair ride yet."

There shouldn't be much to think over, Ignacio Ortiz told himself. There should be no doubt at all. A place of his own to live in—and good work to do! No more jobbing himself out from valley to distant valley as he had done ever since he had run away from the mission at Ramos four years before, four years of drifting work and frightening, half-starved idleness, with more nights spent under the cold stars than he wanted to remember, and not even a saddle of his own to bring along when he sought work as a wrangler's helper or apprentice drover. No, there shouldn't be the smallest doubt. Why not say yes—and quickly? He shook his head, hoping again the big man wasn't looking.

Usually, if he wasn't working from the saddle and a pony nodded along in the sunlight like this creaky mare, he could sleep on the move, but not today. He hadn't really seen this trail five days ago when they drove north to Corona; he had been posted behind the herd, and the frenzied dust and noise blotted everything but the cows from sight and mind. At that it had been no more heart-pounding than this easy ride was turning out to be. Perhaps if he looked about him he could calm his mind and give an answer.

They rode south, dropping deeper into the Ojos Negros Basin with every mile, but still high enough on its sloping rim that the young rider could see sixty miles or more through the afternoon haze to where the double-domed head of Sierra Blanca lorded it over the Sacramentos. Just ahead of him the three horsemen in the lead were beginning to make their way past the ragged line where the piñon opened out on a long sweep of bunch grass. He watched the riders' shoulders bouncing as they let their mounts pick their own route through the first of the ocotillo, the trail boss, Terry, on the left and next to him the tall white-haired brother of the rancher (Angus, was it?) looking far too big for the small gray he rode.

In the lead, riding the handsome young paint Ignacio had looked at longingly for nearly a week now, was another boy. The young Mexican stared at the back of the other youngster, whose red checked shirt danced in front of the small procession like a pennant.

"You'd have company in young Jamie yonder." Ignacio started as if someone had come up behind him and taken him unaware. "True, he's a year shy of you," the rancher went on, "but he'd be good company all the same."

Well, that was where the problem lay. It was the boy who was the key. Something troubled the young Mexican about this Jamie, and he couldn't put his finger on it.

Certainly the boy had been decent enough from the very first, when Ignacio and Terry and the two other hands from the Staked Plains—since paid off at Corona and on their way back home—arrived at the fence of Douglas MacAndrews's D Cross A to join their two small herds together for the drive. They hadn't had much to do with each other during the two days of punishing riding which brought them to the railhead, but in camp at the stock pens after the cattle were loaded on the cars, and last night, when they bedded down in the piñons, their similar ages seemed to draw them together.

Jamie had shared a bag of gum drops with Ignacio after supper, almost demanding that the Mexican take more of them than he really wanted, and when the sun plummeted down behind the far Magdalenas and the evening warned of a night of bitter cold, he went to his pony and returned with a heavy saddle blanket to augment the worn serape the Mexican had been wrapping himself in for the past two years. They had joined the older men around a tiny fire, and Ignacio discovered that Jamie had a pleasant singing voice, although it tended to crack at times.

No, there was nothing Ignacio could name to account for his wary feeling about Jamie, nothing in the way the rancher's son had treated him or spoken to him. The boy had the warmest smile the young Mexican could remember ever having seen.

It had flashed brightly in the firelight every time their eyes met. Why, then, did he hold back? He would have to determine that before they all rode too many more miles. As kindly as he was, and as patient as he seemed, Señor Douglas MacAndrews would want his answer.

Now the five riders reached the great stands of yucca they had been moving toward for an hour, and Ignacio realized that Jamie, Angus, and the trail boss were moving their horses at a faster pace than they had during the middle of the day. Suddenly he realized that not once during the journey had Jamie dropped back beside him. Indeed, he couldn't remember that young MacAndrews had talked to him since they saddled up at dawn— it was as if he had outlived whatever usefulness he might have had for the rancher's son.

Perhaps the wisest course was to return with the trail boss to Las Cruces. Terry would help him look for work. But what excuse could he give the man riding beside him?

Well, he was calm now, and the answers would come out of the calmness. He was sad, too, but the sadness, although deeper, was no different from his feelings at the end of any of the hundred jobs he had taken in the last four years. No, be honest *amigo*, he told himself. It is different. Even if he had known him for just one week, he would miss the big señor.

At this, the sadness became sharper, seemed driven into his chest like a pointed stick. How foolish! He really hadn't been thrown with the rancher much more than he had with Jamie; there was no reason to feel this way. Except—except that this enormous soft-spoken man seemed to know he was there.

The three mounted figures ahead of him urged their ponies up a barren rise, and when he and the rancher crested it in turn, the fence of the D Cross A stretched out in front of them, the posts and the wire strands marching out of sight to right and left as far as he could see.

Jamie, down from his horse, was opening a gate, and Ignacio knew that when he reached the boy he would give his answer. Almost without realizing it, he reined the mare a little, and the rancher moved on past him. A small wind had come up, and the rattle it made passing through the spikes of the yuccas was the loneliest sound he had heard in a long, long time.

Near the gate, not so much guiding the old mare as simply letting her carry him, he saw Jamie watching him with a look of such intensity it seemed it would bore right through him. Ignacio wondered what thoughts had inspired this searching gaze. He would never know, most likely.

Then Jamie, still holding the gate in one hand and his pony's reins in the other, gave Ignacio a smile which exploded in warmth and brilliance. The young rider's heart lurched upward, swelling until he couldn't breathe.

"*Señor,*" he said, hearing his voice as if from a great distance, "*sí,* I will work for you. I will try very hard to please you." While he spoke, his eyes never left Jamie MacAndrews's smiling face.

"Good, Ignacio. It's settled then." The big man spurred his horse gently through the open gate as his son swung himself into the saddle. "High tail it for the house, son. Tell your mother there'll be two extra mouths at table tonight."

Almost before the words had died away, Jamie was gone, taking his smile with him, driving his pony past Angus and the trail boss and through the yuccas, dust rising in sunlit shafts behind him.

"Welcome to the D Cross A, Ignacio," Douglas MacAndrews said, "and close the gate tight, *por favor.* When our fence line's all closed up, everything inside is safe and sound."

2

TIRED AS HE WAS WHEN HE PULLED THE ROUGH HORSE BLANKET UP to his chin, Ignacio was unable to sleep. Remembering everything that had happened since he said yes to the señor took half the night.

When they were riding down the last slope toward the buildings and Douglas MacAndrews said, "There it is, Ignacio. Home," something hard to swallow came into his throat. He couldn't recall ever using the word "home" himself.

Except that it was bigger than most, it looked a very ordinary house, part adobe, with what seemed to be a newer section made of timber. Outcroppings of tawny rock protected it from the full force of the north wind. Down the ranch road, past a piñon post corral and a shack nestled in the shadow of a windmill, a plank bridge crossed an arroyo which skirted a small butte.

Ignacio could see Jamie's paint nodding against a hitch rail, but the rancher's son was nowhere to be found, and for a brief moment he felt strangely deserted. When he and the three other riders reined up he gave up looking for the other boy, remembering that he was now a hand of the D Cross A. He swung from the saddle before the weary mare had stopped, and reached for the bridle of the señor's big horse. When the rancher had eased down to the caliche, Ignacio led the two animals to the wooden trough where Angus and the trail boss were watering their horses.

"Douglas! Welcome home!" It was the light voice of a woman somewhere behind him.

"Hullo, Aggie. Good to be home," he heard the rancher say, his voice warm and strong. There was that word again.

"Jamie says we're to have company for supper, Douglas. Who are our guests?" Beyond the question itself there was curiosity in the voice to equal his.

"Ransom Terry from Cruces," the señor said, "and a new man I've put on. Ransom—Ignacio—this is Mrs. MacAndrews. The last name is Ortiz, isn't it, laddie?"

"Ma'am," he heard the trail boss say. He turned, and blushed when he found that with both hands occupied he couldn't remove his hat. He couldn't speak, either. All he could manage was a clumsy little bow—and this before he'd even really seen the woman of the D Cross A.

She was small, particularly so standing next to her husband, and at a glance he saw where Jamie had inherited his blue-eyed blonde good looks. From that moment those eyes searched him out relentlessly. Well, it was her right.

"*Cómo está*, Ignacio?" she said. There was something commanding in the way she held her head—not tilted back in haughtiness, but certainly lifted high with pride. Her eyes held him for another moment and when she turned to her husband it was as if they had been torn away.

"Supper in half an hour sharp, Douglas," she said, moving toward the house. Ignacio stared after her until the señor's horse tossed its head and jerked him back to attentiveness.

Dios! Even on feast days at the mission he had never seen a table hold so many different kinds of food. Hungry as he was, he scarcely touched a thing. He tried not to look at the others, but he saw the señora eat as sparingly as he did, carrying the food to her straight, careful mouth in tiny forkfuls. Watching him constantly from beneath a cool brow, she made no attempt to hide the looks she gave him. What do you expect, *niño bobo*, he asked himself. Must you be reminded yet again it is her right?

The meal was eaten in silence, with every head but his and the señora's bent to the plates. When they had finished, and the napkins were rolled and pushed back into the silver rings at every place (a rite he watched and imitated with care) talk flooded the room. In a way, this left him feeling more alone than had the quiet. The meager English he possessed, won painfully on the trail or at the dusty edges of towns where he had bunked, wasn't good enough to follow the exchanges which flew across the table with the smoke and laughter.

Angus, he discovered, though mute while on the drive, was a steady, easy talker once his long body was stuffed with food.

"—and if the county don't shore up that bridge over Arroyo Blanco, the next good rain'll wash it clear to Ojo Caliente. I had a word with the county agent last time I—"

"Douglas," the señora broke into the pleasant drone of Angus's words, "I'm sure the boys aren't the least bit interested in all of this." Ignacio looked at Jamie, hoping for another of those dazzling smiles. None came.

"You're right, Aggie," the big man said, "I think they may be excused, provided they're back inside to help you with the dishes."

Jamie made a face and shot from the table like a rabbit, bringing a laugh from Angus and the trail boss. At the door he braked suddenly to a stop, beckoned to Ignacio to follow, and was gone again.

Ignacio looked at the señora, and when she nodded, got to his feet and tried that same little bow he had managed so badly in the yard.

He found Jamie on the low stone wall which surrounded the house, facing westward to where to where the sky reddened as the sun dropped steadily toward to mountain rim. He had a handful of pebbles and was tossing them one by one into the caliche. The air was so still the puffs of dust they kicked up hung there for long seconds.

Ignacio stood behind him, looking at the sunset.

"Well, come on. Sit down. You want to, don't you?" Jamie didn't turn around as he spoke. Ignacio stepped over the wall and found a flat spot ten feet from Jamie.

There must have been five minutes more of silence before the MacAndrews boy spoke again.

"You Spanish or Indian, Ignacio?"

"I—I do not know, *señor.* Maybe both." He felt chilled by something more than the evening air. *Dios,* he must not let such questions upset him so. "In Ramos it didn't seem important," he added softly.

"Well, I'll tell you one thing sure. It's important as all get out in these parts. Where's Ramos?"

"In Chihuahua, *señor.*"

"Mexico—then you're *Mexican.*" Jamie said it as if some petty annoyance were now out of the way.

Ignacio said nothing. The implication of Jamie's remark, unwitting as it likely was, didn't bother him as it might have in those first days north of the river. It was like a slight smell in the air. You got used to it—even if occasionally it became a little stronger. Far worse were those probes which might in some way turn on the hidden past.

He looked hard at Jamie. *Sí,* they were different. He didn't envy the golden hair or the straight nose, the smooth, light skin, or the three extra inches of height, a gap which promised to increase; nor even the fine, soft bed in the big house where Jamie would sleep this night. There were some things, though, things it was useless to hope for—and better not to think about.

"Ignacio," Jamie still hadn't looked in his direction. "Oh, Hell! I ain't going to call you Ignacio. It don't sound right for a man's name. From now on you'll be—let's see—I got it! *Nash.* Shorter and better. Yeah, Nash—savvy?" The words came spitting out and Ignacio winced.

He should not permit this. His name was about the only thing he really owned. He should make some objection—now! But before he could utter a word, Jamie turned his head and smiled, and Ignacio Knew he had lost.

The MacAndrews boy was still smiling when the door behind them opened, and Ignacio turned to see Douglas MacAndrews coming out with Ransom Terry.

"Ride safe then, Ransom," the rancher was saying, "but you know you're welcome to stay the night."

"Thanks, Mr. MacAndrews, but I ain't seen my wife in near three weeks. Besides, I thought I'd stop in Black Springs and have a vet look at that pony of mine. He ain't been acting right. I'll put him on a lead and ride the mare young Ortiz was on. Thanks again."

"All right, Ransom, if your mind's made up. Ignacio, saddle up for Mr. Terry, *por favor.* And Jamie, I think your mother's ready for some kitchen help."

Ignacio raced for the corral, grateful to the señor for giving him man's work this first night at the ranch. Not that he would shirk any chore, but he feared that his hands, sure enough on leather, would find the fragile china more than he could handle.

In minutes, Terry was gone, the horses and the lone rider pounding their way across the plank bridge which sagged over the arroyo, then fading into the twilight gloom of the desert beyond the butte.

"Smart work, Ignacio," Douglas MacAndrews said. "One thing, though. Never rush *quite* so much to saddle a guest's horse." He chuckled, the sound warm and deep in his throat. "He might think we really didn't mean it when we asked him to stay."

"*Sí, señor.*"

"And now, Ignacio, I think we'd best get back inside and see to the rest of those kitchen chores."

The dishes were almost done. A scowling Jamie was placing glassware in a cupboard above the sink. Señora MacAndrews looked up from the table she was wiping.

"We're almost done." She said. "Go on in and make yourself comfortable in the sitting room. When I'm finished here, I'll fix you up with bedding and some other things for the shack, Nash." There it was. Jamie had told the señora about the name he had invented; doubtless the señor himself would be the next.

At first he thought the sitting room deserted, but a sound from the long sofa revealed the lanky figure of Angus stretched out in sleep. The sofa faced a fireplace flanked by an enormous easy chair and a wooden rocker tilting in graceful balance. He stood stock still in the center of the room, peering into shadows not quite dispelled by the lamplight, wondering what he would do or say if Angus stirred. His eyes continued their march around the room.

There was a sampler on the wall whose message he couldn't read, a shelf holding a slender vase stuffed with nothing more than common weeds. He shuddered, something twisting deep inside him, when he saw the rifles and shotguns racked in the corner, and his eye hurried on. The fireplace, cavernous in its unlit state, stood against an adobe wall; he could see outlines of sun-baked brick bleeding through a coating white as bone. Another white wall; fear touched him, but lightly, and perplexity followed. He was glad then to have Angus in the room with him. The man's heavy breathing, regular and even as the gait of a good horse, kept the room to ordinary size. Comforted by this thought, he found his own breathing easier, and his eye swept on to the south wall.

He almost gasped aloud. Here was something Ignacio Ortiz had never seen before in all his life. From right to left across the room, from the floor to the ceiling with its great wooden beams, the wall was filled with books. Books of every size and shape, bound in a hundred different ways, stood in soldiered ranks, leaned against each other carelessly, or rested on their sides in staggered piles. In the padre's study there had been some books, but surely not a dozen. This marvelous wall must hold every book the world had ever known. Ignacio was dizzied by the sight.

He found himself within touching distance of the wall. Leather spines gleamed, gold lettering sparkled, and on one shelf an open volume spread its pages. Heart drumming, he put out his hand and—

"Do you read, Nash?"

Numb, he turned to see the señora standing in the entrance to the sitting room. Wishing he could shrink to nothing, he forced himself to look straight into the blue-gray eyes, certain he would find them narrowed in outrage and accusation.

But there was no sign of this, nothing of indignation, suspicion, or reproach. Instead, he saw an excitement so strong it might have been his own.

"Do you read, Nash?" Agnes MacAndrews said again.

"Just a little, señora—and only Spanish."

"Pity." In a movement so definite and swift it left him blinking, she was gone.

Behind him a sigh came from the sofa where Angus slept.

Bedding piled to his chin, an unlit lantern swinging from the crook of his arm, Ignacio stumbled down the stony pathway. The ponies in the corral moved a little but paid him no real attention. In the east, an orange moon was rising over the brute black shape of Cuchillo Peak, and a few small clouds coursed across the sky. There was some wind at ground level, too; even though the windmill lock was on, he could hear the blades groaning, straining to break free.

He took one more look up the moonlit slope toward the big house before he kicked open the door of the shack.

For what seemed like hours, sleep stayed just out of reach, while his mind whirled so he wished he could lock it in place like the windmill still complaining in its captivity above him. His last waking thought had been of that astonishing wall of books, but sometime during the fitful sleep which did come, the other wall rose again, solid and menacing, as it always did whenever his life began to show a touch of promise.

Awake now, and feeling keen and strong despite the lack of real mind- and body-mending sleep, Ignacio hurried into his clothes and out the door of the shack to find the sun nudging the last of the dark away from the top of big Cuchillo, its bright disc just a little lower in the sky than where he had left the moon last night.

He wasn't surprised to see Douglas MacAndrews standing in the ranch house doorway waving to him.

"Come on, son." The rancher didn't shout, but the strong voice carried well in the crisp morning air. "I've got the coffee going. We'll have a cup together, and then get a real breakfast after the first chores are behind us."

The Mexican boy started up the pathway. As he turned to cross the yard, the big man spoke again.

"We've got a day's work ahead of us, Ignacio."

Ignacio!

The new hand of the D Cross A broke into a run.

3

"A SECTION?" ANGUS MACANDREWS SAID. "WELL, NASH, A SECTION is a square mile. Run your eye from here to the black rock—the malpais. Then look north, to the piñon line. That's two sides of a section. Four hundred of them inside the fence. Not a big ranch— why, in Texas, they'd lose this place. Still, there's near a hundred miles of that same fence."

Angus and Ignacio rested in the cottonwoods which arched over the dry river in the southwest corner of the ranch. Yesterday, long before dawn, they had ridden out, trailing pack horses loaded with coils of wire and a kit of fencing tools. The wire was gone now, hammered length by stubborn length into the great fence for two full days, and all the time they worked Angus had been as silent as he was on the drive to Corona. When they camped last night on the open range, and now, in this pleasant bosque, the pipe and tobacco had come out, and so, too, had the words. Ignacio listened.

How much older was Angus than Señor Douglas? Ten, fifteen years, perhaps? It was high tribute to the rancher that a man as capable as this tall, likeable anglo would willingly accept second place to his younger brother.

Ignacio felt a twinge of shame at his disappointment when Douglas turned him over to Angus after one week at the D Cross A. He hoped his face hadn't shown it. At first he wanted to work for Douglas only, but genuine affection for Angus soon developed, and, besides, it was good to be back in the saddle again after that first week of unfamiliar toil. He had greased harness, hammered, sawed, painted countless shed walls the same dead white which

16

came in the dreams. He didn't mind even that when the señor worked with him, and it was surely better than the stoop work gardening he did at Ramos, but to be on horseback again was like a holiday.

"—and Douglas is dickering to get still more pasturage," Angus was saying. "He's a fine stockman. Studies. Takes care of the land as well as the cows. Never overgrazes—leastways not by plan. He ain't greedy, but he'll make the D Cross A something to see some day.

"Now, laddie, let's check out that last stretch. Maybe we can make it back in time for supper."

As they rode out of the bottom lands, Ignacio thought still more about Douglas MacAndrews. The señor was the best boss he'd ever had. He made Ignacio feel that somehow he was working for himself. That first morning, in the tack room, Ignacio must have looked lost and uncertain, for when Douglas set him to work with a riveting tool and a pile of harness, the rancher stood over him and said, "Look, Ignacio, just work at your own speed. Use your judgment on what to fix and what to throw out. I won't bother you, but I'll watch. I'll let you know *before* you make a mistake, so don't worry."

Angus nodded in satisfaction. The last fence they inspected was in tiptop shape; no need to come out with yet another roll of wire.

"Speaking of sections, Nash. That fifty northeast of the house we picked up cheap back in '78—or rather I did. Douglas was in school in Cruces then. We already had the ten above the arroyo. Old Doc—our Dad—left us a little money, and I had a wee bit more from mustering out at the end of the war. It all went for land."

They rode for an hour in the lee of the malpais, Angus talking all the while.

"We camped on the mesa in the early days. The old part of the house, the adobe, wasn't fit to live in—no roof or nothing. Good thing Douglas didn't have Aggie then."

Mention of the señora stirred an odd excitement in the young rider. If Señor Douglas and Angus were wonderfully open, the woman of the D Cross A was a study in self-containment. At night after he helped her clear the table and wash the dishes, he would carry the memory of her level gaze back to the shack with him, at times absolutely certain she was following him with the blue-gray eyes every step down the pathway. He remembered the look she had given him that first night, when she had surprised him with the books. He hadn't visited the sitting room since, but *Dios,* how he wanted to.

"Yep," Angus was saying, "Aggie sure found life different from what she expected when she married Douglas and came out here."

He wanted to ask a question, but decided not to. At any rate, Angus stopped talking when they turned eastward through the yucca.

Ten days had passed since he'd come to the D Cross A, ten days, and ten nights, too. Only that first night had the dream come to taunt him, and it had faded long before dawn pulled him into the world of Douglas MacAndrews. Perhaps he could be happy here. Certainly his admiration for the señor and the easygoing brother were reason enough. And the señora? He would try to know her better, try to understand the reason for those watchful eyes.

But there was still Jamie. Ignacio had been deserted once again, but this time it wasn't Jamie's fault. Now that school had started, he had gone back to the house in town where he lived, taking with him that look that didn't seem to see, the look which vanished when least expected, dissolved by the broad and winning smile.

There it was. Ignacio couldn't allow happiness to come just yet. One false step and he might slip from the razor's edge and be exposed to even greater misery than he had know—and it was the youngest MacAndrews who might cause the misstep. No, he must stay on guard.

"Too bad you didn't get more time with Jamie before he headed back to school," Angus said.

Ignacio glanced at the horseman riding beside him. *Dios,* had Angus read his mind? Seen Jamie on his face? He must take more care. But the tall rider was paying attention only to the trail, neck-reining his mount through the last of the yucca before they reached the plank bridge.

"He's a good lad," Angus said. "A wee bit stubborn, a touch irresponsible, but it really ain't much wonder, the funny way we raised him." Suddenly Ignacio realized that Angus was now talking to himself and not to him. "Yep—I guess Aggie and I damned near ruined him. Not Douglas, he always had more sense. We'd worked so hard out here, when Jamie came along I suppose Ag and I thought he was just a toy, a pet. We sure spoiled hell out of him. Wouldn't let him out of our sight, and gave in to him on everything. Aggie even tried to tutor him out here—she started out to be a schoolmistress, you know—but Douglas had to put his foot down." Angus chuckled. "Sure glad he did, too. I had to chase the little truant down so much I couldn't work. Relief for everybody when he enrolled in town and Douglas boarded him with the Staffords. Kind of bent poor Aggie's nose, though—and it sure wasn't any picnic for young Jamie. He'd never really known other kids and he just couldn't cotton to them. Hated school as well. I sometimes wonder how he'd be if Aggie hadn't lost the second one."

Suddenly Angus blushed, his rugged face reddening right up to the shaggy white hair. "I talk as much as any old woman, Nash. Just forget some of this—it's probably hogwash, anyway.

"Come on," he said, kicking his spurs hard into his pony, "let's hustle this sorry outfit up to the corral and get some of Aggie's grub!"

4

September slipped away under a blue haze that blurred the horizon and dulled the knife-edge sharpness of Cuchillo's highest ridge.

Except for the fence mending trip, there hadn't been much work to do from the saddle. The herd the brothers had linked with Terry's had been the product of the year's last roundup. Stock which had summered in the high north pastures had all been moved to lower, more protected grazing before Ignacio had arrived at the D Cross A.

Time away from the thousand and one other chores to be done and done again, Ignacio spent fixing up the shack. Angus found him a table and a high-backed wooden chair, saying, as he wedged them through the door, "Why, you're living in the lap of luxury, laddie. When Douglas and I started the D Cross A, both of us lived here, when we weren't in bedrolls on the range, and there's one helluva lot more of the two of us than there is of you."

If the boy felt gratitude, it was nothing to the way his heart swelled when he returned to the shack one afternoon to find a neat pile of clothing on the bunk: Levis, outgrown by Jamie; shirts; a woolen jacket; even long underwear and knit stockings— two luxuries he had never owned before. He hauled a bucket of water from the tank and scrubbed himself until his skin smarted, excited at showing up for supper to thank the señora. But just as he was about to rip up his old white cotton trousers, the thought of Jamie stopped him. For a while, at least, it would be better not to parade the new clothes on weekends, when the other boy came home from school.

Suppers were easier now. Faint alarms still clicked in his head when the señora gave him those unsettling looks, but he was relaxing into the easy camaraderie of Douglas and Angus. Saying nothing himself, he listened, adsorbed, studied, hoarded every word and gesture, from the calm, smiling judgments of the rancher to the rollicking, tobacco smoke blown gossip of the older brother. More, too, he found his guard dropping where Agnes was concerned, and little by little he was able to answer her with something more than a stammer.

Once, though, she shot him a question which made him feel he had lost everything, and he retreated inside himself with the swiftness of a pocket mouse seeking its nest.

"You've never told us where you come from, Nash, or about your people."

He must have looked as threatened as he felt, for silence thick as the smoke from Angus's pipe hung over the table. He didn't breathe until Douglas spoke.

"Aggie, Ignacio will have to tell us some other time. I need his help in the tack room before we all turn in." The ringing in the young rider's ears didn't completely drown out the stern tone, nor did he miss the dark flash in Agnes's eyes before Angus broke in, "I'll set up the chess board and be laying in the weeds for you, lassie."

That was the only time. From that second on Agnes's manner changed in some subtle way. She smiled more often, and if she watched him as carefully as before she took pains not to let him see her, but by no means did he feel she had forgotten him. If anything, she talked to him more, particularly when they did the supper dishes, and with the days growing shorter, she insisted he stay longer in the big house in the evenings. Uneasy at first, he grew to like that. Happy as he was with the shack, it was dismal there sometimes, when darkness fell long before it was time to sleep.

He would watch Agnes and her brother-in-law as they played chess, or Douglas as he worked at the big flat-topped desk. With October's crisp breath at the doors and windows, a fire blazed in the sitting room every night. He would stare into the skipping flames for many minutes, but, inevitably, he would find his head turning to the wall of books. Often, as the nights raced toward winter, he would leave the sofa to stand in front of the shelves, his shadow dancing over the fire-lit leather spines. Sometimes the books seemed to dance as well, and his hands itched to grasp them, to rub against the shiny backs and let the pages ripple like wind-tossed chaparral.

He knew the señora never failed to watch him then.

The days with Douglas, and the more frequent ones with Angus, were good. He decided it was well that he was paired with the older brother. He stood in such awe of the señor he was tongue-tied unless talk was limited to the work at hand. With Angus it was different.

He discovered he could now ask Angus things which would have seemed impertinences when he arrived in the last hot days of August. The tall man welcomed the questions.

"Scotland? It's the wee country north of England. That's where Old Doc and Jamie's grandmother hailed from. Me too. Douglas was born here, but I was already a good sized lad when we came to the Ojos Negros. Old Doc was a veterinary—animal doctor."

Bit by bit, the story of the D Cross A came out. Dr. MacAndrews and his wife had died within a year of each other while Douglas was in college, and Angus, who had been working for the smith in Black Springs, had gone to a bank in El Paso when the old ranch came on the market.

"They knew I wasn't any head for business, but they didn't make a fuss when Douglas co-signed with me."

They started out with a lazy old Mexican bull and a handful of stringy crossbreed cows. Then a man named Burns came out from Illinois on a hunting trip. He was a successful cattle breeder in the middle west and, taking a liking to Douglas and his ideas, shipped out two Hereford bulls on approval.

"When Douglas went to visit Burns, he met Aggie and married her before the trip was done. Don't know what she thought she'd find out here. Douglas brought a Studebaker wagon where the railroad dropped them west of Wichita, and they arrived in town with it piled as high as Cuchillo Peak—furniture, all that fancy china, wedding finery, and the books."

At the mention of the books Ignacio listened even more intently.

"They got rooms at Maude Pelling's while Douglas and I got busy on the house. Aggie poked into every corner in town, even places a lady ain't supposed to go, and she was sure full of the 'wild west'. Kept pestering me to show her my 'six-shooter'. Hell, I ain't never owned a hand gun—never fired one except on the pistol range at Fort Craig.

"Well, we finally got her moved out, right after she learned she was carrying Jamie, and on the day after the biggest gully-washer of the summer. The wagon bogged down in the caliche mud short of the arroyo, and we had to hand carry every blessed thing up the hill.

"Aggie never whimpered—just set her jaw and pitched right in, but, by God, it was them *books* she started with."

Sometimes Ignacio wondered why Douglas had hired him. In his travels since Ramos he had seen good riders by the score who would have jumped at the job at the D Cross A, experienced cowhands as tough as the *riatas* coiled under their saddle horns. So why him? All he could do was shrug his young shoulders.

The señor clearly loved the ranch. There was a special, tangible joy about the way he set about the most mundane task, blue eyes winking from deep creases in a face the wind and sun had turned the shade of sandstone. Sometimes Ignacio wondered if he ever lifted those eyes from his study of the cattle and the rangeland.

His own vision, hawk keen to start, sharpened with every sweep it made across the skyline. Another kind of sight was coming to him here. It could be a rock caught suddenly with the merest corner of his eye, or a distant hillside rippled by the shadow of a cloud, whatever; it was unlike the searching hurried looks he had taken at things since he left Ramos.

He could almost believe that nothing, neither doubts nor dreams, could threaten him again. . . .

One morning, with Angus in town to post some letters, Ignacio and the señor took a wagon and a load of cottonseed cake to one of the southeast pastures. On the way back, Douglas reined in the team and turned to the young Mexican.

"Ignacio," he said. There was a serious darkening of his features. A slight breeze, tugging at the boy's sweaty shirt, brought a touch of chill. "Ignacio, are you happy here at the D Cross A?"

"*Señor?*"

"It isn't any of my business, and Lord knows, I'm satisfied with you—but I don't recall I've ever seen you smile."

There was no sound save for the breeze and a restless move made by one of the horses. Ignacio didn't answer and felt ashamed. All he could do was meet the rancher's steady look. Their eyes locked together.

"Never mind, Ignacio. I didn't mean to pry. I guess that happiness can be a personal, private thing."

Except that the haze had lifted, baring a sky of such indelible blue the clouds were brilliant white explosions against it, October left in the same secret fashion as had September. The first outriders of winter showed themselves on the range: a quick, shuddering wind; a tissue of ice on the windmill tank in the early mornings.

And Jamie came home from school for something Agnes and the others called Thanksgiving.

5

"MEAT!" ANGUS WHOOPED. SMOKE WAS RISING FROM THE BARREL OF the rifle. "It's meat now—make no mistake."

"Fine shot," Douglas said. "Let's get up there and make sure of it. Jamie and Ignacio can bring up the horses."

"Make sure, hell," Angus growled in faked anger. "Critter ain't going to twitch. Meat on the table, I tell you."

Douglas laughed and started up the slope toward the fallen mule deer buck. Ignacio watched Jamie race past him, slipping and stumbling in the snow-dusted shale.

It was a fine shot, perhaps a hundred and fifty yards from where Angus had knelt in the juniper scrub. The buck had made one majestic leap after the report of the rifle, but only one, and Ignacio, although he had never been on a hunt before, knew Angus was right. The deer would never move again.

As he watched Jamie run, he wished he could share the MacAndrews boy's enthusiasm.

"Slow down, Jamie!" Douglas called, the warning sharp in the cold air. "Don't run rifle!" The boy continued his manic scramble, not stopping until he stood over the deer.

Angus was striding up the slope now, rifle over his shoulder, a smile on his craggy face. Ignacio swung in behind him, almost running himself to match the tall man's pace. Well, *he* could run. He was the only one of the four who didn't carry a gun.

There was blood on the snow under the neck of the buck and a strong, sweaty smell came from the dead beast. Angus grasped the antlers, six well-formed points, and lifted the creature's head.

Red trickled in ugly drops from the nostrils and the eyes were two polished black stones.

"Like I said—meat." Angus chuckled in satisfaction. Ignacio shivered. It seemed even colder now.

He was warm enough, though, by the time he had brought up the ponies and helped pull the carcass across the quaking back of one of the two pack horses. The horse, snorting fear and difficult to hold, seemed to know, he thought.

Strange, although he had worried some as he came up the slope with Angus, he didn't have to force himself to touch the deer. It was as if it had been dead a long, long time—or had never lived. The steam rising from its flanks was gone, drifted away on the upland wind.

Jamie, on the other hand, hung back, standing to one side while the three of them tugged the buck into place on the horse.

"That's it today." Douglas said. "Let's head back for Aggie's dinner before she's of a mind to scalp us all."

There was a choked cry from James. "Gee, Pa! I ain't had my chance yet."

"It'll have to come another day, son. We only wanted to take one head—and Angus was the lucky one."

"But, Pa—"

"That's it, Jamie, I'm sorry."

They mounted and started down the stony trail, Douglas and Angus leading, the two boys trailing the pack horses, with Ignacio, handling the one with the deer, just ahead of Jamie. He had forgotten the other boy's protest, intent on guiding his two animals down a steep pitch, when Jamie spoke.

"Don't you hold with hunting, Nash?"

"*Señor?*"

"Oh, hell! Call me Jamie."

And just call me Ignacio, he wanted to say, but instead—

"*Sí,*—Jamie." He didn't turn around.

"How come you ain't carrying a gun?"

What was the answer? He didn't know himself. He had tried to take the rifle from the señor last night, but when he reached for it, he saw the wicked blue steel reflect the warm gleam of the lamp and turn it cold. Something stirred deep within him, something it seemed he should remember, but he couldn't pin it down.

All this might be laughable to Jamie. Better to say nothing. He shook his head.

"Man ought to carry a gun on a hunt," Jamie said. From his tone he was talking to himself now; after his first curiosity he was gone again. "Man ought to shoot on a hunt, too. Can't see why we have to head in just 'cause Angus got a kill. God damn Pa, anyway!"

Ignacio winced. It was unthinkable that anyone, even Jamie, especially Jamie, could talk this way of the señor. He felt more shame at not taking issue about this than he did about the matter of his own name. All he could do was look down the trail to where Douglas and Angus rode, sheepskin collars turned up against the wind, and hope they hadn't heard.

Then, as if it had been struck, his pony lurched wildly, almost falling. Something violent was happening, but even when he saw Jamie's pack horse charge past him, its lead trailing free, he had no time to think. All he could do was try to keep his seat and rein in with all his might.

Then he realized there was something more he had to do, and quickly! Down the trail Douglas and Angus were gingerly making their way through a narrow section. On their left the mountain broke away in a sharp drop of a hundred feet or more. The loose pack horse, panicked, was gaining speed. It would be on the two riders in seconds.

He dug his heels into his pony's sides. *"Vámonos!"* he screamed, and his mount responded, lunging forward like a flash of lightning. He had to get past the crazed pack horse ahead of him before it reached the two MacAndrews men. It meant going off the trail, around the running animal, and on again. He flogged both flanks of his pony with the free end of his reins.

Somehow he did it, and he knew he never would remember how. He grabbed the halter of the loose horse, turned it sideways and blocked the trail with his own pack horse, still loaded with the buck and on its own now, too.

When he got the three animals settled down, he looked at Angus and the rancher. To his surprise, they weren't looking his way at all. Instead, they were staring up the mountain, their faces frozen.

High above them, way off the trail, Jamie was grinding his spurs into his pony, lashing it like fury as Ignacio had his, the pony's hind legs gathering, extending, moving up the mountain in bounding, rock-scattering leaps.

"Jamie!" Ignacio heard Douglas shout, his voice ringing with anger. The rider above them didn't even turn, only beat more wildly with his reins, as if possessed.

As Ignacio and the two brothers watched, Jamie reached down and pulled his rifle from the saddle holster. He stopped laboring his pony long enough to fumble with the gun, and lifting it to his shoulder with just one hand, began to fire. Three, no, four shots echoed from the mountainside, one whining off through the air as it struck a rock, the reports all but drowning out Douglas's second shouted "JAMIE!"

High above the boy and his plunging pony, Ignacio caught a flash of white and brown. In another second he saw it was a deer, smaller than the one draped across the pack horse next to him. As it vanished in the brush, he could see there were no antlers on it.

"Jesus Christ!" He heard Angus's hoarse whisper in the silence which settled on the mountain. *"Jesus Christ."*

It was a dreary meal, this thing the señora called Thanks-giving dinner. She had delayed through the late afternoon as much as she could, still half expecting—Ignacio knew from her frequent trips to the window—Douglas and Angus to return in time. The brothers had ridden up into the high scrub to see if Jamie had hit the deer, after sending the two boys back to the D Cross A.

When Agnes decided her dinner could wait no longer, she and the two boys sat down to a table which sagged with food. Even the simple grace she uttered couldn't lift Ignacio's spirits, but Jamie seemed untouched by what had happened. He was the only one of the three who ate with enthusiasm.

Ignacio was still awake when he heard Douglas and Angus pounding across the plank bridge and up the road, and sleep eluded him long after everything was quiet once again. Just as he finally drifted off, he heard footsteps outside his door and a soft knock.

"Nash—it's me, Jamie. Can I come in?"

Ignacio sat up and found matches for the lantern as the door swung open, letting in a rush of cold. As the inside of the shack filled with light, it struck him that this was the first time Jamie had come to visit since he'd been at the ranch. The boy's hand-some face wore the same smile he'd seen before. There wasn't a trace of trouble or concern. There is too much light in here, Ignacio thought. He lowered the wick of the lantern until it almost flickered out.

"Thought you'd like to know," Jamie said, "they finally found that critter's tracks somewheres up in the snow. No sign of blood, so I guess I must have missed the sonofabitch."

"*Bueno,* Jamie, *bueno.*"

"Anyways, thought I'd drop in and visit. I ain't too damn popular up at the house right now."

Ignacio suddenly felt used, used and in a way he couldn't help, a little traitorous. But, *Dios,* what could he do? In the dim light he could still see the smile.

"Damned if I can figure out," Jamie said, "why there should be such a ruckus over a stinking deer."

6

WORK BEGAN AGAIN IN EARNEST AFTER JAMIE RETURNED TO TOWN AND school the Monday after Thanksgiving.

Angus was forecasting a bitter winter on the basis of certain aches and pains he claimed to have, although, climbing the windmill or astride a cow pony, he certainly looked fit and supple for a man of what, sixty years? Smiling at the gloomy predictions which apparently came every year, Douglas outlined a killing schedule. Ignacio welcomed it. What better way than work was there to fit himself into the life of the ranch?

Still, eager as he was to please, he wondered if they would ever be done with the great outer fence stretched endlessly across the range. It seemed he cut wire from morning to night, pulling it humming tight until he could do it in his sleep. The places where his hands weren't cut and bleeding from the barbs, they burned from the creosote he brushed on piñon posts by the dozen.

Angus spread an ointment on the cuts, saying, "They'll be healed by morning. Same stuff we use on the calves at branding. You'll see—come spring."

There were compensations. With his hands greased with the smelly medicine, he couldn't help with the dishes. If it hadn't happened yet, he dreaded the time he knew was coming, when some precious butter dish or delicate cup would slip from his uncertain hands and crash on the floor. Angus, grousing in his good-natured way, took the boy's place, and with Douglas busy with his desk or newspaper, Ignacio was free to roam the book shelves. With the ointment on his hands, he could easily resist the temptation to reach out and touch.

Sí, getting ready for winter, even if it turned out milder than Angus's warnings, was hard, hard and ceaseless, but when his body could do no more, Douglas would assign him a less demanding task. Sometimes he only asked Ignacio to ride with him "—while I check things out." These were moments of almost unendurable joy.

"See those sections over there, Ignacio?" Douglas would say. "Looks like it would be mighty appetizing to a cow, don't it? That tasty looking stuff is prickly poppy. Cattle won't eat it, and it plain takes over. We won't graze there next year—give the sweet grass a chance to fight its way back in. Year or so we'll have pasture land again."

Often during these excursions they would come across a small herd of horses, old mounts retired out of the working string of the D Cross A. They seemed to make the cottonwood bosque where he and Angus had camped the center of their range. Ignacio was pleased they didn't take flight when he and the señor rode almost into them.

"I could still get something from them," the big man would say, "but they're no good for work unless its pulling a buggy for some fancy lady in town. I think they look kind of nice the way they are." Ignacio would nod. They looked nice indeed, shagged out against the coming winter, breath steaming in the brisk air. *Sí,* they looked just fine—fine and free.

After a dozen such trips, he realized they had now ridden the entire length and breadth of the D Cross A, from the alkali flats in the south to the piñon in the farthest north. There had been a plan in these wanderings. One day had seen them range from where the malpais separated the ranch from the corroded land of the Jornada del Muerto, to the easternmost boundary, the high ground which swept up the lower flank of Cuchillo Peak.

Every time they stopped during one of these fine days in the saddle, whether to eat, inspect some red-eyed steer which didn't look quite right to Douglas, or just to rest the ponies, the rancher would pass along some bit of knowledge, pressed home before Ignacio could sense it was on its way.

Once, Douglas handed him a small whetstone, saying, in answer to Ignacio's questioning look, "For your knife, laddie.

To keep it sharp. A dull knife on a stock ranch is an abomination any time, and in the spring, at branding, it's just plain cruel."

In the spring—branding—roundup! These words triggered an explosion in the young rider's head. There was still so much to learn. With luck and work, especially work, he could please Señor MacAndrews, make some small start on the business of becoming a real vaquero.

"—and when there's nothing else to do, Ignacio, we work the fence. When our fence is closed up tight, everything on the D Cross A is safe and sound."

Halfway through December they made a trip to town; Angus, the señora, and, at Douglas's insistence, Ignacio. The boy felt like an intruder as the rancher brushed aside Agnes's pleas that Douglas go along and leave Ignacio to watch over things.

"I've got a blue million things to do, Aggie, and he's entitled to the holiday. You can do my Christmas shopping."

If he expected any resentment on the señora's part, there was none. With Angus driving the team, as silent as he always was when he was actually doing something, the wagon ride found the lady of the D Cross A talking an enthusiastic streak.

"We'll take Jamie to the Sacramento for a good meal, not that Mary Stafford wouldn't have us, but she's not expecting us. Then, I suppose you'll disappear, Angus—wherever it is you go. It's Friday, so Dr. Clifton's reading group will be at the M.E. Church. Jamie won't hold still for that, so he can spend time with Nash. We'll shop tomorrow. Angus, don't let me forget to see if what's-his-name over at the depot has some new magazines in from the east."

Ignacio had never seen her so alive. She rattled on about the yard goods she needed, the chance to see friends at church on Sunday, and the presents she would buy for Douglas and Jamie. Angus just grunted when she pleaded with him to tell her what he wanted.

"Well, Angus Grant MacAndrews, if you think it's going to be a bottle of whiskey again this year, think again!"

The "good meal" at the Sacramento Hotel dining room was like a bad dream.

If Ignacio felt strange the first several times at Agnes's table at the D Cross A, the mannered formality of the Sacramento filled him with agony. There were too many dishes, too much silver and glassware, and far too much insolent attention from the Mexican waitress. No anglo girl, he thought, would show her contempt so openly. He was above himself, and every plate she thumped in front of him or snatched away told him so.

The señora and Angus didn't seem to notice, but Jamie did. His snickers were silent ones, but they rang in Ignacio's ears all the same. A bubble of anger threatened to swell and burst under his breastbone, while shame bathed his forehead in sweat. *Por favor,* Jamie—he nearly said it aloud—give me that smile that makes things right. This time it didn't come.

Agnes persuaded Mary Stafford to accompany her to her meeting. Angus disappeared as predicted ("either to Sullivan's Bar or that cantina in Mex Town," Jamie said) and the two boys were left with Findlay Stafford and his game of solitaire.

Stafford was a pleasant bespectacled man about the age of Douglas. Quiet, he nonetheless asked thoughtful questions of the younger rider about the D Cross A, the state of Douglas's health, about the condition of the herd and the level in the water tanks. Ignacio in his shyness would have been hard put to answer, but he wished at all costs to avoid making conversation with Jamie as long as possible.

At last, when Stafford pulled up the weights in a tall floor clock, and turned out most of the lamps, there was nothing to do but follow the other boy upstairs to the room he lived in.

"You sore at me about something, Nash?" Jamie asked from his side of the big double bed. In the dark, Ignacio could feel his cheeks redden. He should tell Jamie the truth.

"No, Jamie. *No es nada.*"

"That's good. Couldn't think of what I done."

Dios! He really meant it.

The wagon was loaded and standing in front of the Stafford house. Ignacio, in the box on a stack of salt cakes, looked at Angus, seated alongside the place reserved for the señora. The tall man wore a look Ignacio hadn't seen before, his teeth clenched on his pipe. He turned to glare at where Jamie and his mother were saying goodbye on the Stafford porch.

The MacAndrews boy was deep in a case of the sulks, pulling away when she tried to kiss his cheek. For a second Ignacio though Angus might leave the wagon and stride up the walk, but Agnes suddenly broke away from Jamie as swiftly as he had turned from her.

She came toward the wagon, her face white as gypsum against the upturned collar of her blue coat. Angus helped her into her seat, and they were off, the wagon jolted into motion by a heavier whip hand than Ignacio had ever seen Angus use.

The entire scene left the rider completely in the dark. Nothing had happened this Sunday morning or the day before to account for Jamie's sour mood. When they shopped with Agnes, and later by themselves, he was in soaring spirits, and in such good company Ignacio forgot about his offhand cruelty at the Sacramento. He helped Ignacio pick out a pair of boots at Stafford's general store, showed him around the town, even bought him a soft drink before they went back to the house on Estancia Street for supper.

Jamie kept his mother, his uncle, and the Staffords, in fits of laughter with tales of pranks in school. From the adults' reactions, he had a gift of mimicry. He would begin to quote one of his chums and Stafford would burst out, "That's Will Ed all right—to a tee!" or "Tommy Kinsey, ain't he outgrown that giggle yet?"

No, nothing Ignacio could remember would account for the black look Jamie had given his mother as they left. The rider could still hear the slam of the Staffords's door.

There was no talk as the heavy wagon rolled toward the D Cross A, but when they reached the south pasture gate and Ignacio leaped to the roadway to open up, he heard a sob.

Returning to his place in the wagon box, he saw Angus curl his arm around the slim shoulders of the señora.

"Aggie, Aggie. Never mind. He'll be fine about it by Christmas time."

"I don't know, Angus. I've never seen him act like this."

"Maybe you shouldn't have told him. Left it up to Douglas—or even let him find out for himself, gradual like, when you began to show."

"He didn't come right out with it, Angus, he wouldn't know how"—her voice was thin, tortured—"but he acted like there was something indecent about a woman my age—"

"Hush, Aggie. We'll be home soon. Douglas can handle this."

"Oh, Angus. I'd never tell him!"

"Well, lassie!" Angus shouted, holding the quart of whiskey above his head, his long tough fingers wrapped around it, "So you gave up and took pity on old Angus after all. Merry Christmas!"

"And a Merry Christmas to you," Agnes laughed, "but, mind you, you needn't finish it all today—even with help."

Ignacio was still squatting by the tree, where Agnes had motioned him when the opening of the gifts began. He was stupefied. He wanted to take part in the gaiety, but all he could do was nod when a remark was made to him. Mostly, he stared at the three gifts on their wrappings in front of him: the tough work gloves from Angus ("Now, laddie, maybe I won't always be doctoring those wee, soft paws of yours"), and from Agnes— wonder of wonders—a book. He couldn't even read the title page, but its smooth, blocky squareness, the neat trim of the pages, and the magic of the black type itself made him tremble with excitement. The last one, Douglas's, brought forth such a quick, blurted *"Gracias, señor"* he blushed, fearing Angus and the señora might think the thanks he murmured in English weak and unfelt by comparison. The moment passed quickly, such was his delight in the pair of roweled spurs Douglas had given him.

"*Es nada,* Ignacio," the rancher said. "'Course they aren't new. I didn't even buy them. They were hanging on a peg in that abandoned adobe by the malpais. Spanish, I guess. Hundred years old, maybe more, but what little rust was on them came right off with a touch of oil."

Ignacio held them, one in each hand, the gloves and even the book forgotten for the moment. There was something pleasing about the crude workmanship, the tool marks not quite filed out, the lack of symmetry between the left spur and the right. *Sí,* pleasing—handmade and human.

He hadn't expected anything. Now he felt the calico dish towels Findlay Stafford had wrapped for him pitifully inadequate, even though the señora's thanks were warm.

Jamie, released to his gifts only after Ignacio opened his, tore at the packages like a cat. He pulled a face at the writing set from his mother, but cried aloud with enthusiasm at his other things: a silver-mounted belt; shirts of such fineness they gleamed in the candlelight; a bone handled hunting knife from his uncle.

Douglas prevailed on Angus to open his bottle, saying, "Aggie, don't you suppose the boys could join us in a Christmas drink, just this once?"

Ignacio had never tasted whiskey before, but even though it was strong and alien in his mouth and burned his throat, it seemed right.

"Merry Christmas, everyone," Douglas said over the rim of his glass.

Ignacio felt as close to happiness as he had ever permitted his heart to venture.

"Jesus, Nash. I hate to go back to school," Jamie said. Ignacio was driving Jamie back to town after his holiday.

"I am sorry, too, Jamie." To his surprise, he found he really meant it. The ten days with young MacAndrews had been good ones. They had worked together twice, taking feed out on the range and repairing some faulty timbers in the stock pen where the branding would be done "come spring." Jamie was as strong as many grown men, and took pride in his strength in an offhand, unaffected way which made him a thoroughly enjoyable working partner. He applied himself tirelessly and enthusiastically to any task which required him to display his strength, and the two of them accomplished quite a lot together. True, he grew bored with anything which required time and patience, but there hadn't been much work like that. Douglas had made it clear they were to enjoy themselves during the holidays.

Jamie, with the help of Angus, taught Ignacio the game of dominoes and beat him every time they played, amid such gales of laughter and artless boasting, the rider decided— contentedly—it was just as well he hadn't shown more talent than he had.

He had half expected there might be another flareup of the scene at Stafford's between Jamie and his mother, but none came—or if one did it came in private. He watched Agnes and Jamie together very closely, and for the first time he realized how deeply the mother loved her son. When they were at supper, or in the sitting room, he saw Agnes move close to Jamie at every opportunity, patting his shoulder, stroking his hair, or just gazing at him fondly. Jamie liked the attention, that was obvious, but although he reciprocated, it was with only a fraction of the feeling his mother showed. He seemed to take her affection as a right. You are unfair, Ignacio, the rider told himself. You see this only because it is not yours.

"Oh, I like living in town," Jamie was saying, "but school, ugh! Tell the truth, I'm pretty dumb in school, and it don't bother me a bit. You don't need book learning if you're rich enough. Hey, Nash! Has Ma let you in on her big surprise?"

Ignacio said nothing. Better to appear stupid about this; after all, he had never really been told.

"Yep," Jamie said, "she's going to have a kid—after all these years." Ignacio listened hard for a trace of bitterness, but heard none. Maybe he would never completely know this boy.

On the right, half a mile away, he saw Douglas and Angus herding a dozen head of cattle through the gate to the big south pasture. The two distant riders waved at the pair of them in the buckboard

It had snowed overnight, and now, at half past seven in the morning, the sky was still gray and overcast. Surely the clouds would all be gone by the time he dropped Jamie at the Staffords's and turned about for home.

"Speaking of surprises," Jamie said, "has Ma let you in on the one she's got in store for you?"

"For me?"

"Then you *don't* know. I heard her telling Pa. He didn't let on how he felt, but she sure is all-fired keen on it."

"What is it, Jamie?"

"Hell, Nash—I ain't going to tell you. You'll find out soon enough. One thing, I'm glad it's you and not me!"

He probed his memory, trying to recall everything that had passed between the señora and himself these past weeks, but he was no further ahead when he stopped the buckboard in front of the Staffords's picket fence.

The sky was still cloud-covered when he reached the gate to the D Cross A. Once it was closed behind him, he wheeled a little more speed out of the old horse he had hitched up at dawn. On a bright day he might have let it poke along, but with the sky leaden and unpromising there was no point in lingering. This was the stretch where he had seen Douglas and Angus, but they would be long gone now. The whole vast landscape was empty.

When he topped the next rise he might see the small herd the brothers had been working. They would look like rust on the snow, motionless and winterbound. The wagon road—it was there, if only faintly, under the snow—made a rising curve past a whitened stand of yucca, then disappeared against the gloomy sky where it reached the crest of the ridge. The mountain ring seemed ominously close.

When the buckboard rolled to the top of the ridge, wheels clattering on the rocky roadbed beneath the snow, he halted the old horse. The silence pressed in on him as closely as the mountains and the sky. He stared across the pasture to where the building of the ranch nestled behind the butte, four snow-covered miles away.

Then, off to the left, he saw the cows Douglas and Angus had driven into the pasture in the early morning. They had gathered in a low, flat spot which had been as white and blank as a sheet of paper when Jamie and he had passed. Through the long day they had pressed their mouths against the snow, letting their hot breath melt it so they could get at the grass below. Now they had uncovered a circle a hundred feet or more across. Even in the wettest of Julys he had never seen a section of rangeland of such a deep blue-green.

He used the whip. Something electric passed from his quick hand to the flank of the old horse, and the buckboard shot from the top of the rise.

7

"There's only one order you can't change while we're gone, Ignacio," Douglas said from beside Angus on the wagon seat. "Until Angus gets back day after tomorrow, you aren't to get more than an hour's ride from the house. There won't be any trouble, but it's the first time the señora's been on the D Cross A without one of us, so I want you close by."

"*Sí, señor,*" Ignacio said. He wanted to tell him not to worry, but he knew it wouldn't do to deal in commonplaces with the rancher unless he was completely confident. He wasn't. There were still too many things he didn't know. All he could do now was hope his uncertainty didn't show.

"All right, then," Douglas said. "Let's roll, Angus. That train might just be on time for once."

The rancher hadn't planned for both of them to be away at once. His trip to El Paso had been in the offing for weeks ("If I don't see Ben Hardy at the bank damned soon," he said to Agnes one night, "he'll think I've changed my mind about the loan") but he had no sooner made it firm than word came from town that Angus's oldest wartime friend had died. Douglas wouldn't hear of his brother missing the funeral—that was that.

Ignacio watched the wagon make the last turn past the butte. As he started up the slope to the stable, he saw the señora at the kitchen doorway. Something told him she had been watching him and not the wagon, and he wondered for how long.

Trying not to think about this—or the evening meal he would share with her alone—he decided to stay as busy as he could until suppertime. He could spend an hour straightening up Angus's crude smithy in the open shed by the stable. The tall brother, who was farrier for the ranch as well as engineer and cowhand, and ordinarily as tidy as he was big, had left his shop in rare disorder when the news about his friend had come. Then he could feed the ponies, and after that do some work on the saddle Douglas told him to look on as his own. *Sí,* there was always something for a hand to do.

But the hours and minutes would pass. The time would come when there would be nothing left to do but wash for supper, walk the pathway to the house, settle in at the table, and eat if he could. He took himself to task for his attitude. Why should he feel this nervous fear about the kind señora? *Quién sabe?*

"For pity's sake, don't fret about it, Nash!" Agnes said. "It's only a plate—an old one at that."

It had happened. The piece of china skittered from his hand as if it had a life of its own. The señora was right, it was a small thing, nothing a sensible man should concern himself about, but he had dreaded it for so long he felt worse, once it happened, than he had feared. The shards of the plate lay about his feet, and in the silence which followed the ringing crash, he could hear his heart, and feel the blood flame his face.

"Nash," Agnes said, taking the dish towel from a hand which didn't feel it leave, "I'll finish up. Now don't you go running to the shack. Oh, I know you want to. Tonight I want to talk with you a bit. Go on in the sitting room." *Dios,* she actually pushed him. "Poke up the fire and try to relax until I'm done here."

* * *

Try to relax—impossible. He had thrown another piñon log on the half dead ashes. Every time the heat reached a knot the cracking sound assaulted his nerves until they hummed like new fence in a windstorm. He watched the flames lick away at the fresh log, and gradually his embarrassment faded.

What did the señora want to talk about? Something to do with Jamie? *Sí,* that could be. Perhaps it was only about some chore to be done tomorrow. Or—he hoped this wasn't it—was she about to say something about the baby she was carrying? Did she ever notice how he averted his eyes rather than be seen looking at the bulge under her apron?

"Sit down, Nash. There, in Douglas's chair."

He lowered himself into the big chair with more care than if he were climbing on a fractious horse; it seemed wrong to sit here. It would have been more wrong, though, not to do as he was told.

Agnes took her seat in the rocker and he forced himself to look at her. Behind her loomed the book shelves, the light from the fire bringing them close, as it always did. The books absorbed only a fraction of the light. Its greatest intensity was reflected to him from the eyes of the woman, the flame color changed and heightened by the time it reached him. It seemed that if he returned her look full measure he might be overstepping the safe, restrictive bounds of their relationship, and yet, there was nothing he could do but meet her gaze.

He waited for her to speak, but she only shook her head slowly from side to side, and set the rocking chair in motion. For a long minute, her eyes on him every second, the erect head moving toward him and then receding as she rocked, the only sound was the creaking of the chair and now and again a crackle from the fireplace. Then she stopped and stared even harder.

"Nash!" It was a high, urgent cry, a cry lost some place between a plea and a command.

"*Señora?*" He choked out his reply. Suddenly he remembered Jamie's talk of a surprise. Was it coming now?

Agnes let out a long breath astounding for one so small. "I don't really know how to start this, Nash. But—it's about the books. I've seen you"—she drew her breath in again—"looking at them—reaching for them—touching—so many times."

His stomach churned with such violence he felt ill. "I am truly sorry, *señora*. I meant no wrong."

"Hush, Nash. I didn't say that in criticism—not at all." The fire blazed up, brightened as she spoke, but his face was flushed more from the warmth in her voice and the quick excitement in her eyes, the same excitement he remembered from the first night he stood in front of the wall of books.

"No, Nash. No criticism. Just the opposite." She took her hands from the arms of the rocker and folded them in her lap. "You told me once you could read a little—in Spanish."

"*Sí, señora*"

Agnes MacAndrews squared her shoulders and tipped the rocker forward. *Ahora,* Ignacio thought—now. It comes now.

"How would you like"—she drew still another breath—"to learn to read—in English?"

She paused then and sat straight up, and as if a dam had burst, words spilled out and inundated him. "Learn other things, too, Nash! To cipher, do sums—everything those books hold—I-I could teach you, Nash. Really, I'm a *good* teacher. I *know* I am. No matter what—" she checked herself for the tiniest part of a second and hurried on. "You could learn to read the book I gave you for Christmas." She stopped once more. "It would be a whole new world."

Ignacio searched her face. She looked suddenly tired, drained. He caught the sparkle of a tear jeweled by the light of the fire.

"*I am a good teacher.*" This time it was softer, sadder, and for herself alone.

One moment was all he took.

"*Sí, señora,*" he said. "*Sí,* I would like to—very much."

It was as if he had ridden at breakneck speed off a canyon rim—but knowingly, willingly.

Before sleep, he reached under the bunk and pulled out the wooden box which held his few belongings.

There it was, the book. He riffled the leaves as he had almost every night since Christmas, but it was different. It wasn't just dead leather and paper any more. He breathed on the curved back, rubbed it against his pants and held it up to the lantern to see it shine. As he placed it in the box, his eye fell on the roweled spurs. He hadn't used them yet, or worn the gloves from Angus. That must change—tomorrow.

Some time during the night, figures came stalking from the past, but before he could see their faces or call out to them, the white wall rose in all its sickening, familiar blankness.

"Glory be!" Angus roared, wiping tears of laughter from his seamed face. "Aggie's got her a brand new pupil. Mind you don't blot your copybook, laddie, or she'll take a ruler to you!"

Angus had returned in the middle of Ignacio's second school session. Scarcely glancing up from the big lettered words in the old primer the señora had propped under the globe lamp, the boy had nevertheless heard the low whistle the man gave, and he was aware of Agnes hustling him into the kitchen.

Now, the next day, Angus teased him unmercifully. "Well, scholar, when you learn to write, maybe you can compose some billy-doo to these cows that'll keep them in the right pasture." Ignacio didn't mind at all, even when Angus found him in the tack room, scratching C-A-T in the dirt floor.

He did his chores in a painstaking fury. For all that good-natured Angus seemed to smile on the learning, he couldn't be remiss in any way. Each task was completed right, but he drove himself to finish work before sundown, making sure nothing would call him from the study table after supper. Amazingly, he didn't tire, even though sleep came hard to a brain which ticked like an overwound watch.

Hard as he worked, he felt lazy when he caught sight of Agnes going about her housework. Anxious that nothing should intrude on her one-pupil class, she was a dust-devil in the kitchen. He wasn't to help with the dishes now; she herded him into the sitting room after each evening meal, set him to reviewing the lesson of the night before, and dragooned a mildly protesting Angus into taking Ignacio's place at the sink, as he had when the cut hands were healing.

Ignacio was enthralled by his studies, even the simple-minded stories in the beginning reader, a slim volume about a dog named Rab and assorted little anglo girls who all looked like miniature adults in the gray engravings which took up most of every page. When he puzzled it out, he wanted to ask the señora what was meant by the word "eclectic" on the cover, but saved the question, fearful he might interrupt her teaching.

The second night Angus was home, he heard him say to Agnes in the kitchen, "I know it ain't my business—and you can tell me so. But did you talk this over with Douglas? Remember how it was the last time?" The answer was lost in the sound of dishware.

Five days after the lessons began, Douglas returned from El Paso, bringing Jamie from town to spend the weekend.

"Ben's willing to make the loan," Ignacio heard him tell his wife and brother, "but he's got to get the approval of his board.

One of them is asking for a mortgage on the entire ranch, not just the twenty sections east of the road. I won't go for that, and Ben knows it. We've got time. Shelby doesn't really want to sell until after roundup, maybe not even until midsummer. Maybe by that time Ben can talk his man around."

Ignacio was excited, not so much by the purchase Douglas planned (although he had seen this stretch of rangeland on one of the rides last fall, and remembered it as being thick with grass) as by hearing again the word "roundup." He nearly forgot his schoolwork when he thought of what the spring would bring.

Jamie wasn't impressed by his father's plans. "Beats me why Pa's so all-fired hot to get that land. Ain't as if he was going to buy more stock right quick and make some money. He's got this idea somebody's got to take care of it now that old man Shelby's cashing in."

If anticipation of the roundup put the books temporarily in second place, Ignacio still carried some of them to the shack each night, for reading beyond the pages the señora had assigned. *Dios,* she had been so very right. It was a whole new world.

It was a world Douglas walked in on his second night home. Ignacio, finished for the evening, lifted his head from the books to find the big man looking at him. The boy recalled the question Angus had asked the señora, and he wondered what he could say if Douglas didn't approve.

"Don't let me disturb you, Ignacio," the rancher said.

"I am finished, *señor.*"

"Mrs. MacAndrews tells me you're doing very well." Douglas smiled, not a big smile, but warm enough. Something told Ignacio that even if the señor harbored doubts about the studies, he would never stop them. "Just don't overdo it, Ignacio. Books are gold, but they can weigh as heavy, if they aren't carried right."

The young rider stood up and said goodnight. As he walked past the rancher and through the sitting room, he saw the señora standing in the archway. A look of relief was still making a passage across her features.

Spring had hinted at its coming all through February and March, but its early signals were cancelled by late snows which saw Angus crowing gleefully at his forecasting. Then April slipped in with a burning sun and left with a bounding rush of dust storms, winds at gale force scourging the range with driving yellow sand. A man could look above him and see the sun, a pale, white face hanging aloof and neutral above the battle, but straight ahead—if he dared to peer incautiously against the wind or even safely with it—he could see nothing beyond arm's length.

Regular work was at a standstill, and Angus and Douglas drifted in various degrees of irritation between the house and stable, while the señora and the young rider stuffed rags around the window edges. They carried uncounted buckets of sand from the house, only to see it invade the windward rooms unchecked whenever the storm resumed.

The winds stopped, and three days of soft, cleansing rain marked the last of May. A new, surging stream of life was loosed in the desert. The ocotillo, sending out new growth after each shower, blossomed red as blood, and flowers of pure cream softened the spikes of the yucca.

It was roundup time.

Some of the riding, in the farthest upper pastures bordering the piñon, had already been done by the three of them, with Jamie helping out on weekends. Ignacio was impressed with Jamie as a cowhand. He thought him a bit hard on his ponies, but he readily admitted young MacAndrews's skill and willingness when hard, fast riding was demanded.

"The real work," Angus explained to Ignacio, "don't actually get started until old Tom and his crew get here."

At sundown on the second of June, the three itinerant hands Douglas had hired rode into the yard of the D Cross A. Lean, leathery men, not young, they brought with them a combined chuck and bunk wagon pulled by mules. The señor and Angus talked to Tom, the leader, about the work which was to begin even before first light, while Ignacio watched the old puncher with eyes bright as diamonds. Here was a true vaquero! He would almost give up all the books to be like that.

"Angus, Ignacio," Douglas said, as they left the extra hands to make their camp by the corral, "let's get supper. No school tonight, laddie. Early to bed. Tomorrow's a big day!"

8

By THE TIME THE SUN NOSED OVER BIG CUCHILLO AND SENT ITS RAYS shooting through the early morning clouds, seeking the high places of the basin, Ignacio had already been in the saddle for the better part of two hours.

So far it hadn't been too different from his imaginings in the restless night. Busting out for bunch quitters, chasing laggards from the mesquite, turning the leaders to the pens, it was like the trail herding he had done. The riding was more strenuous, *sí*. He could never slacken the reins and let the pony make its own gait, and he found himself using the spurs Douglas had given him more frequently than he liked. If this pace continued, he would need a fresh horse by noon. At least it was cool, and would stay cool until the sun cleared the last of the ragged clouds on the horizon.

He was doubly grateful for this. The chill breeze kept the pony from lathering up too quickly, and tempered the heat in his face, which was still flushed from the bad start he had made with old Tom in the blue darkness before dawn.

He had gone to the bunk wagon and offered to cut out working mounts for the extra hands. Douglas's agreement with Tom was that the D Cross A would furnish the saddle stock for the roundup, while the three itinerants' sad old horses rested.

"Nope," Tom said, releasing a squirt of tobacco juice into the caliche, "thankee, sonny, but no. Nobody can fit out a cow horse to suit this crew. If you'll just show us the ones we *ain't* to use, we'll fix our own selves up. And, sonny, for Christ's sake, don't stand there like a chill-picking sharecropper!"

His knees gone weak, it was a moment before Ignacio realized he had removed his hat before speaking, and was holding it across his chest, peasant fashion. He had bowed, too, as he did with Douglas and the señora, and Angus, on occasion. Was this wrong? He wanted the good opinion of this vaquero. Was not the way to get respect to show it first?

The hard riding in the cool air helped, and later, when the sun's full force sent sweat streaming down his back, he had almost forgotten the shame of the morning.

With Angus and one of Tom's men, he worked the south pasture, learning a new herding skill every minute. He soon discovered the tall man's trick of working only certain animals, the older calves and yearlings. These, missed in the hasty roundup at the close of summer, must be turned, set to milling, and sent on the rider's way, mothers and newborn following the knotting groups with only rare rebellions.

As the morning wore on and the small herd joined the one Douglas and Tom brought in from the west, the rising din of cattle all but drowned out Angus's gleeful yips. Each moment was so filled with effort and movement Ignacio didn't notice the hours skipping by, but his stomach did. He would have to tighten his belt. Douglas had made it plain there would be no time for food until the day's work was finished.

The big holding pen fenced more confusion than the boy would have thought possible at the tranquil D Cross A. With the sun past its zenith, the full heat of the day came in waves—not from the sky, but blasting upward from the ground. More than two hundred animals were jammed in the holding pen, the grass shredded into chaff by a thousand hoofs, beaten into a pall of dust and fiber which clogged nostrils and streaked sweaty faces. *Riatas* waved above horses and riders like darting snakes.

"All right, Ignacio!" It was Douglas beside him, the usually soft voice a bellow. "From now on we work on foot!"

Tethering his pony outside the gate, Ignacio climbed to the top of the fence, cattle prod in hand. High above the sea of heaving backs, he could see past the squeeze chute to where Angus and Tom were setting up the branding. Smoke, rising from the fire where the stamping irons rested in the coals, all but obscured the work bench which held knives, serum needles, and paint brushes in a crock of healing dope.

Then the rider was down from the fence, afoot in a jarring, tumbling press of horn and muscle. For an hour he and Douglas goaded, pushed, and shoved, cutting calves away from the older stock, getting the fear-crazed beasts into the chute any way they could, sometimes with the prods, often with just their arms and shoulders. Once, Ignacio got a good clear look at the branding area. When he saw Tom busy at a calf held fast in the wooden clamp, he remembered what Douglas told him when he gave him the whetstone, months ago, "Yes, Ignacio, when we notch and castrate, your knife should be sharper than a norther. No point in making the poor dumb brutes suffer more than necessary."

The rider caught a whiff of burnt hair and hide, and the sharp stench of blood. Arm and leg weary, head aching from the relentless bawling of confused and frightened cattle, he was weak from the heat, and grateful when Douglas called a halt for a pull from the water bottles, and to make a fresh assignment of the work.

The other men were lighting smokes and talking when Ignacio joined them. He squatted in the dust and listened.

"This here squeeze chute makes it a lead pipe cinch," Tom was saying, "leastways for a small outfit. On a bigger spread it takes too much time getting the bastards together. I sure ain't sorry. I've hind footed so much in some operations, my roping arm damn near fell off."

"Yep," one of the other others joined in, "ain't used a pigging string in four, five jobs. Not since that place back in the panhandle."

"It's only this doctoring and medicating holds you up," Tom said. "Be bad if there was scabies worrying us this year."

"We've had no trouble here, not inside our fence, or anywhere else in the Ojos Negros." This was Señor Douglas. "Guess it's because we're so protected. That ring of mountains." He lifted his big arm to the skyline.

"And not a case of anthrax I remember, thank God!" Angus said.

The talk subsided and a strange dreamy silence took its place. There seemed to be a greater sense of comradeship among them in the quiet than when they had all been talking, and Ignacio was touched by sadness and loss when Angus stood up abruptly. "Well, let's get at it," he said. "Keep my mind off my empty gizzard."

It was time for Ignacio to work the branding side with Douglas, Angus, and Tom. He watched the old puncher when the first wide-eyed calf came clattering through the chute, hammering the timbers until Angus threw his great weight against the lever and stopped it in its tracks. Tom cropped the ear, a simple angle slash which would say D Cross A to any stockman in the basin. Ignacio moved in with the blackleg serum as Douglas had shown him, while the rancher himself applied the iron, returning it to the fire even before the hissing stopped and the wisp of smoke trailed away. The needle slipped under the hide with surprising ease, without even a quiver from the calf, so busy was it protesting the other ways these men were violating it.

Out of the corner of his eye, he saw Tom cut away the sac which swung between the calf's hind legs and toss the bloody mess to a waiting barrel. Then the old man loaded a brush with the dope from the medicine pot and smeared it on the fresh brand and the red, running cuts. Insects drifted around the chute and blackened the rim of the barrel. What must it be like, Ignacio thought, in the *real* fly time?

Angus released the calf, and Douglas motioned Ignacio to the fire and the glowing irons.

"Easy, easy!" Tom shouted in his ear. "A light touch, sonny, or you'll burn clear through to his innards."

He did better after the first one, but the familiar blush scorched his cheeks until he felt he carried the ranch brand himself.

If Douglas hadn't called another rest, and given Ignacio time to think, he might have done it all. But after he branded a dozen calves and watched them rock away stiff-legged, shaking droplets of blood from their heads, the halt allowed him too long to look at the bloody clutter on the bench and the flies on the barrel, and far too long to choke on the odor of ripped flesh, blood, cow droppings, and burning hair. The complaints of a hundred animals beat against his eardrums.

"Take the knife this trip, Nash," Angus said.

Ignacio turned again to the chute, where Tom now had a big calf pinned motionless. Stepping forward, the rider grabbed an ear and made his cut. Like hot oil, the blood ran down the bone handle of the knife. He moved to the other end of the calf to get the last part over with. Done once it could be done again. *Sí.* When he touched the sac, something in his stomach picked that moment to rebel. He backed away, stumbling. Terrified he would lose whatever remained of his breakfast, he turned to run—and came face to face with Douglas.

"I can't, *señor.*" Was that thin, reedy whine *his* voice? "I am sorry, but—not the *cojones.*" He wished he was not too old to cry.

"Gimme the knife, sonny," Tom said. "It ain't a bit different from picking chilis."

Supper, served outside by Agnes on a long table made from planks laid on sawhorses, was nearly beyond Ignacio's endurance. Jamie was there, ferried from town by Doc Faraday, the Black Springs vet, who always, Angus said, showed up at some time during a D Cross A roundup. The MacAndrews boy didn't have to be told about Ignacio's failure, not the way Angus and Tom carried on, making obscene remarks about the rider's manhood whenever Agnes went inside for another dish, suggesting that Ignacio lacked those parts he refused to remove in the branding pen. Jamie's grin widened with every jibe sent the rider's way, even those Tom uttered in surprisingly fluent Spanish.

All Ignacio could do was hold his tongue and suffer. But when the meal ended near dark, he slipped away and sough out Douglas in the house. The rancher was seated with the señora in front of the dead fireplace.

"What is it, Ignacio?"

"It is about this afternoon, *señor.* Again—I am truly sorry. Would you"—this was the most painful question he had ever asked—"would you like me to leave the D Cross A?"

Agnes gave a strangled cry, but before Ignacio could turn to look at her, the sitting room thundered with Douglas's laugh.

"Not unless you want to, Ignacio," the rancher said when the laugh subsided. "Now look, laddie. I've seen a lot of vaqueros couldn't face that chore, real money-winning cowboys, champions. Maybe you can handle it tomorrow."

"No, *señor*." With this man honesty was all that worked. "I know I will never be able to do this thing."

Douglas turned serious now. "Be that as it may, Ignacio. I want you here, inside our fence, just as long as you want to stay. I—" he looked at Agnes, "—*we* need you."

The second day was like the first, except that with Jamie working and Doc Faraday helping with the medicating, they handled half again as many cattle. Douglas kept Ignacio out of the branding area, sending him out to clean out the two smaller pastures against the side of Cuchillo, those bordering on the twenty sections he wanted to buy.

Alone, away from the knowing smiles of the roundup crew, the boy reflected on his disgrace the day before. Douglas's words had soothed the worst of the hurt, but he knew the affair wasn't finished yet.

There was Jamie. He hadn't seen much of him since last night at supper, and he admitted frankly to himself he was in no hurry. The señor must have guessed as much; the way he laid out the work, their paths hadn't crossed at all.

He rode like a demon through the day, and in the late afternoon, high on the mesa under Cuchillo's brooding crest, he looked down on the D Cross A. He didn't seem part of all that magnificent commotion now. Suddenly he was tired. Night, and the seclusion of the shack, couldn't come too soon.

* * *

"You'll ride with Tom today, Ignacio."

The young rider stiffened. There was no way to tell the señor how much he dreaded spending an entire day with the ornery old cowhand, but he still felt he remained at the ranch only on sufferance. Douglas's face was so purposeful, he decided he had better keep his objections to himself.

"There's only some cleanup left," Douglas said. "The Kansas City people will be in next week, with their own drovers, and after we help them cut out the sale stock we'll be through. Tom doesn't know the country down by the malpais. You'll have to show him."

Ignacio marched off to the corral as erect and rigid as a piñon post. Tom was waiting for him, already up on the gray Angus had lent him for the day.

"Howdy, sonny," he croaked. "So you're going to be my guide. Sure as hell hope you can find this here malpais better than you can find the business end of a calf."

Ignacio continued his stiff march through the corral and into the tack room. Getting his saddle and gear, he could hear Tom talking to one of his crew.

"I was going to try that spotted varmint, but Angus tipped me it was a might shifty and said I should stay in this old rocking chair. Would like to see how that mean-looking buster goes, though."

That settled it for Ignacio. There would be some risk. Calico hadn't been ridden for a week, and even with regular work he was a tricky brute; it was more than possible the pony would pitch him out of the corral the instant he hit the saddle. Well—he couldn't look more pathetic in Tom's eyes than he did. The risk was worth it.

It nearly turned out as he feared. Leaving the ground with all four feet, Calico put daylight between the boy and the leather a dozen times before he got him quieted and under way.

Moments later, as they crossed the bridge with Tom in the lead, the old cowhand turned right around and looked at him. His eyes were narrowed and unreadable, and when he looked ahead again, it seemed he was talking to himself.

* * *

It sounded easy enough to say "make a sweep of the south-west pasture," but it was grueling work and hard, blistering riding. They searched every arroyo for strays, and where the last D Cross A land sloped down to the malpais, the gullies were choked with thorny undergrowth which ripped at their faces. Several times Calico jumped almost unmanageably when he brushed against the bronze pods hanging from the rattleweed. It was hotter, too, in these broken, weed-infested lowlands.

"One lucky thing, sonny," Tom said when Ignacio flushed three old steers out of rocky draw, "we ain't found any unbranded critters. Maybe we won't have to fire up and use the iron, and maybe you can keep that medicine kit buttoned up." They were the first words from either of them, and the older rider's voice betrayed a tired ache which must have come from his very bones.

But if Tom slowed down, Ignacio didn't. He rode as hard and well at three as he had at ten, and little by little he realized he was doing most of the work. When they came across a small isolated herd, it was Ignacio who rode into its center to check for missing brands and ear crops, or signs of illness. It was Ignacio, not Tom, who found the dogied calf mooning in the shade of a yucca, roped it, and trailed the long-faced orphan until they spotted a mother who had lost her own infant. And it was Ignacio who restrung the wire around the bad water at the edge of the alkali flat.

The sun was still warm on their backs as they caught up with their shadows on the slope leading to the corral. Unsaddling, Ignacio saw Tom's two partners loafing at the bunk wagon, one of then trying a tune on a harmonica.

"Sonny," Tom said, "we won't be eating with you. Hitting the hay early to roll out at first light. You won't see our ugly kissers again 'til fall—*if* your big man liked our work." The cowboy paused. The slanting sun softened his features. "Something I want to get off my chest before we say *adiós*. I know we gave you a helluva bad time with that ragging the other day. Now, I ain't apologizing. You'll get worse in this life. I do feel a little bad we spilled it all in front of the MacAndrews kid. I can see that pulls the cinch a mite tight. But what I'm getting at—and your boss feels this way, too, I know—you're going to be one of the best goddamn cowhands in the territory, if you ain't already." Tom stuck out a tough old claw of a hand. "*Hasta la vista,*" he said, "vaquero!"

For the first time in his memory, Ignacio Ortiz smiled.

Despite the long day, Ignacio wasn't tired. He felt giddy, as he imagined he might if he had too much to drink. Washing for supper, stripped to the waist, he realized that during the roundup he had worn the old white cotton shirt and trousers—the only clothes he owned when he first came to the ranch. Jamie or no Jamie, it was time to dress like a vaquero of the D Cross A.

9

JAMIE'S SCHOOL TERM ENDED IN MID-MAY, AND HE SHOULD HAVE BEEN at the ranch long before roundup, but examination time found him failing in almost every subject. He stayed in town for a month of tutoring with Dr. Clifton, although Agnes protested that she could do it while she taught Ignacio. Douglas had placed his large hands flat on the supper table and said (marvelously gently, Ignacio thought), "No, Ag. It won't work. Be content with the fine job you're doing with this young man."

The señora had raced him through the primers and beginning arithmetics. He didn't care for the sums and multiplication tables as he pretended, but he took wild delight in the large, square geography with its great colored maps.

Angus helped here. The tall cowboy knew the face of the world like the back of his hand, although he and Ignacio were both disappointed not to find Ramos on the page that showed Mexico curling like a question mark under the imposing mass of the United States. Aside from Santa Fe, there were no towns shown in the territory, either, and certainly no Black Springs.

By now his skill in reading was such that he could make a shaky start on the book the señora had given him. Word by resisting word, he made his way past the title page which read *Complete Works of William Shakespeare*. It was painful going, written as it was in a tongue bearing faint resemblance to the primers, yet there was something there which held him fast, if a good part of it did elude him.

Angus sniffed, "It's all right, some of it; Macbeth, maybe. But it ain't a patch on Bobbie Burns."

Then Jamie did come home, bringing a dissolute looking blue tick hound named Sam who smelled of every alley in the town. He enlisted Ignacio's help in bathing the dog, fussed mightily over it for a couple of days, and then forgot it.

Sam started sleeping in the shack, and the rider found he was glad of the company, even when Sam chose the middle of the night to ravage his saggy old hide for fleas, his snuffles and yowls robbing Ignacio of precious sleep.

By and large, Jamie and Ignacio got along in a way which gratified the Mexican. The good feelings the rider began to look upon as normal were based mainly on how well they worked together, but they had been strengthened by a little thing which occurred the last night of the roundup. When the rider went in to supper, he stepped right up to the anglo youngster, steeled to do some kind of battle if Jamie made a snide remark about the Levis and the checked shirt he wore.

"Hey!" Jamie said, "You look keen, Nash." His undisguised approval was reinforced by the wide, familiar smile. If Ignacio was pleased, it was nothing to his joy at the MacAndrews boy's next words, uttered with every bit as much sincerity, "Honest, Nash. *You're a regular vaquero!*"

They spent a pleasant day, Sam nosing at their heels, helping Angus plant a row of poplars to shade a kitchen garden Agnes planned. Ignacio thought there was something reminiscent of Douglas in the eager joyful way Jamie used his strong body, lifting the awkward, burlap-bagged trees from the wagon and plopping them in the holes Angus carved from the caliche.

It didn't bother him that it was he, the vaquero, who followed with the water bucket, carefully covering the roots over against the burning sun and squeezing the air away from them with his booted foot.

As June sped to a close, Agnes spent less time with Ignacio and his books. He never heard her say anything, but he saw her put her hands to the small of her back more often, and sensed she was getting close to delivering. Douglas confirmed it when he asked if she didn't think it was time to move to town and finish her waiting with Mary Stafford.

"Douglas," she said, "I'd like to have the baby here. Couldn't we get Angélica Rivera to come out and stay with me?" Douglas beamed, and Angus, too.

"Be damned!" the older brother said. "She went to town to have Jamie. Must figure there's nothing to it now."

Ignacio found himself smiling at this exchange, but he saw that Jamie was sober-faced and silent.

Douglas was off again to El Paso to make the final arrangements with Ben Hardy for the loan he needed to buy the Shelby land. As the rancher thought, the banker had convinced the lone holdout on his board that the parcel MacAndrews had his heart set on would support a mortgage by itself. The vaquero didn't understand these things, but he saw the reason for Douglas's refusal to pledge any part of the present D Cross A, even for grazing as lush as Shelby's unused land.

"Jamie," the señor said at supper the night before he left, "I want you to ride the north fence with Ignacio tomorrow. We haven't really checked it since we were at Corona last summer. And don't try to shunt it off on Angus. He's got enough to do."

"Sure, Pa. We'll take care of it." He sounded definite enough to satisfy any father.

A day later, despite Ignacio's tentative reminders, there had been no move to get it done, and the vaquero told Angus he would make the ride alone. The tall man looked a little vexed.

It didn't surprise Ignacio that afternoon when he heard heated talk in the tack room, but the outcome did.

"All right, *all right*!" It was the first time he had heard Angus shout since roundup. "If you want to go so bad, go ahead, Jamie. At that, *Nash* deserves a trip to town. But I can't make that north fence ride for a couple of days, and if I find a lot of wire needs mending, I'll skin you good—if your daddy don't beat me to it!" Angus, scowling, just nodded to the vaquero when they came out of the tack room.

On Jamie's handsome face there was a huge grin of success. "Break out your best duds, Nash, old buddy," he said to Ignacio. "We're going to Black Springs for the Fourth!" He ran, almost dancing, toward the house.

"I will stay and make the ride, *Señor* Angus," Ignacio said.

"It's all right, laddie. I'll manage. To tell the truth, I'd feel better if you went along. Keep Master Jamie out of trouble. He won't have it, but he's still wet behind the ears. And don't worry about me. I'll be fine."

There was no reason for it, but the vaquero had strong misgivings the next morning when he swung his leg over Calico and followed an exulting Jamie across the plank bridge.

10

"See the way that Martínez girl looked at me, Nash? Sure like to try her. Bet she's a regular little whoor!"

"A what, Jamie?"

"A whoor—you know—a *puta.*"

Ignacio had seen the frank look Concepción Martínez gave the young anglo. He had marked it to simple friendliness, nothing more, but Jamie's smug confidence might be justified. *Quién sabe?* He was good looking enough to attract the girl, and although the daughter of the owner of the Cantina Florida wasn't as poor as others in Mex Town, she would be impressed by the fact that Jamie was *un rico,* rich beyond the comprehension of anyone in her part of Black Springs, New Mexico.

As he had with everyone on this trip, Jamie turned the full force of his high-spirited charm on the girl when she brought the beers he had talked her father out of. Yes, Ignacio had seen Concepción look at Jamie.

He saw, too, the hot macho pride in the glare the girl's brother Jorge had shot at Jamie from behind the bar, and he hurried young MacAndrews as much as he could, claiming anxiety about the ranch.

"All right, *amigo,*" Jamie said. "Just let me finish, will you? I had to argue hard enough to get it."

"It's been three days, Jamie."

"Christ, I know that. Won't hurt Angus to look after things a little longer." Jamie's eyes were so fixed on the girl as she carried trays between the bar and the tables, he almost missed his mouth with the bottle. Ignacio saw her laugh.

Abruptly, Jamie finished, stood up, and looked down at Ignacio. "Well come on, if you're so hell-fired keen to get back."

It was their last sally before heading home. Ignacio had enjoyed the Independence Day celebrations in Black Springs's dusty plaza, and the Staffords had been hospitable to a fault. Still, his expressed concern for the ranch wasn't entirely a ruse to get Jamie out of the Florida. Something had nagged him for the whole three days, even if Angus had insisted on his going.

He felt better as they trotted along the ranch road, and when they passed the stone brow of the butte and thundered across the bridge, he was at ease. Then, as the horses broke into a lope on the climb to the corral, his apprehension returned—stronger than before.

Something was wrong. He felt it even before he saw the windmill whirling unchecked and the tank running over, even before Jamie cried. "Nash! What the blamed hell are those fool ponies up to?"

The working mounts were lined up like the horses in the parade in town, but with heads tossing and chests pressing against the corral fence, pushing so heavily he feared it might give way and spill them into the yard.

"They haven't been fed, Jamie—for a long time."

The vaquero began hauling feed while Jamie ran to the house. Clucking softly to quiet the ponies, wilder now that they smelled food, he noticed deep furrows in the otherwise level ground of the corral. It must have rained torrents while he and Jamie were gone. *Sí*, there were pieces of wood, straw, and other debris, all helter-skelter against the south end of the corral, near his shack, surely swept there by a flood.

After the ponies in the corral had settled down, he unsaddled Calico and Jamie's horse and watered them, grudging them the time it took to drink. Then he hurried across the yard to the ranch house.

It had been months since Ignacio had knocked before entering the kitchen—ever since Agnes told him to stop—and he didn't know why he did so now, unless something of the fear he sensed inside had touched him, too.

Agnes was seated at the table, hands clenched in front of her. Thin lines of fright etched her face. Behind her he could see in the archway shadows the big figure of Angélica Rivera. The midwife tried to smile when she saw him but it didn't work out well at all. Jamie was sitting across from his mother. Of the three of them, he was the only one whose countenance could in any way be considered normal.

"Sorry the chores in the corral weren't done, Nash." Agnes looked up at him.

"Everything is all right now, *señora*."

"Angélica would have seen to it, but when the storms came we didn't dare move outside the door, and we've been busy in the house since they stopped."

Before he could ask the question on his mind, she went on, "—and with Angus gone. Oh, I forgot. You haven't heard. I just now finished telling Jamie." She looked at her son and then back at the vaquero. "Angus checked the north fence the day after you left. He found a break and some animals missing, as many as a dozen, he thought. He came back for his bedroll and another pack horse. Wouldn't wait for morning." She closed her eyes. "We haven't seen him since."

Dios! That was two full days ago. The tall man should have been back by now. Still, it was hard to tell when the truants left the ranch and how far they might have strayed. There was a lot of rocky, broken country north of the fence, and tracking even a dozen head would be slow and difficult. Likely they would see Angus back by sundown and in a fine rage.

"Gee, Ma," Jamie said, "Angus'll be all right. It ain't like this kind of thing ain't happened before." His voice and manner brimmed with confidence and Ignacio blessed him silently.

"*Señora*," he said himself, "we should see *Señor* Angus any time now."

"Well," Agnes said, "I guess there's nothing to be done now but wait." Her spirits, Ignacio saw, were lifting a little with the two of them back. Of course, it was the presence of Jamie which made the difference—he realized that.

Angus didn't come in by sundown, nor did he return in time for the late supper Angélica served them. As the hours went by Ignacio watched Agnes's state of mind erode until it was worse than when he and Jamie had returned. She asked the boys about their trip, but when she repeated questions, he knew she hadn't listened.

After dark he walked the compound looking for damage from the storm. There was nothing which couldn't wait. The windmill had stopped its runaway spin and was turning sedately now, but he locked it all the same. Angus had taught him respect for the level of the water table the deep well sucked from. Even in a good wet year like this it didn't pay to waste.

He went to the shack and tried to study, but, lying down, the book was like a boulder on his chest, and when he sat at the table, it was too easy to stand and walk through the open door.

The stars were out, and the small wind had stopped. From the kitchen came the sound of laughter—Jamie's laughter. *Bueno, Jamie,* he thought, you are doing well, indeed.

The renegade coyote which usually prowled the top of the butte was quiet, and Ignacio was sure that if he couldn't see a rider coming through the north rocks, he most certainly would hear him. He wouldn't undress for bed. Even independent Angus would welcome help after such a ride.

"*Sí, señora.* I know the place. It is a mile west of the new tank, near the line shack." She hadn't put up much of an argument when Ignacio insisted they should wait no longer.

By the time the sun was high enough to bring sweat oozing from under their hatbands, he and Jamie had almost crossed the upper pastures. They reached the tank by noon, let the horses rest while they ate, and, fifteen minutes after they remounted, found the break.

It took some minutes to get through. Angus had made a temporary repair, and Ignacio carefully closed it up again as the tall man had.

In the soft ground among the piñons, they found good tracks they followed easily and swiftly, but once beyond the trees, they could only guess at the line of least resistance taken by a footloose bunch of cows; the rains had scrubbed the rocky uplands of any sign which could have helped.

This was new territory for Ignacio, bad country, littered with great slabs of rock bleached white as skulls. What sparse growth they saw seemed dead or dying, withered, and crusted with gypsum crystals fine as ash.

For three hours they looked for traces of the runaways and the tall cowboy who had chased out after them, bending from the saddle to imagined signs, skirting deep watercourses which split the land. Their eyes burned from peering into the whiteness. Their backs ached from the strain of guiding the horses over the stony ground.

Ignacio called a halt to rest and do some thinking. How far would Angus have followed the strays without giving up? He would have realized by the time he got this far that it would be impossible to drive a dozen or more confused steers back over the terrain Ignacio and Jamie had just traversed. Five times in the last hour they had been forced to dismount and lead their spooked ponies past the knife edges of arroyos deep enough to hold the ranch house. Drive cattle? No! Angus would have stopped, and right here, under that little mesa where he, Ignacio, had reached the same decision. What could have happened then? Flash floods would have roared through these gullies without warning, but an old hand like Angus would have sought the ridges when the first tiny cloud puffed above. There must be another answer.

"Stay here with the ponies, Jamie," the vaquero said. "I am going to walk to the top of that little mesa over there." He didn't think of it as a command but that was exactly what it was. He had, in truth, been giving the orders ever since they left the fence, and he saw Jamie's confidence begin to ebb. It couldn't be helped. This was no time to worry over Jamie and his pride. He climbed the shale-covered slope, slipping back a pace for every two he took.

At the top the mesa feel away from a sharp precipice on its northern side. If Angus had ridden up, he could have gone no farther. The vaquero felt it to be a waste of time to look for tracks on the slick surface near the edge, and he was about to retrace his steps when his eye caught an irregular place on the lip at odds with the general contour.

A raw V in the stone, it looked hacked out by a giant axe. He moved closer and saw that the V was discolored, a sickly yellow-black stain burned into the skin of the rock. Lightning had struck this rim, and from the size and look of the notch it must have been a fearful blow. Satisfied, he turned again to descend and rejoin Jamie, when his foot hit something that skipped away with a clattering noise—not one a rock would make.

When he looked down, he saw it was a briar pipe.

Ignacio stepped back and looked the cairn over carefully when he had put the last stone in place. *Sí*, it was broad enough at the base and high enough. Nothing which skulked above the ground could ever tear at Angus MacAndrews's body. As for the others, the crawlers and burrowers, they would come in their own time anyway, despite the way he had lashed his and Jamie's slickers around his friend's stiffened frame.

He felt sick again, sick from the smell of the body and the carcass of the horse, lying bloated and monstrous thirty feet away, sick from the feel of the blackened flesh he couldn't avoid completely, but above all sick with disgust at the words still running through his mind. "No, Nash, for Christ's sake, no! You'll have to do it by yourself. I couldn't touch the thing!" The MacAndrews boy was still up there, standing on the rim, looking small.

Ignacio had nearly collapsed as he dug the shallow grave with the frying pan Jamie tossed down to him. The arroyo, its steep sides trapping the sun, was like an oven, and the one drink he'd allowed himself from his canteen surged right up again mixed poisonously with bile. His hands were raw to the bone, rubbed so pitilessly against the grainy arroyo bed that no more blood would come—and there was no healing dope to ease the hurt, even if Angus's big warm hand could still smear it on with that surprisingly gentle touch.

The decision to bury Angus almost where he lay had not been hard to reach. The thought of Douglas and the señora looking at the body had made his mind up instantly. The filthy birds now fluttering over the carcass of the fallen horse had torn the flesh obscenely. One of the blue eyes was completely gone, the socket filled with thick, dark, viscous blood.

The cairn finished, he removed his hat and bowed his head. He wondered if he would ever have to come this way again.

Just before they reached the ranch yard Jamie edged his pony over and grabbed Calico's bridle.

"Hold up a second, *amigo*. I want to ask you something." They stopped, but the ponies danced about, puzzled at this halt with the sound and smell of home so close at hand.

"*Sí,* Jamie?"

"Do we have to tell Pa about—you know, not fixing the fence and all?"

"If you mean will I tell him"—Ignacio was glad it was too dark to see Jamie's face—"no, I won't, Jamie."

Dios, but he was tired. After he left the grave his first thought was to look for Angus's pack horses, but he didn't have a sign to go on. Guessing the thoughts of a man was one thing, but leaderless, panicked animals? No, he could spend days, weeks, in this wasteland, risking another disaster, and still not find them. Besides, there could be no excuses for delay. He must go straight back with the news, no matter how he dreaded it.

So he didn't choose the prudent course of camping on the rangeland overnight. He and Calico had led Jamie on a punishing ride. He hadn't let the MacAndrews boy get close to him until just now, coming through the rocks.

All during the ride he had worked on his determination, bracing himself to tell the señora what they, he, had found and done, and now, when he finally felt ready, this weak fool (Did he dare think of the anglo boy this way?) had intruded his own self-serving plea.

Basta! It was enough. Suddenly he felt anger he could scarcely credit boiling inside him. He looked down at Jamie's hand, still on his bridle, and the irritation he felt bubbled the anger out of him before he could stop himself.

He cracked his reins down on Jamie's hand with all his might, and his heart filled with a kind of desperate satisfaction when he heard the vicious sound the blow made.

"No, Jamie—I will tell him nothing!" He shouted it, and spurred Calico forward a few yards, pulled him up and turned him about. "I will tell him nothing—and I will tell you nothing"—his voice dropped, and if it trembled a little, he didn't care—"*but you will tell yourself—always.*"

He gave Calico's head a crueller wrench than he intended, and drove the startled pony pell-mell down the slope.

They reined to a stop at the corral, and it was then the vaquero became aware that all the lamps on the bedroom side of the house were still ablaze. His feet had hardly touched down before the kitchen door flew open and light flooded around the figure of Angélica Rivera.

"Hurry, *señores,* hurry! I need help. The *señora* began her pains this afternoon. She has reached her time!"

11

IT WAS THREE YEARS BEFORE THEY FELT A WINTER SEVERE ENOUGH TO satisfy the annual predictions of dead Angus. Snowfalls came so often and piled up so high the Ojos Negros was white through March. In an ordinary winter, snow which fell at night—seldom more than half an inch—was gone by noon, burned away into the dry air by the never-failing sun. But it was cold enough in 1909 to keep a white mantle on the upper range which seemed prepared to stay forever.

Douglas and Ignacio had mixed feelings about the weather. They were grateful for the moisture the snow would provide as it melted; better that than the torrents which usually came early in the year, brief gullywashers which ran off in taunting rivulets to the arroyos and stripped the soil from the roots of the grass. This way, when the snows melted and winds began, the range could absorb the water at its own pace.

But the cold which came whipping in on the heels of any number of northers that season worked its will on the stock. Unable or unwilling to eat through the snow as Ignacio remembered them doing once, the cattle were weak and wasted, even after Douglas and Ignacio—and Jamie on his weekends—ferried tons of feed into the pastures. A few animals gave up entirely, dying quietly as the hardier ones moved discreetly to other parts of the range.

Douglas was somber, as in the weeks after the death of Angus. That, of course, was different. Beyond being sudden, it was final. The long winter with its relentless cold had to be faced and fought every day, but it would pass. Ignacio knew that now.

Something of Douglas's way of looking at the D Cross A had become his own. The fence was tight.

Yes, the fence was tight, and as Angus forecast, there was a lot more of it, although this hadn't come about in the way Douglas planned. It was the decision he made after Angus's funeral that altered the way the D Cross A was to grow in the next three years.

When the brief ceremony on the rim of the arroyo was done, Ignacio rode down through the piñon a little faster than the others so he could swing back the same section of fence he and Jamie had gone through two weeks earlier.

Only men were in the party of riders he waited for. Agnes wanted to come along, but Douglas pointed out that there was no way to get a buggy or even a wagon into the badlands. Ignacio had tried to apologize for not bringing the body back, but Douglas wouldn't listen. "Don't, Ignacio, don't say anything. You did just right."

Now, while he waited for the honorary pallbearers and the few others who had made the ride, Dr. Clifton's sermon crossed his mind. The language had sounded strangely like the Shakespeare he grappled with in the shack at night, but it did nothing to evoke the tall cowboy lying beneath his pile of rocks. Angus's memorial, for the vaquero, would have to be his memories of him.

When the last of the funeral party was through the fence, and the last wire securely in place, Ignacio climbed on Calico and hurried to catch the other riders. In minutes he came through an opening in the piñons to find Douglas and Ben Hardy, the banker from El Paso, in the rear of the band of riders.

"If this isn't the right time, Douglas, tell me," Hardy was saying, "but as long as I was coming up, I brought the note and the other papers for you to sign."

"I'm sorry, Ben. You've gone to a lot of trouble and work for nothing. The Shelby deal is off."

"Oh?"

"Can't afford it now. I want to buy the land just north of here, but I've got to pick up the entire sixty sections."

"That waste?"

"Yes, Ben. Tell your board I'll secure it with the D Cross A and everything I own—if I have to."

"It won't come to that, Douglas. We'll work something out," the banker said. "But my God man, you can't *ranch* that empty stretch of hell!"

"I know, Ben. It doesn't matter. That arroyo's *got* to be inside our fence."

Douglas perplexed the vaquero in the days and weeks following the service in the arroyo. He didn't seem to grieve, but there were nights when Ignacio heard the crunch of boots somewhere in the compound. Once, he went to the window and saw Douglas pacing back and forth, stopping every now and then to stare hard to the north. Ignacio didn't look after that when he heard the boots.

It almost seemed the señor was intent on removing any sign of Angus, as if he didn't ever wish to be reminded. The smithy was dismantled; from now on horses needing shoeing would have to make the trip to town or await the arrival of a traveling farrier. Angus's scarred old McClellan saddle was stacked in a corner of the tack room with a tarpaulin hiding it from view. Then Angus's room in the ranch house was done over as a nursery for baby Sarah, and most of the tall brother's effects were actually taken out and burned.

Shaking inside, for the first time the vaquero hid something from his employer and friend. He had intended to give Douglas the briar pipe he had found on the rim of the arroyo. Instead, he stowed it deep in the box with the roweled spurs.

By fall, the deed for the sixty new sections came through, and Douglas hired half a dozen men from Black Springs to rush to completion a fence which would enclose the rocky barrens within the D Cross A. When the last post was planted, and the last restricting wire stretched, the rancher and the vaquero rode together to the arroyo. Together they watched as a gentle snow began to cover the cairn.

He had never—as he had more or less sworn to Jamie and himself that awful night in the rocks—said anything about either the young anglo's failure to help him in the arroyo, or how it happened that Angus had made the ride instead of the two of them.

As far as Ignacio could tell, there had never been any confrontation between Douglas and his son about any part of the matter, but for months following the tragedy, Jamie paid an extravagant amount of attention to the vaquero. It was like the visit he made to the shack after the deer hunt, but enlarged, the plea for sympathy now intensified and obvious. It baffled Ignacio. Had he been in Jamie's place, he would have avoided the person who witnessed his dereliction like something contaminated. He wondered if Jamie felt shame. He couldn't see any behind the smile.

Ignacio tried to shrug off the image of Jamie perched on the rim of the arroyo, but he came to realize that this was something he would never be able to forget. This was not just another of the small, nagging irritations he had come to accept as part of the compact he made with himself shortly after he came to work for Douglas MacAndrews and the D Cross A. No, this was larger, immeasurably more important; it went to the heart of the unpredictable youth who lived in the big house.

In vain he sought excuses for Jamie. Perhaps the answer could be found in one of the blurted revelations Angus had made on their early rides together. He tried to conjure up the lonely child running from Agnes's lessons, but the Jamie of the dazzling smile kept getting in the way. Then that image, too, would fade, and its place would be taken once again by the hunched figure above him at the arroyo, and the heat would rise to his face as it had in the moment before he lashed Jamie with the reins that night in the rocks.

He still shuddered at the memory, and he would find himself shaking his head when he tried to reason out how he had generated such boldness. It wouldn't—couldn't—happen again.

There was no question, though, that he must come to terms with the Jamie who was taking shape in his thoughts. He wouldn't allow himself to believe that there was some innate evil in the other youth; weakness perhaps, but not evil or wickedness in the sense of Padre Julian's dark sermons. Whenever he watched Jamie—and he watched him hard these days—all he could see was a laughing, carefree youngster who won people's affection effortlessly. Carefree? Maybe careless was the better word, but careless seemed too weak when you considered the consequences. Was Jamie's treatment of his mother when she carried the new baby nothing more than carelessness?

Perhaps the priest back at Ramos had the truth of such matters after all. It well could be that something black and ugly played with Jamie—but where would such forces come from in the wide, good Ojos Negros?

A thought came to Ignacio which shook him and left him limp. Did the great places of the earth only tolerate certain sorts of people? Was the face of the basin, so friendly and benign to the vaquero and the big señor, turned away from James MacAndrews? *Dios,* he, Ignacio, possessed neither the background nor the brains to consider such lofty matters.

Still, the idea kept returning. Not only the sight of Jamie on the arroyo, his handsome face as dead in its way as that of Angus, but the memory of every foot of the ride back that night was as vivid as if the journey were being made over and over again. He kept seeing the anglo's face as a white oval of fear, dancing against the darkness.

Sometimes Ignacio wondered if a time would come when he wouldn't have to be constantly on guard. He would simply have to train himself to take Jamie as he was. And surely he had enough troubles himself. There was the wall. Each time he dreamed of it, the feeling became stronger, more real, that if only he could uncover his lost past, the dead years before Ramos, perhaps. . . . Jamie, for all his flaws, was complete, a whole man, with nothing missing. Jamie had a beginning. So, times without number, he made efforts to remember which left him cruelly beaten. Nothing came through the wall. What was that passage in the play about the English kings?

> *Glendower: I can call spirits from the vasty deep.*
> *Hotspur: Why, so can I, or so can any man, but will*
> *they come when you do call for them?*

Dios! He did miss Angus.

For two years life was happily uneventful. Good weather, great spring runoffs from the mountains, fine rains in July and August, and very little wind, all combined to make grass in incredible abundance, the blades stiff with moisture, deep green, thick enough to drive the prickly poppy into hiding. Roundup followed good roundup (Tom and his crew returned twice each year) and Douglas began to speak again of the Shelby land.

Sarah, blonde and with blue-gray eyes like her mother's, fascinated the vaquero. It seemed no time at all before the baby's crawl changed to an unsteady toddle, and then to a run which quickly became the only way she moved.

Apparently the child's constant activity appealed to old Sam; the dog followed her into every corner. He still slept with Ignacio, but mornings would find him scratching at the door until Ignacio let him out. Then he would move with more speed than he showed obeying a command or even answering a dinner call, seeming youthful as he bounded up the path to await Sarah's first appearance of the day.

As Sam trailed Sarah, so the tot followed the vaquero, and Ignacio was never alone unless he was on the range. When he studied in the sitting room, Sarah camped beside his chair until bundled off to bed. Far from bothering him, it pleased him. He found he could study better with Sarah there, coloring, playing with a doll, or petting Sam. Sarah seemed to recognize the need for quiet. In contrast to her usual boisterous high spirits, she turned silent as sleep whenever the rider opened his books.

The studies went extremely well. More and more Agnes left him alone, not checking his progress for weeks at a time. She watched him though, peering at him from the archway, or leaning over his shoulder to see what he was reading when she lifted Sarah to kiss his cheek at bedtime.

This goodnight kiss, such an easy ritual now, had confused and embarrassed Ignacio at first. It didn't seem right for the daughter of the señora to be kissing a hired hand—and for once he spoke his mind to Agnes.

"Nonsense, Nash," she said. "You're family."

He would have let himself believe it if he hadn't seen an odd look on Jamie's face one night when Sarah's lips were planted on his dark cheek. It was a bad moment until the look disappeared in the old smile.

He breathed easier and returned the smile. He wanted no trouble with Douglas and Agnes MacAndrews's son, and, indeed, he'd had none these past three years. In fact, as the memory of what had happened when Angus died receded, the cautious liking he had felt for Jamie when he first came to the D Cross A returned.

For his part, Jamie seemed more constant. The charm which Ignacio had once thought merely the other's stock in trade was steadier, if less pronounced—no longer flashed on and off and was then forgotten in those bewildering reversals.

Once when the vaquero had ridden to town to do errands and get the mail for Douglas, Jamie did him a spectacular kindness. He had delivered a box of cookies Agnes baked, and the two of them went to Stafford's store together. Findlay was fetching Ignacio a sack of candy he was taking back to Sarah when a fat, nasty looking youth lounging by the stove yelled, "God damned greasers can go anywhere they please nowadays." Calmly, Jamie walked over to the boy, said, "He's my friend," and then took the speaker out of contention with one thumping fist.

Even this merciless winter and the loss of the stock couldn't entirely dim the bright aura which seemed to come to the D Cross A. The vaquero felt so content and grateful he would have gone to his knees—except that they still ached in memory of the fruitless, unanswered prayers at Ramos.

12

"No, amigo, the anglos don't particularly like it, but we do it all the same," Jorge Martínez said.

Ignacio felt stupid. He had ridden to town with Jamie on their regular monthly excursion with no expectation that this was any special day. After getting the ranch supplies at Stafford's, they had walked across the tracks to Mex Town to find a fiesta in full swing.

Cinco de Mayo. Dios, he had forgotten it completely. The padre and the brothers at the mission never made much of the celebration, but he should have remembered the parade of *santos,* the dancing, the music, and the desperate exulting in the plaza at Ramos on the anniversary of the victory over the French. Jorge looked at him in disbelief when he asked about the festivities, and he felt doubly stupid that Jamie knew about it.

Here was one anglo, at least, who had no objection. Jamie loved a party, no matter where or whose it was. But he could become troublesome if he drank too much. Old Pablo, the porter at the depot and one of the regulars at the Cantina Florida, told Ignacio about one fracas when Jamie was still living with the Staffords. Concepción had given a party for some of the youngsters who were about to graduate from Black Springs High School. Jamie was one of only two or three anglos invited, and although the guests were not paired up boy and girl, young MacAndrews insisted on the exclusive attention of Connie, as he called her. When a boy named Luis Griegos tried to dance with her, Jamie picked him up and threw him bodily out of the cantina. Jorge, who was a year older than anyone in this crowd, hadn't been there, and the vaquero thought it just as well.

According to Pablo, Jamie had spent a lot of time at the cantina in recent months. Ignacio had heard that much from the rancher's son himself, but he doubted if anything had happened between the two, despite Jamie's big talk. Still, the way the girl leaned toward Jamie when she served him, her hand brushing his too frequently to be accidental, it seemed just a question of time. And it was probably just a matter of time before the heat in Jorge's black eyes when he watched them erupted into open flame. With luck Jamie should be off to college before anything dangerous took place, but there was a whole summer to be lived through first.

When the rider and Jamie arrived at the cantina, Concepción and her brother were at the tables on the porch, watching the fiesta crowd. The girl was wearing an apron, and her hair, which ordinarily streamed far down her back, was done up in a drab kerchief. When she saw Jamie, her mouth dropped open and she turned and raced for the door of the cantina as though demons were after her. *Bueno,* Concepción, Ignacio thought, he was too busy looking at the street to see you.

"Hey!" Jamie said to the vaquero, ignoring the nod Jorge gave him, "It's *Cinco de Mayo*—great!"

Ignacio sank into a chair at one of the tables, expecting Jamie to do the same, but just then a willowy girl the rider had never seen detached herself from the throng and smiled at the young anglo before turning and vanishing again. With an eager whoop—"*hasta la vista,* Nash! I may see you later, but don't wait up"—the rancher's son leaped from the porch.

Ignacio breathed easier. For a while he wouldn't have to watch Jorge watching Jamie and Concepción, and away from the Florida all the boy would find to drink would be wine or *pulque.* He smiled remembering how much Jamie detested both—"That crap ain't fit for an American to drink!"

It would be nice to sit here with only Jorge, and drink his own *cerveza* slowly.

"No!" Jorge was saying. "As I said, the anglos—hah! I should say *gringos*—don't like us having this fiesta. *Los cochinos* won't let us be Americans, but they go *loco* if we try to stay Mexican." He was sitting in the wicker armchair, a booted foot propped against the carved post in front of him. In one of the nervous, mercurial gestures the vaquero had noticed in the past, Jorge was tapping a leather riding whip against the side of the chair.

Jorge Martínez intrigued him, but there were times Ignacio despaired of ever being able to call the cantina boy *amigo.* The hot intensity of Jorge's eyes was not reserved for Jamie MacAndrews alone. Ignacio himself had felt a certain few degrees of it. The reason dawned on him bit by bit as Jamie and he made these visits. To Jorge, so strong in his opinions, the rider must appear a traitor to his blood in the way he dressed, the company he kept, and most of all in the happiness he knew he revealed when he talked of his life at the ranch.

"You don't care, though, do you, *cowboy*?" Jorge said suddenly.

"About what, Jorge?"

"No," Martínez said, answering himself, "you don't care. You look as Mexican as I do, but you're not really one of us."

It would do no good to protest. Maybe he *didn't* care. Oh, he knew well enough the thousand little ways the people of Black Springs let their neighbors across the tracks know how they felt about them. Mex Town would be called a barrio if Black Springs were big enough. There were times when he himself brushed up against discrimination, like losing his turn in line to some anglo in a Black Springs shop (not in Stafford's, though), but back at the D Cross A it faded as if it had never happened. It was easy then to decide that it had nothing to do with him. Still, he did wish Jorge would be his friend, and he wished, too, that Jorge would answer him in Spanish instead of English when they talked together.

"Your big anglo friend," Jorge said, "says you are a great scholar—a reader of books."

Fleeting surprise that Jamie would speak of him at all gave way to embarrassment, and he blushed as he managed to nod.

"I have a book you perhaps don't know." Jorge was all earnestness. "*Los grandes problemas nacionales,* by Molina Enríquez."

"I haven't read it, Jorge. About the government—in Washington?"

"*Dios, no!*" Jorge exploded. "These high and mighty *gringos* don't believe they *have* problems. This is about Mexico, *old* Mexico—*your* country."

At that moment Concepción came out of the cantina. The apron was gone, and the black hair tumbled down over a white lace blouse, almost touching a full skirt of deep, lustrous red. Fresh makeup livened her face. She looked about the porch and then stared piercingly at the vaquero. He looked back at her, and heard Jorge go on, "I will lend it to you. Do not forget it when you leave."

"*Gracias,* Jorge," he said, "I will read it happily."

Concepción started wiping the other table. Then she spoke without looking up, her voice coming like the crack of a whip.

"*Señor Ortiz!*"

"*Sí,* Concepción?"

"You did not come to our cantina alone today."

He shook his head.

"No!" she said, in a tone which sounded as if he had denied her statement. "*Señor* MacAndrews was with you. Where is he now, *por favor?*"

He only shrugged. She looked at Jorge then, and so did he. The Martínez youth raised the hand with the whip and waved it slowly back and forth over the dancing crowd in the street. The look on his face could have been put in words, so clearly could its meaning be read.

Suddenly there were hard white lines about her mouth. She tipped back her head and arched her body like a dancer. "When you see him, *señor,* tell him, *por favor*"—again it was a whipcrack—"tell him—" She didn't finish, and Ignacio could see she was looking at something in the noisy street. Then she twisted around and shot through the cantina door.

Jorge looked pleased, with himself and with the turn of events, obviously enjoying his sister's irritation. Jamie, Jamie, the rider thought, are you sure you know what you are getting into with this pair?

The grinning face of the young anglo burst out of the crowd. "Howdy, *amigos,*" he said as he swaggered toward them. His face was slightly flushed under the tan; it made his eyes more blue than gray. "Man! Chasing that slippery *muchacha* sure makes thirsty work." He leaned against the post where Jorge had his foot. Would Jorge lower it? No, it stayed fixed and firm. Jamie didn't seem to notice anyway.

"You should have come out into the stampede with me, Nash," Jamie said. "There was more good stuff out there than—" He broke off, and his grin widened. "Howdy, Connie, that beer for me?"

Ignacio could feel the charge in the air even before he turned to see Concepción bearing down on his table.

"No, *señor*"—the "señor" was drawn out like the long hiss of a branding iron—"this *cerveza* is for your friend." She didn't look at Jamie. The rider worked to suppress the smile he knew was coming. He hadn't ordered a beer.

She banged the glass down on the table and some of the beer splashed out. Then there was a flash of red skirt and brown legs as she left again, tossing back over her shoulder, "Perhaps my brother will take care of you." The words scalded the vaquero, even if they weren't for him.

"Well, how's about it, Martínez?" Jamie said, unruffled.

Even with Concepción gone there was something electric in the air, something contagious; for a moment Ignacio feared Jorge wouldn't move. He could almost feel measurable heat from the other, but, amazingly, Jamie didn't seem to notice this, either.

The moment passed, if not the heat of it, and when Jorge, in a wordless fury, went to fetch the beer, Jamie lowered himself into the chair young Martínez left. He looked huge, sitting where the whip-thin figure had been a moment earlier.

"Nash," Jamie said, "there are times I wish I was a Mexican. They sure as hell know how to have fun." He sighed.

What a blind bull he is, Ignacio thought. Here are two people who would gladly let his blood run out and he doesn't even know it.

Jamie was about to say something more when Jorge reappeared.

"Your *cerveza, señor*." The voice was like a stiletto.

"*Gracias, amigo,*" Jamie said. He flipped a silver dollar toward Jorge, but the cantina boy didn't raise a hand to catch it; it struck him in the chest and fell noisily to the board floor of the porch. Jamie looked surprised, but not disturbed.

Ignacio thought Jorge would leave now, with or without the money, but he stood in front of Jamie as stiff and straight as a lance. It was half a minute before young MacAndrews, busy with his beer and still sweating from his exertions in the fiesta crowd, paid Jorge the slightest attention.

"Yeah, Martínez?" There was nothing threatened, just honest puzzlement. "I paid you—there's the money, on the floor."

Jorge shook his head. *"Señor,"* he said, "my sister's name is not 'Connie,' but Concepción. Be so good as to call her that." Now, the rider thought, even Jamie could recognize the deadly tone.

The anglo picked up his beer in a hand Ignacio knew could smash the slender Jorge to a pulp. If the cantina boy did any thinking about it, he knew it, too, but it was clear it wouldn't make a bit of difference if he felt he had to risk the power of that hand.

"Shit, man," Jamie said, "I know that. Maybe you ain't savvy to the fact she *likes* me to call her Connie." Ignacio was grateful he could detect no anger yet. He pleaded frantically with his eyes, hoping to catch Jorge's. If only he could get him past this ugly second. . . .

It worked. Jorge left them and walked inside the cantina.

"Hey, Martínez!" Jamie called. "You can keep the change out of the dollar."

There was no answer.

"Come on, Nash," Jamie said. "Let's get the hell out of here. This beer's gone flat."

They were across Frontera Street when the rider heard Jorge call him.

"Ignacio! *Por favor,* the book—*amigo."*

* * *

Bedded down in the Staffords's upstairs room, the vaquero wondered if Jamie thought *he* liked it when he called him Nash. He shrugged. It was years too late to make something of it now.

Considered from every reasonable angle, the uneasiness at the Cantina Florida today wasn't Jamie's fault. It was as much a result of Jorge's militancy as anything. After all, Jamie MacAndrews wasn't one of those "high and mighty *gringos*" who made life so—

"Nash, old buddy." Jamie's voice came out of the darkness, soft, pleasant, steeped in drowsiness. "Even if I didn't like screwing Connie so much, I think I'd do it anyway—just to spite that greaser brother of hers."

13

AGNES AND DOUGLAS TOOK JAMIE TO COLLEGE AT LAS CRUCES IN THE
new Buick automobile the vaquero disliked at first sight—or
rather, first sound. Young MacAndrews waved back to Ignacio as
the open car crossed the plank bridge, his gold hair flying in the
breeze, the insouciant smile visible almost until they rounded
the butte. Sarah, in the front seat with her parents, was lost to
sight beneath the high back of the cushions.

The rider was alone at the D Cross A. There was no doubt in
his mind now when he told Douglas he could take care of everything. The dreaded emergencies of the past several years were but
minor breaks in routine any more, and the rancher's confidence
in the young Mexican was boundless, but—"I have one worry,
Ignacio, just one," the señor said out of hearing of the others. "If
it storms—doesn't seem likely, but if it does—I don't want you on
the range, no matter what, *sabe*?" No amount of sunlight would
ever chase away that shadow.

It was three months before he tried the book Jorge lent him.
He neglected all his reading during that time, refusing at first to
admit the reason, but there was at last no denying that it was the
statement he heard Agnes make to Douglas shortly after their
return from Las Cruces. "It seems strange, Douglas, that Jamie—
who couldn't care less—is in college, while my scholar stays here
to mend fences and curry horses." If there was a reply, it was lost
as Ignacio hurried out of earshot, ears ringing.

When he did start on the Molinas book, he found it far more
difficult than his Shakespeare. Beyond the labels on cans or bottles,

79

or an occasional line in the El Paso newspaper Douglas subscribed to, he had not read Spanish since Ramos, and that had been elementary stuff. There was a satisfaction in the discovery that his first tongue could be used to put ideas on paper. He made the struggle. Beyond the sheer fascination of it, there was some duty he felt to Jorge.

He read only a small part of it before deciding that, important as it was, it had little to say to him in his special circumstances. Hordes of pitiful, faceless people came at him from the print, but beyond a genuine sympathy for their plight, his heart could generate no deep feeling like that which moved Jorge to such rage. He felt guilty. His life had been lived free from these particular pressures. His were narrower in focus, and without a doubt would go just as unfelt by Jorge and his masses. He put the book aside. There would be time to tackle it again before he faced his friend at the Florida, and the book told him more about Jorge Martínez than about the *mestizos* and *indios* whose agonies it chronicled.

Although this Molinas thing was too much for him now, he found he wanted to try more in Spanish. "I'm sorry, Nash," Agnes said. "Douglas had a copy of *Don Quixote* once, but I've not the faintest idea where it's gotten to. Actually, I don't think there's a lot in Spanish you could call good reading." This troubled him, the more so when he heard the señor clear his throat in some unmistakable warning to his wife.

He had begun to notice in recent months that in everything of more than day-to-day concern, anything he had to conceptualize, he was now thinking almost exclusively in English. He and Douglas still used a running mixture of the two languages in their work, but more frequently the English term replaced the Spanish one. If he told Jorge the language in the book was too much for him, it would be more than partly true.

"We can't do it by ourselves any more, not the way it should be done," Douglas said one night. "As it is, we just scraped by when Jamie was home. We need another hand, two if we open up the Shelby land and run more stock."

"It's about time!" Agnes said. "I've watched you two drag yourselves in to supper exhausted as much as I care to."

Yes, it had been hard, not only since Jamie went to college, but for the past two years. After Angus died, Douglas had trimmed the herd, selling off more than he wished, not for a desire to decrease the work but to raise cash for the sixty bad sections and later she good land under Cuchillo Peak. Now it was back to the size it was when the vaquero first crossed the ranch with Terry.

"I'll get some men out from Black Springs," Douglas said. "They can throw up a bunkhouse in a month or so, and I'll look for hands."

Recognizing Douglas's decision as the only possible one, Ignacio watched the crew of carpenters erect the new building. Uneasy, he found himself wishing it could be old Tom and one of his men riding the D Cross A as steady hands, but he knew the old puncher would never give up his wandering life as long as he had the strength to push his pony and the chuck wagon from ranch to ranch. It would have to be someone new.

What would the new men be like? How would they take to him, and he to them? Probably, no, certainly, they would be anglos; he couldn't remember the last time he saw riders in the basin with names like Gómez or Romero. He heard at the Florida that anglo cowhands had staked out the Ojos Negros for themselves, discouraging others when it came to jobs—sometimes by means other than words, the *campesinos* at the cantina bar whispered over their tequilas. Jorge would smile. He was thinking like a Mexican.

All the same the worry was real, and became stronger as the bunkhouse neared completion. This would present some new problems for Señor Douglas, too. Would the rancher, with that great sense of fairness, ask him to move in with the new hands? He wouldn't want to treat Ignacio differently by permitting him to live apart. Likely this would end the evening meals with Agnes, Sarah, and Douglas, unless everyone ate together, and that didn't seem probable.

His studies? This was the greatest fear of all. It wasn't that he had to be with Agnes every time he cracked a book, but it helped. There were still times when he needed her advice (although for some reason he never asked about the Shakespeare) and the routine which worked so well, the fire in front of him and the lamp behind, Sarah busy at his feet—that was important, too. If he were part of a ranch crew, he couldn't make special evening trips to the house, even if the señora permitted or encouraged it.

His mood grew somber as the roof went on the bunkhouse, and blackened to despair as he stood with Douglas in front of it.

"You know what this means, Ignacio?" Douglas asked.

"*Señor?*"

"Your personal situation is going to change some."

No need to ask how. Douglas went on in the usual quiet voice, but now it seemed ominous.

"I know it would be nice to move into these shiny new quarters, but I'm going to ask you to stay in the shack. It's important that you be friendly with the new men, but more important that you keep a little distance. Hard to give orders to men you have to bunk with."

Ignacio didn't understand—or maybe he hadn't heard right.

"Cowhands ought to have a right," Douglas went on, "to gripe about the foreman all night long—without him listening."

The rider wasn't sure whether the sweat that washed down over him like a flash flood had been released by joy or terror.

When the two new hands arrived and settled in, first into the bunkhouse and then the work routine, Ignacio discovered it wasn't going to be as difficult as he imagined.

Brothers, Jess and Tim Barlow weren't given much to talk. Ignacio did learn that they had failed in their own stock ranch on the Pecos, forty bleak sections homesteaded originally by their father. Bad water, taxes, and huge medical bills when their mother followed the elder Barlow into the Fort Sumner cemetery put them under the auctioneer's hammer, and they gratefully accepted Douglas's offer of the jobs, relayed by their banker.

The señor must have talked to them at great length before he put them on. They treated the foreman with respect from the first day, and Douglas made it immeasurably easier by never giving orders directly to the Barlows; anything he wanted done he asked for through Ignacio. By the time the desert broke out in its annual rash of spring color the two new men were so much a part of the ranch the vaquero wondered how Douglas and he had done as much as they had.

To his wry amusement, Ignacio found himself in great demand at the Cantina Florida. Jorge delighted in the vaquero's company, and although he disparaged the appointment to foreman to Ignacio's face, he would break off his harangues about the evil doings in Mexico City, Sante Fe, or Washington, to introduce him to newcomers as "the *hombre* who runs the D Cross A."

With Concepción it was always the same. "What is the news from your big anglo friend? Does he never write? Do the college girls take up all his time? Tell me the truth, Ignacio!"

It was a changed Jamie who came home at Thanksgiving, Christmas, and Easter. He was strangely subdued, and it set the vaquero wondering. Snatches of conversation between the boy and his parents provided part of the answer, and Ignacio was able to guess the rest.

Jamie was unhappy and homesick, and it came as a shock to discover that once out of the Ojos Negros and away from Black Springs, he was standoffish with new people and had made no friends. Stranger still, in sharp contrast with high school, his grades were remarkably good, nothing like honors, but safely above the passing mark. Agnes was ecstatic.

"Well!" she said one night as she was settling in at the study table with Ignacio, "It just goes to show you should never give up. All these years of drilling Jamie have been worth it!"

The vaquero was puzzled. Gradually it dawned on him that the señora was confusing some of her work with him, thinking it had been Jamie bent over the books the past five years. No, impossible! She couldn't delude herself that much, could she? Of course, he had never fooled himself about Agnes's real desires. It *should* have been Jamie sitting there. Her, Ignacio, was just a substitute; but it was enough that he had benefited from the señora's needs.

One fine, hot, August morning, Ignacio Ortiz awoke with the thought that, give or take a month or two, he must now be twenty-one. This, by all accounts, was when one became a man. *Chihuahua!* He felt no different, was no different, from a day, a week, a month, or even a year ago. He looked into the cloudy old mirror on the wall, and saw much the same face as had looked back when he first came to the D Cross A. Truth was, he guessed, he had never been a boy—not, in the sense Jamie had, or Jorge. To "become a man" didn't happen in a day. Still, there was some particular magic, some "medicine" as the Indians would say, about reaching any milestone. He would let himself enjoy it.

It was a blazing August day in the Ojos Negros basin. Through the late morning and early afternoon at least a dozen storms made small attempts on the crown of big Cuchillo, but none of them could wait for the others to join in a real assault, and one by one the sun scorched their darkness into blue again, often before they could send even so much as one stab of lightning into the mountain's side. Ignacio considered that most of his storms had been burned away as well. Even if the dream still came now and then, life at twenty-one was good.

He had to ride down near the malpais today to check the stock in the southwest corner. Roundup would start next week, bigger than ever before. Old Tom would be back to help. Jess and Tim had proven themselves a thousand times, and Jamie wasn't due back for his final year at Las Cruces for another month. *Bueno.* Whatever else he was, at roundup Jamie was a wonder. The weight of years would fall from Douglas, too, when roundup came. The excitement, born fresh every time, was beginning to rise in him again.

He gave Calico his head going through the yucca. The pony no longer possessed the wild strength of former years, but he was steady now and could be trusted on any ride. The day would come when Ignacio would have to turn him out on the range with the other horses, but he would be a fine mount for a long time yet.

The heat on his back felt good. If only Jorge Martínez were riding along beside him, he would see how good life could be. *Sí,* it was too bad Jorge couldn't be a vaquero, too. "Ay-aah! Calico." He slapped the pony on the rump. There was work to do.

14

"Do you mind a spectator?" the girl named Ann Jennings said behind his back, and Ignacio spun about swiftly in a reflex he couldn't check. Last night at supper he had watched Jamie's friend from Santa Fe as closely as he dared, avoiding the glances she sent his way, casting his eyes down into his plate as he hadn't done since those early days at the D Cross A. Now she had walked up unnoticed while he was intent on Sarah's riding lesson. He wondered how long she had been standing there.

He stammered out a weak "señorita" and swept his hat from his head reluctantly. Beneath it he had felt more secure. The brim pulled down against the bright sunlight had kept his eyes from view; now this disturbing young woman could look straight into them. Hers were incredibly deep, dark as his own, startling after the accustomed blue and blue-gray of the MacAndrews clan, and with a gaze of such directness it was as if she had put out a hand and touched him.

"Howdy, Ann!" Sarah yelled from Calico's back, and the vaquero felt grateful for the sudden rescue. "Why don't you"— Sarah urged Calico to the section of corral fence where they were standing—"have Nash saddle you a pony, too? He's promised we can go up in the rocks today." The gratitude faded and panic took its place. He would have his hands full today with Sarah, never mind the added worry of looking after Jamie's friend. Still—

"No, thank you, Sarah," Ann Jennings said, laughing and turning back to Ignacio. "All my riding has been flat saddle, Nash, even in Santa Fe. I'm not ready for you two western types yet."

He should feel relieved at the refusal. It should be Jamie who rode with her, not the hired hand. They should have many fine hours together—and he, the rider, should feel good about it. Why didn't he then? Enough, Ignacio, enough! Think of other things.

With an effort he got his attention back on Sarah. There were still a few exercises he wanted the eager nine-year-old to run through here in the corral, mildly difficult work to drain away a little of her abundant energy before they reached the heavy going in the rocks. He barked out orders and suddenly was embarrassed at the self-importance he heard in his voice. He was showing off, letting this young woman know what a brilliant teacher he was. It was childish, but in his own defense he could claim it wasn't something entirely new. As if it were yesterday, he could hear again the quick lift of Agnes's voice when Angus had walked in on one of his early lessons.

The sudden entrance of the señora in his reflections brought something else to mind: last night's supper, and his discomfiture at the way the Santa Fe visitor had been grilled. There hadn't been much Ann Jennings could have kept hidden in the face of the storm of questions Agnes and Sarah loosed at her. He remembered how he had writhed at the inquisition, only relaxing when he saw the easy way Ann answered them, sitting marvelously still the entire time, only turning her head from one MacAndrews to another as she spoke.

Yes, she was from the East—Boston, where she was born, New York, and several other places before Washington, D.C. The "District," as she called it, was "home, really." Her father, not robust, had held a succession of "minor" government positions. When her mother died unexpectedly six years ago, his health turned worse, and the doctors advised a change of climate. He wangled a post on the staff of the Territorial Governor in Santa Fe, and Ann came out with him as housekeeper and hostess. When statehood came to New Mexico in 1912, two years ago, they stayed on. "Very contentedly," she added.

Once during the recital Ann's eyes caught the rider's, and he felt such a palpable shock that from then on he didn't look at her, only watched the member of the family she spoke to. Douglas beamed, and it warmed Ignacio to know that the young woman had already won the señor's approval. Jamie looked smug, and from time to time the vaquero felt guilty satisfaction when young MacAndrews was shushed into silence while trying to help Ann with an answer.

Sarah wore an expression Ignacio could only characterize as a "birthday" look, as if Ann had been brought here as her particular gift. Her pigtails danced as she nodded when the young woman spoke, and the smile on her face seemed to say that she knew all the answers beforehand.

The questioning went along warmly enough until Agnes asked, "And just how did you manage to meet *our Jamie,* Miss Jennings?" Ignacio wondered if he was imagining the challenge he heard in the seemingly innocent question. He looked around the table. Agnes's tone hadn't bothered Jamie, or dulled the edge of Sarah's enthusiasm. He couldn't read the rocky features of the señor.

He watched Agnes, hurt by the suspicious look he saw on her face, as Ann explained how Jamie had come to the Capitol for the Admission Day celebration with some of his college acquaintances. He and Ann had met at a party given by the Chupadera County senator. "We saw a lot of each other after that, Mrs. MacAndrews."

"But—working for the governor as you do—aren't you and your father *Democrats?*" There was no mistaking Agnes's feelings in the way she said the word, and the rider was stupefied. Why, Findlay and Mary Stafford were Democrats, as were any number of other Black Springs people he knew the señora esteemed. Besides, he couldn't remember Agnes voicing an opinion on politics in all the years he had been at the ranch. A gauntlet had been thrown down, and Ignacio held his breath, wondering if the calm young woman from Santa Fe would pick it up.

"Well—yes," Ann Jennings said. For a moment a tiny undercurrent of concern seemed to trouble the surface of her voice, but when she spoke again the words came steadily, unhurried, with a measured, soft control which reminded the rider of Douglas. "But in Santa Fe, Mrs. MacAndrews, we're all government people first, I suppose, then Republicans or Democrats. We do see quite a bit of each other, you know."

Ignacio saw Agnes fix her mouth in the ruler-straight line he knew so well. The words themselves hadn't mattered, but clearly the señora was vexed at the young woman's refusal to join battle.

Douglas suggested brandy in the sitting room, and the vaquero knew that the señor, too, was aware of what was happening. Ann, of course, wouldn't have recognized the tone of slight command in the big rancher's voice.

From his seat in the corner of the big room, Ignacio looked at Ann. In the light from the oil lamp she was nearly as dark as he, not with the Latin brownness he had worn all his years, but with a deep russet glow. She was the kind of woman who seemed taller than she really was, partly, he was sure, because of the way she carried herself in the shiny long dress which rustled when she walked, but more because of the quiet pride which marked every movement she made.

Her body was slim, almost lean, but with curves swelling in subtle unbroken lines along the entire length of it. Her hair, black as the rock of the malpais but with hints of the same russet in certain lights, was piled high on her head, sweeping upward from a neck which in spite of its delicacy looked strong and resilient.

From his corner, Ignacio couldn't see her eyes, but he remembered them from the furtive glances he had permitted himself at supper, and he was glad he couldn't see them. For the first time in his life he wondered how he looked to someone else. He blushed in the shadows of his corner. *Bobo!* This splendid being hasn't even seen you.

The conversation of the group around the fireplace droned in his ears. Suddenly, Ignacio stood up, muttered something which he hoped sounded like a goodnight, a decent one, and left, his confusion swirling about him like a cloud.

He stared into the murky old mirror. No, there was surely nothing in the face which stared back at him to interest or excite anyone. It was not a face like Jamie's.

An attempt at his books proved futile, and a search for sleep turned out to be even more useless. He turned on the narrow bunk until the bedding was twisted into knots.

"No, Nash, not today—but thank you," Ann was saying as she and the vaquero watched Sarah race Calico smartly around the barrels he had set out in the center of the corral. "Someday, perhaps, you can teach me to ride the way you're teaching Sarah. I think Mrs. MacAndrews and Jamie have something planned."

Nothing in her placid features told him she had noticed his odd departure the night before. He was right in what he had told himself then. There was nothing about him to notice.

Behind her he saw Jamie come out of the kitchen. The rancher's son waved and the rider waved back. Ann turned, saw Jamie, and ran toward him.

"*Adiós, señorita,* Sarah and I must ride now," Ignacio said. But she didn't hear him, he guessed.

Calico stepped briskly through the rocks, all his years apparently forgotten under the slight weight of Sarah, and Ignacio had to coax more pace out of his own mount just to keep up. The little girl didn't rein up for nearly half an hour, not until they reached the pinnacles and crags which broke the line of the ridge well above the ranch. From here the buildings of the D Cross A were no bigger than Sarah's doll house.

"Penny for your thoughts, Nash," Sarah said.

"You would waste your money, *muchachita.* They are not worth even that."

"Nash." He turned to look at her. She was leaning forward in the saddle, her chin almost resting on the horn, eyes gazing down toward the compound. "Jamie's going to marry that eastern lady, isn't he?"

"I have not been told, Sarah," he said.

Sarah turned in the saddle and looked at him, something shrewd and quizzical moving across her freckled features. "How about you, Nash? Will you ever get married?"

Ann stayed on at the D Cross A for the better part of a week. The vaquero, knowing and admitting to himself exactly why, avoided her. He spent more time than he had in many months with the two Barlows, riding fence like a fury, checking tanks, doing a dozen little things he ordinarily left to them. He even invented a useless tally of the stock on the Cuchillo pastures which kept him on the range overnight, wrapped in his bedroll like a mummy, his eyes wide open and staring at the stars until they moved halfway across the sky.

Saturday came, and Jamie loaded Ann Jennings's luggage in the car for the trip to Santa Fe. It would be easier now. With hardly a word to Douglas, and none at all to the señora, he bathed, put on his newest clothes, and rode to Black Springs to see Jorge.

"Where is your *amigo*?" Concepción Martínez asked, even before Ignacio could order a beer from Papá Andreas. Her eyes sparked black heat, as if he, the rider, had committed some transgression. He almost laughed, thinking of Cleopatra and the messenger. "*El caballero grande* promised to see me last Saturday night. I waited until almost midnight for him."

Ignacio shrugged. Perhaps he should tell her Jamie most likely wouldn't be seeing her any more, but it was really up to the young man himself to close this particular fence. She didn't seem to know yet, or her anger would have been more specific than this general blaze, and more intense. No, her face wore just the look of vexation it always did when he entered the cantina without Jamie.

"Is Jorge here?" he asked.

"*Sí*, in back, helping Mamá with the little ones." It was said grudgingly, indicating she would make no move to get her brother until asked directly, and even then only when she chose. He smiled a little and played it the way she wished.

"*Por favor*, tell him I would like to see him."

She didn't answer, only walked behind the bar with a tray of empty glasses and bottles, and Ignacio found himself looking at her with more interest than usual.

As he watched her, though, he discovered that his inner eye was seeing not Concepción but Ann Jennings, and he wondered why. He couldn't think of two more dissimilar women. Oh, they were both dark, and almost of a height, but against the careful, almost cool control of the young woman from the East, Concepción was all dancing flame. Although he admitted more than just the possibility of high warmth, even heat, in Ann, he was sure that whatever fires smouldered beneath the smooth luster would be more carefully banked than those which consumed the Martínez girl.

Well, one of them had belonged to Jamie. The other was his as well. Suddenly, Ignacio's stomach burned, and a sour, acid taste filled his mouth. He felt ashamed.

"You tell Jamie *'Con-nee'* wants to see him, *pronto!*" Concepción was washing glassware in the sink behind the bar. The vaquero nodded, and as if she had been waiting for this show of compliance, she abruptly dried her hands and walked swiftly toward the living quarters at the rear of the cantina.

Except for Papá Andreas and two quiet drinkers in the alcove, the place was empty. Ignacio wished it would fill with the usual Saturday crowd. He didn't want Ann Jennings—or Jamie—in his thoughts. *Dios*, that was why he had deserted the D Cross A for the Florida today.

"*Qué pasa, mi amigo?*" It was Jorge—greeting him in Spanish. He must look as tormented and derelict as he felt.

"*Nada,* Jorge, *nada.*" His voice sounded dreary.

"*Amigo!*" There was forced brightness in Jorge's words. "You read the El Paso *Herald?* Villa is sweeping across Tamaulipas like a—"

"*Por favor,* Jorge. Not tonight my friend."

There was no talk at all for a long while. Smoke filled the cantina as men wandered in from Frontera Street. It looked like there would not be many anglos in the Florida tonight, and that was just as well. It surprised Ignacio that he should think this way, but many thoughts had surprised him lately.

Concepción was back in the room again, her red skirt flashing like a cape in a bull ring as she took care of the now-busy tables. Voices rose and fell like the waves on the ocean he had seen on that one run from Ramos.

"I don't know what troubles you, Ignacio," Jorge said, after they had drunk a good many beers and not a few tequilas, "but there are only two things would do you any good right now."

"*Sí,* Jorge?"

"You should either stick a knife in a man—or something else in a woman."

Perhaps it was the tequila—there had been more of it than he could remember ever having—but Ignacio laughed longer and louder than he had in his entire life.

The Jamie who returned from taking Ann to Santa Fe was more like the old Jamie than the perplexed college boy of the last four years.

Ignacio had long since given up trying to get a vicarious share of the young anglo's education. Every time he had asked Jamie to talk about his studies he was turned aside by a snorted "it was all a lot of crap." Sadly, the vaquero concluded that the four years had been a total waste.

Agnes, however, was impressed with her son's diploma, returning from the graduation exercises with a glow which lit the ranch for weeks. Douglas was silent, unless one could count the conversation Ignacio overheard—and wished he hadn't.

He left a book in the sitting room one night, and returned to get it. It was a warm evening, and with the kitchen door ajar, Agnes and Douglas hadn't heard him enter the house. When he heard his name, he would have retreated immediately, but something in the urgency of the voices held him fast.

"Aggie," Douglas said, "it appears to me that since Jamie got home from Cruces, you haven't paid any attention to Ignacio's studies."

"I suppose it's a lot of foolishness when you get right down to it, Douglas," Agnes said. "I don't know what possible use Nash could make of an education, anyway."

"It isn't a question of 'use,' Aggie. The lad's got a right fine mind—and if the project was worth starting, it's worth—"

Ignacio moved out of the house before he heard more.

For two weeks he didn't crack a book. The one he had returned for gathered dust on the table by the sofa, alternately beckoning and repelling him.

The rest of the summer Jamie scampered off to Santa Fe at every opportunity, and in August Ann made another visit.

Once, when Douglas assigned his son a task he couldn't foist off on Ignacio or the Barlows, the vaquero and the dark girl rode together—at her insistence. Western saddle or not, she handled a horse beautifully, and old Calico seemed to know he was on show.

The rider took the girl into the highlands on the eastern side, those sections, once Shelby's, which were now such a part of the

D Cross A it was all one broad blue-green sweep of grass tilting up toward the lofty top of Cuchillo. They stopped to rest on a swale of grass which opened toward the entire southern reach of the Ojos Negros. In the middle distance the Oscuras and the San Andres swelled above the buff bottomlands like great blue welts, and beyond them, under the distant haze, they could make out the beginnings of the awesome white sand sea, rolling away to invisibility like some ghostly snowfield.

"If you didn't know," Ann said, "you'd swear man had never been here. There's a kind of empty . . . sadness. But there's beauty and peace, too. It brings an ache to my throat."

"*Sí, señorita.*" It was the only thing he could find to say, no matter what profundities his poor head held. He was helpless now; he must have known he would be, even at his first meeting with Ann Jennings.

"Nash—" Ann started to say something and checked herself. "But your name is really Ignacio, isn't it?"

"*Sí.*"

"Where did the 'Nash' come from?"

"*Señor* Jamie called me that, when I first came here."

"Mr. MacAndrews still uses "Ignacio'."

"Yes, he is the only one."

For a moment he feared there might be other questions, ones whose answers were hidden by the wall, but she fell silent, gazing out over the Ojos Negros with what seemed a new, sharper intensity. In a flash of intuitive certainty the rider knew those questions would never come from Ann Jennings, as they had never come from Douglas.

His eyes followed hers out over the basin, and he knew that his examination of all this familiar, dearly loved expanse of lonely beauty matched hers exactly. His glance rested on each butte just as hers did, hurrying, as hers did, across each sweep of desert, each green line of bosque. And most assuredly she was unaware of this, unaware of him. That—he swallowed hard—was the way it had to be. *Verdad.*

Ann Jennings and the young man of the D Cross A would have to occupy his mind together from this time forward. It would not be easy, but it must be done. No matter that "alarums and excursions" clanged faintly in his soul's inner space, he would suppress every doubt about the rightness of this pairing.

Was one rising now? He watched Ann's face as she looked across the land, saw the quiet passion in it. Could she be happy with the boy who stood once on the rim of a lost arroyo, with fear and loathing as his companions?

Her horse tossed its head and she turned to face him. "May I call you 'Ignacio', too, as Mr. MacAndrews does?"

If he had felt helpless before—what was he feeling now?

"That's it, *amigo*," Jamie said. "We'll be married here in Black Springs soon as Ma can make arrangements with Dr. Clifton. Ann doesn't have any people but her father, so she's pretty happy about it."

As long as it had to come, Ignacio was glad it came here in the Florida. Removed from the realities of the ranch, he could sink back into the murmured Spanish he heard around him, let the soft words wash over him—and forget.

This sort of thing had happened to him with increasing frequency these past few months. Even with Jorge's arguments ringing in his ears, the place had become a haven. The people, dark-eyed like him, seen dimly through the cigar smoke, the guitar old Romero strummed gently in the corner for his free tequilas, the rich smells from the kitchen where Mamá was working magic with *albóndigas* and a dozen *salsas*; it was a balm to him when the books in the sitting room or the company of the MacAndrewses or the silent Barlows weren't enough.

With this new change on the horizon, he would need this solace even more as the years went by.

"When will it be, Jamie?" he said.

"What?"

"The wedding."

"Hell, man, I don't know. Ask Ann—or better yet, ask Ma. Look, Nash, old buddy, you don't have to hang around here waiting for me. I got a hunch Connie is going to get over her mad tonight."

15

FROM AUGUST THROUGH OCTOBER LETTERS FLEW BACK AND FORTH between Agnes and Ann in Sante Fe. Ignacio took the señora's to the post office and dutifully fetched back those addressed to her. Only once in that time did he post one from the young man to the girl he was engaged to.

The vaquero guessed most of the correspondence had to do with wedding plans, but he couldn't know exactly what was passing between the pair until one evening Douglas, grousing just a little, said, "Don't know if this long engagement is such an all-fired good idea, Aggie. Ours lasted three days—and things have worked out fine, haven't they?"

"Things are different now, Douglas!" Agnes snapped. "Jamie has a position to think about. It won't hurt to take our time and do it right."

Douglas turned to Jamie, "How do you feel about it, son?"

"Hell, Pa," Jamie shrugged and grinned, "I'd as soon let Ma and Ann work it out. I ain't in no particular hurry."

Ignacio was astounded. If it were he . . .

* * *

Twice the time was set, and twice Agnes changed her mind, answering Douglas evasively when he questioned her. When the señor began to look dark at the mention of the subject, Ignacio knew the woman of the D Cross A would have to forego any more postponements, and at last she fixed another day. This time she sounded positive.

Ann would come to the ranch just before Christmas, and the wedding would take place in the First Methodist

Episcopal Church, Dr. Dudley Clifton officiating, on New Year's Day, 1915.

Then, a week before the holidays, Jim Gibbon, the telegrapher from the depot, sent a car to the ranch with a frantic message from Ann. The wedding was off again—indefinitely this time.

Her father had been recalled to Washington. The war raging in Europe since August had scarcely been noticed in the cattle-lands; New Mexicans were far more interested in Pancho Villa. But it had created a demand for anyone with a knowledge of Germany, and Spencer Jennings, it turned out, had spent two years there as a youth. Ann felt honor bound to help him move and stay with him until he was resettled in the East.

The impact of the news absorbed, the vaquero was sure the señora would exult in some way, but he couldn't have been more mistaken. Agnes actually sulked. He could only speculate that she was vexed because this delay wasn't of *her* making, that, or the fact that Jamie for once was upset and anxious. He was supremely sure of Ann, or had been.

Ignacio took a small but very real pleasure in seeing the mother and sons' wishes thwarted by Ann's determination, but it hurt a little to see Douglas so disappointed.

The same war which had cancelled the wedding plans brought a flurry of activity to the D Cross A. The great armies colliding across the ocean were fast becoming ravenous, as were the civilian populations all over Europe, and the demand for American beef grew beyond belief. Buyers from Kansas City and Chicago besieged Douglas by letter and telegram, and when spring broke across the Ojos Negros, they appeared at the ranch in person, begging, cajoling, promising unheard of bonuses, in the end threatening reprisals "when the shooting's over and the market's back to normal."

Some of the basin ranchers unloaded animals as fast as weary cowhands could run them to the railside yard in town. Last summer's square of rickety pens burgeoned to five, then ten times its former size, but Douglas was adamant. The fall roundup had been uncommonly large, and the big man stated that he had no intention of stripping his pastures for these windfall profits, or selling stock too young for finishing. "When this war is over, those poor people over there will need food even more than they do right now.

If we do our job, Ignacio, we'll be ready for it." Jamie—it didn't surprise Ignacio—disagreed, but not in his father's hearing.

The señor held fast to the course he set for the D Cross A, but still they worked in a frenzy, doing the myriad things necessary for the herd to increase on his patient schedule. The Barlows, under Ignacio's sure hand, were titans, and Jamie showed the strength and energy characteristic of him when things had enough immediacy and excitement to hold his interest.

Often, though, he was gone from the ranch for days at a time. He took the car when he left, and while Douglas may have fumed privately, he said nothing, only doubled his own efforts so that the rider and the Barlows wouldn't have to take up the slack. It wasn't difficult to figure out the object of these excursions— Concepción Martínez—there was no doubt of it. The vaquero's next visit to the Florida brought enough bad language from Jorge to last the summer. Surely, Ignacio thought, when Ann gets back from Washington that will be the end of it.

One afternoon early in July, after the first hard, hot weather rains had come, Jamie came home from town at noon. His face was gray, with a strange set to it, and there wasn't the trace of a smile. He disappeared inside the house without a word to Agnes, who was hanging out a wash behind the low stone wall.

Jamie didn't come to supper, and with Douglas gone for the night, down in Otero County looking up old Tom and his crew for the fall roundup, Ignacio shared the evening meal with an obviously troubled Agnes. She didn't utter a word until she shooed him back to the shack when he tried to help with the dishes. He went to sleep with her anxious look still in his mind's eye.

Next morning, after posting Jess Barlow to the north fence and Tim to repairs on the windmill at tank five, he walked to the corral to cut out a mount for his own sweep over toward Cuchillo. Down the old south road, he saw in the morning sunlight a plume of dust rising through the yucca. Was it a rider or a vehicle? He couldn't be sure at this distance. Douglas? No, he couldn't get back yet. Perhaps another message from Ann; his heart picked up its rhythm sharply. He stood with his feet rooted in the caliche and his hand on the corral gate, unmindful that Calico and the new paint had wandered over to him.

Now he could see it was a buggy under the dust, moving at a good pace, too. To be this far out the driver must have left Black Springs in the dark. By the time the rig was at the butte, and less than a hundred yards short of the bridge, he had half convinced himself it carried a woman—or a girl. Impossible. What woman would hitch a horse and buggy, or even rent one at the livery, in the middle of the night? But it *was* a woman. He could see the flowered print of her dress and the rebozo drawn about her shoulders. As the buggy rattled over the bridge, he saw who the driver was, and his heart dropped in his chest.

"*Buenos dias,* Ignacio," Concepción Martínez said. She looked out of breath. "*Por favor,* tell Jamie I want to see him."

"*Sí,* Concepción. But first let me care for your *caballo.*" The poor beast was in a heavy lather. The girl must have used the whip recklessly.

"Never mind that, vaquero. Get Jamie. Now!" There was more than just the promise of hysteria in her voice.

"I will see if he is here, Concepción."

"He is here, all right. Make no mistake." She pointed at the Buick, parked where Jamie had left it the afternoon before.

Quaking, the rider started for the house. If he had any hope of getting Jamie out in the yard before Agnes appeared it vanished when the kitchen door opened.

"What is it, Nash?" she said. As far as he could tell, she hadn't so much as glanced at the figure in the buggy.

"It is Concepción Martínez, *señora.* She wishes to talk—to *Señor* Jamie."

"He's not here!" It was blurted out with defiance, but a little too quickly to hide the hint of panic.

"I will tell her so." His voice was so soft he hardly heard it himself. Behind him, Concepción started the buggy up again, wheeling it around to get it closer to the house. When she stopped it, she looked over his head to where Agnes MacAndrews stood rigid and alert, as if she would guard the kitchen door against an army.

"I know he is here, *señora.* I *will* see him—*por favor!*"

"Look, Miss Martínez, or whatever your name is"—there was no panic now—"if I tell you my son's not here, he's not! State your business with him, and I'll tell him when he returns."

Ignacio looked at Concepción. Suddenly, he knew what was coming next, knew it as if the words already hung in the bright, dry air, but he felt detached, light-headed, as if this were happening to other people in a faraway place. A wave of pity, something he never thought he would feel for Concepción Martínez, swept over him. She didn't look as wild and striking as he remembered her from the Florida. The flowered dress was garish, the high heeled shoes which replaced the rope soled sandals she wore when she raced about the cantina looked out of place, and the heavy coat of rouge and lipstick spoiled her lips and the smooth brown cheeks. She looked tawdry, commonplace, and yet—there was this brave attempt at dignity.

"Do you really wish to know my *business* with your son, *señora?*" Her head was high, as she looked calm, but the little muscles in her throat trembled.

"Yes, certainly."

"Well, I will tell you then. There will be no need for you to tell *him*. I told him yesterday, before he left me and—"

"Get on with it, girl!" Agnes almost screamed. She *will* know, she will have to hear it, Ignacio thought.

Concepción was in no hurry now. She had come to face Jamie, but he could see this suited her just as well. When she spoke again her voice was low, and deadly quiet. "*Señora*—I am *encinta,* with child—pregnant. Your son Jamie is—"

"Wait!" Agnes threw up a small hand, but the girl went on, as deliberately as before.

"—the father. He knows about me, and he knows the child is his." She waited then, and the vaquero wondered if the control she showed could stand up against the storm he knew was coming.

"What would my son"—Agnes's voice was lower, too, in an effort to match the girl's—"*have to do with the likes of you?*" The last part carried such a heavy load of revulsion that Ignacio felt anger scorch him like a flame. In one sickening moment he knew that the net of contempt cast over the girl covered him as well. *Jorge, Jorge, you were right in everything, amigo.*

"Ask his friend here," Concepción said, but Agnes wasn't through.

"How, might I ask, can you be sure my son is the father of this . . . *child* you say you're carrying?"

When Concepción answered, the vaquero knew the strength was going out of her. "*Señora,* he was the only one—ever."

"Young woman," Agnes said, sure triumph in her voice, "I've heard enough. Get your buggy off the D Cross A as quickly as you can—and never bother us with this again!" She turned and walked to the kitchen and the door slammed behind her, but even before it did, the vaquero's eye caught a movement in the curtains at the kitchen window. He wondered if the girl had seen it, and turned to her.

"Is there anything I can do to help, Concepción?"

"No, Ignacio, *gracias*. It is enough that you were here."

He camped in a grove of ponderosa near a stream which gurgled between grassy banks, high on the back side of Cuchillo. From here he couldn't see the D Cross A or the Ojos Negros.

He wondered what Douglas would make of the note he left telling him he had decided to take a horse and get away for a day or two. If the big man had not been gone, if he had been able to talk to him, he would have left the D Cross A for good and all, but there was no way he could ever quit without telling Señor Douglas face to face. Here on the mountain he had thought things out as best he could.

The anger, bitterness, and yes, the actual physical sickness which accompanied him on the long ride up had largely dissipated in this restful place. If he could hold the newest thoughts firmly in his mind, he could go back down and get about his life again.

Not all the people he had known were like Jamie and his mother. There was the señor, of course, and there had been Angus. Old Tom and the Barlows, Findlay and Mary Stafford— and above all the dark girl somewhere in the faraway East—none of *them* had put the poison in him. For that matter, he could forgive Agnes readily enough. He would have fought as tigerishly as she in her place. As for Jamie—well, he would have to reason his feelings out another time.

Yes, he would stay at the D Cross A for another little while, at least. He would camp here on the mountain a day or two, and then go down and get to work. After all—there was a roundup close at hand. He would be needed.

The telegram from Ann Jennings said she would arrive in Black Springs within the month, and that Agnes should make arrangements for the wedding as she thought best.

16

"No, Jamie," Ignacio said, "it is a bad idea."

"For Christ's sake, *amigo,* I'm not a complete bastard—and I promise, God damn it, I won't see or bother her again."

"But *Señorita* Jennings's train will be here in an hour."

"We'll be back in plenty of time. Besides, that train ain't been on time once this year."

They were on Frontera Street, heading toward the tracks and Mex Town, Jamie striding along powerfully, Ignacio drawn in his wake, reluctantly. After dropping Douglas at Stafford's store, the rider and the rancher's son had gone to the depot to check on the train. "On time at Tucumcari," Jim Gibbon reported. It was then Jamie proposed the visit to the cantina.

Thank God Jorge would not be there. He was down in Mesilla, becoming a godfather for a new cousin in the Martínez tribe, and not expected back until Tuesday. With luck, they could pay their respects, have one drink for the sake of decency, and then get out. With even more luck, Concepción would be sleeping, and unable to see them.

Ann's train was on time at Tucumcari. *Bueno.* His heart beat wildly at the thought of seeing her again. It calmed, though, when he made himself remember that in only two weeks time the dark girl and the man swinging along in front of him would be husband and wife. The thought provoked little pain now. At night in the shack, and days at work, he had drilled himself too thoroughly for that.

Perhaps this trip to quiet Jamie's conscience wasn't such a bad idea. It would be good to bury the ugly episode once and for all before Ann arrived. Maybe Concepción would be mollified enough by the visit that nothing would be said, and Ann would never know.

His heart still ached when he thought of what Concepción had looked like when he went to see her three days after coming off the mountain. Mamá had sent him back to the girl's room, and he had walked through the dimly lit hall feeling guilty himself, simply because he, too, was from the D Cross A. When he reached her, all he could do was stare in shock.

"Concepción!"

"*Cómo estás,* Ignacio?"

This couldn't be the lively, sinuous girl who worked the bar, nor even the pathetic, counterfeit *dama* who had tried to face down Agnes MacAndrews a week ago. Horror had paid a visit here. The girl was wasted. Hard lines of pain still marked her face.

"The baby, Concepción?"

"Tell your friend to forget about it. There will be none."

"But—"

"By myself! I did it by myself. Don't ask me how."

"And you, *pobrecita*?"

She laughed a little, bitterness ringing such changes on the laughter it was something terrible to hear, for all that it wasn't very loud.

"*Muy bien*, Ignacio. I am fine. That doctor says I can have all the fun I want now, and never have to worry. There will never be another child."

He hadn't said a word to Jamie, and Jamie hadn't asked.

As they reached the steps of the cantina, he realized Jamie still thought there was something left undone. "After all, Nash, Connie's a good kid, a real sport," he was saying as he pushed his ways inside. "Only thing I don't cotton to—she had no right to make that fuss with Ma."

Once his eyes adjusted to the light inside, the rider saw the usual Saturday afternoon crowd. These were the field workers and small farmers from the Río Concho, southeast of Black Springs. He knew almost every one by sight, and some by name. Unlike the macho riders who made the cantina rock with drunkenness at night, these were quiet men, husbands and fathers in for the marketing and a quick tequila. Dressed alike in white cotton from head to toe, they huddled at the tables in dignified silence. Tomorrow they would be in the Mex Town church with their families; during the week they would disappear into their work. They spent little, but were still the Florida's most respected patrons.

Ignacio wasn't sure he wanted them for an audience when Jamie spoke with Concepción, if he did. He couldn't see the girl anywhere, and breathed more easily.

"I got to have a drink first, Nash," Jamie said.

As Andreas came up to serve them, putting out a whiskey bottle at Jamie's command, his hand shook visibly. The family knew, the vaquero was sure of it.

"Tell your daughter I'd like to see her, *viejo*," Jamie said. Andreas nodded and left the bar.

"Let's go, Jamie," Ignacio pleaded.

"Keep your pants on, Nash!" Jamie snapped. "We'll do what we came for." The rider wondered about the "we."

In less than a minute Andreas was back, wiping glasses furiously. Jamie signaled him for another whiskey, and as the cantina owner moved in front of the two of them, Ignacio saw him look to the back. The eyes in the dark brown face were white with fear. Jamie saw it, too, for he turned when the rider did, expecting, no doubt, to see Concepción standing there.

It was Jorge. He stood in the hall doorway, a light from somewhere behind him casting him in half silhouette. The fine head was inclined a little, and his body was turned slightly, the back straight, rigid, his arms close to his sides. His face, what could be seen of it, was as white as the clothes of the drinkers at the tables.

Jamie's voice broke across the crowded room, "Howdy, Martínez. I'd like to see your sister." The boom of it crushed the soft drone of Spanish into silence, and Jorge answered into the echoes.

"*Mí hermana está muy enferma, señor.*"

"Aw, come on!" Jamie said. "Speak English, *hombre.*"

"My-sister-is-still-not-well," Jorge said, spacing the words out slowly, as if speaking to an infant or an idiot.

"Still?" Jamie said. "Didn't know she was sick."

"There are many things you do not know, *Señor Bufón.*"

Ignacio could feel the anglo stiffen. "Now look, you little shit!" Jamie roared, "I know how you feel, and I don't want trouble with you—but if you get smart with me, I'll kick your greasy ass to Kingdom Come!"

Every pair of black eyes in the room was on them now, and the quiet was deathly. This is when it will come, Ignacio thought—but the slim youth in the doorway stood his ground. *Sí, sí,* he was playing the charade to its only possible conclusion. The best, the only way he could protect his sister's name was to stand for this abuse—if it cost him every ounce of pride he had.

Ignacio tugged at Jamie's sleeve. *"Por favor,"* he said.

"All right, all God damned right! We'll go." Young Mac-Andrews reached in his pocket, pulled out a wad of bills, and threw two of them on the bar. Still holding the rest in his hand, he started for the door, his face flushing crimson. *Por favor, Dios,* the rider prayed, *get us through that door.*

If Jamie had held his anger, it might have ended there. Maybe it was a fraud, maybe he was only bent on proving to the vaquero that he wasn't a "complete bastard," or maybe it was, as it seemed to Ignacio later, sincere decency—but before he reached the door Jamie stopped, turned, and flashed the same seductive smile which had won the rider so many, many times.

"Look, Martínez. I'm sorry, sorry as hell." His big face lighted up more brightly still. "Hey, *amigo!* I'd like to leave a little *dinero* for Connie." He waved the money in his hand. "She'll need it when the baby comes!"

Jorge shot across the twenty feet of bar room. A knife rose and fell—two, three times—before Jamie could move or flinch. All Ignacio could do was throw his weight against the arm which wielded it. Jorge's screaming cry rang in his ears.

"MARRANO!"

James MacAndrews lay on the floor of the Cantina Florida, blood welling up through the gabardine covering his chest. Five and ten dollar bills were scattered on the floor about him, and his eyes, as he lay, grew wider in surprise. Nothing else about his face had changed.

Ignacio sat in the doctor's outer office, and tried to keep his mind on the ticking of the big wall clock. Dr. Colvin had been with Jamie for over an hour, and he wished he knew how things were going. The nurse—the doctor's widowed sister, Sally Bannister—had bustled in and out of the inner room a dozen times, carrying bottles, pans, and bloodied dressings, but she hadn't told him a solitary thing, and she looked too busy and concerned for him to ask. He was still covered with Jamie's blood himself, and he wanted to wash it off.

How had he carried Jamie across the tracks and down three blocks of Frontera Street to Dr. Colvin's? Some of the *campesinos* from the Florida must have helped; Jamie hadn't helped himself. He had passed out long before they laid him out on the table in the doctor's office and Mrs. Bannister cut away his shirt.

He did remember holding Jorge after the attack, surprised at how strong he was, as if he had been tempered into steel in the crucible of his insane, seething anger. What happened to Jorge after that he didn't know—but he could guess. Andreas, or Mamá, or someone, would have convinced him he couldn't stay in Black Springs, and he would have begun a long journey an hour ago or more. Perhaps Ignacio would never see him again. He would have to think about that later.

Sally Bannister came out again, this time empty-handed. She sank into the chair behind her desk with a tired sigh.

"*Señora?*" Ignacio said.

"Please don't ask me, Mr. Ortiz." It wasn't said in a cold or unkindly way. "The doctor should be through in a few more minutes. He'll come out and talk to you then." She seemed to be studying him as she spoke, but his mind was too full of other things to wonder why.

As soon as he was convinced Jamie was out of danger, he would have to find Douglas and bring him to his son. Then— Ann! He had heard the train pull in a half hour earlier. Most likely she had gone to Stafford's when she found no one at the depot from the D Cross A. Who would tell her what had happened? And how would the señora take it?

Probably they would spend the night in town, and as much more time as needed for Jamie's wounds to heal. Then—when Jamie was back at the D Cross A, and as soon as Ignacio could be alone with the señor—he would tell Douglas MacAndrews he was leaving, right after roundup. It couldn't wait past then. He would force the words out while his resolve was at its peak.

The door to the inner office opened and Dr. Colvin stood there in his long white coat. "Mr. Ortiz—Nash," he began, but he had no sooner started than the hall door opened and Douglas entered. When the vaquero saw his face, he realized for the first time in all their years together that this great rock might someday crack.

"He's out of danger, Douglas, weak from loss of blood, and in shock, of course," Dr. Colvin said. "I don't expect he'll be out from under the anaesthesia for thirty, forty minutes yet, so there's no point in going in to see him now. You'll need your car to take him out of here, when he comes to—and handle him with care. Don't worry, though. He's tough—and lucky. An inch lower . . ."

Douglas turned to the vaquero. "Ignacio, let's walk a bit. I have some questions." The rancher thanked the doctor and left the office. The rider, before he followed, murmured "gracias" to the doctor and then the woman. He saw Sally Bannister give him a look which, even in his modesty, he knew as one of admiration. He couldn't think of what he'd done to merit it.

On the bench in Black Springs plaza, the señor's interrogation was insistent, almost brutal. "Spare me nothing, Ignacio," he said.

The rider told it simply, fully. With anyone else but Douglas he might have shaded the facts a little, but before he was halfway through he knew the rancher had swift, sure instincts about it, anyway.

When he finished, Douglas looked out across the plaza. "Thank you, Ignacio. I'm grateful to you—again." Then he buried his face in his hands and was silent for a while. Once, the vaquero saw the powerful shoulders heave, but when at last he raised his head and spoke again, the face was calm and the eyes clear.

"Ignacio, I've got to get the car and get back to the doctor's office. I wouldn't ask you to do this for me, but Ann's waited far too long already. I want you to tell her. Tell her as much as you think is right. Tell her as gently as you just told me, but tell her.

She'll hear it all eventually, this town being what it is, and I'd rather it came from one of us. It should come from Jamie, but we can't count on that."

"*Sí, señor.*" Now he must set about the most difficult task the rancher had ever given him. Well, someday soon, when he was gone from the D Cross A, he could set about forgetting all this. He started off for Estancia Street and Stafford's, but not quickly enough to miss hearing Douglas Mac-Andrews—talking only to himself, the rider knew—say one more thing.

"Who'll pick up after Jamie when I'm gone—and who'll look after Ann?"

17

Ignacio Ortiz was the only non-Anglo present at the reception for Ann and James MacAndrews. With the family in the receiving line, and each of them the center of an excited group afterward, he was left completely to his own devices for more than an hour. He watched each MacAndrews in turn: Douglas, imposing in the unaccustomed dress suit (surprisingly, the big man wore it with as much ease as he did his old sheepskin jacket), looking radiant every time his eyes settled on the bride; Sarah, pigtails flying, her hands still fierce about the bouquet she had held at the altar. Jamie, more handsome than he had ever seen him, smiled his abandoned smile at every handshake and embrace. And Agnes? It was impossible to read the señora's face. Ignacio wasn't sure she had completely returned to normal since they brought the bandaged Jamie home from Black Springs. The terror and pain were still visible to anyone who knew how to look. Strange, he had seen a face remarkably like Agnes's not long ago.

He had, of course, been wrong in thinking himself the only *Mexicano* here in the top floor ballroom of the Sacramento. Two of the musicians were regulars at the Florida, and all the servants had Spanish names. María Gómez, trim in her black uniform, had given him that familiar look of half contempt as she served him a glass of champagne. He took the glass to the corner farthest from the orchestra and the bridal couple, too far away for anyone to press upon him a piece of the wedding cake Ann cut with Jamie's hand on hers.

That was where he stayed until Sally Bannister found him.

108

"Hello, Mr. Ortiz," she said. In her hand was a glass of champagne, too, held with a good deal more ease and confidence.

"*Señora.*" He tried the same little bow he had never really mastered. Her smile made him feel even clumsier.

"Your friend Jamie looks as good as new, doesn't he?" She lifted her glass in the direction of the groom. "A stunning couple." She looked back at the vaquero. "Will you be next, Mr. Ortiz? Oh, but I forget. You scarcely *talk* to women, do you?" He wished he could speak fine, rolling sentences and prove her wrong, but he didn't say a word, as her smile became a challenge.

This was his third encounter with Sally Bannister. The second had come when he went with Jamie to have his dressings changed. While young MacAndrews was with the doctor, he idly picked up a magazine and began to read. He was halfway through an article on the war in France when he saw her watching him with an intensity and directness he had never known in a woman.

"You're really *reading,* aren't you?" The moment's irritation he felt gave way to embarrassment, and he couldn't say a word. She had smiled then as she was smiling now. Upset as he was, he couldn't help noticing that Sally Bannister was striking in the extreme, handsome rather than pretty, fair and blue-eyed but with a deep tan which only heightened her blondness. Like her brother, the doctor, her accents were clearly not of the Ojos Negros.

Now, here in the ballroom, he racked his brain for something to say to her, but before he could find a word, he saw Ann break away from the knot of guests around her and Jamie and come toward him, and the other woman was forgotten.

Ann stood in front of him, her face, set off by the white gown, more darkly beautiful than he had ever seen it.

"Jamie and I are leaving now, Ignacio," she said. "It seems every man here has kissed the bride but you."

She stepped closer, and he braced himself to keep his knees from buckling. Timidly, he leaned toward her and placed his lips against the offered cheek. He blushed, the heat and color rising in his face as if he faced an open fire.

"Thank you, Ignacio—or rather, *muchas gracias,*" Ann said, and moved on. He scarcely saw her go with Jamie, as a laughing throng closed in around them.

Behind him, like an echo, he heard Sally Bannister laugh: a deep, throaty, earthy—and yet sympathetic—sound.

"So," Concepción Martínez said from behind the bar, "they are now married—*esposo y esposa.*"

"*Sí*, Concepción."

"*Bueno!* Now I can think of something else. *Esta terminado, verdad.*"

"*Sí.*"

"Let us drink to the future, Ignacio, *amigo.*"

The same mail which brought Ann's letter from the honeymoon in Colorado Springs brought a picture postcard for Sarah and one for the vaquero.

There was a letter, too, from Jorge, postmarked Ciudad Juárez. It was an odd mixture of English and Spanish, telling Ignacio he was with the army of Pancho Villa, that he had actually seen one of the Madero brothers, and that he expected to see fighting soon. Above the signature Jorge had printed in big letters, "WISH YOU WERE HERE!" There was no return address, so Ignacio couldn't send him Douglas's message.

"Tell him and his people there'll be no charges, Ignacio. I've spoken to Sheriff Lane—and *Jamie* will make no trouble."

The vaquero had passed the word along at the Florida, but the family had received nothing more from Jorge than he had.

Agnes read her letter from Ann and tossed it on the kitchen table. "Must be nice to honeymoon at a place as fancy as the Broadmoor. I spent mine in a wagon."

"Ag-gie!" Douglas chided.

Ann and Jamie stayed in Colorado Springs just ten days, but with their rented rooms in Black Springs to furnish, and a thousand other newlywed chores, it was a month before the bridegroom showed up at the D Cross A, his old breezy confidence rippling across his face.

Douglas decided his son would work four days on and three off, living in his old room at the house when at the ranch, and returning to town and Ann for each long weekend. It was the rancher's idea they live in town. Agnes made no comment about the arrangement.

After his first time back with Ann, Jamie showed up with a roll of yard-wide paper under his arm. "Drawings for a house," he said in answer to Douglas's question, as he rolled the big sheets out on the dining room table. "Thought we could build between here and the highway, where that little arroyo runs alongside the wagon road."

"Good place," Douglas said. "Smart looking set of plans, Jamie. Who did them?"

"Well, most of the work is Ann's. Truth is, she thought up the whole idea."

To that point Agnes hadn't seemed to pay attention. Now she pushed her way between the MacAndrews men, and bent over the drawings. "Seems a scandalous waste of money to me. We could add more than enough room here for a tenth of what that will cost."

"Aggie, Aggie," Douglas broke in, "these youngsters don't want to live with us."

"Still seems a lot of foolishness to me!" With that, Agnes marched into the kitchen. There was silence until she was gone.

"You get started on it, son," Douglas said.

By the time Ann came out for Thanksgiving dinner, the trenches for the stone foundation were already done, but it was the señor, not Jamie, who had arranged for the work. The younger MacAndrews hadn't even seen them, until he and Ann, together with Sarah and the vaquero, rode out to the site on the morning of the holiday.

The Saturday after Thanksgiving, the rider came to the house for a cup of coffee two hours earlier than usual. He was to make his regular trip to Black Springs for some things Agnes wanted, then pick up mail at the post office.

Pushing his way as quietly as he could through the kitchen door, he was amazed to find Ann sitting at the table in her dressing gown. Something had blanched the high color from her cheeks.

"*Qué pasa, Señora Ann?* Are you ill?" he said.

"No, Ignacio. It is nothing, just something I must work out for myself."

Ignacio was almost sure he saw another figure, also in a dressing gown, far back in the shadows of the dining room.

"If there is anything I can do, *señora*—" The girl shook her head. When he looked again at the dining room there was no one there—if there ever had been.

Christmas came and went, and for Ignacio Ortiz it was a bad and lonely rime. For the first time, Douglas and Agnes spent the holidays in Black Springs. The rancher asked the vaquero to come in at least for the day itself, but he lamely pleaded too much work, and although the big man looked disappointed, he didn't insist. Sarah broke into tears when told the rider wasn't coming, but in the end it was decided that now Tim Barlow could go off to the Pecos country to see the girl he was writing to.

Ignacio avoided Jess until he feared the poor man would take it personally, and he finally sought the elder Barlow out on Christmas day and shared a bottle of whiskey with him. The drinks only put him in a more troubled mood.

He spent all his time away from work in the shack, trying to read—and failing miserably. The decision he had made in Black Springs plaza after Jorge's attack on Jamie came back to haunt him. He knew now he would stay on at the D Cross A until the day he died. There had been a time, not so long ago, when such a prospect would have raced his heart with joy. Now—though he *would* stay—the joy was thinned by gall. Could he hope for something more than an uneasy peace?

The senior MacAndrewses returned to the ranch the day before New Year's Eve, earlier than planned. For twenty-four hours they maintained a stony silence at odds with Sarah's bright chatter. In his years with them the rider had seen no such gulf separating the rancher and his wife.

When Jamie came back after New Year's Day, he spoke little and set to work immediately—to the vaquero's surprise—on the new house, coming in later for supper each night and retiring early.

Ignacio, wondering what could possibly have happened, and how it might affect the dark girl alone in town, nursed his uneasiness in the silence of the shack.

Late in January, in an urge so foreign to his usual instincts it frightened him a little, Ignacio saddled a horse and rode to Black Springs to see Ann. He pushed the young pony, broken only the summer before, so hard he felt ashamed. In front of the house where Jamie and Ann had their apartment, he walked the heaving animal for long minutes, and he was still wiping its wet flanks when Ann appeared on the porch.

"*Bienvenido*, Ignacio!" Her smile was so broad and her voice held such delight he was taken aback. He had expected to see a face like Señor Douglas's when he returned after Christmas. That was a month ago. Whatever happened then must now be quite forgotten. He was wrong to come.

"*Buenos días, Señora* Ann," he said. What would he say next?

"Come up, won't you?" she said, "Can I give you coffee?"

"No, *señora, gracias*. I cannot stay." He felt confused and foolish. She must know he had made this trip just to see her, and yet he said nothing. Surely she must think he had gone *loco*.

Then the smile of greeting fled her face. He could see the small beginnings of sadness pull at the corners of her mouth and the outer edges of her brown eyes. No, he was not imagining this, it was there. The first insidious start of the things he had begun to fear for this woman were happening. He would speak, knowing full well the terrible chance he took.

"*Señora*—I—wondered about your happiness." The words were out, and could not be recalled.

She dropped her eyes. A tumbleweed rattled against the wooden steps of the porch and behind him the pony whinnied. Then Ann MacAndrews lifted her eyes and met those of the vaquero. The winter sun brushed pale highlights on her gold-dark features.

"Thank you, Ignacio—my friend. I will be all right, truly I will," she said, "if you will help me."

Never in all his life had he known such strength.

"*Sí, señora*. Always—and in every way I can."

There was too much to think about to hurry back to the D Cross A. He gave the pony its own way along the yucca-lined track, letting it walk slowly and rest often. The poor beast had earned it after the wild ride in.

Everything in the wide basin was without motion on this windless, gray day. Even the images in his mind were still, hanging suspended just beyond the reach of thought. The sun was over his left shoulder, the only thing in all his view which moved, speeding toward the cloud banks on the western peaks. For all the cold decay and fallow winter dreariness which lay about him, his heart had lost its weight.

Even if the white wall rose again, he could deal with it.

18

JAMIE'S TRUCULENT SILENCE ENDED AS QUICKLY AS IT BEGAN—BUT
so did his work on the new house. He would nod smiling
agreement whenever Douglas urged him about his task, but by
the time February had come and gone, only three sides of the
stone foundation were in place. Ignacio avoided traveling the new
road to the highway.

The second letter from Jorge Martínez was as useless as the
first as far as sending Douglas's message was concerned. It was
postmarked "Las Palomas, Sonora – 28 FEB 16," but Ignacio
couldn't find the place in the old geography book. Just the same,
he wrote a letter to his friend, to send off the very second he had
an address, and he made a copy and left it at the Florida in case
they heard something between his visits.

Jorge's letter wasn't long, but the hurried scrawl breathed
excitement from every line. One passage in particular screamed for
his attention ". . . and I have been given special work because I am
an americano. Someday I will be able to tell you all about it. I can
tell you that soon—very soon—something will happen to open the
eyes of every gringo." The last part was underlined with a heavy
hand. Ignacio was disturbed without knowing exactly why.

"Damn it, I don't know!" Jim Gibbon shouted above the excited
hubbub in Stafford's general store. "It was a company report advis-
ing us to keep an eye peeled for trouble. All I know is what it said.
Villa crossed the border yesterday with maybe a thousand men, and
there's a hell of a lot of people dead on both sides."

"Where did it happen, Jim?" Findlay Stafford asked, the one quiet voice in a storm of loud ones.

"Columbus—about fifty miles west of El Paso."

"I know the place," Ignacio didn't know the speaker. "Used to run cattle there," the man said. "Cross over and buy them in Las Palomas on the Sonora side and run them to an agent in Columbus. Real stealing, more ways than one. The greasers we dealt with couldn't read a tally stick for sour apples." He laughed.

Ignacio shrank further into the corner where he was standing. *Las Palomas!* Jorge had taken part in this!

He had felt something in the air as he drove the wagon down Frontera Street. Men and women walking the wooden sidewalks had stared at him and he had checked himself and the wagon carefully. Dismissing it as fancy, he walked through the rear of the store to find this angry knot of men besieging Gibbon with their questions.

"War!" one of them was screaming now. "It's the only thing. God damn it. Kill every one of the sneaky bastards!" The veins on the man's face were standing out like fence wire.

"Wait just a minute." This was Findlay Stafford, his spectacles far down his nose, face as thoughtful looking as ever. "Who you going to declare war *on?* Last I heard, Pancho was at odds with Mexico City. Can't blame *them*."

"Don't make no never mind." It was another unknown man. "A Mex is a Mex. Wouldn't trust that stinking crowd across the tracks, either."

"Has anybody"—Stafford ignored the man—"checked with Hendry over at the *Chupadera County News?* Maybe he's heard something." Ignacio had seen Findlay glance his way just before he spoke.

In seconds the store was empty, save for the merchant and the rider.

"Nash," Findlay said, "I don't think there'll be real trouble in town, but it might be a good idea to get your load on board and get on back to the D Cross A."

"*Sí, Señor* Stafford." He recognized the wisdom of the storekeeper's advice. It would be well after dark, anyway, when he reached the ranch, so he might as well get started.

The two of them worked steadily, but without haste, loading the salt and cottonseed cake, the sacks of beans and flour he had hauled out countless times before. He had just finished tying down his load when Stafford, who had gone inside to answer the bell announcing a customer, appeared on the dock again.

"Nash," he said, "there's an ugly crowd out front, just kids, but I don't like the look of them. I want you to take the alley when you pull out, swing over toward Stanton Street, and take the back way out of town."

In the doorway the rider saw someone else. It was Sally Bannister.

"Findlay," she said, "Mr. Ortiz can give me a ride home. I live out that way, and I don't think anybody would start anything if I were in the wagon with him."

"Good idea, Sally."

She hadn't so much as said hello to the vaquero, but she hadn't taken her eyes off him all the time she talked to Stafford.

Nor did she speak to him as they rolled through the alley, turned, and took a shortcut through a vacant lot, but she looked at him constantly, as she had back at the store. He knew it, even if he did keep his own eyes firmly on the horses.

When they reached her gate—she had suddenly reached across and pointed it out, her arm brushing his—he set the brake and climbed down to help her out. Back down the street, he could see three big youngsters. They must have followed the wagon from the store, but he hadn't noticed. You were too busy thinking about the woman next to you, *amigo,* he told himself. They were just standing there, but one of them had a good sized rock clutched in his hand.

"You're coming inside with me," Sally Bannister said.

"Señora?"

"I said you're coming inside with me. Don't worry about the wagon. Nobody in Black Springs would dare to touch it with that 'D Cross A' on its side. You can get it out of here after dark. They'll be gone by then." Her voice was so firm, the command so clear and strong, he didn't think to argue.

He followed her up the path, carrying the bags she had thrown in the back of the wagon at Stafford's. As they reached the steps, he considered telling her he would be on his way after all, but she moved across the porch too quickly. With the bags in his hands he had to follow her inside. She locked the door behind them. It had, he remembered, only taken a push to open.

"I'll put on a pot of coffee," she said, "unless you'd like something stronger."

"*Gracias, señora.* Coffee will be enough." Why had he accepted anything? He should go.

"Put those things in the kitchen, Mr. Ortiz." She turned and looked at him. "Would you object if I just called you Nash?"

"No, *señora.*"

"And my name is Sally."

"*Sí, Señora* Sally."

"No—not *Señora* Sally. Just Sally!"

He swallowed hard. At no time in his life had he ever called an anglo woman by her first name only. Somehow it seemed an unearned intimacy, and it frightened him more than those young ruffians out in Stanton Street.

"Just Sally," she repeated. "Come on, try it. It's not so difficult." The smile he remembered from the reception danced its way across her face.

"*Sí, Señ*—Sally!" She laughed out loud and an alarming warmth crept up the length of his body. He was glad the bags were still in hands he was sure would otherwise be shaking.

She turned, still laughing, and he followed her into the kitchen. "There, put the bags on the table, Nash," she said, "and while I make the coffee, go out to the sitting room window and see if those three hooligans are still in sight."

"*Sí*—Sally." She was right. It wasn't so difficult.

At the window he could see them, lounging idly against the picket fence of the house across the street, the one with the rock tossing it in the air, catching it, all the while keeping his eyes on Sally Bannister's front door. They looked bored. They would leave soon. *Sí,* they would leave soon, and he could go.

But the fact was that Ignacio didn't want to go. He looked over the heads of the three boys, past the house with the picket fence, to Estancia Street. He could just see the Stafford's big house. Across from it, out of sight, was where Ann Jennings MacAndrews lived.

"Sit down, Nash." Sally Bannister had come up behind him, and he jumped at her voice as if he'd been caught thinking aloud. "The coffee will be ready in a minute."

Sally took his place at the window, while he found a chair, a severe, straight one, to sit in.

"Uh-huh, still there," she said. "Why, that big one is Billy Joe McIntosh. Just wait until I see his mother." She turned to the vaquero. "It seems you're stuck here for a little while, Nash." She moved across the room and sank into an armchair facing him.

What would they find to say to each other now, he wondered.

"Mary Stafford tells me," she said suddenly, "that Aggie MacAndrews was your teacher for a long time."

He nodded.

"What sort of things do you read, Nash?"

He looked at her blankly for a moment, and then an amazing thing happened. Ignacio Ortiz began to talk. It came in fits and starts at first, then in a gushing torrent of words. When he finished, he realized she had never gone to get the coffee. It must have boiled away.

Dios! Had he really told her about the Shakespeare, the other poets, the histories, and all those books even Señora MacAndrews didn't know about? He should feel embarrassed and ashamed; he didn't.

Then she told him about herself, how, after her husband died in a boating accident, she had lost the child she carried, and, with nothing left for her in New York City, had followed her brother, the doctor, to New Mexico. Her voice was strong and forthright in the telling, and the smile still played over her face, bit it didn't hide the loneliness.

It almost seemed he was reading this somewhere. No one he knew, not even Agnes, spoke as Sally did. It was a dimension he had found only in books—he never expected it in Black Springs.

"Hunter College. I still miss it." She had been talking about her schooling, but he'd lost some of it along the way.

It was dark out now. Hours had skipped by unnoticed.

"I must go now—Sally," he said.

She went to the window.

"Yes, they're gone." She turned to him. "Promise me you'll come again, Nash."

"I promise," he said.

They were at the door, and she put out her hand like a man. He took it, wondering that he could be so calm, touching a woman like this.

"I'll walk out to the wagon with you," she said.

"It is too cold."

"Never mind."

As they moved across the porch, the vaquero became aware that the darkness they walked into wasn't total. The wagon and the two nodding horses were bathed in an orange light, a glow which came from somewhere south of them. He smelled smoke, if only faintly. One glance beyond the railroad tracks half a mile away was enough to tell him that Mex Town was in flames.

"That should do it, Ortiz, and *muchas gracias* for your help." Sheriff Corey Lane sat down on the wet earth in front of the Florida, his back against one of the veranda posts. The sheriff's face was gray, partly from smeared grime and soot, but from strain and fatigue as well, Ignacio knew.

The vaquero was bone tired, too. He hadn't drawn a normal breath since he raced from Sally Bannister's front porch with her protest echoing in his ears. "No, Nash, no! Stay here. Something terrible is going on there!"

They had fought the fires all night: the sheriff, the rider, every man and boy in Mex Town, and most of the women, too. Only now, with the sun rising over the last columns of smoke and the choking haze, were they under control. Of all the buildings on Frontera Street, only the cantina itself had escaped the flames. It almost seemed as if the riders who galloped the length of the dirt street the night before had thrown their brands intentionally wide of the Florida; it was the one place in Mex Town they had use for. Ignacio had looked at the Martínez place first when he broke through the line of Sheriff Lane's mounted deputies, and his heart only began to beat again when he saw the cantina standing dark and placid in the holocaust of blazing vigas, roofs buckling under the attack of flame and smoke, and the wild-eyed crowds hurrying with their water buckets, shovels, and wetted blankets.

The last of the deputies moved off to get some breakfast, his horse slogging through the puddles where water spills had turned the caliche into sludge.

"Couldn't have done it without you," the sheriff said. "Oh, I can handle the lingo well enough to get food and drink, but without you to organize your *paisanos* only the adobe would be left."

Not so, Señor Sheriff, Ignacio thought, I saw how you worked, and fought, and commanded. My people will not forget. *My people?* Pay close attention, Jorge.

He looked around. With the sun lifting over the rooftops he could assess the damage. It was a miracle how well Mex Town had survived. Well, in this poor place there wasn't much of value to burn. Feed for livestock was all charred to ash, or else so soaked it was sure to rot, but without a doubt the *campesinos* from the Río Concho would make good that loss. Some of the dwellings were now open to the sky, true, but he knew a month wouldn't go by before the barrio looked much the same again. These people (my people?) knew how to work—their lives had consisted of little else.

Twice during the night he had seen Concepción, hauling buckets like the strongest man. They hadn't spoken, but she had smiled at him—a sharing smile. With her hair in disarray, the familiar red skirt billowing as she ran, and the leaping flames reflecting from eyes he had seen provide their own wild fire often enough, she looked tough and confident, unlike the girl who had confronted Agnes, or the wan, bereft creature he had visited in her room in the cantina.

"It's a damned good thing," Sheriff Lane was saying now, "your people aren't given much to packing guns. They're quiet, but they're sore as hell—and they've got guts. Wish my neighbors across the tracks had seen the things I saw last night."

The men who had fought the fires had drifted off for food and comfort before the dawn. Now they were beginning to fill Frontera Street again, looking around as Ignacio had, trying to decide, no doubt, where to make a start. He could leave now; there was nothing more for him to do. The wagon was still at Sally Bannister's and the horses would need attention. He said goodbye to the sheriff, and made a little bow. He did it very well.

Where Frontera cut across the tracks, and on the farther side, anglos were forming in small, silent groups. A few had been there the whole night through, watched by the deputies of Corey Lane, but now it looked as if the whole town would be coming out. The Black Springs fire volunteers, who hadn't crossed the tracks all night, were packing their equipment now that there was no danger to the anglo side of town. Ignacio knew he could cross the tracks without the slightest worry. There would be no more trouble for a long, long time.

He turned for a last look at Frontera Street. There, against one of the few unscorched walls, lined up as quietly as the crowd of anglos gathering behind him, stood a Mex Town family; father, mother, and two brown-faced little girls. Their clothes were spotless, put on clean this morning. All four of them looked untouched and pure, the white of their garments shone in the sun, and their faces were astonishingly alike. Whatever it was the faces held—fright, sadness, or shock, he couldn't tell—they stared at the anglos on the street behind him.

Something stirred so deep inside him he didn't know the place. He didn't know this family—and yet he did. Somewhere in the past, the dead past, he had seen them all before. Where? When he was sure it all would come, the white wall loomed before him.

* * *

It was three weeks before he saw Sally Bannister again. A note left for him at Stafford's reminded him of his promise. Yes, he meant to keep it, but he put off seeing her for most of a long day, lingering first over his beer at the Florida while he found out from Andreas there had been no further word from Jorge. Concepción was visiting friends on the far side of Mex Town or he might have stayed in the cantina even longer than he did.

He wandered across the tracks, not idly but at a snail's pace. On the surface, things were much the same in Black Springs as before the fire. Pershing's expedition into Chihuahua and Sonora was a ten-day wonder; after the first excitement no one spoke of it. It was certain things would never be the same again between

Mex Town and Black Springs itself—not that they had ever been what they might have been. With all the friction where the two villages met, there had, at least, been accommodation of a sort. Now that was gone. In its place were ill-concealed black looks, a little darker on the anglo side, oddly enough, as if to say that they were the injured parties.

Delaying still, he stopped at the apartment to see Ann and Jamie, but they were gone. Finally he decided he had better keep his promise to Sally and get it over with, but, reluctant as he imagined himself to be, when he started up Stanton Street, he found his pace quickening.

"Come in, Nash. It's so good to see you."

It wasn't either of the faces he remembered, not the terrified one he had left to fight the fire, nor the one which smiled its relief from the window the next morning when he came to get the wagon. Sally Bannister's face was more the one which had taunted him at the reception, only softer. She held out her hands to him, and he took them, surprised at how strong they were, but more surprised at himself that he hadn't hesitated.

"Sit down, Nash," she said. "Supper will be ready in half an hour." She had known he would come. There was a shine about the room which told him so. It hadn't been untidy before, but now it looked as if a great deal of time had gone into making it exactly right. On the back of the couch was an antimacassar he was sure hadn't been there before, and there were flowers in the room which must have been cut this very day.

They dined by the glow of candles set in silver holders which caught the light and sent it skipping across a gleaming tablecloth. There was wine, a great, red, shimmering decanter of it, and food unlike any he could remember having, lighter by far than any the señora had ever served. They didn't talk, but while he ate, she looked questions at him from eyes which hardly left his face.

After a dessert so delicate and frothy he wasn't aware it had come and gone, she sent him back into the sitting room with the first words she uttered since they sat at table. "Make yourself comfortable, Nash. I'll just clear part of this and be right with you."

When he settled himself, he heard her call again. "I've some fine old cognac, Nash. Would you like some?" Yes, he would. He was finding it easier every second to say yes to Sally. The cognac was heady stuff. Rich fumes spiralled from the queer, outsized glass with such strength it seemed the drink would reach his head before he even sipped it.

He leaned back in the chair and reached for one of the *cigarros* he had bought at the Florida on an impulse he hadn't understood. He had only smoked two or three times before, when old Tom had rolled cigarettes for him at roundup time. Somehow it seemed exactly the thing to do with the exotic brandy in his hand, and Sally now across from him on the couch. As he lit his smoke, he watched her hold her own glass between the palms of her hands whose pressure when he first arrived he still could feel. As she leaned forward, the material at the neck of her low-cut dress fell away from her body a little, and the soft light from the lamp threw a deep shadow in the place between her breasts. He could scarcely breathe until she straightened up again.

Then, quite suddenly she asked him for one of his *cigarros*. Amazed he felt no shock—he hadn't seen anglo women smoke— he walked to her on unsteady legs and gave her one. When she leaned forward to the match he held, the shadow deepened once again, and even if he couldn't see the trembling of his hand with his eyes on her, he felt it.

He returned to his chair and looked at her. Her arm lay motionless across the back of the brocaded couch; smoke hung in the air, but stirred with life as she moved her hand to put the cognac glass on the table at her elbow. His head swam in a way that liquor alone could not account for, his throat ached, and something familiar and yet new stirred in his body.

Then, just as anger at the futility of it took hold of him, she put the cigarro in a dish, got to her feet, and smoothed her dress by running her two hands down her body. She moved toward him, not hurriedly but with steps so sure and steady it was like the coming of a distant cloud. She sank to her knees when she reached him, and put one hand on an arm which suddenly went numb, while with her other hand she captured one of his, studied it, turned it palm toward her, and pressed her lips against it. Then, looking into his eyes with hers, now darker, deeper, but with a burning light behind the blue, she placed his hand on the place where the dress, the shadow, and the flesh all came together.

His breathing stopped, and then his heart. As his hand slipped beneath the drooping neckline and cupped one breast, Sally Bannister whispered, "Nash—" as soft as sleep, and leaned to kiss him.

Afterward, when they lay together on the bed whose coverlet and sheets had slipped unnoticed to the floor, he looked at her with curiosity so strong it drove his shyness and uncertainty completely into hiding.

"Nash," she said, propping her weight on her elbows as she turned to him, her chin cupped in her hands, and with the old teasing smile lifting the corners of her mouth, "you were a virgin until just this moment, weren't you?"

He didn't answer, but his face must have told her readily enough, and she rolled on her naked back and rocked the bed with laughter so free and clean and hearty that before he knew it, his own was echoing hers.

Tears had streaked her cheeks by the time it subsided, and, looking at him again, the brows above her bright eyes arched wickedly, and with the smile still playing secret games with the otherwise open face, she cried out in mock despair. "My God! What would the Black Springs Woman's Club say about what I've just done to you? And all the things I'm going to do. . . ."

Throughout the spring, all through the sun soaked, burning summer, and on through a winter whose bitterness he scarcely noticed, the vaquero spent every second he could spare with Sally Bannister. They weren't just two bodies straining to break free of clothes and tumble into bed, not by any means. She had the widest range of interests of anyone he had ever met, and he soon discovered she was intent on taking Agnes's old place as his teacher. She fed him on eastern newspapers and magazines, and insisted he read the new books she ordered in by mail as well as the classics he had all but mastered. And she made him talk. He had, until then, no inkling of how much he knew. She would listen, rapt, and then she would attack his Mexican cowhand-cantina accent without mercy.

"Look, Nash," she would say, "your Spanish, considering your background, is beautiful, but when you use English—ugh!

If you say 'theenk' once more, I'll retch." He took no offense. There was a selfless ring to her criticism, and he would collapse with laughter at her imitations of him.

There was never any talk of love, and he was grateful. Once in a while, the fact that it could never come to this on his part brought pangs of something close to guilt, but her bold confidence, the absence of any demands, and the obvious delight she took in him eased his conscience.

They only saw him at the Florida when he looked in to see if there was word from Jorge. No one there had heard a thing since he had, before the Villa raid. He sent his letters off in care of general delivery at Juárez, and when two months went by without it coming back, he let himself become convinced that Jorge must be still alive.

One night, Concepción fixed him with eyes which were black points of anger and suspicion. "*Amigo!*" she said, her face showing the high fire he remembered when she was just a girl, "What are you up to with *la viuda,* that Bannister *puta?* Aren't the girls on this side of the tracks good enough?" She sounded just like Jorge.

Then, one day at the number four tank, as he and Jamie were having lunch together, the younger MacAndrews brought it up out of the blue. "*Amigo*, it ain't none of my business, but don't you think you're asking for a mite more trouble than you can handle, fucking around with an anglo woman?"

For once, the anger which rose to the top of his head spilled over. "What is it that worries you, Jamie? Are you afraid her brother might stab me with the needle he used to sew you up?" Jamie's look of blank surprise was satisfying.

The only thing that troubled him was what Ann might be thinking, if she knew, and after the scene with Jamie he was sure she did.

19

"It's Jamie in the Buick," Douglas said. Far down the road to the highway a long tail of dust was drifting over the rangeland. "Wonder why the boy is tearing up the road like that."

"Is he alone—or is Ann with him?" Agnes asked. Ignacio felt his heart sink. The cold tone was still there.

"Can't see much under that cloud of dust," Douglas said. "Damn it! It had better be something important for him to beat up that car like that."

Ignacio dropped the training lead of the new pony he was gentling for Sarah, and walked out of the corral, helping the youngster down from the fence as he did. He followed Douglas's gaze to see the Buick round the butte, bump wildly over the bridge, and start up the ranch road. When he saw that Jamie was alone and remembered the rancher's son still had another day of his weekend coming, he felt something twist in the pit of his stomach. Something must have happened to Ann! The fear didn't leave him until the car was near enough for him to see Jamie's face.

Young MacAndrews was hatless, and his hair was blown in every direction; his features were caked with dust—but he was smiling. An enormous grin split his face.

The Buick had barely come to rest before Jamie bounded over the side.

"Jamie!" Agnes shrieked. "The car—it's rolling!"

Already halfway across the yard, he raced back, diving over the side of the moving car and grasping for the hand brake, his long body balanced precariously atop the door. Twenty feet back down the road he got it stopped, and then he was running, coming toward the four of them, his heeled boots clumping across the gravel in a galloping run.

"Jamie," Agnes said when he reached them, "have you been drinking?"

"No, Ma. Not a drop. But I sure as hell *feel* drunk!"

"What's up, son?" Douglas asked.

Jamie drew himself up to his full height. He took a deep breath, and his voice thundered across the yard.

"WAR! Congress has declared war on the Kaiser. We're at war with Germany!"

With that one word the outside world advanced within the borders of the ranch, its outriders striking to the heart of the world the vaquero knew. It was as if the fence were down in a thousand places.

Ann moved out from town three days after Jamie's frenzied drive to bring the news. She was quiet and withdrawn and the rider worried about this, but at least Agnes was civil, if not actually friendly. It seemed the señora had decided a truce might be in order, at least until the first confusion was resolved.

"Yep, I'm joining up," Jamie announced right after he delivered the shocking news. "Right away. I ain't waiting for Uncle Sam to call me." The statement had echoed through every conversation since.

Douglas said very little, but his face was as grave as Ignacio had ever seen it. When he did talk, he spoke of the coming roundup, and although the rider listened, the sound of guns, however muffled and distant, rumbled behind the rancher's words.

Jamie didn't work, couldn't. He spent far too much time racing between the ranch and town, the happy smile a permanent part of his face. A telegram from the congressman in Washington brought word that he would be granted a commission, and he drove to Fort Bliss to get his uniform. He wore it to supper every night for a week. "I can't wait to see my orders!" If he shouted it into their faces once, he did it a hundred times, his impatience to be gone showing itself in every word.

Jess and Tim Barlow left the D Cross A the day after Jamie brought the news. They said goodbye to Douglas quietly and in private, and did the same with Ignacio, apology and pride mixed in their tan faces. They promised to stop in town and ask about replacements for the spring work before going off to enlist. As they rode off across the bridge, the war suddenly visited Ignacio in personal terms, and he wondered if he would ever see the two reliable cowhands again.

"What will *you* do, Nash?" Sally Bannister asked. He hadn't given the matter a moment's thought, and now he wondered why. It wasn't a question of evading responsibility, for he realized he felt none—none at all. In some strange way Jamie had made the war his personal domain, with no place in it for Ignacio Ortiz. Would Sally think him a coward if he answered "nothing"? Did he dare tell her how he was with guns? She seemed satisfied—no, grateful—when he said he wouldn't be a soldier.

Still, he went to Douglas for advice. "No, Ignacio," the big man said, "I won't risk the two of you. Besides, you're not even a citizen. They'd likely throw you out of the country if you tried to join. And I need you—you'll do your bit right here."

Ignacio Ortiz looked hard at James MacAndrews in the days before the young man of the D Cross A went off to war. When he thought about the danger Jamie would be facing, he knew it would be difficult to keep his heart—bruised so thoughtlessly by the anglo so many times—from following along. They had been together as boys and men for nearly a dozen years now, had ridden together *Dios* knew how many thousand miles of fence, sweated their way through more than twenty roundups. It wouldn't be easy to say goodbye to this laughing warrior.

He spent more time with the rancher's son in those last few weeks than he had since before the college days. Jamie still didn't do much work, but he did help Ignacio with the two new hands who had come to take the Barlows's places, an old puncher pitifully past his prime and a boy who scarcely knew one end of a cow from the other. The vaquero feared Douglas might think he was loafing, spending so much time with Jamie, but the señor insisted he stay at his son's side as much as he could. "He'll need you near him sometime before he goes. This first enthusiasm won't see him through completely."

If this was so, the rider never saw any evidence of it. Once, when they rode together, he tried to talk with Jamie. They stopped to rest by a water tank whose windmill wasn't turning. Ignacio climbed it to find the trouble, a tumbleweed which had jammed the gearwork behind the blades. While he freed the mechanism he looked down to where Jamie sat with his back against the spill trough where the two horses watered. From Ignacio's vantage point Jamie looked so small the rider was reminded of Angus's revelations about his lonely, isolated childhood. Perhaps the señor was right. He hurried down.

When he looked at Jamie's face all he saw was the same smile he had seen for weeks. From the windmill, though—*quién sabe?*

"Jamie," he said, as he pulled the horses away from the water, "when did you become so keen to fight this war?"

For a second, Jamie didn't answer. He picked up a handful of pebbles, stood up, and began throwing them into the tank, one by one.

"Crying out loud, Nash. That's a silly question. It's what a man does when his country's in it." He didn't look at the rider.

"But"—could the vaquero bring this up?—"what about Señora Ann?"

"Oh hell, *amigo*," Jamie looked at Ignacio with a smile as disarming as ever, "she'll be glad to see me go."

* * *

The unfamiliar sound woke him from a troubled sleep. Something, and not one of the ponies, was moving around by the corral fence. He pulled his pants on, but left the shack without bothering about his boots. He padded silently up the path, and was almost opposite the house, when he saw the two figures. When he realized it was Ann and Jamie, he headed back, but not in time to escape the sound of their whispered, urgent voices.

"Oh, Christ, Ann! You're making something out of nothing. She don't mean no harm—it's just her way."

"Look, Jamie. I'm not imagining things. She resents me, and shows it in every way she can, particularly when your father isn't there. But that's not the point. I could cope with it, if I had your help—and that's what this is all about, your running away to war."

"Running away? Jesus! I'm fighting for my country."

"Oh, I know you'd most likely go anyway, Jamie, but it's the *way* you're going. The change that came over you when we got in it, well—" She was silent for a while. "Jamie, I love you, but if you weren't going into the army—I'd leave you. When this is over, we've got to come to terms, or it will be over for us, too."

In two days, Jamie's orders came and he went off to war. He left on the back of a D Cross A saddle horse, in his uniform, with a few things stuffed in his saddle bags. His father offered to drive him to town to catch the train for Fort Riley, but he insisted on going in to Black Springs all alone. He would leave his pony at Kelly's livery stable, and Ignacio could pick it up when he went in for the mail. He embraced his mother, Sarah, and his wife in turn, with hugs so brief they revealed his haste to leave.

Douglas simply wouldn't be put off riding with his son as far as the south pasture gate. "You mount up, too, Ignacio," he said. "I've a feeling I'll need company riding back."

The rider kept a respectful distance behind the two MacAndrews men as they crossed the bridge and struck out through the yucca.

"Do well, Jamie—and take care," Douglas said at the gate.

"Don't worry, Pa. There ain't no bullet with my name on it."

"We'll look after Ann. Rest your mind on that."

"Oh—yeah." Jamie turned to the vaquero. "So long, *amigo*. Keep your nose clean."

Ignacio opened the gate for him, and when it closed again they shook hands across the highest bar. Then the señor and the vaquero sat their horses until Jamie topped a low ridge a mile south of the fence.

Not once did he turn and look back.

There was a letter at the post office from Jorge. He took it to the Florida before he opened it, and read it with Andreas, Mamá, and Concepción looking over his shoulder. It embarrassed him that they hadn't heard—had he known he wouldn't have said a thing about it—but they didn't seem to mind.

"Read it out loud, Ignacio," Concepción said. "Mamá and Papá can't read English."

Jorge was well. Oh, a little stomach trouble a few months back—nothing serious. It looked like there would be no fighting for a while. "It is no big secret things have not gone well for the General or our army." He missed Black Springs, and the cantina, and all of them.

Ignacio stammered when he came to the part which said, "I have been living with a girl who travels with our unit. She is very nice; young, but wise, and *muy valiente*." To his surprise, the old people laughed pleasurably. Concepción said nothing. The letter closed by begging Ignacio to thank Señor MacAndrews, a "fine, fine hombre." There was no hint of a political message, no "wish you were here."

Beyond a brief note to Ann and one to Agnes after he reached Fort Riley, no letters came from Jamie for many months. The first they knew he had gone overseas was when Douglas found his son's regiment mentioned in the El Paso paper after Chateau Thierry. Some minor action on the fringes of the battle had turned out well for Jamie's unit. The vaquero read the brief dispatch over several times, sure that Jamie should be singled out in it somewhere.

Then, letters arrived at last, and a photograph. Jamie had been promoted—a second time—and the shiny bars of his captaincy were clearly visible in the sepia snapshot he sent along from Paris. Everyone who saw the picture commented on how well he looked, but Ignacio was thoughtful. The smile was there, all right, but there was something else. *Sí,* he had seen that face before, when Jamie sat on the rim of an arroyo by himself, long ago.

The letters sent him to his books. He brought out the old geography once more. Paris, Metz, the large cities and rivers Jamie wrote about, were easy enough, but many things had happened in towns and villages he couldn't find. War, it seemed, took perverse delight in conferring a fame on the smallest places with the strangest names, places like Thiau-court, Vigneulles (or Las Palomas

and Columbus) which had no public life at all before they were
visited by death.

The dictionary he bought at Stafford's failed him, too, when
it came to words like "star shell," "Very Pistol," and "railroad
gun." The ominous "creeping barrage" he figured out for himself, and shuddered. After puzzling out as much as he could
on his own he turned for help—diplomatically, he thought—to
Agnes instead of Ann, and received a jolt which shook him
for days.

"Don't ask me!" The señora was almost savage. "Why
don't you take it up with Mrs. Bannister. I understand *she's* your
teacher now."

If Ignacio suffered from Agnes's tongue, it was nothing to
what Ann faced every day. The uneasy peace following the out-
break of war, and extending more or less until Jamie left, was
shattered beyond repair. Nothing Ann did or said escaped the
señora's scathing comments. When Ann took Sarah to town to
get her fitted for winter clothes and bought the child an enameled
music box at Stafford's, Agnes railed. "You want everything at
the D Cross A, don't you Ann? Sarah, too." Looking at the girl's
face, Ignacio was heartsick, but helpless.

"No, Ignacio, there's nothing you can do," Ann said. "It is
enough that you are here." Someone had said that to him once
before.

* * *

Agnes was withdrawing more and more into a world of her
own making. To anyone not intimately familiar with her moods,
it would have appeared she was totally without emotion about
the son now in combat. When she talked to the others at any
length, it was of Jamie, but never, by look or word, did she
betray the fear and worry Ignacio knew must be her constant,
unrelenting companions. If she said, "When Jamie comes home,
we should take a trip, California or somewhere like that," it
sounded as if he was just in Black Springs for the day, and soon
would be churning up the dust on the ranch road. But if she said,
"When Jamie comes home" once, she said it fifty times a week.
There were occasions, though, when the iron control seemed to
rust through.

Ann, Douglas, Sarah, and the vaquero had good times together, all things considered. The young woman, aided by the rancher, drew Ignacio deeper into the family's life than he had ever dared to venture, even in the old days when the books were still new to him. But whenever their camaraderie was too obviously enjoyed, Agnes tried to stop it.

"How can you all laugh like that," she would say, "with poor Jamie over there?"

"Aggie, Aggie," Douglas would rebuke her, his voice floating across the room as gentle as the down from a cottonwood, "we can't help Jamie by curling up and dying."

After one of these exchanges, Agnes burst into tears. The rider had never seen her cry before. Wrong. He had. That first Christmas, when she was pregnant with Sarah.

Feeling treasonous, he told Sally about the state of things at the D Cross A, and his bewilderment at Agnes's behavior.

"I'm surprised at you, Nash," Sally said. "You've lived with that woman for what, a dozen, thirteen years? Don't you know the only soul she's ever loved is that handsome lout of a son of hers?"

Ignacio was staggered. How could Sally know this, he asked her. She shrugged. "Talk, gossip, I'll admit, but the people I know, know Aggie MacAndrews very well indeed. In Black Springs she's nowhere near the great lady you think she is, and she's got a case on Jamie. Every time, he hurts her it gets stronger, oddly enough."

It was a revelation, if he could believe it. The intimation that town society didn't see the woman of the D Cross A as he did shocked and confused him. Sally must be wrong.

And the señor?

"Nothing wrong with him," Sally laughed. "Douglas MacAndrews is all he seems—a gentleman."

Ignacio was deeply troubled, not so much by what Sally told him as by the fact that he had talked about Agnes and Douglas with anyone. The truth was that his concern for Ann had caused his indiscretion. But he never spoke of *her* to Sally.

Strangely, Ann's nature became again what it was in the few days the vaquero had known her before her marriage; not frivolous or carefree, to be sure, but she smiled more freely and frequently than she had in the year before her husband left. Remembering the conversation he had heard the night by the corral fence, he wondered what would happen when Jamie came home.

"What's she up to, Nash?" Sarah asked.

"Do not speak, *muchachita*" Ignacio whispered.

Ann had stopped the big touring car halfway between the highway and the ranch house, without giving any warning.

It was an overcast, raw day in early spring, but the three of them had been in high spirits on the way home from Black Springs. They had seen almost everyone they knew in town (Ignacio spent more time in the cantina than usual, and Ann and Sarah teased him about it), the shopping had gone well, and the El Paso paper was filled with good news from France. Best of all, there were letters from Jamie for all of them. Ann and Sarah had decided to save theirs until they got home and Ignacio had agreed.

Looking at the stock they passed, the rider hadn't paid much attention to where they were when suddenly he felt the car slowing to a stop. On the right was the foundation of Ann and Jamie's unfinished house. Without a word, with the motor still running, Ann pulled the hand brake on, opened the door, and left the car. She walked steadily through the sage and ocotillo which partially screened the stones from the road.

Sarah and the vaquero watched as she circled the U-shaped foundation, with the wind blowing her dark hair wildly about her head. She seemed wary, like an animal who suspects a trap. Finally she settled down on the stones themselves and turned her head toward the main buildings of the D Cross A, unseen behind the butte five miles away. For perhaps ten minutes she sat like that, hands folded in her lap, her head high. Then she rose and returned to the car with the same steady steps as the ones which had taken her to the weed-covered rocks.

In seconds they were bouncing along through the ruts as if they had never stopped. It was remarkable, Ignacio thought, the way Sarah looked at her sister-in-law.

As the middle months of 1918 rolled by with increasing speed, confidence that the Central Powers could not last much longer climbed to dizzy heights, blunting the effect of the lengthening casualty lists they scanned.

The unspoken conviction that nothing bad can happen when your side is winning left the people of the D Cross A doubly vulnerable when the official telegram arrived. Jamie had been wounded. A second wire, a long cable letter from Jamie's commanding officer, left them shuddering as they read. "At this writing, amputation is not indicated, but only time will tell."

Jamie's last letter, shouting his eagerness as he sniffed the winds of triumph, only depressed their spirits further. It had been written two days before the armistice, just before the action in which the mortar shell blew a staff car on its side and pinned him under it. It was a cocky letter.

In contrast to the other four, Agnes was exultant. "He's alive—and that's all that counts!"

With the Great War ended, word came that Jamie would be moved from Paris. The Royal Navy flashed the signal that the seas were safe again. The battle grounds were empty, and the doors of the French ports were swinging the other way. The A.E.F. was coming home.

Even though the wounded had priority, it was still the middle of December before Jamie was settled in the great hospital outside Chicago. Not one word had come from the wounded man himself.

* * *

"I'm going day after tomorrow," Ann told them early in Christmas week. She had driven to Black Springs to use the telephone. "They wouldn't let me through to Jamie, or couldn't, I don't know which. I talked to a Captain Martin—she's his nurse. The leg is healing as well as can be expected."

Douglas and Ann had just begun to plan her trip, when Agnes broke in with a cry of such shrillness it froze the rest of them. "Make no mistake! I'm going, too!"

Douglas tried to talk her out of it, reminding her time and time again of Ann's first rights as Jamie's wife. No pleading, no entreaty, reached her. Ignacio watched the rancher's temper rise, threatening to break the chains of self-control forged through a lifetime.

When he entered the kitchen the next morning, it looked as if neither of the MacAndrewses had slept. Agnes was red-eyed, but not from crying as Ignacio thought at first. Overnight she had developed a heavy cold, with a hacking cough punctuating obviously painful breathing. Douglas was making one last attempt.

"For God's sake, Aggie! It doesn't make any sense at all. You're in no condition to travel. Don't you know people up there have been *dying* this past six months from this influenza thing? Won't you please, please give up this crazy notion?"

Agnes made no reply, but shook her head from side to side and buried her mouth in her handkerchief when a fit of coughing seized her.

Douglas MacAndrews sighed his defeat. "All right, Aggie, you can go. You'll have to take Sarah with you, because I'll use the time to go to El Paso and talk with Ben. And I'm sending Ignacio along with the three of you. I've got my reasons, but I don't intend to discuss them now."

The rider, staggered, scarcely heard the rest of the rancher's words. Half-formed thoughts collided in his mind like cows in a holding pen at roundup time.

"Now Aggie," Douglas went on, "you'd better get to bed and nurse that cold."

20

His last sight of Douglas was a painful one. After seeing them off, the big man drove out ahead of the train to where the highway crossed the tracks, and stood up in the front seat of the Buick like a charioteer, waving his arms to the passing coaches. It was a forlorn gesture, made with no hope of reply.

Nothing had prepared Ignacio for the train. It was hard to take in the running water in the washrooms, toilets which flushed, electric lights, and a hundred other wonders; all this while the train ate up miles of track faster than he had ever taken Calico, faster even than the Buick on the rough roads of the Ojos Negros.

There was an awkward moment when they went to supper in the dining car. The man in charge, holding a stack of menus like a shield in front of him, announced that all the tables were already taken, and the old bad smell assailed the rider's nostrils. Ann brushed past him. "Don't be impertinent, steward!" she blazed. "Half the places in this car are empty. You'll seat us immediately, all of us, or we'll have a word with the conductor." Well, that was behind him, and of no importance now.

He watched the porter fold down the beds in the stateroom he had shared with the other three in the afternoon, said goodnight, and headed for his own smaller berth in the other sleeping car. When he reached the vestibule, the thought of sleep left him. He would feel cheated if he missed any of this speeding night.

The evening star had almost dipped beneath the horizon. He had no way of knowing exactly where they were; they had already left behind all the places whose names he knew: Ancho,

Corona, Vaughn, Pastura, Santa Rosa. Signposts, water towers, stockpens, and each lonely depot rolled by like riffled pages in a picture book. Book? *Sí.* They really were out on the battered old geography with its colored maps now; probably had crossed that squared off part of Texas called the Panhandle, and perhaps reached Oklahoma.

Without a moon, the dark was shapeless, and the quick rocking of the train made the stars shake as if they couldn't stay aloft the whole night through. There were lights from time to time, small lights, but sometimes bright enough to silhouette the edges of a barn or silo, and sometimes clusters of them took courage in their numbers to try to fold back the dark from empty streets in secret, sleeping towns.

The sky had been clear when first he stopped in the vestibule. It was changing now. Speeding headlong through the blackness, faster, it seemed, than in the day, when distant objects moved to match its pace, the long train raced beneath an overcast which turned the stars off, rank by quaking rank.

Melancholy seized him. He wished Sally were standing by his side. He needed a little help on this awkward journey, and he knew he couldn't get it from anyone in the car ahead. Sarah was still too young, and Ann and Agnes too heavily involved with their own bitter struggle—and the things they would face when they came to the son and husband. It wasn't the first time he had been alone.

"We're here to see Captain James MacAndrews," Agnes said, before Ann could so much as open her mouth. "He's in Ward T-102."

"Just a second, ma'am, let me check," the soldier said, turning to a cabinet behind him. "Let's see—Lundberg, Maas, Mabley—here it is, MacAndrews, James H. Hey! I guess you ladies didn't know. He's not a captain any more—been a major since last Monday."

"That's just fine, young man," Agnes said. She was almost severe, but Ignacio could see her back straighten with pride.

"Now—how do we get to him?"

"Well, ma'am," the boy said, looking at the card he held, "there's a notation here says you're to see Captain Elizabeth Martin before you visit."

"That's the nurse I talked with on the telephone," Ann said.

"Nonsense!" Agnes said. "I want to see Jamie, now!"

"Sorry, ma'am." The soldier smiled an apology. "If it's on this card—that's orders. If you ladies and the gentleman will just sit right over there, I'll send for Captain Martin right away." He pointed to a long wooden bench by a Christmas tree which was taller and gaudier by far than any the rider had ever seen in Black Springs or at the D Cross A.

The huge lobby seemed as hot as the malpais in June, hotter, so confining was it. A number of men and women rustled along in whispers of starched white cotton. There was a bad smell to the place the vaquero couldn't identify, medicine no doubt, but he wondered how anything that smelled so sick could heal. Over the bench hung a long, framed picture of rank upon rank of soldiers carrying rifles on their shoulders, a regiment on its way to war. He wondered if any of these warriors lay broken in the wards behind him, he wondered how many of them—

"Mrs. MacAndrews? Oh, I imagine both of you are. I'm Betty Martin." Ignacio turned to see the nurse.

"I'm Ann MacAndrews, Captain, Jamie's wife," Ann said. The rider was gratified that Ann had spoken first. When he glanced at Agnes he could see how the younger woman had managed it. The señora's lips were set too tight for speech, her suspicion of this pink-faced pleasant woman who was caring for her son plain to see.

"May we see him now?" Ann asked.

"I'm having him wheeled from his ward to the officer's solarium," the nurse said. She paused, and a shadow dimmed the bright face. "He should be there any minute now—but, could we talk a little first?"

A small cry escaped Ann, and she turned as pale as the nurse's uniform. "He *is* all right, isn't he? There's nothing *wrong*, nothing we've not been told?"

"No, Mrs. MacAndrews, there's nothing wrong, not in the usual sense, at any rate."

"The leg's not healing!" Agnes blurted.

"It's not that. As a matter of fact, he should walk within a week, not without a limp, of course, but he *should* walk. If—if he'll—" the nurse looked around at all of them, "—try."

The silence was heavy, and the heat, a mere annoyance until now, became oppressive.

"What can *we* do, Captain Martin?" Ann said. Ignacio picked up a thin note of fright in her voice. "What can we say to him?"

"This is what I wanted to talk to you about." There was genuine concern on the nurse's face. "You see, he doesn't know you're here."

"WHAT?" Agnes's cry was so shrill Sarah jumped.

"Well, the truth is, and I hope you'll try to understand,"— Captain Martin's voice was low, and Ignacio thought she must sound like this when she tells a family one of theirs has died— *"Major MacAndrews doesn't want to see you."*

They waited at the door of the solarium, while the nurse crossed the big, sunlit room to where Jamie sat in his wheelchair with his back to them. There were other people in the room, patients and visitors, and she bent over and whispered in Jamie's ear. He nodded once or twice, but Ignacio knew the precise moment when she told him they were there. The broad shoulders stiffened, and the blonde head snapped up and back as if he had been struck.

The nurse, doubt clouding her face, signaled them to come ahead, and Ann and Agnes crossed the room almost at a run. The vaquero hesitated, and before he took a step, he felt Sarah put her hand in his. Together, slowly, the rider and the girl approached the wheelchair.

Ann and Agnes had circled Jamie, and were now facing him.

"God damn it," the man in the wheelchair said, the voice low and under control, but charged with such a load of hate Ignacio almost staggered, "I told them I didn't want to see anyone, and I *meant* anyone."

Ignacio watched the faces of the two women, saw them drained of blood in half a second. *Dios!* Like lightning in a storm his mind was lit by the meaning of what he saw. For the first time in all the time they had known each other, Ann and Agnes MacAndrews, these two so different women, were experiencing a thing together, and with identical reactions. Whatever they saw in Jamie's face must have included both of them with brute impartiality. "Jamie!" was all they said, but it came from both their mouths in one small cry.

In a movement so violent Ignacio knew he had forgotten Jamie's strength, young MacAndrews wrenched the chair around and started rolling toward the door. When he recognized Sarah and the rider, he stopped the chair and stared at them. Then Ignacio Ortiz saw for himself what Ann and Agnes must have seen. There was hate in Jamie's face, all right, but not for them—it was all directed inward and thinned by self-pity. This was a defeat more total than when the terrible thing with Angus happened.

The man in the wheelchair buried his face in hands, and the voice which came from behind the hands was a muffled sob. "No, no, no."

Sarah's hand tightened in Ignacio's. He looked across Jamie's head to Ann and Agnes.

"*Señoras,*" he said softly, "you should be alone with Señor Jamie for a while, I think. I will wait just outside if you should need me." He looked down at Sarah. "Come, *niña*. We will speak with Jamie later."

He didn't see Jamie again that day. Agnes and Ann spent an hour with him, and when they finally came out of the solarium—their anguish and confusion still eerily alike—they almost swept Ignacio and Sarah down the corridor and out of the hospital.

"Can't Nash and I talk to Jamie?" Sarah said.

"Not today, Sarah," Agnes said. "Ann and I want to spend tomorrow with your brother, then we'll see." Her voice, when she said "Ann and I," was a strange sound in the rider's ear. "Nash," she went on, "will you please take Sarah around the city tomorrow?"

"*Sí, señora.*"

Agnes's voice had been oddly subdued. In a way, it was a relief to hear her flare up again in the old familiar manner. "They're not doing something right in that hospital, you can be sure of that."

They went in the morning to the big art museum on the lake front, and the rider, no less than the youngster, was stupefied by the wonder of the place. The galleries were jammed with people, but Ignacio felt somehow insulated against the hubbub. It would be easy to become intoxicated by all of this.

The streets teemed with shoppers, bands played tunes which he vaguely recognized as having some religious meaning, and the automobile horns raised a din which would have shamed the noisiest herd of Herefords. At last, buffeted by too much clamor and excitement, Sarah and he sought refuge in the hotel coffee shop. Made bold by the calm of the place, and the smile on the waitress's face, he asked a question. "*Señorita.*" The girl's smile broadened at the title. "Please. There are people in the street with pieces of cloth across their mouths. *Porqué*—why?"

"Surgical masks, mister," she said. "Against the flu, the influenza. It's mostly over now, but some people are still scared. A few months ago almost everybody wore them. Never bothered with one myself. If you go, you go."

He looked carefully at Agnes at supper. Her cough had disappeared during the train ride, but she looked worn, her body frailer than he had ever seen it, the rawhide toughness which had sustained it through the years gone into hiding.

They must have had a bad time with Jamie today, she and Señora Ann. Both of them were silent when they returned to the hotel, but the pain in their faces, mirroring each other, could be read as easily as the headlines in the newspaper he bought while waiting for their return.

Neither of them had spoken of the visit until just now, and it was Ann who told most of the story. Jamie had gone wild every time they mentioned his coming home. He was convinced he would never walk again, despite, according to Captain Martin, every assurance a battery of doctors could give him. Ann and Agnes had confirmed the nurse's hopeful outlook with one of the doctors themselves, but Jamie wouldn't have it, wouldn't listen.

Agnes didn't eat a bite, seemed lost in thought all the while Ann talked, and brightened only when Sarah began to tell them of her excursion with Ignacio.

After supper, he took a *cigarro* and walked out through the arcade of shops to Wabash Avenue. In front of him were the blackened girders which supported the train tracks he could see from his room. Near the hotel door, shaking a little bell, stood one of the gaunt men dressed to resemble the anglos's

Christmas saint. With his hollow cheeks and burning, red eyes, the man looked as pious as any martyr, but Ignacio wondered if this one, like the others Sarah and he had seen in the afternoon, reeked of rotted whiskey, too.

A few feet away a man was selling newspapers by a fire which burned weakly in a metal bucket. For several minutes, Ignacio looked at the newshawk without seeing him. His mind was too full of tomorrow, too full of Jamie. All four of them would go tomorrow on the third visit. How many visits would there have to be?

"Merry Christmas, buddy!" the newspaper vendor said, and Ignacio let the man drift into his consciousness. Despite the grin he was sending the vaquero, the man was a pitiful sight. He was toothless, and his face was seamed and gray, the chin covered with whiskers of considerably more than one day's growth. Under a dirty cap, two watery eyes looked out, eyes too old, or sad, or both, to light up even in the fire's glow.

"Merry Christmas, buddy!" the man said again.

"*Feliz Navidad*—" the rider stammered. He made his little bow, and turned back to the hotel. He was in the lobby before the thought struck him: that man was an anglo!

Ignacio sat on a chair just inside the door of Jamie's room. The man in the wheelchair and the other three formed their own group by the window, Jamie against the wall, Sarah perched on his bed, and the two women with their backs to the thin sunlight coming through. It made it hard to see the expressions on their faces.

The first storm had passed, and Jamie, if not pleasant, was at least civil. He had spared none of them when they entered the room, and his viciousness made the vaquero realize how wise Captain Martin had been in arranging the first visit in the solarium. Had they come here first, Jamie would have attacked his wife and mother without mercy; in the solarium he was obliged to mind his manners a little bit.

If young MacAndrews's language and manner with his little sister in the room were typical, Ignacio could guess how much worse it had been for Ann and the señora yesterday. No wonder they had returned to the hotel drained and beaten.

"If you don't return to Black Springs," Agnes said, "just what will you do?"

"God damned if I know yet," Jamie said. "I suppose they'll move me over to the disabled wing in a couple of weeks. Free room and board for as long as I like, and now that I'm field grade, I rate my own personal orderly. Plenty of cripples like me over there."

"Don't say cripple, Jamie, please." Ann's voice was so low the rider hardly caught her words.

"For Christ's sake, Ann!" Jamie raged. "If I ain't a cripple with this useless thing, what the shit do you call it?"

"The doctor we talked to yesterday, Colonel Rainey, I think it was, says it's absolutely certain that—"

"Yeah? Well, it ain't his leg, is it?" Jamie's voice was spiralling up to hysteria, and Ignacio was suddenly grateful they would soon be leaving for the day. They had been here three hours now, and nothing had been accomplished.

"I've got to go to the bathroom," Sarah said. The rider was startled to hear the youngster's voice. Neither he nor Sarah had uttered so much as a single word since they greeted Jamie upon arrival.

"All right, Sarah," Agnes said, rising, "I'll help you find a ladies room." She looked down at her son. "We're going out to the car then, James. I don't know if Sarah and I will come tomorrow, but we'll be here the day after, you can count on it. Merry Christmas, son."

She called him James; Ignacio could only remember that once or twice before. And not coming tomorrow?

He thought Agnes would tell him to come now, too, but she said nothing as she and Sarah went out the door. He should leave, he knew, but a force was real and palpable as if Cuchillo Peak had settled on his shoulders kept him in his seat.

More was going to be played out here. The man in the wheelchair and the dark girl staring out the window had reached a place they had never been before. Some awful, endless thing was beginning.

"Jamie," Ann said. (*Ahora.* Now—it begins now.)

"What?"

"Do you love me?"

"What has that got to do with the fix I'm in?"

"Do you?"

"Well, sure. You're my wife."

Ann MacAndrews rose and faced her husband. "Jamie, do you remember the talk we had, before you left? When I said we'd have to come to terms?"

"So—that's it! You want out." A fury blazed in Jamie's face. "All right, *clear out*. Here's your big chance. It's what you've wanted for a hell of a long time!"

Ann looked as if she had been struck. The pale rays of the winter sun had no power to heal the blow, and for long moments she stood there, hurt and disbelief setting like wax on her features. Then, and Ignacio could see the effort, she gathered strength to speak.

No, no, Señora Ann, he pleaded silently. I beg of you. Do not say it. Do not step into the same trap as your poor *amigo* here.

Ann MacAndrews didn't step, she leaped.

"Jamie, Jamie. Is that what you thought I meant? My God! Don't you know? No matter what has happened, this, or anything, I will *never* leave you!"

The tears came then, a torrent of them, and she rushed from the room. She didn't look at the vaquero as she left.

From somewhere down the corridor came a moan of pain. A hospital cart was pushed noisily past the door. In the courtyard outside the window a sudden gust of wind stripped the last leaf from a spindly tree, and from a great distance he could hear the hum of a gramophone. His back had begun to ache. Sitting so long on this unyielding chair was like two days in the saddle

Jamie turned the wheelchair until he faced Ignacio. "Well, *amigo*. What have you got to say about all this?"

"I have nothing to say, Jamie." He stood and turned to go.

Then, first as a tiny stirring, something began to move inside him. It grew, flowing outward from the center of him. He had never known a thing like this before, a power which should have shaken him to pieces, but instead forged him into a weapon of awesome strength. "*. . . for though I am not splenitiue and rash— oh, sí, sí—yet have I in me something dangerous.*"

"Sí, Jamie!" he said, turning back, "I do have things to say, *mi caballero grande!* But I do not think that you will like them."

The words rolled out without his choosing them, touched with a life of their own, hammering against the walls and echoing like hoofbeats.

"*Basta*, Jamie, *basta!* We have had enough of you, all of us, but I, Ignacio, more than anyone. Since we were boys together I have watched while life was trotted out for you like a great, fine horse, and I have seen you ride over things and smile—and break things, and *smile*—and hurt and hurt, and SMILE! Where is that smile now, my friend, *mi amigo magnífico?* Can you smile for Concepción, or Jorge, or Angus, or Señora Ann? Come—tell me. Where is that smile which has bought you so much of everything? Have you lost it with your manhood? You *are* a cripple, *verdad!* Not because of that poor leg, though. You are crippled in more important ways. *Adiós, Don* Jamie. Talk to me again when you decide to become a man."

It was as if a norther had blown right through him and left him clean. He stayed in the room just long enough to see Jamie's mouth open in an astonished O, and then he left.

In the corridor he came face to face with Agnes. She must have seen the distraught Ann and come back for him. He knew as surely as he had ever known anything that she had been in the corridor, right outside the open door, during his entire attack on Jamie. He stood stock still and looked at her, and he knew, too, that his look must be much the same as the direct, piercing gaze she had given him in the early days. He bowed, murmured "*Señora,*" and walked swiftly past her.

At the corner which led to the lobby, he turned and looked at her again. She was staring at him, too far away now for him to attempt to read her thoughts. They watched each other for a moment—the student and the teacher. Then, suddenly, she squared the slim, fine shoulders, lifted the ash blonde head, and entered Jamie's room.

21

"You'll have to leave the train now, ma'am," the conductor said. "We'll be pulling out in two minutes."

Ann stood up. It's not happiness I see, Ignacio thought, but there is a radiance which fills the stateroom. Will it last while she stays here with Jamie?

The young woman bent over and kissed Sarah, then turned to the vaquero. "*Gracias*, Ignacio—for everything," she said.

She faced the señora. "I don't know quite what to say, Agnes. 'Thank you' isn't nearly enough."

The older woman reddened and glanced at Ignacio. "Please, Ann," she said, "no thanks are necessary. We're leaving you with a terrible job, not helping you a bit."

Ann moved to the compartment door. "Well, I'll do my best," she said. "Somehow I'll make him walk—and I'll bring him home."

She disappeared, but in seconds Ignacio saw her on the platform. The train lurched to a start, and she raised her arm. She was smiling. He pressed his cheek against the window, and watched her until she was lost from view.

* * *

It was dark by the time they cleared the yards and the train made the big turn westward out of the city. The blackness outside the window reflected Agnes's face to him, and Ignacio could study it unnoticed. It would fade when the lights of a small town or a grade crossing whipped by in the night, only to reappear when they reached the pitch black countryside again, a ghostly, mirrored image. What was that line from the Bible again? *"For now we see as through a glass, darkly."* Sí.

As he had for a night and a day, he wondered what had gone on in Jamie's room after Agnes went in for that last time. None of them had talked much on the drive from the hospital or at supper, but the señora hadn't talked at all. When she finally did speak, her words, soft as they were, seemed a detonation.

"Nash," she said, "I'd like you to go to the hotel desk. Have them make a reservation for us on tomorrow's train for home." Ann gasped, but Agnes went right on, "Just for Sarah, you, and me. Make sure they know that Ann is staying on, and will keep this room."

Now, on the train, he watched her face in the window, and when Sarah stirred from sleep, and the señora turned to look at her, her eyes caught his before moving on.

"Sarah," she said, "you had a nice nap, honey. Why don't you go back to the observation car and see if there are any magazines? Nash will come and get you in time for supper." She fished in her purse and handed Sarah a dollar bill. The hand she held it out with trembled. Sarah yawned widely, and, dreamy looking and half asleep, left the compartment.

They were alone, closeted together in a way far different from the spacious sitting room at the D Cross A. He turned to the window again, and now he could see that she looked at him as he had at her. The clicking of the train wheels became almost unbearably loud, and the gentle rocking of the coach seemed violent.

"Nash," she said. He started. *Dios*, but his nerves had been scraped raw by the past few days.

"*Señora?*"

"You know all about us, don't you, Nash?" The sound of the wheels seemed to stop. "Yes, you know all about us," she went on, "and you never say a word. Not until—" She stopped. His heart hammered in his chest. She shook her head. "No reproach, Nash. Not ever. My God, what we've owed you. And we never faced up to it. Well, Douglas has, but not the rest of us."

Then came more, much more. It came in fits and starts at first, then in a cataract, fragments of the past falling about them like the shards of the plate he had once broken.

"I guess I've never really *seen* you there," she said. "Even when we studied together, I thought I was seeing—"

No, señora, he thought, that admission is far too much for you to make—and your vaquero does not require it.

"It will be different, Nash, I promise you!" There was too much passion in the voice to call it just determination; it *was* a promise—and he believed it. He almost knew what was coming next, but his heart thumped *por favor, por favor* until he heard her say it. "I'll make it up to Ann."

She closed her eyes and leaned back against the seat. "In my foolishness, and yes, wickedness, I somewhere got the notion that if I ever made a place for Ann within me—I'd be giving up on Jamie. Well, a lot of new things are going to happen to Master Jamie when he gets home. With your help, and Ann's, somehow I'll find the strength to undo the harm I've done. And I'll use the strength of Douglas, too."

She opened her eyes and looked at him. "Don't believe I'll go to supper, Nash. I've still some things to think about, and I'm very tired. I must have aged a million years since we left the D Cross A."

"Shall I get Sarah now, *señora?*"

"Please. I'll just rest."

At the door, he looked back at her. Her eyes were closed again. Even with the tinge of red in her cheeks, he thought perhaps her color wasn't good.

"*Hasta la vista, mi señora.*" She didn't answer. Already she seemed to have gone to sleep.

Supper with Sarah was a lark. He ordered wine with a French name he couldn't pronounce; he just pointed with his finger and the smiling black waiter nodded. He even shared it with a laughing Sarah, although the bit he poured in her glass was scarcely enough to fill a thimble.

"You're in a jim dandy mood," Sarah said.

"*Sí, muchachita.* And why not? We are going home, and the world is *muy bonito.*"

"How about Jamie, Nash? Will he get better?"

He thought this over. "*Sí.* He will get much, much better."

Well, it was true. The world was fine indeed, Jamie would be fine, everything would turn out *perfectamente.* They were going home. Suddenly, he thought of how good it would be to see Sally once again. Ah, *sí!*

When he took Sarah back to the stateroom, he found the beds made up, and Agnes already in hers, sound asleep. He returned to his own berth, smiling broadly, finding that he, too, was pleasantly tired. It was a long time since he had had a good restful night.

"Mister, mister! Wake up! Got to talk to you."

The voice was hoarse with urgency and the hand which shook him was rough on his shoulder.

"*Qué pasa?*" Sitting upright in his berth he tried to see who was parting the curtains.

"Ain't you the gentleman traveling with the lady and the little girl in 4-B in the next car?"

He made out the porter now. "*Sí. What is wrong, señor?*"

"You better get dressed and come down there. We got us a sick woman and a mighty frightened child!"

Still dressing as he followed the porter's white jacket through the vestibule to the other car, Ignacio thought of the people in the hospital and shivered.

At the compartment door, the porter turned to him. "Yes, sir, a mighty sick woman, mighty sick."

Hurry, *hombre*, hurry! He wanted to burst through the door, but he wanted forewarning, too, so he let the man continue. "She complained about a headache when I fixed her berth. Then, about ten minutes ago, she rang me to go get you. Said she was hot and had me feel her forehead. Man! She's burning up, and she—"

Ignacio could wait no longer. Almost pushing the black man aside, he flung the compartment door wide open. Sarah, in her nightgown, was kneeling beside Agnes's lower berth. The ceiling light was on, too dim to reach into the señora's bed, yet strong enough to show him Sarah's face, white with terror, when she turned it up to him.

Ignacio sank to his knees, touched Sarah lightly on the shoulder, and peered into the berth. He could see Agnes clearly; the blanket which had covered her was pushed down to her waist and her chest was rising and falling wildly. The strap of her nightdress had slipped off one white shoulder, laying bare the upper part of a tiny breast so pale it gleamed like gypsum even in the faint light which reached it. His own face felt fevered, she looked so naked and exposed.

With trembling hands he reached down to bring the covers up about her neck. The train slowed without warning, throwing him forward, and he came to rest with his face pressed hard on hers. The touch of her flaming skin burned away the dampness of his own. *Dios!* No one, not even Agnes at her wiry best, could withstand this holocaust for long.

She moved as he pulled away from her. "Douglas?"

"No, *señora*, it is Ignacio."

"Oh—yes—Nash. Been dreaming. Where are we?" Small as the voice was, and pathetic, it was made more so by the realization that she had put every bit of her feeble strength behind it, as if she were shouting against the wind.

"Kansas, I think, *señora. Qué pasa?*"

"Caught a touch of something. I'm so *hot*, Nash."

"It is nothing, *nada, señora.* You will feel better in the morning." The lie choked him. He turned to where the porter blocked the narrow doorway. "*Por favor*—please. Could you get some cold, wet cloths? And see if there is a doctor on this train—as quickly as you can!"

He turned back to see Agnes run her tongue across her lips, and felt his own crack dry at the sight of the fever turning the fragile body into a torch, the gray eyes flickering like candle wicks.

It seemed as if no time at all had passed before the porter was handing him a bucket crammed with ice and towels, "I done told the conductor about a doctor, mister."

"*Gracias.*" Ignacio squeezed the towels with hands which didn't feel the cold, gently draping one across the burning forehead, using another to sponge the face and neck.

"That felt good, Nash. I can sleep now—" She closed her eyes.

The vaquero sank back on his heels, eyes riveted to the señora's neck where a small blood vessel pulsed.

"Nash—" It was Sarah. He looked and saw her huddled in a corner, and felt a wave of shame that he had forgotten her. "Is she going to be all right, Nash?"

He knew at once no lies would fool her. "We will have to wait and see, *niña.*"

She moved over and laid her head against his shoulder, and together they watched the woman in the lower berth. From time to time, Agnes moved a little, but for the most part she rested quietly, the raging fires seemingly banked inside her. Once or twice she seemed to speak, but her words, if words they were, made no sense at all.

"Can you step out here, Mr.—ah," the conductor said, glancing at a leather notebook, "Ortiz?"

"*Sí, señor.*" Ignacio looked at Sarah, and stepped into the corridor.

"Mr. Ortiz," the conductor said, "there's no doctor on the passenger list. We've checked. I'm sorry, but I'm making arrangements to have the lady removed from the train at the next scheduled stop."

The rider felt his heart stop. The porter was standing behind the conductor, and there was compassion in the black man's face, but all the same Ignacio knew he was quite alone. No doctor! Well, his instincts, and he hated them, told him it would make little difference if Agnes had a doctor, but—to take her from the train, into the grasp of the cold out there? Impossible!

"That will not do, *señor*," he said to the conductor, softly.

"What?"

"It will not be necessary to take the *señora* from the train."

The conductor's eyes widened. "Maybe I didn't make myself clear," he said. "I'm not asking or suggesting. I'm telling you."

"I understood quite well, *señor*, but the answer still is no."

While the conductor drew a breath which tightened the gold watch chain across his blue vest, the train rumbled through a crossing. Red lights flooded the corridor, and the ringing bell sounded angry.

"Look here, Ortiz!" It was a shout, but Ignacio only noticed the absence of the "mister" this time. "The woman has *influenza!* I won't have her die aboard my train."

"The *señora* stays," Ignacio said, as simply as he could.

The conductor's face twisted. "By God! I'll get the law aboard!"

Ignacio shrugged.

"Do you think a little spick punk like you can hold off a squad of cops?"

"I do not know, *señor*." He was tired, but he would find the strength for this preposterous test. "All I know is that I must take this lady home. And I will."

At the next stop—he had no idea what city or town it was—he saw the conductor on the platform. The man was obviously confused, shaking his head as he paced back and forth under the window where the vaquero watched. No lawmen came aboard.

Agnes had remained asleep as long as the train was in motion, but when it stopped, she opened her eyes and moved her head frantically from side to side. Ignacio, at the window with his eye on the conductor, saw Sarah crawl from her corner to the lower berth.

"Mama?" The señora didn't answer, but suddenly sat bolt upright, throwing the blanket from her with a wild motion. Her body was rigid, but all at once she started a violent quivering. "Douglas! Douglas!" she screamed—and the raving began.

For an hour, while the train ripped its way through the dark flatlands, Agnes MacAndrews raged. Fervently the vaquero hoped none of it was clear to Sarah, whose sobs tore his heart in the few moments the woman in the berth was silent. But the names, surely the girl could miss none of them—Angus, Concepción, and the others. Every delirious reference was in one way or another a defense of Jamie—and herself.

Then, at last, she was still again. Ignacio urged Sarah to get some sleep, and after the girl closed the curtains of the upper berth, he took a post on the stateroom floor, his eyes staring into the blackness above the window sill.

A few miles east of Amarillo, the train pulled off on a siding to let an eastbound express go by. Agnes stirred, and he shot to the side of the lower berth.

"Nash—"

"I am here, *señora*."

"When we reach Black Springs, remind me to take care of something." *Bueno!* She was clear as a bell, no ranting now.

"Of course, *señora*."

"Before we go out to the D Cross A, I want to talk with Findlay Stafford. I'd like him to get some men to work on Ann's and Jamie's house. It could be almost done before they're back with us." She closed her eyes again.

Somewhere in the high plains country, where the land slides away from sight in a great ascending swell toward the mountains, Agnes Hall MacAndrews died.

Ignacio wouldn't be able to tell Señor Douglas exactly when it happened. He had moved across the stateroom floor just to see if she was covered. One look told him she was gone. He didn't even need to touch her.

For a long time he did absolutely nothing. He didn't awaken Sarah. He wanted her rested when he told her. Finally, at dawn, he sought the porter and asked him to get the conductor to send a message on from Tucumcari.

Back in the compartment, he knelt beside the lower berth. Wasn't he supposed to draw the sheet up over the lifeless face? He couldn't do that. Closing the curtains would have to be enough. Agnes's eyes were closed, and that was good. He had heard of putting pennies on the lids if they weren't. It made him shudder to think how the metal might bruise those delicate folds of flesh. Hadn't he read, too, how the ancient Greeks would put a copper inside the mouth for the traveler to pay the ferryman who took the dead across the river? Well, the señora would go copperless to Charon—she could pay her passage in other coin.

Sarah slept through the stops at Tucumcari and Santa Rosa, and didn't wake when the conductor entered half an hour later. The man acknowledged the finger Ignacio held to his lips, and spoke to the rider in a low, decent voice. "The telegrapher at Black Springs report, they're trying locate your man MacAndrews. Got to send out to some ranch to get him. We're going to pull up short of the depot, so's you'll have a little privacy when you take the lady off. Take all the time you want, Mr. Ortiz—there'll be no need to hurry."

22

Major James MacAndrews, D.S.C., D.S.O., was not the last of the Ojos Negros men to return from the Great War. A few still rotted in veterans's hospitals in the East, their homecoming delayed so long that when it came, the war and their part in it had been long forgotten. Some, of course, did not come back at all.

Jamie could have had a hero's welcome, had the family wished it. His decorations, the wounded leg whose condition no one really seemed to know, and the rank he had reached for one so young, would have brought speeches from the mayor or the county judge, and an enthusiastic, if off-key, fanfare from the newly formed Chupadera County Drum and Bugle Corps.

But his train arrived at two in the morning, delayed thirteen hours by a freakish spring snowstorm in the Panhandle, and it was past three when Douglas finally got Ann and her husband to the D Cross A.

Hard rains had fallen on and off, and by the time the car reached it, the arroyo was running full to the top of its banks, the plank bridge awash and impassable, except on foot.

Ignacio, his poncho shedding water like the steep sides of the arroyo itself, waited on the compound side in a wagon, with a lantern on the seat beside him. He had seen the lights of the Buick long before it reached the butte, and had worked frantically to hitch a team and reach the streaming gully before the car. Now, while Douglas kept the engine running, he watched as Ann helped Jamie across the bridge, the two of them quickly soaked, gleaming in the headlights.

He only nodded to Jamie as he got down from the wagon. Talk would have to wait until they were all inside and Douglas and Sarah had had their chance. He saw the limp as Jamie neared the wagon, saw the cane, a thick, dark, gnarled thing which looked more like a weapon than a crutch.

In moments he was helping Douglas with the baggage, and the two of them struggled wordlessly together across the bridge, treacherous now that the Buick's lights were extinguished. In the wavering light of the lantern he could see Ann with Jamie in the wagon, pressing close to him, her face buried in the drab, wet wool of Jamie's army coat.

No one slept that night. They talked in front of the fire while the rain, unable to sustain the assault, finally stopped. Ignacio sat quietly in a corner of the big room by himself, listening to a conversation which seemed to have no aim, and in the end went nowhere. He sat in wooden silence until the sunrise, with that special power it always seems to have after heavy weather, burst through the east windows. Excusing himself, he started for the shack, pausing only to grip Jamie's hand, tipping his head almost formally. Young MacAndrews nodded back, but didn't say a word.

In the shack, stripped naked, he hung his still-damp clothing up to dry and stretched out full length on the narrow bunk, pulling a thin blanket over himself, without bothering to build a fire in the little stove. Perhaps he could sleep for an hour or two. He should ride to the north pastures today, check the cows there before plans were made for the coming roundup.

Douglas, even though he had just made this trip to get Jamie, was going in to Black Springs in the next day or so. He must ask the señor to make another payment for him on the Mexican saddle they were holding at Stafford's. Three more payments and it would be his. No, he wouldn't ask him. It would take away an excuse to see Sally.

"It's a terrible thing to say, Ignacio," Ann said, looking down at Agnes's grave, "but I'm glad I wasn't here for the funeral. It must have been awful for you, after that nightmare on the train."

"It was not so bad, *Señora* Ann," he said. It was true. Nothing could have been so bad as the look he had seen on

Douglas's face when he caught sight of him, before the train had even stopped, waiting out by the Black Springs stock pens.

He looked at the headstone. It was only three months, but already the fine dust which blew ceaselessly from the basin up through Las Sombras Canyon was piling up on the lower parts of the chiseled letters which read, "Agnes MacAndrews 1870–1918." The grave, too, was showing the first ragged growth of spring. Ignacio remembered how the señor had bought the barren lands around Angus's arroyo, to get his brother inside the fence, and he wondered if the rancher would someday try to run a salient of the D Cross A clear up here, to enclose Agnes, too.

"I wonder where she is, and what she's thinking," Ann said. "Well, wherever she is, I guess she's found peace."

No! he protested silently, not the señora. If the señora's soul was still intact, she was most assuredly not at peace. The woman who had slipped from life on that racing train was far from finished with this world.

Shadows were beginning to stretch over the cemetery, and the old ghost mining town was darkening. Coming up to Las Sombras had been Ann's idea, and a sudden one at that. Originally, she and Jamie were going to make the trip together, and Ann had already pulled the car up to the door. She left the engine running while she went in to help her husband. It was fifteen minutes before she appeared again, and Ignacio, who had been helping the new hand Pepe load feed into the wagon, had wandered over to see if he could turn the engine off.

"Ignacio," Ann called from the kitchen door, "could you saddle a horse for me? Jamie's not going. He's having a lot of trouble with his leg this morning."

"Would you like me to ride with you, *señora?*"

"Oh, would you, Ignacio? Please, please—I'll change and be with you in just five minutes."

She kept her face turned from him when she came out, but the effort was a futile one. One glimpse was enough to tell him she'd been crying. By the time he got in the saddle, she was far down the road to the bridge, and she didn't slacken her pace until they rounded the base of Cuchillo Peak and were starting up the canyon.

At the grave, though, she was as calm as if she had just awakened from a restful sleep. For a long time there was no sound but the humming of the wind in the jack pines above the old ruined town. He hadn't really looked at Las Sombras at the funeral. Only Douglas had held his attention as they lowered the coffin into the gaping hole hacked out with such neat precision in the frozen ground.

"I think it's time to start back down, *señora*," he said.

"You're right, Ignacio, but somehow I hate to leave."

Riding back down the switchbacks on the canyon road, the vaquero wondered if Jamie would come to the supper table tonight. He hadn't put in an appearance in the ten days since he and Ann returned. As a matter of fact, the rider had seen him on so few occasions there was no escaping the conclusion that Jamie was avoiding him.

Angélica Rivera, brought out from town by Douglas to run the house so Ann could care for Jamie, complained a little at the trays she had to prepare for the young woman to carry in to her husband every night. Apparently this kind of catering went on at other meals as well. "*Qué cosa!*" Angélica said to Ignacio. "*El patroncito* can walk *muy bien* when you and the big *señor* are not around!" So— Jamie was avoiding Douglas, too. What a fool he, Ignacio, had been when he told Sarah on the train how fine the world would be.

At the corral, Ignacio took the reins of both the horses. He looked at Ann. She was staring at the ranch house, but it was too dark to see the expression on her face. He was glad.

"*Gracias*, Ignacio," she said without turning. "You are always there."

* * *

Just before spring roundup the first letter came. When Ann stopped the Buick at the shack and shouted that there was mail for him, he was sure it was from Jorge Martínez. Except for the card from Ann on the honeymoon, and the brief note from Jamie during the war, Jorge was the only one who had ever written him.

It was a good thing Ann was in a rush to get to the house, or she would have seen him stagger. He had opened the letter, postmarked in Black Springs and addressed to N. Ortiss, Forman, D Cross A Ranch, even before she put the car in gear.

"Dear Ortiss—" it began, and the irony of the opening didn't strike him until he had read the letter a second time.

Dear Ortiss—

You dont no but we been watching you an that widdo whoar if you dont quit stiking your cock in her we will each you some night an make a steer out of you wich will stop you sure as hell ha ha tell her same goes for her she coud get her ass branded she coudent spred it no mor you an her insultted black Spring long enouf

—a sitizenn

He couldn't choke down a morsel at supper, and made a lame excuse to go to the shack.

It was beyond his understanding. He and Sally hadn't been secretive, but neither had they been arrogantly indiscreet. They met only at her house, and then only at night. Anyone who *wanted* to know about them could have, easily enough, but why this now? He had been seeing Sally for almost three years.

His first thought was to burn the grease-smeared thing and forget about it. Hadn't he read that only cowards wrote such letters; they never acted out their threats. But what about Sally's safety? The writer or writers, if there were more than one, might not be cowardly where a woman was concerned. He buried the letter beneath a rock in back of the shack, unable to stomach the thought of it inside with him, and looked to see if it was still there every time he passed it, jumping as if with guilt once when he saw Pepe watching him. He jammed it into his pocket and later hid it under a different rock.

Roundup would prevent him from seeing Sally for at least a week, and he fretted through his work. It must have shown.

"Ignacio," Douglas said, "are you a little under the weather? You haven't looked yourself the past few days."

"My stomach, *señor*." Well, it wasn't really a lie. He certainly couldn't eat.

"Perhaps you ought to see a doctor," Ann said.

He shook his head, but later he realized it was just the alibi he needed to go to town and see Sally.

When he came to the ranch house that night to tell the señor he was taking the next day off he found that Douglas had already gone to bed. Ann and Jamie were sitting in front of the fireplace, and the look on Jamie's face told the rider he was taken by surprise.

"Howdy, *amigo*," Jamie said. Ignacio realized he hadn't heard the voice in weeks. "How's the operation going?"

"*Muy bien*, Jamie. It will be a good roundup." It was a safe beginning, but he felt uncomfortable until he saw Ann smiling.

"I thought I might look in on it tomorrow," Jamie said. "'Course I won't be any earthly good." He pointed to his leg with the heavy stick.

Instantly, Ignacio decided he would have to put off the trip to town for another day. Someone might have to look after this tall young man, and he would have to be the one.

Dios, keep Sally safe until I come to her.

Jamie did show up at the holding pens next morning. Ann drove him to the flats west of the corral, and Ignacio saw her open the door for him. With her arm around his waist, the two of them made their way slowly to the fence near where Douglas, Pepe, and the rider were working.

It was an ugly limp. The right foot brushed the caliche awkwardly, as if one leg were miles shorter than the other. Angélica was wrong, the vaquero thought, his heart aching as he saw Jamie throw his weight heavily on the cane each time the foot came down.

When they reached the fence near the squeeze chute, Jamie leaned against it, breathing hard. "Damn it, Ann! It ain't going to work, I tell you."

"You'll be fine when I get you all set up," Ann said. She walked to the car, came back with a kitchen chair, and helped Jamie into it. "The sun will do you a world of good, and I'll be back for you in an hour."

Douglas waved to his son from the far end of the chute, waved again to Ann as she drove off.

Trying his best to stay busy, the vaquero couldn't keep his eyes from the man in the chair. Pity burned in the rider's chest, and remorse, too, when he remembered his cruel attack in the hospital in Chicago—no matter how much Jamie had deserved it. To shake these feelings, he turned to his work with a will, as Douglas and Pepe drifted off to the far end of the holding pen.

A runty calf, bawling louder than the car horn Ann had blown in answer to the señor's wave, was pushing under the bottom rail of the fence on the other side of the chute. One hand higher and the little animal couldn't have made it through, but before Ignacio could move to head it off, the calf was free, romping loose on the side of the fence where Jamie sat. The confused, frightened creature, hidden from Jamie by the squeeze chute, rocketed along, hugging the fence, unmindful of where its stiff white legs took it. It was on young MacAndrews before the rider could shout a warning.

With one swift, flashing, graceful movement, Jamie was on his feet, dancing to one side, fending the calf away with the heavy cane. It was the kind of action Ignacio had seen many times before. He tried to look away, but much too late. Jamie's blue eyes met his.

"You won't have to show me the hateful, filthy thing, Nash!" Sally Bannister said. "I got one, too." He should have known from the look on her face, and the way she hurried him through the door and closed it behind him. "My God!" she said, "I know there's been talk, but this—" There was white rage in her face, and something else. Fear?

"Perhaps, Sally—" he began.

"NO! No, Nash, no!" Her low scream was like a winter wind. "Don't say it. Don't ever say it! I can stand anything, *bear* anything but that."

He stayed the night with her. In the morning she turned to him as pathetic as a child. "See, Nash," she said, "it's right. It's good. It's us. . . ."

Four years—almost to the day—after he had run from the Cantina Florida with a little food, less money, and a change of clothing tied up in a serape, Jorge Martínez came home. He didn't send word to his friend at the D Cross A, and since none of the anglos who came to the ranch were patrons of the cantina, it was three weeks before Ignacio walked into the Florida on a busy Saturday afternoon and found Jorge working behind the bar. He looked so right and natural there that for a moment the rider could almost believe nothing had changed, and the young man had never been away.

When Jorge saw him, he raced from the bar. Ignacio didn't get a good look at him until after they embraced and Jorge pressed a hard kiss against his cheek.

"Ignacio! *Cómo estás?*"

"When, Jorge?"

"Almost a month ago."

"*Porqué el secreto?* Why didn't you let me know?"

"I wanted you to just walk in and find me. Just like this." The cantina owner's son was smiling, and Ignacio looked carefully at his friend.

Under the smile was a face which reminded him of Jorge Martínez, but it wasn't the one he had kept in memory these past four years. It was a weathered face, with lines around the eyes which could only have come from squinting against sun and dust, and the eyes themselves—blacker, it seemed—looked as though they had been burned into the tough skin below the forehead. There were creases in the forehead, too, which hadn't been there before the run from Mex Town. Even with the smile the face was that of a man who had been used hard. Why, he could be a vaquero, Ignacio thought.

He looked fit, lean, durable, as supple as Ignacio remembered, but tougher somehow. His sleeves were rolled up, and the rider saw that the muscles in his arms had a mature set they hadn't had four years ago.

"You have been well, Jorge?"

"*Sí!*"

"Were you never hurt?"

"Not a scratch, *amigo*. My friend Álvarez used to say angels rode with me, before he died." The smile faded and then returned. In the fraction of a second it was gone, Ignacio thought of Jamie, who never smiled these days.

"Then you are all right, *verdad?*"

"*Sí.* You worry too much, *viejo.* You always did. Come, let us have a drink together."

Concepción joined them. She shook her head at Jorge's offer of a drink, but stood close to the two of them, not speaking. She didn't have to. Love for her brother and affection for the rider were plain enough for anyone to see, even though her joy seemed diluted when she looked at Ignacio, her smile lightly brushed with sorrow.

Suddenly he felt warm, wanted, at home. The cantina, with these two waiting for him, would always be a refuge.

Another letter came, but this time it was addressed to Douglas. Never, never had Ignacio known the sickening mortification he felt when the big rancher spoke to him about it.

"It isn't any of my business, Ignacio, and I wouldn't have mentioned it, except—it's a nasty threat. I don't think the sick soul who wrote this thing would have the nerve to carry it out, but if anything happened, I'd never forgive myself if I hadn't told you." He looked at the vaquero, who could hardly meet his eyes. "Does the lady know?"

Ignacio nodded.

"Hmm. That makes it worse." Douglas looked thoughtful. "I've got a lot of respect for Mrs. Bannister, Ignacio, but if I'm any judge at all, she's got a sight more courage than common sense. I'll bet she feels it doesn't make a particle of difference. Right?"

Again the rider nodded.

"I'm not sure," Douglas went on, embarrassment now clear in his manner, "that I entirely approve of the lady and you together. In the long run, the way our small world is constituted, marriage is the only place for this kind of thing." *Dios!* The señor was blushing like a red sunset.

"Forgive me, Ignacio," Douglas said. "I had no right to say that. I realize marriage might not work out in a case like yours. Oh, hell! I'm making a damned fool of myself." He walked a few paces from the vaquero, and turned back to him. "For what it's worth," his face broke out in a wide smile, "I sure do admire the lady's taste in men."

At Sally's insistence, he tried to put the sordid business out of his mind, but it preyed on him more sharply after each time he had been with her. In the long run, he knew, there was only one possible decision, and he would have made it immediately except for one inescapable fact. Setting modesty aside, he knew that Sally would have to make the greater sacrifice of the two if they went separate ways. He admired her, delighted in her bright, quick mind, and yes, reveled in her skillful body, which he had come to know even better than his own, but—the feelings were deeper, stronger by far, on Sally's side.

They had begun their time together out of simple common need, respect, and friendship. If the letters served good in any way, it was because they pointed out how Sally's professed casualness, if such it had truly ever been, had changed into something else.

"Why," she asked once, of the empty air, it seemed, "did they have to wait so long? If it had happened right away, before I'd come to—" Tears streaked her face. She almost never cried; when she did it devastated him.

He saw her more often than in the days before the letters started coming, partly to check on her and see how she was bearing up, and partly out of their shared defiance. He agonized at how much worse it must be for her, there in town, wondering as she passed her fellow villagers if *they* could be the ones, while he was sheltered at the D Cross A, insulated against all of this by the work he had to do. He would have to decide, and soon, for both of them. Every time he thought he had reached the point of no return, however, something Sally would say or do would cause him to put the decision off until they met again.

Strangely, he spent no time at all wondering where the letters came from. He had at first, of course, but when Sally got another, and he a second and a third, careful study pointed up the grisly truth—at least three different hands had penned them. Douglas had said "sick," and sick it was—contagious, too.

Each time, before they parted, their lovemaking took on a quality of desperation which had a touch of doom about it.

Suddenly, Jamie made a return of sorts. By the time the summer had run its course and brought them to another roundup, he was coming to supper regularly. Once in a while he even smiled, although it was but a hint of the wide, reckless grin of the Jamie who romped off to France.

In August, Ann got him in the car for a trip to Black Springs. He said he could "walk a fair distance" now, and with the vaquero carrying packages, they shopped all of Frontera Street, winding up in Stafford's to visit Findlay.

"Come on in the office for a drink," the storekeeper said. "We could mosey over to the Sacramento, but they've got the street side of the saloon boarded up on account of this prohibition nonsense, and you'd have to climb the stairs and go through the lobby entrance. Besides, I don't fancy my liquor from a coffee cup."

Only Jamie accepted. Ann had a dress fitting at Esther Kimball's and the vaquero begged off as well. He mumbled something about getting a haircut, maybe, but the truth was he didn't want Jamie thinking he was watching him every second.

There wasn't time to go to Sally's, and he hoped he wouldn't run into her somewhere in town. For some reason that he didn't care to think about—and this had nothing to do with their current troubles—he never felt easy about seeing her when he came to town with Ann.

Sarah had asked him to check at the express agency for a package she was expecting, and then he could slip over to the Florida for a drink with Jorge.

Jim Gibbon was tapping away at his key when the rider entered the depot office. With his head bent over his apparatus, the green eye shade hid the telegrapher's face from view. The expressman wasn't in sight, and the vaquero knew he would have to wait until Gibbon finished sending off his message.

Ignacio had run into the Western Union man once or twice before the war, usually at the Sacramento when he had gone there for a drink with Jamie. Rumor had it the man was in Black Springs because of trouble he had in a better post. Fights, Ignacio had heard—over women, mostly. The man was as big as a breed bull, and looked ten times as mean. Still, Jeffers, the station master, had once said, "Say what you like about Jim Gibbon, he's got the sweetest fist on the entire line." Someone explained this was shop talk, indicating how good Gibbon was with his equipment. Well, the rider could see it now. There was something almost dainty in the way the huge cupped hand moved up and down on the brass key.

"Yeah?" Gibbon said, when he finished and turned his chair.

"*Por favor*, is there any package for Miss MacAndrews?"

"Ain't been anything in today for anyone."

"*Gracias, señor*. We will ask again next week."

"Yeah, you do that, Mac."

The vaquero turned to go.

"Hey!" Gibbon said behind him, "ain't you Ortiz, the so-called foreman out at the MacAndrews's place?"

"*Sí, señor.*"

"Thought so, seen you out there. You're the one that's—uh—*friendly* with the widow Bannister, ain't you?"

Ignacio said nothing.

"Understand you've picked up a couple of pen pals along the line." The man leered, his big face naked, brutal. Ignacio saw for the first time what an unhealthy white it was for anyone who lived in this sunny country. It frightened him, that face. He turned to go again.

"I'd watch myself, if I was you, pal," he heard Gibbon say as he left the depot

Could this be one of them? No. He had seen the man's elegant script on the telegrams that had come to the ranch, nothing like the crude, badly managed printing in the letters. But Gibbon knew; more than that, Gibbon was enjoying their torment—and he didn't even know him or Sally. What kind of man—? Yes, he frightened him.

He would be seeing more of Gibbon in the future, too. Already a number of anglos like him were beginning to come to the Florida, now that the new law had made drinking at the Sacramento difficult, and had actually closed the other saloons in Black Springs.

He hurried back to Stafford's.

By roundup time, Jamie was riding again. He didn't take part in any of the work on foot, even though the limp had become less noticeable—except when Douglas was on the scene—but he did do some heavy riding with Ignacio once.

Moving around the pens on horseback, his cane stuck into a saddle holster like a rifle, he was loudly critical of the old man and the boy who had stayed on in place of the Barlows, and little short of vicious with Pepe, who threatened to quit until Ignacio calmed him down. His behavior made the vaquero wonder what had happened in France—there must have been something besides the wound—to create a man like this. The Jamie of the old days could be an unthinking, careless menace, but he didn't deliberately try to destroy people as this one did.

And this one almost never smiled.

It was a long time, before Sally, since he had been in the Florida this late on a Saturday night. He would see her tonight, too, but it would be late. She was stuck at the office, helping her brother rebuild the rib cage of a young puncher who had been half kicked to death by the raw bronc he was breaking. The cantina was almost empty. The November wind seemed to blow right through the adobe walls, and the tequila did little to dull its moaning, cold lament. It had been a bad day all around.

There was a letter from Tim Barlow for one thing. The younger of the two good cowhands penned his apologies for not having written sooner. He'd been with the army of occupation in Europe, and "well, you know how time slips by." He wouldn't be coming back to the D Cross A. The girl he was seeing before the war had been left a little money, and they had bought a small place near Dalhart, Texas. And "maybe you haven't heard," brother Jess was dead. Like Tim he had made it untouched through all the fighting, only to die at Camp Shanks in New York, a week off the boat from France—victim of the same influenza which took Agnes. Ignacio tried not to take too many drinks too quickly, in case Sally would be free later on.

Jorge looked glum, listless. The raw weather must have affected him, too. The place was empty, the old Andreas, Mamá, and even Concepción had gone to bed. He watched Jorge move silently around the bar room, extinguishing the lamps in the niches in the walls.

"How is your big anglo friend Jamie?" Jorge said, when he settled in across the bar from Ignacio. The vaquero shrugged.

"Not bad, Jorge. His leg gives him trouble, but it improves." There must have been something wary in his voice, for he saw Jorge look at him with suddenly narrowed eyes.

"Don't worry, *amigo.*" There was a smile of contempt on Jorge's face. "He has nothing to fear from me. It wouldn't help Concepción, and—I've had all the killing I ever want." As he said the word "killing," Ignacio saw Jorge's black eyes flare with pain.

Jorge poured himself a drink, lifted it in front of him, and for several moments stared at the rim of the glass. "Did you know"—he looked at Ignacio now—"I was a *commandante,* a major, like your friend?"

"No, Jorge. That is *magnífico, verdad.*" A foolish comment, but what else was there to say?

"*Sí, magnífico!*"—Jorge's laugh was a mocking, bitter thing which echoed derisively from the cantina walls—"and I have medals, too, enough that if I wore them all, this shirt would be a *traje de luces,* a suit of lights." He drained his glass and filled it up again. "*Seriamente,*" he said. He *looked* serious, the smile gone. "It was no big thing to become an officer. Patience, survival, that was all it took. Álvarez had them for a while. He was our major before me—until a machine gun burst gave me my promotion." He drank again. It wasn't like Jorge to drink this way, the rider thought.

Then it came, and perhaps the fact that Jorge's voice never rose above a whisper made it worse. Certainly it did nothing to mask the horror, the cynicism, the complete and crushing disillusionment—and the heartbreak. For two hours—maybe three—Jorge made him walk the bloody ground which *he* had walked.

With Jorge he lived the first bright days, looked with the same hopeful eyes at the proud banners of the struggle, and felt the touch of the girl Juanita, could almost see himself the raw place on her shoulder left by the rifle sling. He knew the joy of dancing and the wine, the harsh exhilaration of the first great fighting—and the resting afterward.

Then, with Jorge and his *compadres,* he felt it change. He saw the first, tiny, winked-at compromises for the "cause," felt the first disgust Jorge felt when the *gran general* began to change into something other than a crusader, and then the killing, not war, not *revolución,* just *killing*—done because they had all forgotten there was anything else to do.

"Columbus, hah! *Nada.* I didn't know enough when we hit the *gringos* at Columbus." Jorge's black eyes grayed, went dead. "It was the *padre* at Camargo. I came home because of him. He had hidden a boy who tried to put a bullet in our Pancho, so there was never any doubt about what we had to do. We were kind, *muy simpático.* We let him finish his Mass that Sunday morning. Then we shot him against the wall of his little church—efficiently."

The old wall clock ticked away. It sounded like a bomb preparing to go off.

"And Juanita?" Ignacio asked.

Jorge didn't answer. He only laid his head in his folded arms, and the sobs gently moved his back.

Ignacio placed his hand on Jorge's head. "Cry, *amigo*, cry. But, *por favor*, remember, *estás en tu país*. You are home."

He couldn't see Sally now. He would be no good to her as a man—and telling her of his decision would have to wait. It would be cruel to tell her in the middle of this dark night. He could catch a couple of hours sleep in the stall at Kelly's where he had left the new horse, Gavilán, and then get back to the D Cross A.

The year would soon be over. Beginning with Agnes on the train, it was all a homecoming of a sort. Jess Barlow had come home, yes, and Jorge, drained and ravaged back in the cantina. Jamie, too. He knew now he would never want to find out what had happened to laughing Jamie over there.

As if they had been spoken in his ear, he heard the words of the Bastard after King John's death: *"Now these, her princes, are come home again. Come the three corners of the world in arms, and we shall shock them."* Perhaps. The man from Stratford didn't know the Ojos Negros, or these princes.

"I'll go back East," Sally Bannister said, "just as soon as I can sell or rent the house, and Dr. Sam can find someone to take my place." She hadn't cried, just sat there with her hands folded in her lap, her head held perhaps a shade too high. "No," she went on, "if I can't have a life here with you—I most certainly can't stay. You had better go now, Nash. Don't kiss me—don't touch me. I couldn't bear your touch right now."

He stood up and started for the door.

"Nash." He turned to her.

"Sí, Sally?"

"Merry Christmas—and Happy New Year."

She was smiling. It was a good smile. Anyone who didn't know would have thought they were parting just for the moment.

23

CHANGE TOUCHED THE OJOS NEGROS BASIN AS REGULARLY AS THE sun swept across the sky, a sun seen fully or in part almost every day.

In the high country, the cold of winter struck to the very heart of the rimrock and the limestone ridges, but when the noon sun poured down—even on January days—the skin of the stone expanded, cracked, flaked away from the core, and sent rock fragments skipping and bounding down the canyon walls toward the valley. Thousands of tons a year settled from the heights, raising the level of the canyon bottoms year by year, but so imperceptibly even the most discerning pair of eyes at the D Cross A failed to notice.

Some of the falling rocks, those large enough, cut a pathway of destruction through the piñon and the scrub, in random disregard of any process of natural selection, leveling with fine impartiality the sturdiest and fittest which tried to block their way, as well as the scrawny stuff which clung to the stony hillsides.

The rains would come, some so high in the ranges they were hidden from the valley floor, gathering in the dish-shaped meadows which separated the stands of ponderosa, and spilling over in floods which hastened the crumbled rock on its journey down the gullies and arroyos. Some of the water, left behind in the mountain meadows, sank into the soil and seeped its way through substrate passages, leaching gypsum from the dark stones along its course.

Far to the south, flat, eye-burning miles beyond the sands which were its one creation, an ancient lake, dry now, sucked this lime-rich, watery load into its secret bowels, held it there until the waters all were gone, then spewed it up as dust to catch the light summer winds which followed on the wilder ones of spring. Season after season the wind settled still another coat of white on the dunes which loomed above the alkali—and not a particle was ever lost in the great closed system which was the Ojos Negros.

If these changes went unseen by Ignacio Ortiz, his searching black eyes couldn't fail to register those in the human world close at hand. Erosion and redistribution had been at work there, too, and the peaks and valleys of his psyche had begun to round and fill. More and more, his books lured him to the quiet of the shack.

When Douglas brought in a crew to install a generator in the pump house, he watched with mere curiosity, until the rancher said, "Yes, Ignacio, we're taking a step into the twentieth century. There'll be electric lights in the house and stable, and we can pump water even when the wind doesn't blow. Be nice for you in the shack, too."

Without knowing why, the rider balked at this, his stomach fluttering at going counter to any wish Douglas had.

The big man shook his head in smiling disbelief, but told the vaquero he could keep the place in stygian blackness if he wished—the shack was his, Ignacio's. He did talk the rider into having the old board and batting walls recovered with tar paper, however. Ignacio, remembering how northers would sometimes cut through the shack, made no fuss.

He would sit in the shack at night, alone but seldom lonely, while the kerosene lamp's yellow light washed over the pages of his books. He must, he thought, smiling, look marvelously like those old alchemists in their haunted cells. Well, at least no one was there to see him struggling to turn the base metal of his ignorance into gold.

No one but Sarah. The girl, staying for the most part at Mary Stafford's as Jamie had done during school, would often seek him out in his hideaway after supper. He couldn't swallow back the lump in his throat when she curled up at his feet as she had as a tot.

Over his blushing objections, they would do scenes from the plays together. If Sarah's drawl, every final *g* dropped irretrievably (he could hear Sally's crisp accent as she drilled *him*), failed to produce a suitably judicious Portia—his was surely a comic Shylock. There were times when she did soar above her limitations, and her young voice brought the shack an Ophelia a touch too mad. She offered him his "rosemary for remembrance" and it was with rue, *verdad*, that he followed her to "where a willow grows aslant a stream."

The change in Jamie seemed permanent. The flashing smile was gone, and would seldom come again. Ignacio tried to convince himself that in some ways the change was for the better. Bad-tempered as the man was nowadays, he was, in a peculiar way, more *aware* of the people around him than the old Jamie—that blundering, unconscious, but natural boy. The awareness, though, too often showed itself as distrust, suspicion, and impatience.

Ignacio wouldn't have cared, except for the effect he knew it had on Señora Ann (more and more just *the* señora, now). In her there had been a change, too. Some of the bright pain was gone from her eyes, but in its place he saw a dim, lifeless ache.

Against all this, there was one blessed constant, the señor. Douglas moved across the rider's sky like the sun, a sun whose warmth he had never known to fail. Without the big man the D Cross A would be as cold and barren as the moon. Ignacio felt secure when he saw that the señor still looked as durable as the rocks above the ranch, even after his monthly rides to high Las Sombras.

Jorge married. He surprised Mamá, Concepción, and the rider by taking a wife three weeks after old Andreas died in his sleep. Now the full task of running the cantina was his.

The bride was a shy, faintly pretty thing from the Río Concho, and Ignacio wasn't conscious of hearing her say a solitary word in the first year the pair were man and wife. Jorge just seemed to have adorned himself with her much in the same way he put on his father's apron and stepped behind the bar. *Adíos, guerrero,* Ignacio said to himself, and *bueno.*

At the wedding, the vaquero spent most of his time watching Concepción. Jorge's sister drifted through the celebrants in the cantina in a dreamlike way which set him thinking. He knew she had no man, and wondered why. The beauty of maturity had long since replaced the wild, exotic look which had lured Jamie and the others, and in spite of what had happened to her, he knew she could have her pick of the *campesinos* who came to the Florida—and no few of the anglos, too. Like Jorge, she seemed devoid of passion.

Well, passion had been a poor provider. It was just as well it had departed. All of them could do with less of it—Jamie (*sí*, his sourness *was* a passion of a sort); Ann; himself. They should all find the deeper, sounder thing which Douglas had. *"Give me that man who is not passion's slave, and I shall wear him in my heart of hearts, Horatio. . . ."*

24

"IT's A BOY!" ANGÉLICA RIVERA ANNOUNCED, BEAMING. SHE BLOCKED the door a good deal more now than she had sixteen years ago at Sarah's birth, but the extra weight seemed to have softened her nature. The old midwife-turned-housekeeper had gotten over the pique she showed when Dr. Colvin rattled up the ranch road in his Model T. "Dr. Sam says you can all come in and see them in ten minutes."

"They're both all right?" Douglas asked.

"*Sí, Señor* Douglas. *Muy bien—madre y niño.*"

Ignacio relaxed. Ann had carried well enough through the heat of summer and into this gray November weather— but what did he know? The moaning which had come from the room was terrifying, and the fact that it wasn't loud or frequent hadn't comforted him—this was Señora Ann. When he heard the baby's first cries, he was sure something had gone wrong.

Angélica appeared in the doorway again and motioned for them, but the rider hung back, until Douglas gripped his arm and led him through the door. At first, intent on Ann, he didn't see the tiny head in the curve of her arm. Douglas released him and moved with Sarah to the huge old bed, and then, with the rancher and his daughter at the foot of it, he couldn't see much of anything, except Dr. Colvin packing his black bag. Douglas and Sarah were both talking at once and Angélica was clucking in his ear. "*Pequeño!* Only seven pounds. When I was young *todos los niños* were bigger."

Then, Ann called to him. *Dios!*

He moved to the side of the bed opposite Sarah, walking as if a heavy step might shatter something. "*Sí, Señora* Ann, I am here."

There were still a few beads of perspiration on her forehead and upper lip, but the look on her face made his heart swell. Angélica must have brushed out her hair, for it spread on either side of her head like shiny, black wings.

"You haven't looked at him, Ignacio," she said.

The baby's eyes were closed, but he could have wagered then that when the blue changed (they are all blue at first, aren't they?) they would take color from the mother's—deep onyx dark. Already the few damp hairs he saw were as black as hers. The little face—the mouth pursed tightly—seemed screwed up in thought. Impossible, of course, but when *did* they start to think? His own memory was of no use in this regard.

"He is splendid, *señora. Magnifico!*"

Douglas and Angélica left with the doctor, and he started after them, but Ann reached out and took his hand. "Ignacio," she said, "would you do something for me, *por favor?*" Would he? He nodded happily. "Please find Jamie for me, if he isn't back by supper time." She wasn't smiling now.

His spirit dropped like a stone. *Dios.* He had been so caught up in this wonderful excitement he had forgotten the worst trouble of the whole long day. Across the bed he saw Sarah's smile disappear, anger coming to her face so swiftly he knew at once she had forgotten, too. They must have both wanted to forget that Jamie hadn't been there, not for his wife's heavy labor, or the birth of his son. Ignacio looked from the sixteen-year-old back down to the woman in the bed. For the first time he noticed how pale she was under the dark complexion.

"*Sí, Señora* Ann," he said, "of course I will find him." He said goodnight and hurried out the door.

When he reached the sitting room, Douglas and Dr. Colvin were standing by the fireplace. "Don't know, Douglas," Sam Colvin was saying, "he rapped on my door about noon yesterday—told me Ann was going into labor, and was gone before I could say more than 'yes, I'll come.' " The doctor stopped talking when he saw Ignacio.

"Thank you, Sam," Douglas said. The voice carried such a burden, it made the rider wince. The señor turned and walked past him. He is going out in the yard to wait again, Ignacio thought, just as he did all last night, and today until the baby came.

Dr. Sam left, too, and in a moment he could hear him in the kitchen, giving instructions to Angélica. Ignacio moved to the place by the fire where the señor and the doctor had been standing.

It was almost out. No one had thought to take care of it the past two hours. He went to the wood box and picked up two piñon logs, selecting them carefully, as if their size and shape made a difference. As he took them to the fireplace, he saw Sarah enter the sitting room.

"I suppose you'll have to go and look for him, Nash, for her sake, but for all of me—he can't stay away long enough now!" If no sparks flew from the half-dead fire, Sarah's eyes snapped like lightning.

"*Muchachita*—" He tried to keep his voice low, reassuring. "Perhaps he has trouble with the car. We should see him soon." He turned to lay the logs on the fire, quickly, so she wouldn't see his face.

"I don't believe it!" The scorn in her voice was like acid. "*And neither do you!*"

Jamie had left the ranch in the Buick more than twenty-four hours earlier, soon after Ann began her pains. Ignacio was coming to the house for breakfast as the car bucked and lurched down the road in the half darkness, nearly hitting him. He couldn't see the driver behind the headlights, but only Jamie drove like that. Señora Ann had reached her time, he knew it.

He hurried up the pathway, until he thought perhaps he would only be in the way, and he slowed his steps. The señor was there, and Angélica, of course, which was even more important. Maybe he shouldn't go at all. But he did, he had to.

Ann sat at the table, smiling. Once in a while her face twisted, and once in a while she put her hand on the swollen place under her robe, but still she smiled. "I won't be too much longer now, Ignacio," she said. Never, never had he seen eyes with a shine like that, not even hers.

Sarah squirmed with excitement—she could have been sitting on the kitchen stove instead of her wooden chair—and the señor, well, Ignacio couldn't hold back his own smile when he saw the foolish joy, barely touched with anxiety, on the big man's face. Only Angélica seemed unaffected. She served up breakfast as if it were the beginning of an ordinary day.

"Did Jamie tell you, Ignacio?" Ann asked. "We decided on a name. Ian. After Jamie's grandfather."

"And if it should be a girl, *señora?*"

"Agnes." He saw her look at Douglas.

Then Angélica spoke up. *"Bueno!"* She sounded like a trail boss. "And now you will *eat!* You have work to do today, *señora.*"

None of them really missed Jamie until after the doctor had arrived. When Sam Colvin announced that it would be several hours yet, Sarah said, "I guess that's good. Jamie will be back." At the girl's remark, Ignacio realized that, yes, he should have returned by now. The same thought must have struck Douglas, for he left the house without a word. In seconds the rider could see him standing in the compound, rubbing the chin he hadn't had time to shave.

Supper wasn't a bit like breakfast. All the smiles were gone. Dr. Sam told them the pains were close enough together now, and Ignacio saw that the man was clearly troubled. "She should deliver, damn it!" the doctor said. "It almost seems she's *trying* to hang on. Wish that husband of hers would show up soon."

Back in the shack, Ignacio tried to read, and couldn't. He didn't sleep, either. He dressed again, stepped out of his door, and watched the Little Dipper spin around a cold North Star through the entire night. He couldn't count the times he saw Douglas come out to look for headlights on the road.

"I'll bet," Sarah said suddenly, "that bastard brother of mine is with that woman over in Mex Town!"

The vaquero wasn't sure which shocked him more—hearing Sarah speak that way, or learning she knew about Sofía Gutiérrez. It shouldn't have surprised him. Sarah, in town for school, was bound to hear. Nothing remained hidden in Black

Springs for very long. He knew Sarah was wrong about this, though, if he didn't know how he knew it. This time it wouldn't be Sofía. It was simpler and at the same time far more complicated than that.

Jamie was off and running again, had been, the rider recognized, since before Ann had told her news to the others at spring roundup time. He had seen the look on Jamie's face, but of all people, he couldn't tell Sarah when it was.

"I think I'll saddle up, *niña*," he said, "just in case."

He was already up on Gavilán when he saw the headlights. They came so slowly he wasn't sure it was Jamie driving, but no one else would be coming out at this time of night.

He didn't unsaddle his pony, but he loosed him back into the corral, and by the time he shut the gate the Buick was crunching to a stop by the house. When Jamie left the car, he saw him stagger. At first he thought of the limp, but a second look, even across the yard, was enough to convince him the rancher's son was drunk.

Then a flood of light came from the kitchen door, and Sarah ran out through it. She flew at her brother. Her small fists beat against his chest, and Ignacio saw Jamie drop his cane and grapple for them.

"You son of a bitch!" Sarah screamed. "I'll never forgive you for this—even if Ann does. And someday I'll see that that baby boy in there finds out what a bastard you are!"

No, no, *muchachita*, the vaquero pleaded silently across the night, Señora Ann will hear you. He found himself running toward the struggling pair, wondering as he ran what on earth he would do when he got there.

By the time he did, Sarah had pulled her hands out of Jamie's grip and had moved to the attack again, this time clawing him with her nails. As the rider wedged himself between the two of them, he saw Jamie bleeding from an ugly gash on his cheek. Ignacio was rough with Sarah, pushing her to one side, and standing in front of Jamie to keep her off him.

"*Gracias, amigo*," Jamie said behind him. "You're a pal. Who would have thought the little shit could fight like that?" His speech was thick, and the air around the three of them reeked.

"I am sorry, *niña*," he said to Sarah.

"Me too, Nash." Sarah said, quietly. She turned and walked into the house.

Ignacio left Jamie, and went to the corral to take care of Gavilán. At the gate he looked back. Jamie bent over and picked up his cane. He took an unsteady step forward, stopped, squared his shoulders, and limped through the kitchen door.

25

WHEN IAN JENNINGS MACANDREWS SQUALLED HIS WAY INTO LIFE
on November 22, 1921, the D Cross A cattle ranch owned by
his grandfather covered more than a thousand square miles of
Chupadera County, New Mexico. A few hundred were actually
national forest lands grazed under permit, but nine hundred and
sixty sections were the outright holding of the Cuchillo Livestock
Co., D. MacAndrews, President. Over one hundred and fifty
miles of four-strand wire fence, running from a low point near
the malpais to the foot of the dominating mountain in the east,
a gain in elevation of a quarter of a mile, enclosed twenty-five
hundred cattle, twelve working ponies, two milk cows, perhaps
a dozen chickens, one regular dog, and *Dios* knew how many
drifters. On the range, moving where the weather and their fancy
took them, were a score of old horses, let out to roam when their
working life was done.

Also within the fence, in the center of a choppy sea of good
grass and bad, sand, ocotillo, greasewood, mesquite, rock,
horned toads, alkali, and lizards, were buildings which housed
nine other creatures. The oldest of these was Curly Decker,
cowhand, born in Utah in 1854, who suffered mightily nowadays when he sat a horse for more than an hour; the youngest,
of course, was the baby boy. Ignacio Ortiz, vaquero and foreman, at thirty-one (it was supposed) almost struck a balance
point between the two.

If the D Cross A wasn't the largest Chupadera County ranch
(Kincaid's Rocking T, to the north, was twice as big in animals
and land), Ortiz was sure it was the finest; perhaps not the

181

"showplace" one Angus MacAndrews had predicted many years ago, but close to it.

Ian himself was a healthy child. As he grew, walking and talking in regulation time, alarming no one with either precocity or sluggishness, it became apparent he would favor his mother Ann, a handsome woman originally from the eastern seaboard. He was darker and finer-boned than the MacAndrewses, and he had his mother's eyes, dark brown really, but black in certain lights like hers, although his were given more to blazing up with fire. After his fourth birthday Ian never cried. On that day his father, a tall, good-looking man who limped sometimes, not only failed to show up for his birthday party, but forgot the event entirely.

His tears dried when his friend Ortiz (Ian called him Tío Nash) took him riding in the corral. Neither the youngster nor his friend could know they were the last ones he would ever shed.

All in all, though, life was "trotted out" for Ian like a "big, fine horse." It was the near perfection of the prospect which caused the vaquero Ortiz to wonder if it would all turn out as promised.

"No, Jamie!" Douglas was firm. "We'll go ahead with the grazing plan Ignacio worked out."

"Jesus, Pa." Jamie was so exasperated Ignacio was sure he would limp when this was over. "We could run another five hundred head in here if we'd open up that pasturage. We're losing money being so Goddamned conservative."

"That's enough, Jamie." The señor's tone was more of resignation than rebuke, but the rider knew, and so did Jamie, Douglas really *meant* "enough."

He wished the rancher would defer to Jamie a little more often. It was flattering always to be right in his employer's eyes, but the black looks Jamie sometimes gave his father—and by indirection the vaquero—didn't promise well for the day when it would be the younger man giving orders.

It was always painful when he thought like this, but he had to face it. Douglas, if still strong as an ox at nearly seventy, had lost more than a step or two in this, Ignacio's twenty-second year at the D Cross A. Whenever the rider visited Agnes's grave at Las Sombras (he never told anyone he went there), he would look with growing sadness at the headstone. Agnes's carved name was well toward the left of the marker, the other side blank and waiting.

Well, it was foolishness to expect this steady man to change or compromise. He could only run the D Cross A arrow straight. No matter how it looked to Jamie, he wasn't playing favorites.

One thing had made life a little more tolerable at the ranch. With Sarah at the university in Albuquerque these past four years, there hadn't been any of the terrible angry scenes—like the one at Ian's birth—which had occurred with such alarming regularity until the girl went off to school. Ignacio missed her, though, oh how he missed her.

Ann—it was no surprise—never by word and seldom by look took any side counter to the one she knew to be Jamie's, but neither did she extend herself on his behalf. Douglas understood, Ignacio was confident of that, and would have understood if Ann had been fiercely supportive of her husband.

Ian, moving toward his sixth birthday, and another party, only watched.

Generally, Douglas smiled in tolerance at his son's wilder schemes to make the ranch wealthier, but on one occasion he exploded with more force than Ignacio had ever seen him use. That was when he discovered that Jamie had been corresponding with a firm of geophysicists in Tulsa, with an eye to drilling for oil on the flat sections between the house and the highway.

"Not on the D Cross A!" the big man bellowed. "This is a stock ranch, not a sink hole!"

"But, Pa. Half a dozen wells bringing up a few barrels a day sure beats pushing cowhide all year long. Simpson down near Hobbs turned his—"

"That's enough!" This time it *was* a rebuke. "We're already taking enough out of this land of ours—maybe too much."

There was a strange feeling in Ignacio when the señor said "this land of ours." They were at supper, and Douglas spread his big arms to include everyone at the table.

Taking too much from the land was something the rider had thought of himself from time to time. Where on earth did all the beef go which they shipped each spring and fall? He remembered pictures of the gigantic stockyards in Chicago, but it only increased his bewilderment. Was it right, he wondered, for the Chupadera ranchers to produce five thousand times more food each year than the less than five thousand people in the county could possibly use? Surely it was no plan of nature.

He tried to find a book which might tell him something, but the Black Springs library, one small room tacked on the back of city hall, was no help, nor was Hattie Spletter, the librarian. Her attitude seemed to be that he had taken leave of his senses, trying, as he was, to find something which might do him out of his job. As he left the library and walked across the tracks to see Jorge, the idea chased around in his head. There was something else, too.

Last week he had driven with Douglas to a small ranch near Socorro to look at some breeding stock being auctioned off. The place was run down, its pastures plainly overgrazed. Heavy rains had played havoc with the denuded grasslands, cutting countless arroyos in the range, arroyos unlike the natural watercourses of the D Cross A. The gullies exposed the subsoil several feet below the level of the terrain, and red rocks jutted out. They were the angriest red he had ever seen, as if they had waited, buried, long enough, and now were fangs ready to rip at man.

Driving back across the Jornada del Muerto, the desiccated wasteland bordering the big river, he silently urged the rancher to greater speed, so impatient was he to get within the shadow of Cuchillo and the almost-tailored plains of the Ojos Negros.

As he walked Frontera Street, the memory of the corroded little ranch, its forlorn owner standing alone at the edge of the crowd of bidders, haunted him. He remembered, too, how, from his vantage point at the shack, he had cast his eye in every direction. If any violent force lurked beneath the sweet grass and the familiar ageless rocks, it didn't reveal itself, but he puzzled about it all the same.

Well, once inside the Cantina Florida he could forget these thoughts. He picked his times at the cantina carefully nowadays. As he had supposed, the anglos had made it *their* water hole on certain days and evenings. There seemed to be no effort to apply the drinking law in Mex Town. Jorge's business was thriving.

Even the government man who closed the Sacramento for good and all stopped in now and then to get a drink, acting as if the Florida and Mex Town were foreign soil beyond his jurisdiction. Jorge enjoyed it all immensely.

"Think, *amigo!*" he said. "*Los gringos espléndidos* have such poor regard for us they don't care what we do. *Oigan! Qué chanza!* Their prejudice will make me rich."

It seemed every anglo drinker in the Ojos Negros showed up at the Florida, but only at those chosen times which, to his surprise, he found he was avoiding. Well, almost every one. There were two notable exceptions. Jamie, of course, hadn't set foot in the Martínez place for ten years now—never would again, in all likelihood. The other was Jim Gibbon, the Western Union man, who did his drinking there, all right, but not with the other anglos.

"It's not that he has such a great love for us, Ignacio," Concepción said. "The other *gringos* can't stand *him.*"

Jorge had heard gossip to the effect that Gibbon, as telegrapher, knew too much. Certainly he was way ahead of the *Chupadera County News* in anything that mattered. Concepción, Ignacio noted, was partly wrong about his not having "such great love for us," however. Gibbon couldn't keep his eyes from Jorge's sister. True, he never did more than pass the time of day with her, but the vaquero saw the small round eyes light up in the man's pale, brutish face when he watched her.

Ignacio wondered if Concepción would ever take another man. As far as he knew, there had been none since Jamie. She was what, thirty-five now? He thought her more beautiful than ever. Unlike so many of her Mex Town sisters, her waist hadn't thickened, and her skin hadn't been coarsened by too much sun as had that of the wives of the *campesinos*. All she did, as far as Ignacio could tell, was work, go to church, and spend what free time she had with tiny Josefina, Jorge and María's three-year-old.

She never spoke of Jamie, but when a new anglo patron would call her "Connie," her face would darken, and the baffled newcomer would find the service slack indeed, until he tumbled to the fact that Señorita Martínez only answered to "Concepción."

She was attentive to the rider, and Ignacio thought back to those days when Jamie was her sun and moon, and when, if she spoke to him at all, it was only to ask where Jamie was. Time, time, he smiled, you devious old *brujo*.

If the Florida had been a haven, he found to his amusement the cantina was becoming, for him, a school of sorts. Here, in the quiet times he chose to come, he was learning how to be a Mexican.

Ignacio Ortiz was certainly split in two, he considered, or perhaps three. There was the vaquero, the *paisano* at the Florida, and the Ortiz who opened the books at night and soared off to worlds no one knew he visited. Wait! There was a fourth. That one waited before a high, white wall. *Basta!*

Sí, it was a school, this Cantina Florida, but the tuition was paid in pleasant coin. When he could, he did things for the men from the Río Concho. He loved, truly loved, these kind, softspoken farmers, who, no matter how they scrubbed to come to town, always gave off a faint odor of earth and manure and things which grew. The smell touched something deep inside him; when it reached him it seemed sometimes he could hear a bucket striking water in a dark well, the promise of something cool and satisfying, something half remembered, something. . . .

Sí, he did things for the *campesinos*, gladly. Take today. Old Carlos Sánchez, whose rocky farm was just below the piñon line in the Concho hills, came to Ignacio's table timidly.

"*Por favor*, Ignacio. May I speak with you?"

"*Sí*. Carlos, of course. *Qué tal, amigo?*"

"It goes well with me, Ignacio, except—there is a letter I must write about my taxes, and I wondered—"

"A letter? Certainly, my friend." Ignacio smiled at the old man and the way he bowed, holding his hat in front of him. "If you will borrow some paper and a pen from Jorge, we shall take care of it, you and I."

"Forgive me, Ignacio, but I have already."

How many times had he written letters such as this, and at this table? Mostly the *viejos* like Carlos asked for this kind of help, but a few of the younger men did, too. They had forgotten their spectacles, they would say, or had injured their writing hand at work (sometimes the alleged injury was bandaged most convincingly). The wives, he knew, got this help from the padre whose crumbling adobe church was down the block from the cantina, and he never passed the priest without thinking of the common cause they shared, smiling at some things he had put in black and white he was sure never sounded in the hush of the confessional.

He often speculated on what Agnes might say about this "use" he made of the education she had given him.

Ian was getting an education, too. He spent a good part of every day in the corral with Ignacio. The vaquero had been putting him upon Gavilán for two years now, and the time had almost come to take him into the wider world of the D Cross A.

It wasn't just the riding part Ian learned. Small as he was, the rider had him saddling the pony from the moment he discovered that the boy was strong enough to lift the tack. He had to build a platform of sawhorses and planks for Ian to stand on, and once, throwing the saddle across Gavilán's back, the youngster held on a fraction of a second too long and flipped over the startled animal in a wild somersault. After the terrified vaquero was satisfied Ian hadn't suffered injury, the two of them rolled in the caliche laughing until they cried.

He would miss the boy when he went to Black Springs in the fall, to stay, as had his father and his aunt, with the Staffords. Miss? *Dios!*

In the evenings he sometimes read to him. He had been shy about this, but both Douglas and Ann had urged him, and soon he began to look forward to the sessions, often neglecting reading of his own to spend more time with Ian—but never when Jamie was on the premises. It seemed the only time Jamie paid attention to his son was when he was involved with Ignacio. It didn't happen often. The anglo was spending more and more evenings away from the D Cross A.

If it hadn't been for the look on Ann's face, the rider shamefully admitted to himself he would have been glad for these absences. Few pleasures in his life could compare with those times when Douglas worked at his desk, Ann busied herself with sewing or chatting with Angélica, and the vaquero and the dark youngster nestled side by side on the couch, an open book spread in front of them.

Ian had one interest, though, in which Ignacio couldn't help. Early—he had been five, or a bit younger—the boy had begun to draw. From the start the rider saw that the sketches weren't at all like the crude stick figures and the distorted buildings and mountains he remembered Sarah turning out at about that age. Certainly it wasn't finished work, but the people emerging under Ian's crayon or pencil were clearly recognizable, just a line or a shadow capturing something in their character. There was one of Ignacio the rider couldn't look at without embarrassment. He was riding a horse which looked at least a hundred hands high compared to his own tiny figure—and clearly mastering it.

Sarah, of course, saw Ian's pictures on her trips home from the university, and a fresh supply of sketch pads, pencils, watercolors, and instruction books arrived from Albuquerque every other month.

Two people at the D Cross A never looked out from Ian's pile of drawings on the long table. There were dozens of beginnings of Ann, but none completed. There were none at all of Jamie. It didn't matter, though, that last. Jamie never looked, and Ignacio doubted if the man who raced off to town almost every night was distantly aware of what the boy was up to.

Jamie made no attempt to conceal his truancy. Twice Ignacio found articles of women's clothing in the Buick, once just seconds before Ann came from the house to drive him and Ian into town. He disposed of them himself, and then got into the habit of checking the car when he walked the path to breakfast any morning after Jamie had gone flying out the night before. He was certain Jamie knew of these inspections, and even more certain the two of them would never mention it.

Douglas, he was convinced, didn't know. Well, who in town would tell him? Besides, he went to town a good deal less than in former years. At any rate, he prayed the señor didn't know. There was enough sadness in his eyes already after quarrels with his son about the running of the ranch.

Jamie would present some course of action for the D Cross A and at first Douglas would listen patiently. When the older man would at last point out the folly of Jamie's often crack-brained schemes, the young anglo would erupt with a spate of venom.

"That's enough!" Douglas would say again (it seemed wearier and less emphatic every time) and Jamie would either collapse, deflated, or limp away to sulk.

Well, at least—and this outweighed all else—*the fence was tight*. This was the D Cross A, not that ravaged patch of misery they had looked at near Socorro.

There had been, of course, many changes. The new pickup truck had eliminated the need for so many ponies in the working string, and the power running to every building on the ranch except Ignacio's shack had unquestionably made work a good deal easier.

Ann loved the running water the new pumps provided, and the indoor plumbing which made frigid outside trips a thing of the past. She told Ignacio he should use the family bathroom any time he wished, but after thanking her he went right on bathing at the windmill tank.

They experimented with running a hundred black Angus on the range, handsome beasts ("a superior type of beef," the county agent said) but without the ornery instincts for survival of the Hereford they had known and worked so long.

"One thing," Douglas said. "As long as I've anything to say about it, we won't try any of those Brahma critters they're running over in Texas. They could be the finest things on four legs, for all I know, but they'd look a sight better in a circus or a zoo than on a stock ranch."

Ignacio couldn't help laughing at the big, blunt, practical rancher's sudden revelation of an aesthetic streak.

Then Ian went to town to start in school.

26

"YOU HAVEN'T TOLD ME," CONCEPCIÓN SAID WITHOUT LOOKING AT him, "that you got a letter from *la viuda*." She put his bottle of beer in front of him and walked away as stiff as a board. She hadn't even brought him a glass. *Dios*, she was angry!

How did she find out so quickly he had heard from Sally? He had picked up the letter just an hour earlier, and had only stopped at the Staffords to see Ian. If the boy had been there, and not off playing with friends, he wouldn't even have had time to read it yet.

It wasn't the first time Concepción had surprised him like this. She always knew things about him, almost as if one of the principal functions of her life was to check on him. Well, he *was* one of her brother Jorge's closest friends; it was bound to be.

He wanted to read the letter again, but with Concepción watching him from the bar, something told him it would be just as well to wait. She never talked so contemptuously about anglos as her brother did, but—and he couldn't figure out the reason—she had never so much as mentioned Sally Bannister without something close to a sneer on her face. It made no sense. As far as the vaquero knew, Concepción hadn't had ten words with Sally all the time she lived in Black Springs.

The letter (at that he didn't need to read it another time) could have been written by a stranger, except for the very end. Sally had remarried, and there was a child, a girl named Courtney. Her new husband was kind, considerate, and devoted to Sally and his daughter; well off but by no means rich. Sally said nothing about love for her husband—Ignacio hoped there was some. She asked the vaquero not to write. "There was nothing between us

190

I regret, Nash, nothing, but you can understand, I'm sure, that explanations might be awkward." The closing was like a blow. "I shall always love you." In all their time it had never come to this. He put his hand to the letter in his pocket, but didn't take it out.

Concepción was still watching him when Jim Gibbon entered the cantina. Perhaps it was the letter, and the vivid picture of Sally it brought to mind, but his thoughts raced back to the day in the depot when the telegrapher had taunted him about those other letters. It was foolish, but from that day he had never seen the man without feeling the momentary twinge of fear. Gibbon had never brought it up again, in fact Ignacio couldn't remember him ever talking to him on his visits to the Florida, and when they met on the streets of Black Springs, the Western Union man didn't even seem to see him.

Something of all this must have shown in his face, for when Concepción—her temper cooler—brought him another beer, and a glass this time, she sank into the chair beside him, saying, "You don't like that Gibbon very much, do you, *amigo?*"

Ignacio shrugged, hoping the gesture was vague enough to end the matter, but the woman wasn't put off that easily. "No," she said, "you don't like him very much at all. Why? Jorge says he has never seen a man like you—one who hates no one. Why this Gibbon then?" She looked at the letter peeping out of his shirt pocket, and pointed to it. "Is it because of her?"

He smiled, thinking there might just be something in this "woman's intuition" business. Of course, there was more to it than that. Sally was gone. Even if Gibbon had been involved in the letters (he didn't believe that, anyway) it would sooner or later have ended much the same way. Still, the fear had something to do with Sally after all. If it hadn't been for the man's scornful, insulting words in the depot he never would have focused on Gibbon quite so sharply.

He stared hard at the man's broad back. Gibbon looked heavy, massive, and yet it had nothing to do with size, although certainly he had that, too. It was a look Ignacio had seen before. Some bulls on the range had it. Often, one animal, no heavier or bulkier man his fellows, would appear bigger by far, fixed to the ground as if part of it, and yet capable of sudden, blinding motion which would leave an onlooker gasping. Such creatures were the only ones in an entire herd you had to worry about.

The space at the bar on either side of Gibbon was empty. There were only a few early afternoon drinkers, but it wasn't much different when the telegrapher came in when it was crowded. The *campesinos* moved aside whenever he stationed himself there, as he had now, right in the center of the bar.

He took great pains with his appearance, this Jim Gibbon. The white shirt stretched across his back gleamed like snow, and above the collar the hair was neatly trimmed and combed down carefully. Like most of the men who drank at the Florida, he wore his hat, but Ignacio remembered the hair as being thin on top, and straw pale in color, washed out and faded looking, like the curiously small eyes.

Suddenly, Gibbon turned around and looked at Ignacio's table, and the vaquero felt the tremor of fear again deep in his stomach, and then felt ashamed when he saw that Gibbon wasn't even looking at him. It was Concepción the small eyes were fixed on. Then the telegrapher nodded to the girl and left the cantina.

"What would you say if I went out with that one?" Concepción said.

He was stunned, and several seconds went by before he realized just how sick the question had made him. He said nothing.

"He has asked me many times," Concepción said. "He would like to take me to El Paso, too. He is an important anglo, *amigo*. Good job—lots of money."

Ignacio stared at her in disbelief. Surely she wouldn't! "What does Jorge say?" he said. No sooner had he heard his own weak voice than he regretted having spoken, even before she turned on him with the savagery of an attacking cat.

"*Jorge?* Why should it be *Jorge* who says yes or no? My brother is not my owner! Nor is anybody else!" She sprang to her feet and started to run from the table, only to stop and whirl about, her red skirt billowing into a flaming circle. With her black eyes making holes in him, and the color in her cheeks like the red of fever, she spat at him, the words scalding. "Ignacio Ortiz— *estúpido, bobo!* You are the stupidest, most hateful man I have ever known!"

27

SARAH CAME HOME FROM THE UNIVERSITY WITH A DEGREE IN education and a piece of paper which said she could look for a job as a teacher in the public schools of the state of New Mexico, but no one at the D Cross A, least of all Sarah herself, seriously expected that the girl would ever stand in front of a class and diagram sentences on a blackboard.

Ignacio helped her carry her school gear from the car into her room, dismayed at the weight of the wooden club she had used to lead her sorority to the college championship in field hockey. She spent ten minutes sticking dance programs in the side of her dressing table mirror, two more persuading a grumbling Angélica to finish unpacking for her and to do a wash, and then she sprinted for the corral to join the vaquero for a ride "up in the rocks like we used to, Nash!"

She was all ranch girl again half an hour after Ann and Douglas brought her down from graduation (Jamie didn't go), and Ignacio feared for a moment that the great experience she had just completed would be laid aside and forgotten, after making no more change in her than Jamie's had. He needn't have worried.

"I'm not like Ian, Nash, no matter how much I wish I were," she said, as they sat on the rocks while the ponies nodded in the afternoon sun. "I tried some art courses this year, but I couldn't paint or sculpt or any of the things I tried. But I still have this terrible urge to *do* something, something creative. I still remember that art museum in Chicago."

Then she told him that after the fiasco of trying to do something artistic with her hands, she had discovered writing. It was

193

too late in the year to get into any classes, but she struggled along on her own. Nobody had seen the stories she wrote. "Would you take a look at them, Nash?" she asked. "Nobody I know, even in Albuquerque, reads as much as you do."

Sarah brought her stories to the shack that night, and read one and parts of several others to the rider, while Ian sat quietly on the bunk. They were wild tales, full of scenes from city life he was sure were reworkings of things Sarah must have read in other books, or else flights of the imagination so erratic and obscure he couldn't make head or tail of them. As softly and uncritically as he could, he told her so.

"Well, for heaven's sake, Nash, what else could I do? The things I know from my own experience simply wouldn't interest anybody!"

"Perhaps you will have to live a little more, *niña*," he said, not entirely sure he knew what he meant.

She looked at him with a funny smile on her face, glanced at Ian, half hidden in the shadows, then looked at the rider again. "You mean like you and Mrs. Bannister?"

Dios! He wondered what his face looked like. Even if he had been able to recognize that Sarah was no longer the *muchachita* who had curled at his feet in the sitting room all those years, he would still have been unprepared to enter this kind of conversational ground with her. Surely they had been through much together: the anguished, horrible night on the train from Chicago; the fight with Jamie when Ian was born; and she, maybe even more than he, himself, had been a witness all through Ann's trials with her husband—but . . .

The next question was, if anything, more embarrassing. "Has there been anybody since, Nash?"

He didn't know if he shook his head in answer to that or to the last thing she said before she and Ian said goodnight, "Will there ever be again?"

When the girl—no, *amigo*, woman—and the boy had gone, he sat at the table and pondered his personal situation as he hadn't done in years. The old, cold constriction was in his chest again as it used to be when he was questioned. What right, he asked himself, did he have to be so private? People like Sarah—there were others, too—cared about him. In his twenty-two years at the D Cross A his condition had changed immeasurably. In some strange way he and Jamie had changed positions, and it was the younger MacAndrews who was alone and orphaned now, even if he didn't know or show it. It made the vaquero feel guilty—as if he had stolen the anglo's birthright.

He dreamed of the wall again that night.

Usually, Douglas MacAndrews cut his activities sharply after roundup, but that summer of 1927 the rancher set himself a pace which disturbed Ignacio and Ann. It was as if there were some time limit set on everything he did.

"Oh, he looks good, Ignacio," Ann said, "but I know for a fact he isn't sleeping well. Sometimes I can hear him prowling the sitting room 'til daybreak. When I say anything he just shushes me." She had wrung a promise from the rider, one he didn't want to keep. *Sí*, he would speak with the señor.

He put it off for a week, ten days, watching Douglas like a hawk and marshalling his courage to talk to him.

Once, when the two of them were on their way to the old grove of cottonwoods where Ignacio had first camped with Angus, Douglas motioned for the vaquero to hold up. "Thought I saw something in that little draw, Ignacio. Wait here for just a second while I check it out." He was on a horse almost identical to the huge brute he had ridden to Corona when Ignacio first knew him, and perhaps it was the sameness of the horse and the difference in the rider which brought the image so quickly and forcibly to mind. As Douglas moved down the slope, the vaquero remembered something he had seen near Deming just days before he came to the D Cross A.

He had been working as a stable boy in a little crossroads town. A crew had been sinking a well behind the livery, and had brought a Studebaker wagon full of iron tools and gear. Parked in a steep place a hundred yards above an arroyo, the wagon unaccountably began to roll, picking up speed too rapidly for any of the workmen to get to it and pull the brake. Ignacio watched as helplessly as the others as the great wagon, with perhaps a ton of weight aboard, rumbled toward the arroyo's edge.

It wasn't a new wagon, but it was in splendid condition, the sides recently varnished and all the brightwork oiled and polished. As it neared the brink of the gully it underwent a change the boy Ignacio could scarcely credit. Doomed as it was, it changed visibly as he watched, becoming a wreck even before its dizzy plunge over the edge began, as if the seeds of destruction had been waiting for this moment to start their growth. He couldn't even recall the crash itself. It didn't matter any more.

He watched Douglas ride into the draw and a cold shiver moved up his spine.

"Guess I was wrong, Ignacio. Nothing down here but horny toads and mice!" the big man shouted back up to his vaquero.

On the return ride, Ignacio kept his promise to Ann.

"Don't worry, Ignacio," Douglas said. "The fact that you and Ann have concerns about me eliminates any I might have myself."

Nevertheless, it didn't escape Ignacio that the señor worked even harder in the days that followed.

28

It was hot in the Cantina Florida. A succession of afternoon suns had worked the heat through the two-feet-thick adobe walls. Old Pablo was sitting in one of the wicker chairs on the porch.

"*Cómo está, viejo?*" Ignacio said. He liked this courtly old man. "*Qué pasa?*"

"I am looking for rain, Ignacio," Pablo said. "Oh, I know this is not truly one of the bad dry times—but I wish it would rain, *verdad*."

Pablo, the vaquero knew, didn't wish it would rain for himself—in his job it didn't matter if it never rained—but for his friends, the *campesinos*. They suffered a good deal more when the rains didn't come than even the most marginal Chupadera rancher. A dry, undernourished cow could make a recovery; it didn't take too many waterless summer days in a row to ruin a Río Concho crop.

He went inside, and finding Jorge busy, opened two bottles of beer, took them back out to the porch, and gave one to the porter.

"I have known a bad, *bad*, dry time," Pablo said. He was talking to himself more than to Ignacio. "It was many years ago— I do not know how many. There is nothing worse in any country. Every year that goes by brings us closer to the next one."

Ignacio patted the old man gently on the shoulder. Together they looked westward across the adobes of Mex Town. A narrowing band of gold was all that remained of another torrid day—that and a fringe of red which warned of a clear night and another hot, fair day tomorrow. Down the street, toward the church,

197

strummed by unseen hands on another porch, a guitar sent a few plaintive notes through the still air. Somewhere a goat bleated. A baby was whimpering, as if in answer, in the house across from the cantina. Ignacio felt a wave of melancholy wash over him. It wasn't an unpleasant feeling, but he knew he should go inside before it changed. He left Pablo and sought his familiar table.

In less than half a minute he heard the door to the family's quarters open and close, and in a flicker of white and red, Concepción moved past him, making her way to the bar where three drinkers had already made their start on the evening.

Without so much as looking over her shoulder, Concepción said, "Good evening, *Mister* Ortiz." No matter that the room was like an oven, ice frosted the greeting, and Ignacio smiled, thinking back to the days when Jorge used to employ this method of exclusion.

When she picked up a tray and passed by him to clear the table next to his, he hid his smile, and in a voice every bit as cold— if forced—said, "*Señorita*, bring me a tequila—no, a bottle, *por favor*." He accented the *por favor* heavily, sarcastically, suddenly feeling a little vexed himself. Foolish woman, he thought, foolish, silly woman. Why should you be angry with this old friend? I wasn't trying to run your life that last time we talked.

Basta! Enough, he would leave, go across the tracks to the Black Springs plaza and listen to the town band. Old Señor Kelly at the livery stable would be grateful for his company. He didn't find much to occupy him nowadays, with his son concentrating more on the filling station end of the business than on horses. Then he could bed down in the stall with Gavilán and ride home again in the morning. It might be his last long ride on the old pony. He would turn Gavilán out to pasture next week, most likely. Well, he would leave after one more drink. It wouldn't do to take only one after insisting on a bottle.

Three drinks later he was still deciding to go. That was when Jim Gibbon came through the doorway from the porch. Ignacio stared at him dully. The fear didn't stir immediately, probably the tequila held it back a bit, but Concepción was right—he hated this massive brute. As a matter of pride he couldn't leave now, couldn't let this man who never even looked at him or talked to him push him out of *his* cantina.

The Western Union man was in a suit which had been pressed until it shined, the fabric stretched so tight across his back it looked as hard and unyielding as sheet metal. Ignacio stared hard at Gibbon's back, and had two more tequilas while he stared.

Then Concepción was at the bar, standing next to the telegrapher. Gibbon turned and spoke to her, and Ignacio poured himself another drink—and another.

"Wake up, Ignacio! *Amigo! Por favor.* I must close up now." It was Jorge, shaking him.

Ignacio raised his head from an arm numb from the weight of it, and looked around. Except for Jorge and himself the bar room was empty. It must be very late. Most of the lamps were out, and Jorge had already turned the chairs upside down and put them on all the tables except Ignacio's. The rider was still a little drunk and very sleepy. He tried to shake his head to clear it, but the motion gave him a headache and he stopped at once. At least the stab of pain had done the trick. His eyes focused better and he felt he could begin to think.

Sí, thoughts came—but the first one brought a surge of panic. "Concepción! Where is she, Jorge?"

He was amazed Jorge only smiled. What was the matter with the man that he didn't share his alarm?

"I do not know, *amigo.*" Jorge was grinning widely now. "Somewhere in back, I think—asleep. It is nearly three in the morning, Ignacio, but I'll go back and wake her if you wish." The grin was pleasantly wicked, and at another time the rider would have been covered with embarrassment, but now the look was reassuring. Jorge went on, "*Amigo,* never have I seen you *borracho* like this!"

Ignacio found his hat, said, "*Buenas noches*, Jorge," and left the cantina.

He stood on the porch for a while, as he had earlier in the evening. Earlier in the evening? Hah! Last night, yesterday. The air had chilled, and he removed his hat to let a slight breeze blow through his damp hair. A glance at the sky, full of stars and without out a patch of cloud around to hide them, told him the red sunset he had watched with Pablo had been an accurate forecaster. It wouldn't rain tonight.

The cooler air drove some of the mists from his memory of the evening in the cantina. It had been like a weird dance, the way Concepción had moved around Gibbon while Ignacio drank. From time to time she would glance toward his table, and he remembered the spiteful looks she gave him. Once she stuck out her tongue at him. He had tried to dismiss this as childishness, but he had promptly doubled the size of the drinks he poured himself.

It was all of no consequence now. Jorge had just assured him Concepción was in her own bed, asleep, hadn't he? Besides, need he remind himself it was none of his business? Yes, he did remember her going to the back, and Gibbon leaving the cantina. The vision he had in front of him now, of the Western Union man handing a note to Concepción just before they parted company, was pure imagination. He could forget about the whole thing and go on to Kelly's.

The vaquero left the porch. There wasn't a sound except for the plop of his boots in the dust of Frontera Street all the way to the tracks. His progress was unsteady, and as he started down the embankment he tripped, rolling wildly to the gravel ballast which leveled out where the goathead weed stopped. He lay there for a moment, while a dog barked somewhere over in Black Springs. Struggling to his feet again, he stepped with care between the wooden ties and the smooth, worn rails, seeing just the faintest reflection of the stars on the polished iron.

As he left the tracks behind him he saw the street lights on the anglo side of town go out. He felt alone, useless, and disgusted with himself to have gotten so drunk. Concepción must have looked at him with nausea—and he hadn't even been aware of it. Her hot, angry words of recent weeks would turn to no words at all, and Jorge must, in spite of his smile, be ready to cross him off the cantina list.

To add to his discomfort, a pressure on his groin reminded him he hadn't relieved himself since he reached the cantina. If he didn't do something quickly, something else would happen and really crown the humiliation he had already brought upon himself. He could take care of this chore right here—there surely was no one about at this ungodly hour—but a nagging desire to restore some small measure of dignity made him seek the alley between the freight house and the depot.

Once in the junk-littered passageway, he realized he was only a matter of feet from where Gibbon lived in a couple of rooms built on to the depot itself. In spite of the way he was feeling about himself, he smiled at the thought of what simple justice it was to urinate almost on Gibbon's doorsill.

He leaned against the freight house wall and fumbled with the buttons of his pants, only then noticing the razor thin line of light around the shade edges in the window across the alley. Gibbon was still awake? As late as this?

Then he heard the voices behind the shade, and he froze.

The telegrapher's voice ripped savagely at someone in the room with him. "Don't give me that shit, *señorita*! It's a little late to beg off now."

The answering voice was muted and indistinct, freighted with terror, but full of defiance, too. *Concepción!*

Before her voice died away, Gibbon, raging now, spoke again. "Huh-uh, *Connie*, baby. It's what you came here for—and you'll get it! Better you relax and not get hurt. Won't do no good to holler rape. Ain't one soul in the whole fucking town would take the word of a greaser cunt like you! Now, GET BACK ON THAT BED!"

Horror gripped Ignacio. What in the name of *Dios* could he do? He could shout, try the door, take a beating from Gibbon if necessary—but would it stop him? The ox in the room could stretch him senseless and still complete the obscene violence he was starting now. And even if he did stop him, there would be other times. For the first time in his life, Ignacio Ortiz would willingly, gladly, have used a weapon.

Trying to part the blackness with his eyes, he looked about him in the dark alley for a club, a rock, *anything*. He moved toward Gibbon's door, and as he did his foot struck something and he bent to pick it up. Heavy, terribly heavy, it slipped from his fingers, and he dropped to his knees and groped in the dirt until he found it and secured it as well as he could in his two trembling hands. He guessed it to be some forgotten railroad gear, perhaps a pinch bar. *Sí*, that's what it was. He lifted it and its weight left him in despair. There was no way he could swing the heavy thing.

From the room he could hear Concepción more clearly now. The defiance was gone. Pleading took its place.

He discovered he was holding the iron as if it were a lance. He braced himself and looked at Gibbon's door, then, at the last second, he shifted from this target to the window, and charged across the narrow alley with every bit of force he could muster.

The tip of the bar struck the window sash squarely between the upper and lower panes of glass, and he felt the shock of impact for a fraction of a second before the whole frame gave way. It sailed into the room, the breaking glass and splintering wood hitting the floor inside with a crash which roared out and echoed off the freight house wall behind him.

Gibbon was naked. His body, half turned to the window, was white as a slug. Immediately the rider knew he wouldn't stay motionless like this for long, and he prepared to withdraw the pinch bar and run it right into the belly of the telegrapher. Then, he caught sight of Concepción and stopped.

She was crouched on a bed against the wall, the red skirt pulled up to her waist and whatever she had worn beneath it torn to shreds. Her blouse was gone, too, and tatters of flimsy clothing were tangled with the unkempt bedding.

Gibbon moved, just an arm, and only a fraction of an inch, but Ignacio knew all the time he could hope for had about run out.

"Concepción!" he called. "Get your clothes and leave!" When she didn't move at once, just lay there on the rumpled bed as if paralyzed or dead, he nearly shrieked. "*Vámonos*, Concepción! *AHORA!*"

She sat up, and her legs swung crazily over the edge of the bed. The red skirt, vivid as a splotch of blood in the dim light, cascaded down over her brown thighs as she stood. He saw her breasts quiver, hanging away from her body when she bent to pick up the pitiful remnants of her white lace blouse.

She clutched the rags of her undergarments to her and slid around Gibbon, and in less than a breath the door opened and she was in the street beside him. In the light from the window he found her eyes, and then, without a word, she was past him, running out of the alley and across the tracks.

He looked back in the room. Gibbon hadn't really moved, but the blank surprise was leaving his face. Ignacio turned and left the alley, walking, but swiftly, toward Frontera Street.

Then he realized his pants were soaking. The fear he hadn't had time for had caught up with him.

A dozen savage line squalls marched across the Ojos Negros like assault troops, following electrical displays of awesome power and ferocity. Between the storms and after them, undaunted by the high voltage commotion in the basin, the sun beat down even more intensely than in the static days before the rain. Drenched, streaked, and scored by the waters which became a hundred little rivers on the D Cross A, coddled by the sun's heat crusting these rough-edged wounds, the pastures made the grass.

October only whispered its arrival, pushing warm, dry breezes through the arroyos, breezes that spun the windmills and set their off-key reassurances creaking above tanks suddenly and joyfully overflowing.

When the D Cross A was as ready for winter as it would ever be, Ignacio knew he had to get to town and see Concepción.

29

"DON'T EVEN TRY TO GET UP UNTIL I SAY SO, ORTIZ, UNDERSTAND?"
Dr. Sam Colvin said, withdrawing the needle from Ignacio's arm.
"And I mean not for *anything*. I'll give you another shot for the
pain tonight, and when you can take something by mouth I'll
have Joe Lenzinger fix some pills.

"Far as I can tell, there's no internal damage, apart from the
cracked ribs, but whoever beat you up sure as hell did a good job.
I understand Mrs. Martínez and her sister-in-law will be looking
after you."

The doctor snapped the black bag shut and left the room at
the back of the Cantina Florida. Jorge and María were standing
in the hall, and Dr. Sam crooked his finger at the woman, who
followed him out of sight.

Jorge came in and sat in the chair the doctor had used.
"Cómo estás, amigo?" he said. He held up his hand in a quick,
fluttering movement. "No, no, Ignacio. Do not try to talk, *por
favor*! You might tear out those wires in your jaws, and the
doctor would have it all to do again." Jorge was silent for a
moment. "Perhaps," he said, "we can prepare some way for you
to write. It is necessary for me to know who did this."

Two hours earlier, Ignacio couldn't have told him if he
wanted to. When he regained consciousness, he knew he had to
be somewhere in Mex Town. Anglo rooms didn't usually have a
picture of the Virgin on the wall, and there were few with wooden
chests like the crude one in the corner with the carved handles. He
guessed he must be in the Florida, but what he was doing there,
and why he was in such agony, he hadn't the dimmest notion.

It must have been a full minute before he realized that the small figure at the end of the bed was Ian MacAndrews.

"How are you, Tío Nash?" the boy said, and as Ignacio tried to lift his head and was defeated by the pain, he could see Ian's face, white with worry—and the whole thing flooded back in on him again. "I came right here for Señor Martínez," Ian said. "After what you said before you passed out, I figured you didn't want me to go for Sheriff Lane."

Yes, he remembered it all now. He remembered how he had ridden Pavo, the new young spotted horse who looked so much like Calico, down the old yucca bordered south road, and he remembered picking Ian up at Stafford's and letting the boy ride Pavo down to Kelly's, and how fine Ian had looked on the frisky newly broken pony. How fine he himself had felt on his way to see Concepción Martínez to tell her what she had to do to take care of herself—and that it was in a way, "his business."

What he didn't remember—and knew he never would—was what stupidity had prompted him to go through the alley where Gibbon lived.

"When you quit talking, I thought you were dead," Ian said.

At that, he had almost cleared the alley and reached the tracks. He saw the pinch bar lying there, and the new sash, still unpainted, in the window of the room.

"Ortiz!" It was a harsh, animal cry, and even before he turned, he knew it was Jim Gibbon. There was no mistaking the man's intentions. He was out for blood, lust for it clear in the distorted face, but the telegrapher had blundered. Calling out like that had given the vaquero all the time he needed. With fifty feet between them, Ignacio could run for it, easily make Mex Town and the ·cantina before Gibbon could catch him. Once at the Florida it was unlikely the Western Union man would start a fracas. As Gibbon took the first step, Ignacio set himself for flight.

Then, his eye caught something else beyond the man. At the far end of the alley, he saw Ian. How long the boy had been there, or what his errand was, the vaquero had no way of knowing, but he did know that any thought of fleeing now was gone. He couldn't run—not with Ian there. He waited for whatever impact Gibbon's rush would bring.

He caught the first blow on his forearm, but the second, crashing through, landed with staggering force squarely on his chin. It was as if the bones at the back of his jaw had become unhinged, and splintered ends had been driven through his eardrums. The pain from that blow screamed inside his head, but with each one after that the sound diminished until the whole affair was wrapped in silence.

Gibbon held him by the shirt front with one hand and beat him with the other, steadily—endlessly it seemed—working his way up and down the rider's body and about his head. Then, suddenly, it was over. The hand which held him was withdrawn, and Ignacio toppled forward, clutching at Gibbon in one desperate attempt to remain erect, but the telegrapher stepped back and let him fall. When he struck the ground, the vaquero wondered, almost idly, how the earth could shake so much when struck by a body whose very weight and substance had been clubbed away.

He tasted blood spilling over his chin, sweet, warm, red lakes of it, and he knew his nose must be a shapeless mass, but he breathed easily, and the pain was gone.

Gibbon had left, and Ignacio looked up to see Ian standing over him. "Tío Nash!" The small voice seemed to come from miles away. "Tell me what to do!"

"Just tell no one, Ian. Tell *no one* who did this thing!"

Then the pain returned. It hurt to breathe, and he knew something terrible had happened inside his chest, and the blood in his nose began to clot, and some of it in his throat was choking him—and he began a long, spiralling descent into the dark.

Now, here was Jorge, good, earnest Jorge, asking him who had done it. Oh, he would tell him eventually, would have to, or it would be a flat denial of their friendship, but not until he was on his feet again. Told now, Jorge would set off on a rampage of his own.

"What I do not understand," Jorge was saying, "is *why*. There isn't one man in the Ojos Negros I would call your enemy."

So, the rider thought, Concepción has never talked about that night.

A shadow led someone down the hall, and then Concepción came into the room. Jorge had left his lamp burning when he left, and he hadn't slept, even as tired as he was. When Concepción came in he gave up trying. On the tray she carried, a bowl of soup steamed its fragrance through the room. He saw a piece of glass tubing in the bowl, and turned his head so she could feed him. Looking toward her, he faced the lamp, and the light hurt his eyes, even though they were still almost swollen shut. She must have noticed, for she reached behind her and lowered the wick until the flame was almost gone. He could see her better now, and he saw the sorrow and apology he hoped she would never voice.

"The little snip won't tell me a thing, Ignacio," Ann said, while Ian smiled a rare smile. "No matter that I remind him I'm his mother—he just says he promised you."

Ignacio tried to mumble through his wired jaws, but gave it up. He wanted to tell Señora Ann how good it was to see her, tell her how unnecessary her apology for Jamie was. It was just as well he couldn't. He had seen the shadow cross Ian's face when Ann said Jamie was in El Paso. Hadn't the boy been in the hall yesterday when Jorge gossiped about the rancher's son spending the last three nights in Black Springs with the anglo woman whose name Ignacio, drowsy from drugs, hadn't caught? He hadn't expected Jamie, anyway. The Cantina Florida hadn't seen his blonde head for thirteen years.

The question the vaquero really wanted to ask was where was Señor Douglas? He couldn't think of anything to keep *him* away, but it had been over a week now, and there hadn't been so much as a word from the rancher. There had been something strained about Ann's face when she came through the door, and it puzzled and worried him. It planted a nagging seed of fear in his mind. Douglas was angry with him. Well, he couldn't blame him. He remembered the big man's reaction, the look of personal humiliation, when Jamie's trouble happened, and Ignacio's affair must have shocked and disappointed the owner of the D Cross A to a terrible degree.

"Tío Nash," Ian said, "I've got to get back to school, but I'll come and see you again tomorrow."

The youngster hadn't missed a day. Usually, he brought some of his art work, and would spend an hour making sketches. He seldom spoke, but it was good to have him there.

"Run along, Ian," Ann said. "I'll stop by Stafford's after shopping, to say goodbye."

When the boy disappeared, she turned to the rider. Suddenly her face darkened, and she shook her head. She is having more trouble with Jamie, he thought. It must be that, but even so he had seldom seen her look so defeated, so despairing. Silently he cursed the circumstances which kept him chained here. He should be at the D Cross A. There probably wasn't a great deal he could do for her, but he would *be* there. Long ago he had convinced himself that if he suffered when she suffered, it helped a little—helped him, anyway.

She seemed about to speak again, when Concepción came in. "Excuse me, *señora*," she said to Ann. "It is nearly time for Ignacio to bathe himself."

"Of course, Miss Martínez," Ann said. (Out of the past he heard Agnes say "Miss Martínez," but so differently.) The woman from the D Cross A went on, "I was just leaving. And Miss Martínez, thank you for looking after him the way you are. Bless you for it."

"*De nada, señora*. Ignacio *es mi amigo*." The vaquero would have smiled—but for the wires in his jaw—at the way Concepción was acting so *Mexican*, and comic Mexican at that, casting her eyes down, slurring the Spanish. Under the tape and the pain, he felt much, much better.

When Concepción had gone, Ann said, "One thing, Ignacio, you have a truly beautiful nurse." Her brow furrowed. "Wasn't she the girl who—?" She stopped, and her blush seemed to warm the room. No, she had not forgotten, but she harbored no ill will.

Then, as she rose and looked down at him, he could see that Concepción Martínez was no longer on her mind. With his head flat on the pillow he hadn't seen her as clearly when she was seated as he did now. She was smiling down at him, but something was wrong, terribly wrong. He must hurry and get well and return to her.

It was another two weeks before he could even get out of bed. The wires were gone from his jaw and he could eat some solid food again, but the liquid diet had left him weak as a shoot of new spring grass, and it was all he could do to move down the hall to the toilet. His ribs and neck pained him fearfully as he walked, but it was so much better to make the trip than to use the bedpan Dr. Sam had insisted on, which Concepción, to his mortification, had to empty several times a day.

Gradually, the pain diminished, leaving behind only those twinges which told him the tortured sinew and bone were knitting. He was on the mend, but much as he wanted to get back to the D Cross A and make amends to Douglas—the rancher still hadn't come to see him, and it weighed on him—he wasn't in any condition to return to the ranch just yet.

For one thing, there was the trouble with his right eye. When he first found himself in what turned out to be Concepción's room, there had been bad double vision, and although it had cleared up in a couple of days, it returned when least expected. Worse, however, was the needle pain which seemed to pierce the eyeball from time to time—and the sudden momentary dimming of his sight. With his jaw wired shut, he couldn't tell Dr. Sam, and now, for some reason, he didn't want to.

To his surprise, he received a "hurry and get well" card from Jamie. At the bottom was a scribbled not, "Get back quick, amigo. Big doings at the D Cross A. You'll want in on them."

He wondered if the señor would want him "in on them."

The only time he thought of Gibbon was when Jorge was camped in the chair beside the bed, but that was often enough. When Dr. Sam took the wires from his jaw and he could talk, he feared his friend would badger him for the name of his assailant, but Jorge brought the subject up only that once—the day he awoke in the cantina. The vaquero didn't fool himself, though. The curiosity was still there, tucked away someplace in the fine, dark head.

They talked books—and politics; or rather, Jorge did.

"You mean you aren't even registered to vote?" Jorge asked.

"Jorge, you forget. I am not even a citizen. If I should ask to vote, they might deport me."

"Too bad, *amigo*. We will need every vote next year, when the New York governor, Smith, runs for the presidency."

"Why are you so strong for him, Jorge?"

"He is a Catholic, like you and me, Ignacio. He will understand some things," Jorge said, his voice strong and positive. Ignacio thought it over.

"Jorge, aren't you afraid he'll turn out to be much more anglo than Catholic? You have always said these *'gringos'* are all alike."

The cantina owner tried to look confident, but the vaquero could see some doubt in his face, and he smiled.

After five weeks, he was able to make it to the bar room. He tried to pick times when the place was empty, when even the *campesinos* weren't around. The thought of answering questions, particularly in front of Jorge, made him quake inside, and he would nurse one small beer and get back down the hall whenever any patron—friend or stranger—entered.

Pepe came to see him once. The cowhand was uneasy, and Ignacio thought it must be because of his condition. He stammered the usual things, but kept his eyes averted from the traces of the battering still evident on the vaquero's face, and Ignacio was relieved when he took his leave.

The visit reminded him that he had seen Señora Ann only once. As cautiously as he could, he asked Ian if *he* had seen his mother, and when the youngster said he hadn't, Ignacio decided it was time to go.

"When you see her, Ian, tell her, *por favor*, I would like her to come and get me when she can. It is time for me to return to work."

"*Sí*, a party. Tonight, *amigo*!" Jorge said, his eyes gleaming. "*Señora* MacAndrews sent word she will come for you tomorrow, so tonight is the only chance we have."

"It is not necessary, Jorge," Ignacio said. "Really, my friend, I would prefer you didn't."

"You misunderstand, Ignacio." Jorge's mouth opened in mock surprise. "This party is not for *you*. I wouldn't embarrass you like that, *amigo*. Unfortunately, the real guest of honor won't be there either. Well, we shall do our best without him."

"Who is this 'guest of honor', Jorge?"

"Why, *Señor* Gibbon, of course, the big Western Union *hombre* from the depot. We all wished to say *'adiós'* to him here at the Florida—tonight, a farewell party—but he had to leave for El Paso on the train this morning."

"Gibbon has gone?"

"*Sí*. A very sudden thing. He resigned his job last night."
Jorge smiled broadly and then went on, "He hadn't come to the
cantina in a month and a half, and his friends worried about him
and paid a call—to see if he had troubles they could help with."

"Friends?"

"Yes, *amigo*, the *campesinos* and the others he drank with
here: old Sánchez from the Río Concho; Lobo Mendoza, that
big *paisano* who did some fighting a few years back; many
others—and oh, yes, I, Martínez, I was there. I simply couldn't
stay away. He didn't really want to leave. Well, we helped him
pack his things, and took them to the freight dock for him. Then
some of us spent the night with him, so he wouldn't get too
lonely." Jorge sighed, and rolled his black eyes toward the ceiling.
"Ah, but at the train this morning," he went on, "that was wonderful, *magnifico verdad*! There were speeches, flowers—even a
mariachi band. Gibbon was so choked up he couldn't say a word.
And he didn't look well, either—not well at all."

So Concepción had told her brother.

"You see, *amigo*," Jorge said, "you must come to the
party."

"*Sí*, Jorge. I will come."

It began quietly enough, but by midnight it was a lively
affair. He had never seen the *campesinos* so gay. They trooped
in singly and in small groups, each of them pausing at Ignacio's
table to shake his hand in smiling silence. The music from the
mariachi band—it must have been the same one which piped
Gibbon off that morning—made the walls of the old bar room
throb.

Jorge, like so many of the others, drank far too much. He
toasted Mendoza, Carlos, and Ignacio several times, but never
so much as mentioned the "guest of honor," nor did any of the
others. At last, as the crowd thinned out and the musicians
departed with their instruments, he sank bleary-eyed and weary
into the empty chair at the vaquero's table.

"Fine *hombres*, are they not, *amigo*?" Jorge said, waving
grandly to the last of the *campesinos*. "Even the ones who weren't
with us know they are men—always have been. And it is because

of *you*! Don't shake your head, my friend, it is true. You have always known some things we didn't."

Jorge looked sober now. "There is something I didn't tell you this morning, Ignacio. Last night, when we called on Gibbon, some of the men who helped us were from the railroad crews—anglos."

He was back in the room, preparing to undress for bed when she came in. "*Sí*, Concepción?" he said.

"May I speak with you now, Ignacio?"

He motioned her to the big chair but she shook her head.

"You must know," she said, "that I was the one who told Jorge. I am sorry if this makes you angry, Ignacio, and I know you made Ian promise not to tell—but I could take no chance on something else happening to you."

"It worked out, Concepción."

"Now don't say goodnight just yet, Ignacio." She crossed the room to the chair. "I think I *will* sit down. My legs feel weak."

So did his, and he leaned back against the bed. Concepción was breathing heavily, and her color was high, as if she had just come in from the sun.

"Ignacio," she said, "I want to be your woman!" It was said with considerable force, as if she expected resistance from her vocal cords. "There, Ignacio. It is out. The rest will be easier."

When she went on, her voice was earnest, but not pleading. "Why not, Ignacio? Sally Bannister is gone now—and you can never have the other one. Don't look so pained, of course I know. I have no one either. No one. And it's been how many years since her husband—" She paused for breath. "You need someone, and so do I. Is that so bad a thing to say?"

He took a moment before he answered. "No, Concepción. Between us nothing could be bad, but—what about your people, Jorge?"

"Ignacio!" For the tiniest part of a second her eyes blazed, and he thought she would leave. Then softly, "Do you have loyalty to everyone but yourself?"

He didn't answer.

"Do you want me, Ignacio?"

Yes, he did. He nodded.

"Then don't make me come to you—take me."

He walked across the room, pulled her to her feet and took her in his arms. His poor battered chest should have hurt, but it didn't.

Ann didn't say a word after he got into the car in front of the cantina, but Ignacio was grateful for the opportunity to be alone with himself. Even with the señora alongside him, Concepción ruled his thoughts. With luck he could keep his mind too busy to think about seeing Señor Douglas, until he had to. Then he would just have to face up to whatever the rancher had to say. There was no point in worrying about it now.

From time to time, though, he glanced at Ann as they hummed along the blacktop toward the ranch road. It was a gray day, and with the canvas top up, her face was in partial shadow; but that only accounted for part of its lowered color, and with every mile closer to the ranch her features darkened. Then they made the turn and were thumping over the cattle guard opposite the big sign which read, Cuchillo Livestock Company— D Cross A—MacAndrews.

In another mile they would reach the high ground and he would see the butte, the arroyo, and beyond them, the ranch itself. Even with the prospect facing him—and Concepción back in town—it would be good to be home. They passed a small group of cattle and he saw they were in good shape to go into winter. The summer rains had done their work, and even if the grass was browning out a little, there was still a wealth of nourishment in it. Yes, it was good to see that the D Cross A hadn't changed.

Then, as they rolled to the top of the high ground, he saw it. Rising out of the ground near the foundation of the house which was never finished, looking like a black, ugly growth, was an oil derrick. Grouped around it were trucks, buildings—one of them an outhouse—and a donkey engine belching black smoke into a dismal sky. There were perhaps a dozen overall-clad men on the scene. None of them looked up as the car moved down the slope toward them, and when Ann stopped the car and switched it off he could see why. The donkey engine was sounding away like a stampede on slickrock. Even when Ann leaned over and yelled in his ear he could hardly hear.

"Well, you've seen it, Ignacio. Horrible, isn't it?"

One of the men detached himself from the others and pointed with a finger of authority toward the engine. In a moment it was idling and the man who had pointed was walking toward them.

"Howdy, Mrs. MacAndrews," he said.

"Mr. Shepard, this is our foreman, Ignacio Ortiz," Ann said, and the man nodded to the vaquero.

"Nothing yet, ma'am," Shepard said. "You know, I sure don't want to kid anybody. It just don't look promising to me."

Ann nodded as the man went on, "If you would, ma'am, tell your husband I'll come by the house tomorrow and give him my report. Hope it's better news than I've got right now."

"I'll tell him, Mr. Shepard—and thank you." Ann started the car again and they rolled away toward the butte. When Ignacio looked at her, he saw that her eyes were streaming tears.

Once more she stopped the car, this time to take a handkerchief from her purse. When her cheeks were dry the rider dared the question which had burned his tongue since his first sight of the rig and the drilling crew.

"How did it come about, *Señora* Ann, that *Señor* Douglas permitted this?"

She drew a breath. "Oh, Ignacio, he doesn't know—*he doesn't know!*" Great sobs came then, and they cracked his heart.

He saw the woman struggle to control them, and he waited in silence until they had run their course. Finally, they stopped, and she turned to him.

"I didn't tell you when I came to see you at the Florida, Ignacio—too afraid it might hurt your recovery. And I didn't come again, because I knew you'd ask—and I couldn't lie to you."

"*Qué pasa, señora?* Tell me, *por favor!* What has happened to *Señor* Douglas?" He felt nothing, but heard the fright in his voice.

"He's had a stroke—a bad one, Ignacio. It happened the day you rode to town—in the afternoon, probably at about the time you—well, anyway, Jamie was gone, too, with the car, and the hands were all out somewhere in the pastures. I didn't miss Douglas until supper time, but when he didn't come in I went looking for him. I found him in the tack room, slumped over that old tarp-covered saddle in the corner. It took all three of us, Sarah, Angélica, and me, to get him to the house. I'd never realized,

I guess, just how big he was—he's such a gentle man. When the hands came in, we sent Pepe for file doctor."

She stopped talking. The pain in her face was more than he could bear, and he looked away. The clouds in the west had parted, but the November sun provided no warmth at all.

"You won't know him, Ignacio. And—he won't know you either. The worst of it is—he won't get better, ever, according to Dr. Sam."

* * *

Ignacio waited in the sitting room for Ann, who had stopped in the kitchen with Angélica. She had told him to go right in to Douglas, but he couldn't—not without her. He wondered where Sarah was. He could understand now why she hadn't come to the Florida, either. Ann had told him, as they parked the car, of the fights between the girl and Jamie, after Douglas's stroke.

"Now she rides, almost all day long, whenever Jamie is on the D Cross A," Ann said.

Something was wrong in the sitting room. Douglas's big overstuffed chair was missing. The only thing in front of the fireplace was the delicate little rocker Agnes used, and he was amazed it had survived unbroken all these years. He felt empty as he looked to where the big chair had been; the one with the Navaho blanket thrown across it. It had probably gone no further than the bedroom, but that could be another country.

Beckoning, Ann moved past him toward the hall.

"It is Ignacio, *Señor* Douglas," the vaquero said. There was no answer from the man in the big chair. He was looking out the window of the bedroom, and didn't move when the rider spoke. Ignacio couldn't see his face. Perhaps he hadn't spoken loudly enough. He tried again.

"It is Ignacio, *señor*. Ignacio Ortiz."

Douglas MacAndrews turned and faced his foreman. The mouth Ignacio remembered as being so firm was slack, and Douglas's left shoulder sagged. The arm on that side lay across the huge chest as if it had been draped there, the once-strong hand limp in the rancher's lap, seemingly devoid of life. The big man's mouth worked a little, as if it were trying to form words, but no sound came out.

There was a terrible ache in Ignacio's chest which had nothing at all to do with his injuries. He couldn't fool himself for an instant that there was even a flicker of recognition in those eyes which had faded from strong, deep blue to the pale gray of the sky outside the window. It was over.

Talk with this ruin would be useless, but Ignacio didn't leave. Maybe—*por favor, Dios*—maybe something above and beyond words and recognition could take place here! Maybe there could be, just this once, some higher, stronger touching between Ignacio Ortiz and Douglas MacAndrews of the D Cross A. He forced his mind upward and outward until the blood pounded in his head. Listen to your vaquero, *Señor* Douglas—listen!

He stayed until the window was just four square panes of blackness, until the hulk in the chair gave itself to restless, tormented sleep, bound, like great Lear, "upon a wheel of fire."

He turned to go, stopped at the door, and turned back again. "*Señor* Douglas," he whispered, "I have come back to tell you that—*the fence is tight*."

In twenty-three years at the D Cross A, it was the only real lie he had ever told.

With the door shut for six weeks now, the shack was as musty as a tomb. He lay down on his bunk and stared sightlessly at the black ceiling, unaware that time was passing. He hadn't the faintest idea how long he had lain there when the knock came. It was Sarah.

"Oh, God but it's good to have you back here, Nash! Hey! You don't look near as bad as I expected from what I'd heard."

Suddenly he was appalled, then angered, that this pretty girl in front of him could be smiling, laughing. Then, blessedly before he could say a word, he realized she had already lived with this horror for six weeks. It was only for him, Ignacio, that the blow had real immediacy. Life, after all, did possess this criminal habit of continuing—even when it shouldn't.

"*Cómo estás, muchachita?*"

She was fine, she said. Well, things *could* be better. Jamie was being a genuine bastard, but she'd fix *his* clock. Damned good thing he, Nash, was back to run the D Cross A. Pepe had told her about the feed not ordered, and the salt blocks needed at number three. She'd ridden out to see for herself.

Five hundred head should be run to other pastures, too, and it shouldn't wait.

"If he'd only move the cattle with half the speed he moved his father," she said. Oh, *sí*, the sorrow was still there under the bitterness and anger.

"Moved?"

"Wouldn't have him in the sitting room. Said he couldn't bear it. Hell of a lot he cares. Truth is, it keeps him from feeling guilty about the drilling if he doesn't have to look at Daddy."

"Where is Jamie, *niña*?"

"God only knows! Probably out in the truck, looking for more places to punch his filthy holes in the D Cross A!"

Ignacio didn't see Jamie until the next afternoon. The rider didn't go in for supper, and he had breakfast in the bunk house with Curly Decker and Pepe, telling himself there were things to talk about with them and the boy Billy Joe that couldn't wait.

He knew he shouldn't—Dr. Sam had been stern about this—but he saddled a horse and rode up toward the rocks, thinking he had to get to town one day and bring back Pavo. The jolting ride took a great deal out of him, and when he rēached the outcropping he had to dismount and rest.

Back in the compound he could see Jamie leave the house and walk toward the truck. In the middle of the yard he stopped and the vaquero saw him look up to where he sat. Thirty seconds must have gone by before Jamie waved. It was a careless, offhand gesture, the kind he could have made, Ignacio thought, if the rider had never been away. Then, Jamie was in the truck, and roaring down the road.

The vaquero did go in for lunch, and he made another visit to the rancher. Prepared as he was, it wasn't any better, but the worst of it was the realization that he would get used to it.

At three in the afternoon, Jamie drove up the road. When Ignacio saw Dr. Sam's Model T behind him, he thought for one foolish moment that young MacAndrews had gone to town to fetch him, but the way the two greeted each other when they parked the vehicles, he knew this joint arrival was mere coincidence.

"After I've seen Mr. MacAndrews, I'd like a look at you, Ortiz," the doctor said.

"Good to see you, *amigo*," Jamie said.

"It is very good to be back, Jamie."

"Tough break for the old man."

"*Sí.*"

"'Course, he wasn't young, and we couldn't expect him to last forever. He had a damned good life, you know."

Dios, he is not dead yet, Jamie!

"But you, Nash. Jesus you're a tough little *hombre*! From what I hear, a lot of men would be dead—what you took."

Jamie walked toward the truck, turned and came back. "I got a million things to do, but I guess it wouldn't look right if I moseyed out of here before Doc Sam's had his say." He walked back to the truck again and sat on the running board, picked up a handful of stones and began pitching them into the dust.

Can't you at least go inside and be with the doctor, Jamie, Ignacio thought.

The soft thud of the stones hitting the caliche dust seemed as loud as drumbeats. When Jamie had thrown them all he got another handful and started in again.

In no more than ten minutes (it seemed ten hours) the doctor came out through the kitchen door. Ignacio could see Ann's figure in the doorway. She disappeared without speaking to her husband.

"It's like I told you, Jamie," the doctor said. "We don't know a lot about these things. One thing sure, the brain damage is massive—recovery of the mental faculties absolutely out of the question—and if another comes, most likely it will take him.

"There you are, Ortiz. Why don't you go on down to that place of yours? Strip to the waist and I'll be right with you."

The doctor had finished with him, but before he left the shack, he looked searchingly at the vaquero. "Have you had trouble with that right eye you haven't told me about, Ortiz?"

Not wishing to lie to someone as intent as Dr. Sam on helping him, Ignacio decided to say nothing.

"All right, don't tell me. You'll soon be as sound as a dollar every place else, but there's something there I plain don't like the look of. We'd need an eye man if anything goes wrong, so keep in touch, hear?"

30

THE FIRST TIME IAN MACANDREWS SAW HIS GRANDFATHER AFTER the stroke was at Thanksgiving. His mother took the boy into Douglas's room and came out alone. It was nearly an hour before Ian came back into the sitting room and joined Ignacio on the couch in front of the fire, where the vaquero was reading a magazine—or trying to.

If Ian is ever going to cry, the rider thought, now will be the time, but the dark eyes remained as dry as they had in Ignacio's sick room at the Florida.

"Where's my Dad, Tío Nash?" Ian said.

"I think he's out at the oil rig, Ian."

The fire spat and crackled. A bad wind outside was causing an uneven draft.

"Tío Nash—who is Angus?"

Douglas must have been talking. He did sometimes.

"He was your grandfather's brother."

"Was?"

"*Sí*, Ian. He has been dead many years. His grave is in the badlands, way to the north."

"But still on the D Cross A." It wasn't quite a question. "Will you take me there some time, Tío Nash?"

"*Sí*, Ian."

"I guess I do remember hearing about this Angus, but it wasn't my Dad who told me. How come, Tío Nash?"

"I—I do not know, Ian."

Dios! This one would be hard to lie to.

Jamie's oil venture was a failure, but he wouldn't admit it.

The rider was impressed with the drilling boss, Shepard—a man of real integrity, beyond a doubt.

"Look, Mr. MacAndrews," he told Jamie, "I could go right on taking your money, and I don't suppose the people back in Tulsa would blame me, but it's time for you to face facts. There just plain isn't any oil here. I've spudded in three holes for you against my better judgment, and in this last one we've sunk every foot of casing available between here and Odessa. Nothing but salt water in any of them. I'm pulling my rig tomorrow, and that's flat and final."

Jamie was furious. He pleaded with Shepard to try once more, finally shouting at the man. Ignacio feared the two of them would come to blows. It would have been fearsome. The oil man was every bit as big as Jamie. When Shepard wouldn't budge, and quietly repeated he would take his men and gear off the D Cross A as soon as he could manage it, Jamie at last fell silent, and walked away—limping.

"Well," Sarah said, "maybe that will calm down old get-rich-quick MacAndrews for a while." The girl clearly enjoyed her brother's setback, but her enjoyment was short-lived.

Jamie petitioned the county court to have Douglas declared incompetent, and he hauled Sarah along for the hearing. Even Ignacio saw the necessity for this. Hands had to be paid, feed and equipment must be bought, and plainly someone had to have the authority to act for the livestock company and the D Cross A.

When Sarah returned from the hearings—alone—she was seething. "Oh, that Judge Adamson!" she railed at supper with Ann and Ignacio, "Polite as all get out, but he sure doesn't think a woman has any rights at all. 'I'm confident,' he said, 'your brother will do what's best for all concerned.' Turned everything over to Jamie, lock, stock, and barrel. I wanted a peek at Daddy's will, to see what *he* wanted, but I couldn't get him to listen, on account of poor Daddy not being dead."

"Where *is* Jamie, Sarah?" Ann said. Strange, the rider thought, the pain of having to ask isn't in her voice any more.

"Gone to El Paso," Sarah said. "He got them on the phone after Judge Adamson turned the bank account over to him. Wanted to talk to Ben Hardy, but Ben's retired and some new young bank officer is looking after us. There was something about starting a 'stock portfolio' or something. And get this! Jamie's got some crazy notion about starting a bank in Black Springs."

When Jamie returned from El Paso two days later, there wasn't the slightest sign of any limp. He was in such high spirits that the smile almost flashed with his old boyhood brilliance.

If the vaquero's heart hung in his chest like a lead weight about Douglas, and if he was disquieted by some of the things going on at the D Cross A, one part of his life was becoming comfortable and steady—the time he spent with Concepción.

They were good together, the two of them, and she filled the need he hadn't realized he had before Sally Bannister. Concepción wasn't as skilled in bed as the anglo woman, and he was surprised to find what a deep modesty hid behind the bold, free exterior she presented in the bar room. For his part, he was as patient, gentle, and softly tender as he could be, with the result that little by little, her passion welled up into something powerful indeed, but still so private and hesitant that, Jamie or no Jamie, she could have been a virgin.

One night as they lay together drained and happy, something clicked inside his head, and he offered marriage. She raised herself from the pillow, and looked at him for several moments before she answered. "*Gracias*, Ignacio." There was the shining beginning of tears in her black eyes. "No, my good, good friend—my love. We cannot."

"*Porqué?*"

Again she hesitated. "Would you, Ignacio, ever leave the D Cross A?"

He didn't answer, couldn't.

"I thought not—and I think I understand, but you must know, too, I could never live there."

He felt ashamed and stupid that he hadn't thought of this.

Jorge was frank and open—and approving—about the relationship, and to the mild discomfort of the rider, pleasantly vulgar about the intimacies they shared.

"I told you long ago you needed a woman to put it into, *amigo*. For your sake I hope she's good at it."

Apparently Concepción told her brother of Ignacio's offer. The cantina owner shrugged it off as "of no importance," but he thanked him warmly. Still, in the next sentence, Jorge revealed how much bitterness still remained.

"Look, Ignacio. She is my sister and you are my friend—but no man really wants to marry a woman who can't produce a son!"

As the spring of 1929 grew near, the vaquero began to worry hard about the ranch. With both Douglas and he out of action the previous fall, and Jamie spending all his time on the fruitless hunt for oil, the last roundup was only a fraction of what it should have been. The herd now stood at an all-time high, not a dangerous level yet, but after calving, if they didn't make a truly formidable shipment, the grazing problem would get serious. Jamie, busy with plans for the new bank, and running the new Pierce Arrow to El Paso twice a month, wasn't interested in their predicament. When Ignacio as foreman tried to turn Jamie's attention to the coming roundup, the anglo finally snapped, "Run the God damned thing any way you want to! I've got more important things to do." Ignacio set about doing just that.

First, he had to find more hands. Riders had left the Ojos Negros in droves in recent years, lured away by easier, higher-paying jobs in the booming cities in the East. It took *un loco*, he admitted, to earn a hard living in the saddle these days, when the big shippers in the towns were paying two, three times the wages ranchers were. He enlisted Sarah in the search, and with Ian in the Buick with them, they scoured the basin and the valleys which opened away from it.

They found old Tom, living in a boarding house in a crossroads hamlet east of Tularosa.

"Nope," the old timer said, "I had a real bad fall last year—up in Valencia County—and I'm ree-tired. Thankee all the same, sonny." The vaquero smiled that, at thirty-nine, he could be called "sonny" by anyone. Well, Tom must be seventy now, and he looked it when you saw the tired, watery eyes.

After clucking sympathetically over Douglas (he didn't dwell on it—the same kind of thing was happening to all his friends these days) Tom offered to help them find some men, and piled into the back of the car, barking directions like a trail boss.

"How come you need extra hands, vaquero?" Tom said when they were under way. "Ain't you already got five able-bodied riders even with MacAndrews laid up the way he is?"

Ignacio explained, omitting the fact that he couldn't count on Jamie. While he talked he saw Sarah glance at him from the wheel, and he knew that Ian, in the back with Tom, was looking at him steadily.

They finally succeeded in finding two men Ignacio thought might do, an anglo and an Indian boy down from the Mescalero who had ridden in Otero County the past two summers.

They let Tom out at his boarding house. The old man waved goodbye and as the car pulled away, he shouted after them, "Come again, vaquero. Sometimes I get so lonely I—"

Ignacio wondered if maybe Douglas wasn't better off.

The roundup was a nightmare, but somehow, even with the new men to train, Ignacio managed to hold the thing together. When it was finished, and he had paid the spare hands off with money Sarah made a frantic trip to town to get from Findlay Stafford—since Jamie was nowhere to be found—the tally sheets amazed him.

It was the biggest roundup in the history of the D Cross A. The pastures, after the buyers loaded their big stock trailers and went their way, were back in balance once again, and with the price of beef nearly as high as during the war in France, the money was more than anything the records in the sitting room desk revealed. The vaquero's heart was still a heavy weight. Douglas MacAndrews didn't know.

Late in August Sarah had a visitor at the D Cross A. Leila Balutan was a dark, almost swarthy girl from New York City, a friend from Sarah's days at the university.

Jamie looked at her with ill-concealed suspicion all through her first supper at the ranch, and when the girl excused herself for a moment at the end of the meal, he said to Sarah, "She's a Jewess, isn't she?"

Sarah dropped her fork into her plate. "For God's sake, Jamie! Nobody uses that term anymore."

"Well, she is, isn't she?"

"I suppose so. I hadn't thought about it. You needn't say it as if it were some kind of disease."

Next morning, Sarah asked the vaquero to cut out and saddle horses for her and her friend. He had them ready at the hitch rail when the two young women came out of the kitchen door.

"No, no, Nash," Sarah said, "not just two of them. I'd like you to ride with us—and Ian, too." The rider looked at the boy, who had helped him with the mounts.

"How about it, Tío Nash?" Ian said. Ignacio nodded, and Ian raced for the corral again.

"I've packed a lunch," Sarah said, "so we can make it an all-day affair."

When they were all in the saddle, the rider said to Sarah, "Where would you like to go, *muchachita*?"

"Tío Nash," Ian said, "could we go to that place where Angus is?"

To Ignacio's surprise, Sarah siezed on the idea. "Swell! I've never been there myself."

They dismounted at the edge of the arroyo which overlooked Angus's grave. While he tethered the horse to the rocks, and Sarah put out the picnic lunch, Ignacio tried to sort out his feelings. On the ride up he had grown more depressed with every mile; now that he was here his mood had actually lightened. It was about time the arroyo heard the sounds of youth and laughter—and knowing Angus, he was sure the dead cowboy would like the company.

"It's so beautiful here," the New York girl said when they finished eating, "but I suppose you people are too used to it."

Beautiful? For a second he recoiled. Well, in fairness, this young woman couldn't judge the place with a cowman's eyes. Yes, if you didn't have to concern yourself with water, or how cattle could graze on this barren rock, the arroyo had a certain dramatic, stark appeal.

The cairn—his hands felt raw again just looking at it—had held up pretty well. A few stones had rolled from the top, but the marker would surely be standing long after he was gone.

Ian had brought a sketch pad and was working away while Leila looked over his shoulder. "You're right, Sarah," she whispered. "He's good—and I don't mean just for his age. It's too early to tell just how good, but I'd sure like to show his stuff to a friend of mine in Taos."

Ignacio's heart swelled with pride. He had heard at the table the night before that Leila was opening an art gallery in Taos, where her brother was a sculptor, so these fine words meant even more than the praise which came from Ian's teacher in the Black Springs school.

It had been a good day, but it was time to get them in the saddle if they were to get back by dark.

An awkward little scene took place that evening after supper, although everything had started well enough.

Jamie, in one of those turnabouts of his which still left Ignacio blinking, played the role of genial host to the hilt. He brought out brandy and glasses for everybody, and pressed drink after drink on Leila Balutan, all the while asking her about herself with what seemed genuine interest.

"And how do you like our neck of the woods, Leila?" he said.

"Marvelous, especially the place we went today."

"Where was that?" He looked at Sarah and Ignacio for the answer, but before either of them could think, Ian spoke.

"Tío Nash took us up to Angus's grave, Dad."

Jamie hardly said a word the rest of the evening.

Ignacio could feel the effects of the brandy, and he wasn't surprised that Leila, who was obviously not an experienced drinker, was getting just a little tipsy. He was surprised, though, when the conversation shifted to him. The New Yorker already knew quite a bit about him, it turned out; the books, how long he had been with the MacAndrews family—enough to embarrass him. But embarrassment was too mild a word for his feelings when he heard her say, "I can understand some things now, Sarah. Now I know why you didn't have time for any of the men at school. You had him"—she pointed to Ignacio—"hidden away back here." Sarah put her hand to her throat and blushed right up to her hairline—and he saw Jamie almost choke.

On October 28, 1929, the cornerstone was laid in Black Springs for the Chupadera Stockman's Bank, James MacAndrews, Chairman of the Board.

Even the Governor came down from Santa Fe for the big party Jamie gave in the ballroom of the Sacramento. So many champagne corks were popped the old place sounded like a shooting gallery. If there were any prohibition agents there they looked the other way.

Once again Ignacio was the only one on the guest list with a Spanish surname. He didn't stay long. Concepción was waiting for him.

It was All Saint's Eve before Ignacio learned what happened in New York on October 29th, and more than a week before he knew of the effect it would have on Jamie MacAndrews and the D Cross A. No one had mentioned Wall Street in Mex Town, and it was at Stafford's store that the disaster took shape for him.

"Well, it don't make no never mind to me," one of Findlay's customers was saying. "Never had enough of the ready to put in the market myself. I understand the biggest plunger in these parts is young MacAndrews, Douglas's boy. Bought everything in sight on as little margin as they'd let him. Ain't that so, Findlay?"

"I'm sure I wouldn't know," Findlay said, looking anxiously at the vaquero.

Ann, in town to pick Ignacio up, bought a copy of the extra the *Chupadera County News* brought out, as well as the El Paso and Albuquerque papers, but she didn't talk about the crash on the drive back to the D Cross A.

When Jamie read the papers in the sitting room, his face turned gray as death and his hands shook until he could hardly hold them. To the rider he looked every bit as stricken as his father.

There was no way of telling just how much Jamie's speculation had cost the ranch. Ann and Sarah (they didn't even wait until the vaquero was out of earshot) implored Jamie to take them into his confidence, but he had turned so withdrawn and morose he wouldn't answer.

Fortunately, Jamie had repaid Findlay Stafford the money Sarah borrowed at roundup time, and no other creditors had materialized by Christmas.

"Maybe all he used was the savings account in El Paso that Daddy used to talk about," Sarah said. "If that's the case we're not flat broke."

With Ann's help, Sarah did prevail upon Jamie to turn over the checkbook of the Cuchillo Livestock Co. It turned out there was indeed enough of a balance to take care of the small operating costs which would see the ranch through the winter.

Just before Easter, a group of men motored out from Black Springs to see Jamie. He must have spotted the approaching car as it came around the butte, and recognized it or the occupants, for he streaked for his bedroom, shouting over his shoulder to Ann, "For Christ's sake, Ann, tell them I'm sick. Tell them I can't see anyone!" The vaquero and Sarah were both in the kitchen with her, and Ignacio rose to leave, but the señora begged him to stay.

There were five men in the party, only one of them from Black Springs, the lawyer Heygood. The four others, from their clothes, and the city pallor of their faces, weren't even from Chupadera County or close to it, the rider guessed. Heygood did the talking.

"You see, Mrs. MacAndrews," the lawyer said, his polite voice not hiding for a second his firm determination, "your husband hasn't met his bank stock pledge. He hasn't replied to our letters, either, and we simply can't wait much longer. The contractor for the bank building has requested another payout, too, so, you see, if we don't get the funds Mr. MacAndrews has promised by the first of May, well, much as we regret it—we'll have to close him out.

"Now, we realize there's more than enough collateral in the holdings of the Cuchillo Livestock Co., but Judge Adamson has told us Mr. MacAndrews and his sister"—he nodded toward Sarah—"can't use or pledge the assets as long as the old gentleman is still alive, and we rather doubt the earnings will suffice."

"How much money is involved?" Sarah asked.

"Seventy-seven thousand on the stock, and fourteen thousand for the contractor."

Ignacio almost gasped aloud. He had never heard that much money mentioned in one breath in all his life.

"Close him out!" Sarah said. Her voice was like the ringing steel sound of a coyote trap snapping shut.

Ignacio saw the lawyer look to Ann, and saw her nod. In the silence which followed, his quick ears picked up a tiny sound, and he knew that Jamie was listening in the hall. In his minds eye he could see the rustle of the kitchen curtains on that distant day when Concepción sat in the buggy in the yard.

Douglas MacAndrews died sometime during the afternoon of June 15, 1930.

Ignacio remembered hearing somewhere that people generally died in the early morning, before sunrise, dreading to face another day. No dread would have influenced the señor in his decision, if he had one, and the vaquero was sure he had. For one thing, he outlived the first of May. There would be no chance for Jamie to pillage the D Cross A to provide the money for his bank. What's more,—and the rider was certain of it—Douglas had waited until after roundup.

It was Ignacio who found Douglas dead, sprawled on the floor in front of the chest of drawers. The big man, whom he had thought no longer capable of movement, had left his chair somehow, and pulled the lace scarf from the top of the chest, spilling everything on it in wild confusion. In the huge, still hand Ignacio found a small, silver framed picture of Agnes.

As always, the wind was blowing at Las Sombras. The headstone had fresh lettering on it now, the serifs on Douglas's side of the marker knife-sharp and immaculate. They will wear, too, Ignacio thought. The wind, whistling through the pines about the town, would have its way.

The wind would have its way with the living, too. It had already left old Dr. Clifton as worn and pitted as the carving over Agnes's mound. How many more trips up the switchbacks could the ninety-year-old pastor make?

As the minister read from the book he held, Ignacio registered every face around the grave. There was Jamie, of course, Ann, Sarah, an Ian who looked suddenly older. Findlay Stafford, yes, he was there, and his wife Mary (dying herself of cancer, he had heard), Sheriff Lane, Ben Hardy and his son Jonathan the lawyer,

Hendry of the *News*, old Tom, Kincaid whose huge Rocking T stretched away on the north of the D Cross A. Curly Decker, Billy Joe and Pepe, Dr. Colvin and Hattie Spletter, and nearly every merchant from the entire length of Frontera Street.

It came to the vaquero then that this was a completely different gathering from those he had seen in his twenty-five years in the Ojos Negros. In back of the others, he could see Jorge and Concepción, and behind them Carlos Sánchez, Pablo the porter, Romero minus his guitar for the first time in Ignacio's memory, and fifteen or more of the *campesinos*. For the first time, Ignacio Ortiz was not the only non-anglo present.

"I can't begin to tell you folk," Jonathan Hardy said, "how much I appreciate your letting me do the reading now, so I won't have another trip to make."

Everyone in the sitting room was motionless and hushed, everyone except Jamie. What made the man so restless, Ignacio wondered, expectancy? For shame, vaquero, he told himself—Jamie didn't force those tears at the cemetery. Since Douglas died, though, the change in the man had been dramatic.

"Just go right ahead, Jonathan," Jamie said. "As head of the family now, I'd like to go on record as to the kind of trust we have in you."

Ignacio had been watching Sarah, and as Jamie said "head of the family" the look he saw on her face was like an act of murder.

"Hmm—yes," Hardy said, "well, let me begin by saying this is the *damnedest* will I've ever seen, and don't misunderstand, that's not said in a critical way at all. Douglas left a holographic will in a sealed envelope in my office safe, and a copy which he had me file with the county clerk in Black Springs. Now, this will Douglas wrote is a shrewd, thorough piece of work, technically sound, and I've no doubt it will go through probate without a hitch—something rare with holographs. My only regret is that I can't claim authorship. I guess it's the language in it that I marvel at. So—I'll get to the reading without boring you with any more remarks."

The first paragraph expressed Douglas's sorrow that he couldn't name one Ignacio Ortiz as administrator. That post went to Corey Lane, "but I know Mr. Ortiz will understand my reasons." It took Ignacio several seconds to recover from the shock of hearing *his* name first in the last words of the señor, and then he guessed the reasons; he wasn't a citizen, and—Jamie. Even now the son was looking at him with a peculiar, dazed expression.

Small bequests—none of them *really* small—came first. It turned out Douglas held the mortgage on Angélica Rivera's house in Mex Town. It was hers free and clear on any day she chose "to stop looking after others less deserving, and turn her loving care and kindness on herself." She was also endowed with a monthly sum equal to one half her pay at the D Cross A, the funds for this and the other bequests to come from a trust in Ben Hardy's bank—a trust which no one but Ben and Douglas had known about.

There was money set aside for an "Angus MacAndrews Scholarship" at Las Cruces, and the proceeds from another trust were to be divided equally "amongst all hands in the employ of the D Cross A at the time of my demise. Ignacio Ortiz will not, of course, share in this distribution, as he is not, nor has he ever been a 'hand'."

Some charities were named in varying amounts totalling about six thousand dollars.

"Now," Jonathan Hardy said, "this is where we get to the main body of Douglas's will." Ignacio could feel the tension in the sitting room mount. He didn't have to look to know that most of it came from Jamie. The lawyer's flat voice cut into the heavy quiet like a blade. As he read, though, it was almost like hearing the señor himself.

Ignacio heard the sharp intake of Jamie's breath when the lawyer read that "my friend, my companion and associate, Ignacio Ortiz" was to receive shares of common stock in the Cuchillo Livestock Co. amounting to twenty-five percent of the corporation's ownership, *and* the sixty sections of land which enclose "my brother Angus MacAndrews's grave, as a freehold, small recompense to this good man whom I and mine have used so much."

The rest of the livestock company was divided equally between James and Sarah.

Then, sliding down over them like an avalanche, came the rest of it. The grazing land of the D Cross A was parcelled out between the two MacAndrews children in such a way that none of it could be sold, mortgaged, pledged, leased, or given away without the *"joining and mutual consent of both parties."*

The house and outbuildings, even Ignacio's shack, and the fifty sections comprising the original ranch, the property Angus bought when Douglas was in school, were Ann's because "this was the hearth she kept for me."

Beyond the operating account of the corporation and what was left in household moneys, there wasn't a red cent of cash in anyone's inheritance.

As the lawyer stuffed papers in his briefcase, Jamie rose unsteadily to his feet. For a moment the rider thought he would fall, the way his tall body shook, but he turned and left the room. The limp was more ungainly than the rider had ever seen it.

31

"Now that he's finally got hold of himself, and can talk straight, Jamie says he'll fight it," Sarah said. She and Ian were in the shack with Ignacio two nights after the meeting in the sitting room.

The vaquero felt uneasy with Ian listening, and the way his eyes kept scanning the youngster's features must have shown it.

"Don't let it bother you, Nash," Sarah said. Yes, she had read him right. "The poor kid was in the middle of the fight last night—and the night before."

"Is there anything I can do, Sarah? Perhaps if I told Jamie he could have my part of—"

"NO! You will *not*!" she exploded. "He'll just have to get used to it and accept it. It's the way Daddy wanted it. And you heard Mr. Hardy. There's not a thing he can do."

Ignacio thought for a moment. "*Niña,*" he said at last, "*por favor*, do not misunderstand me, but Jamie is the *señor* now. I must always remember I work for him."

She sighed. "Oh, Nash—when all's said and done, I guess I really wouldn't have it any other way. We'll calm him down, and try to make him happy. At least he'll be forced to *ranch* now. Please, get that sad look off your face. I never completely forget he's my brother—and Daddy's son."

Ignacio saw that Ian was smiling, just a small smile, but enough to make the world a little brighter.

Then, like a crash of thunder, someone hammered on the door. "Sarah!" It was Jamie. "I don't know what the hell you're up to in there, but cut it out—and get your ass back to the house!"

Jamie scarcely spoke to Ann and Sarah in the next few weeks, and he didn't talk to Ignacio at all. There was work to be done, and the vaquero needed to discuss a number of things with the new "señor." He thought back to the days when Jamie used to come to the shack to have Ignacio lick the wounds he had received in the big house. It would be better if Jamie would use him like that again; perhaps, then, they could get about their business.

The rider couldn't decide if it was the effect the reading of Douglas's will had on Jamie, but in a sudden alteration of his habits, the anglo stopped going in to Black Springs. Except for one daytime trip to town he hadn't left the D Cross A since the funeral—but he wasn't in the house much, either. In dry weather, he took the truck out on the rangeland, and if the tracks which served as roads became too bad for driving, he rode a horse.

Ignacio, making his own rounds on Pavo, would see him sitting on the running board, or standing beside his pony, looking out across the D Cross A like a lost traveler seeking a new direction.

With Jamie constantly on the ranch, Sarah found a thousand things to take her into town, sometimes with Ian, more often with her sister-in-law. Some inner prudence made the vaquero decline her repeated offers of a ride. Whenever he needed Concepción and the peace of the Florida, he saddled Pavo, or waited until Ann went to Black Springs by herself.

Surprisingly, Ann's spirits hadn't sunk nearly as much as he expected. Like Sarah in recent months, she began to concern herself with the operation of the ranch, and even rode occasionally, something she hadn't done since the war. Sometimes, if the vaquero was working the close-in pastures, she begged to go with him, asking questions constantly about the stock, the grass, and his plans for the fall roundup—"your roundup" was the way she put it. His joy on these trips was like the taste of wine in his mouth, and as he answered her, he thought of his own rides with Douglas in the early days.

It was on one such day on horseback that he learned there had been many more bitter fights between Jamie and Sarah than he had known about. It surprised him. In the past the brother and sister had shown no reluctance to quarrel openly and loudly in front of him. "I don't even know what they're all about, Ignacio. They stop talking when I enter the room."

By the time Ian returned to school in Black Springs the day after Labor Day, Ignacio had come to the slow realization that he hadn't spent so much as five minutes alone with Sarah since the night she and Ian came to the shack.

At suppers in the house (Jamie sat with them infrequently and in stony silence) he would look up from his plate to find Sarah regarding him with a look he couldn't fathom. Clearly, she was troubled, but if her face revealed anything beyond a general discontent, it showed a woman in the process of making up her mind.

When the answer came, it came from Ian. Ignacio had spent a weekend with Concepción, and had walked across the tracks to meet Ann at Stafford's and return with her to the D Cross A. Ian was on the porch swing, his sketch pad in his lap.

"*Cómo estás*, Ian," the rider said. "Has *Señora* Ann come in with the car?"

"She's with Aunt Sarah at the depot. They're making a train reservation." The boy looked up with eyes darker than Ignacio had seen them since Douglas's funeral.

"*Qué pasa, niño?*"

"Aunt Sarah is leaving us. She's moving to Taos to live with that Miss Balutan who was here last summer."

The vaquero almost staggered. This hit as hard as any blow from Gibbon's fists.

"Come on, Nash. Cheer up! Your face is as long as a dogied calf's," Sarah said, as they waited for the northbound train. "I'm not going to the moon, you know!"

In the week since he had heard the news from Ian, he had only seen her once. While Ann drove him back to the ranch, as mystified as he was by the sudden decision, Sarah moved in with Ian at the Stafford's, and came to the ranch just to pack.

She hadn't told him the reason for her leaving. It wasn't hard to determine why, although it surprised him just a little.

Sarah had always rushed into battle with her brother with more than a touch of eagerness. What had been different in these last engagements?

"What will you do in Taos, *niña*," he said, not looking at her, letting his eyes stray to where Ann and Ian were checking Sarah's luggage through with Pablo, farther down the platform.

"Work in Leila's gallery. It's probably as close to art as I'll ever get. Oh, and I'll write. Maybe this is what you had in mind when you said I had to 'live a little more' remember?"

He hadn't *known* what he meant—but surely it wasn't this.

"Nash"—now her tone was low and serious—"I'm going to put a terrible responsibility on you. You'd probably be better off if you left the D Cross A, too, and I couldn't blame you—but I hope you'll stay. Ann needs you, the ranch couldn't survive without you—and there's Ian. I guess Jamie can't help himself, but he'll wreck that little boy, the way things are going. So, even though I've got no right to ask—promise me you'll stay."

He only nodded. There was no need to mention how unnecessary his promise was, how there was a prior one—more binding if unspoken—made sixteen years before.

Suddenly the girl started to laugh. "There's one more thing before they get here." She motioned toward Ann and Ian, who had left the porter and were now walking toward them. "Don't get upset, but Jamie said some pretty nasty things to me. Accused me of being in love with you. Said that if I hadn't been to bed with you, I was intent on getting there pronto. Those weren't his exact words, but I'll spare you *them*!"

"*Niña!*" He was horrified. This was *Sarah*, his *muchachita*, the little girl he would always—*Dios!* How *could* Jamie?

Sarah pulled a face. Then the big smile changed to something softer, and his heart pained a little when he realized the *niña* was gone forever.

"I guess I'll have to set you straight on something, vaquero. For once, Jamie's managed to be right. If I stayed on, that nice friend of yours at the Florida wouldn't stand a chance. Most likely she'll never know—because you won't tell her—but in a way, Jamie's kind of paying the debt he's owed her all these years."

He didn't know whether the throbbing in his head came from the blood pounding through it, or from the noise of the approaching locomotive. Thank God there was no more time for talk!

Then, Sarah was looking down at the three of them from the coach steps, and waving goodbye. "Come and see me—all of you! Yes, bring Jamie, too, if he'll come."

32

FOR A LONG TIME AFTER SARAH LEFT, THE VAQUERO HAD ALL HE COULD do to check the resentment he felt toward the brother who had driven her away.

Despite his efforts to be circumspect in his letters to Taos, some of his bitterness must have shown, for about a year after her departure she wrote him, taking him to task, gently. Didn't he realize, she asked, there was more to her leaving than "Jamie throwing me out"? She was tough enough to have stuck it, if it would have done some good, but if she had stayed she would have been a reproach to Jamie, and there would have been more and worse bloodletting. "I never would have been able to keep my big mouth shut about the bank, the oil fiasco, the other financial adventuring—and, above all, *Ian*. With Ignacio's help," she said, Jamie would have a chance to straighten out—without "me as a burr under his saddle."

She liked her new life, and Ignacio need not think she was "in exile." She had taken her small share of the D Cross A earnings this past year, and had bought into Leila's gallery. She was writing—"nothing good, *yet*, but lots of it"—and (the rider's relief was tempered by a tiny stirring of loss) there was a man, Max Balutan, Leila's sculptor brother. "There's no sense upsetting Jamie. He'd take to his bed about my Jew."

Another accommodation was being made for the willful man who was now the boss of the D Cross A. Sarah might be right, though. Jamie had returned to something like the easy good nature the vaquero remembered before the war, and there were even hints, small ones, of the disarming smiles of those early days.

More gratifying to Ignacio, Jamie's involvements in Black Springs seemed to have ended, and the effect this had on Ann, although not remarkable, eased the rider's heart.

It was good Jamie was on the ranch so much now, as there was a formidable amount of work to do. Curly Decker took his money and retired, and Billy Joe left soon afterward, using his legacy from Douglas to finance him on the rodeo circuit; every few months Ignacio would get a scrawled postcard from Cheyenne or Calgary or wherever the younger cowboy found time to write. Jamie gave Ignacio no argument when the vaquero suggested they not replace the two. With Pepe and Ian—suddenly a man in the saddle—they shouldn't need extra hands for several seasons.

Grass was plentiful, disease shied away from the Ojos Negros as it always had, and Jamie gave every indication of becoming a cattle rancher once again. Ignacio felt he wouldn't be lying if he could see Douglas now, and tell him the fence was tight.

"It is a landslide, Ignacio!" Jorge Martínez shouted, holding his glass out toward the radio as if he were toasting it. "Roosevelt will carry every state except Maine and Vermont, and maybe two, three others." Jorge was in a splendid mood. This must have been the fourth round of drinks he had bought for his customers since they flocked into the Florida to listen to the election returns.

"But Jorge," Ignacio said, trying to keep the smile from his face, "if they repeal the law against drinking, won't the anglos across the tracks take some of your business away?"

"Who cares, *amigo*? Maybe I will retire from the cantina— become a politician. People like you and me—*paisanos*—are winning places in the government all over the state tonight."

Concepción put her tray down on the bar beside her brother. "If you take one more drink," she said, "you couldn't be elected dog catcher here in Mex Town."

Nothing could dull the fine edge of Jorge's spirits—not tonight. "I wonder," he said, ignoring Concepción, "how they are feeling at the Sacramento. *Los pobrecitos* over there don't even have a drop to drown their sorrows."

Ignacio wondered, too. Jamie was at the Sacramento with the Republicans. Aside from regular shopping and business trips, the election and the long campaign were the only things to bring the man to town in nearly three years now. He hoped, no, he had to be confident, this breach of Jamie's self-imposed isolation would not become the excess of the past. Things had gone too well for anything to happen now.

The anglo certainly had been rabid about this election. How was it possible for Jamie to hate a man he had never met as he did this Roosevelt? He had asked the rancher once, and there followed a ten-minute tirade of invective and obscenity ending with Jamie saying, "—and every God damned pinko in the country is riding on the bastard's coattails. Jesus, *you* ain't going to vote for him, are you, Nash?"

"You forget, Jamie, I can't vote."

"Well, I'd make an exception in your case, of course, but it might not be a bad idea if none of the Mexicans in this state could vote. They don't understand these things."

Ignacio didn't mention this conversation to his friend Jorge, who, when it came right down to it, didn't know the Democratic candidate any better than Jamie did.

"Those children in back will grow up in a different world," Jorge was saying. "Let's drink to justice, Ignacio."

Well, he could drink to it, but he couldn't tell Jorge of his doubts that a new face, or even a thousand, would make the difference real. It was his own shortcoming. Jorge had what one of Jamie's friends had called the "big picture." The rider's world was only big enough to hold the people at the ranch, Concepción, Jorge and María, and the two brown *niños* who had followed Josefina into life. He didn't even want a larger world.

Yes, Jorge had the big picture—pity it was only in black and white. To the cantina owner the gringos were still all alike. Ignacio tried to tell him that old Mr. Stafford was voting for his man, and that Sheriff Lane, retiring, had backed as his replacement the young deputy Ortega out of the Río Concho.

"*Sí!*" Jorge flung Jamie back at him. "I hear your *gringo* friend isn't speaking to either one of them."

Over the radio the song "Happy Days Are Here Again" was coming from some campaign headquarters in New York. Somehow, it seemed desperately out of place in the Cantina Florida.

"Can you stay with me tonight, Ignacio?" Concepción asked at his elbow. "It will be late before I am through with work, with this nonsense going on." She gestured toward the radio.

He nodded. Concepción wouldn't burden him with the big picture. Her world matched his in size, and he doubted if she had paid even as much attention to this world-shaking campaign as he had.

He watched her now as she moved among the tables. What a lucky man he was, undeserving, too. It twisted his heart that he couldn't return the love she never put in words, but which he had watched build in her these past few years.

All at once he felt terribly depressed. The bar room, even Jorge's ebullience, was closing in on him. He could go over to Estancia Street and spend some time with Ian; the boy wouldn't be in bed for another hour. Yes, that was exactly what he would do.

He told Concepción he would be back.

While the Great Depression settled like fog on the rest of the country, the clean winds of the Ojos Negros kept Chupadera County free of it. To be sure, beef prices were down, way down, but so was the cost of everything they bought, and if the fortunes of the D Cross A surged upward no faster than the grass, they surged as steadily.

Jamie's moods kept pace with the improvement. He looked better than he had in years. Tanned by the sun, his body lean and fit from the increased work load he assigned himself, it was as though the calendar had been turned back a dozen years. Ignacio reflected that it had been many months since he had seen the limp. He paid a good deal more attention to Ann now, too, and the vaquero saw smiles lighten her face more frequently than he could remember at any time since the war. In fact, there was only one thing at the D Cross A which disturbed him at all these days—Jamie's relationship with his son.

Ian had begun to paint in oil. The sketchbooks he had filled so diligently, and even the watercolors, had been private things; he never showed any of his work unless asked. But the big easel, a Christmas present sent down by Sarah, whether in the sitting room or out on the kitchen patio, claimed a lot of attention.

"Sissy stuff!" Jamie snorted once, when the boy was finishing a view of Ignacio's shack and the wooden windmill. "That crap sure smells the house up, too." The intensity of the look Ian gave his father was almost frightening. Ian didn't say a word, though—just moved the easel into his bedroom and painted there.

He was twelve now. He would never be as tall as his father, and with his darkness a powerful reminder of Ann, there seemed little MacAndrews in him at all. Serious, somber, he seldom spoke, and the constant air of tension about him was at odds with a face almost too much claimed by calmness. Quiet, yes, but not tranquil. *"For though I am not splenitive and rash . . ."* Hadn't the words of the melancholy prince occurred to the rider once before? Surely they applied more to Ian than to him.

If the boy was, in many respects, an enigma, there was one thing about him not hidden from Ignacio. His love for the D Cross A, and for the vast Ojos Negros as well, would have been plain enough even if he hadn't signaled it so strongly in his paintings. When they rode together—and that was every time Ian came out from town—the boy would seek some high route where he could see across the empty miles without restriction. His silence then would assume a deeper tone, and his eyes would burn with a passion the vaquero had never seen before, not even in Douglas's blue ones.

Wait! He had seen that look before. Concepción had it, and maybe Sally. Not that it was a woman's look, not with Ian, but it evoked the same feeling, as if there were an erotic shading to it. It was consuming, and yes—sexual.

Sarah came to visit. Although his first fear had faded, Ignacio dreaded her return. With this Max Balutan in her letters all the time, he needn't worry about another conversation like the one on the station platform; but the fact that things were going so well with Jamie gave him pause.

This was a far different Sarah, though. "You can believe it, Nash. There are other places in this world besides the D Cross A. I've never been as happy in my life as I am in Taos."

Again it was Max Balutan. When she was with Ignacio she talked of little else. The rider took himself to task for the unexpected stab of jealousy he felt. Sarah was so sure, so secure in this relationship, apparently, that she only laughed lightly when Jamie made a remark about "this Hebe chiseler you're getting cozy with."

When Sarah saw Ian's oils, she took Ann and the vaquero aside. "Look. That boy deserves real instruction. I'm going to take a couple of canvases back with me—and you get him up to Taos soon. He might be as good as I think he is."

She rode once with Ignacio before she left. "I'm so grateful to you, Nash. Got to admit I'm proud of Jamie, too. He sure seems to have learned his lesson, and if he's getting a little cocky, I guess we can indulge him."

The night after Sarah left, Ignacio dreamed of the wall again. It had been so long—years—since the awful vision haunted his sleep he had begun to think it wouldn't come again. This time was as bad as any he could remember, and the afterimage burned his mind for weeks.

"Jesus, Nash!" Jamie looked up from the desk in the sitting room. "Do you realize that was the smallest spring roundup we've had in more than thirty years?"

"*Sí*, Jamie,"

"Well, for Christ's sake, *amigo*, don't you think it's time we got off our asses and did ourselves some good?"

"I suppose we could run another hundred head this season, Jamie. We could put on another rider in the fall, and—"

"No, no! You ain't getting the idea yet, Nash!"

Ignacio felt a lump grow in his stomach. He had wondered about Jamie's restlessness since roundup, but he hadn't foreseen this.

"I want a lot more cattle on the place," Jamie said. "We've got credit again, and I mean to use it. Get ready to put on five or six more hands—permanent."

"But, Jamie—"

"No 'buts,' *amigo*. Hell, we can handle it. Look, Nash, there's something in this for you, too, you know. After all, you're a high-muck-a-muck *stockholder* in this operation."

Ignacio stared at the man seated at the old desk, Douglas's old desk. How many times had he stood here while Douglas, in those easy gentle words which never prodded, laid down some wise strategy for the D Cross A? He couldn't remember a time, almost from the very first, when the big señor hadn't sought his foreman's advice—and listened to it, no matter what the outcome. The lump in his stomach swelled. How wrong he had been, trying to convince himself that Jamie was Prince Hal, that maturity and responsibility would turn him into another strong, discerning, good King Harry for the D Cross A.

"God damn it!" Jamie said. "You ain't one bit brighter than my old man was."

The lump in Ignacio's stomach burst like an abscess, spreading through him in a rage of fire. "You will ruin the D Cross A, Jamie!" *Dios*, he was shouting! The sound was the harshest, most painful cry he had ever heard cross his lips. "*Por favor*, Jamie—I beg you. Don't overload our land!"

Jamie turned to some papers on the desk without answering. It was plain he was finished, but the rider knew that, however it all turned out, he couldn't leave it there.

"I can't do it, Jamie." If there was a tiny bubble of fear in his chest, the sustained anger washed it away.

Jamie didn't look at him. "It's too late for your opinions, Nash," he said. "I've already made some deals. You'll just have to make the best of it." The blonde head was still bent over the desk and Ignacio realized that his small fear was nothing to the terror which gripped Jamie at that instant.

Anger swept over him in another giant wave and he knew that if he stayed there for a second longer, he would strike the man, with far more fury than he had that night in the rocks so many years before.

He spun about to leave—and looked into the dark eyes of Ian MacAndrews.

When the first of the new stock arrived, Ignacio tried to tell himself that everything would turn out well.

If the weather held, the grass could take the increase. He had jealously guarded some of the pastures, and there were even a few which hadn't seen a hoofprint in a year. Even Douglas would have agreed the time had come to grow—*a little*. But he was aghast when trailer after trailer rolled up to the D Cross A, unloading animals for an entire week. Pepe and Ian and Ignacio rode and worked for eight straight days, running beef to the pastures from sunup until the western sky gave up its last red glimmering.

He didn't speak to Jamie, nor did they get any help from the architect of all this frantic activity. Jamie had started spending most of his nights in town again.

Then came the inferno summers when the grass left the Ojos Negros Basin.

33

"I DON'T BELIEVE," FINDLAY STAFFORD SAID, "I'VE EVER SEEN A BURN-UP as bad as this one!" There wasn't an old-timer in Chupadera County who didn't echo his despairing words.

At first Ignacio, like almost everybody else, was not too concerned. A month without rain was unpleasant, but certainly no catastrophe, and definitely not the "bad dry time" Pablo had talked about. But as the hot summer followed a dry spring, and was chased in turn by an autumn just as arid, he knew that if rain didn't come in quantity next season, they faced disaster.

There was no way they could sell off stock fast enough; it seemed the markets in the East had simply closed up shop, and the few buyers who came to the basin offered next to nothing for the emaciated creatures who staggered under the blowtorch sun.

Ignacio lost count of the stock that died. Those that managed to survive needed looking after more than ever now, and he felt guilty, taking a pull from his canteen when surrounded by the thirsty, hungry animals they drove from clump to scraggly clump of withered grass.

They did sell some, and they got a few dollars from the sale of hides, but as tanks ran out and grass was chewed to the very roots, it took no genius for finance to figure out that Jamie wouldn't be able to meet the notes he had signed for the money to stock the D Cross A. Nor would there be cash to pay the "five or six more hands" Ignacio, luckily, hadn't had time to hire.

The first winter after the drought began, they did get moisture, but it came in the shape of terrible, sweeping rains that looted the range of its thin layer of soil and carried it away in a dismal flood to the mouths of the arroyos. When it dried, and the spring winds blew, they saw the precious silt lifted into a dirty sky, saw it gust away to the north and east, carrying with it any hope of summer grass.

It would take a generation, Findlay Stafford said, to build that base again, a score of years of dying plants and cattle droppings—if enough stock made it through—before the grass would thicken.

After the winter storms, no real rain came that year—or the next. Sky after burning sky appeared each day, cloudless, the scorching sun firing the caliche to the hardness of porcelain.

Then the people came, people unlike any the Ojos Negros had ever seen. They streamed out of the distant, unnamed places the Chupadera dust had blown to. First they came in tiny groups, a family or two, then in caravans, red-eyed men, gaunt women who never smiled, and children. Their dilapidated cars and trucks choked the highway into Black Springs and out again, crawling along the blacktop like some great, disjointed, rusty snake.

"What in hell are they doing down this way?" Jamie said. "They sure can't be aiming to push those heaps to California by way of Phoenix. Why, they couldn't carry enough water to get them across the mountains to Las Cruces."

"Don't know, Jamie," Findlay Stafford said. "That tall one there says they meant to stay on U.S. 66 all the way, but at Santa Rosa the state troopers turned them down our way. Been some trouble at Gallup, and I reckon the state figured we'd be a mite more tolerant, since we ain't seen very many of them—until now."

"God!" Jamie said, "I've never seen a sorrier bunch of critters—human or otherwise!" Ignacio winced. Did Jamie have to be so loud? These "critters" weren't deaf; in fact they looked like they had that special, keen alertness which comes with thirst and hunger.

It was blistering hot on Stafford's loading dock where Ignacio sat with Jamie. The dock was on the side where the highway crossed Frontera Street, and the rider could see Ian in the back lot, loading the pump parts they had come to town to get.

He had stopped for the moment, and was standing by the pickup, staring intently at the people his father and the old merchant had been discussing. Ignacio could almost bet that someday one of these travelers would appear in one of Ian's paintings.

This wasn't the first lot the rider had seen, but it was easily the biggest. There were three battered cars and a truck, all piled to the sky with furniture, poultry cages, boxes, barrels, and odd rags of clothing and bedding crammed in every space.

On top of the loads perched the children. They stared at the men on the dock with huge, unblinking eyes. The eyes were the same cornflower blue the vaquero saw about him every day, but washed out, faded.

"Just look at those wrecks they're driving," Jamie said. "Two of them ain't even got licenses."

"Well," Stafford said, "I guess they're letting them get by with it. They ain't got money to pay fines, I expect—and you sure can't jail them all."

The nearest car was still running, thrashing away while the driver was inside the store. Ignacio guessed the man felt he couldn't start it again if he turned it off. The people, the adults anyway, looked the same as this old car, fidgeting and shuffling as if they, too, were reluctant to stop for fear they couldn't get under way again, either.

The women, the first to go inside Stafford's while their men pumped gas and watered radiators, were coming out, carrying unbagged pieces of penny candy for the children. None of the children left their places. They just reached bony hands down to grasp the licorice whips and jawbreakers and clutched them to their chests. Not one ate while Ignacio watched.

"Look at the man by the Oakland, Dad." Ian, finished with his loading, had come to stand by the rider. "He looks enough like you to be your brother."

Ignacio could feel Jamie stiffen as he looked at the man. *Dios*, he did look like the rancher. Not so much in the physical sense; his hair was darker and thinner and he wasn't as tall or husky as Jamie. The resemblance came from inside the man, a look of damaged pride like the head of the D Cross A sometimes wore. Those dark eyes of Ian's see more than things to paint, the vaquero thought.

"You've got rocks in your head, Ian," Jamie said. "I ain't like him at all, not in looks or any other way. Ain't no power on earth could push *me* off land that belonged to me."

"Maybe so, Jamie," Findlay Stafford said, "but it must be pretty bad where these folk come from. The Kelloggs dragged me to the movie in Almo the other night. They had a March of Time on these Okies—couldn't believe my eyes."

"Don't give a damn!" Jamie was openly angry now. "Still couldn't drive me off my land!" Ian looked at his father with a face completely without expression.

Then, the cars and the truck were gone, throbbing and steaming their way down the blacktop and out of town.

Jamie and Findlay went inside the store, and Ian hopped on the loading dock beside Ignacio. "When are you going to see Doc Colvin?" Ian asked suddenly. Ignacio jumped.

"Why should I see the doctor, Ian?" It was a lame question, and it sounded it.

"Look, Nash. I saw you out by the tank the other day, holding that wet towel to your head. It's that right eye again, isn't it?"

"No, Ian!" he protested, "I had too much to drink—that's all."

"All right, Nash. Have it your own way." The rider knew the boy wouldn't press him too hard on this.

Maybe he should see Dr. Sam. The pain in the eye had come more often recently. Yes, he would see the doctor soon, but right now there was too much to worry about, the way things were going at the ranch, and there was no way he could go to the doctor's office without Señora Ann finding out. Colvin wouldn't say a word if he asked him, but in Black Springs everybody would know; the word would be out in five minutes. Besides, the pain—and the dizziness and momentary loss of vision—never lasted long.

"You heading over to the Florida?" Ian asked.

"*Sí*, Ian, for a little while."

"Mind if I tag along? I haven't seen Mr. Martínez in a year."

They had turned the corner and started up Frontera Street when Jamie appeared on the front steps of the store. "Where the hell are you two going?" He was still angry. There seemed to be a smell in the air, like after a road crew had been blasting.

"We're going to the cantina," Ian said.

"O.K.," Jamie said. Ignacio could see the effort he was making to hide his dislike of the idea. "I'm going to the post office and check the box. I'll park the pickup somewhere near the Sacramento. Mind you, I'm going home at four, and I ain't waiting."

They started off again, and as they walked, Ignacio looked hard at Ian. It was important he observe him well now. In a month he would go off to the military school at Roswell, and it would be Thanksgiving, maybe Christmas, before they would be together for any time again.

There had been a bad scene when the decision had been made—by Jamie. Ann, in rare tears, had tried to intercede, until Ian himself had begged her not to. For once, shaking inside, Ignacio had spoken out, but not where the boy and his mother could hear.

"Why, Jamie?"

"Make a man of him."

"He will become a man anyway, Jamie, and he doesn't want this."

"God damn it! He's going to Roswell—and that's that!" Jamie had limped off to the corral.

Ian felt strongly about this, but after stating his objections once, he never said another word. The rider noted the boy taking an even keener interest in things around him, and his brush and painting knife were busier than ever.

He was two inches taller than the vaquero now, and tough as harness, though still a far way from the strength and power of his father. Ignacio was never happier than when they rode together, and his joy was inexpressible when he saw Ian in the saddle. Sarah had become a fine rider, too, but there hadn't been the same centaur joining with the horse which Ian had.

"Nash," Ian said, as they reached the tracks, "did you notice something about those people on the road back there?"

Yes, he had. His mind reached all the way back to Chicago. Jamie might have had some uncanny resemblance to the man by the Oakland, but wherever they were, the poor always looked alike.

"They were all anglos," Ian said. *Dios,* again?

It was quiet in the cantina, uncrowded. The Black Springs crowd had returned to the reopened bar in the Sacramento, and the *campesinos* didn't have the money any more, with their tiny farms burned to a crisp. After the heat of the walk from Stafford's, the shadows in the bar room were almost cool enough to bring a shiver.

Josefina was working the tables, and the vaquero was struck as always by how much like the young Concepción she looked.

"Howdy, Jo," Ian said, pronouncing the *J* as he would if it were an anglo name.

"Hello, Ian," the girl said. That's right, they must know each other very well from school. Looking at both of them, he realized they weren't children any longer, and he wondered if Concepción, who seemed as much a mother to Jorge's three as Maria did, realized it too. If ever a woman should have had her own—well, it didn't pay to dwell on that.

Ignacio settled in at the bar, where Jorge had his nose deep in a newspaper while Ian and the girl drifted off toward the alcove.

"*Qué tal*, Jorge?" the rider said.

"*Bien*, Ignacio, *bien*."

Jorge didn't look at him, but glanced sharply instead to where the two young people were huddling together. It was a momentary thing, but enough to send a little tremor through the vaquero. Jorge was a fair man, true, but his memory was long.

"He leaves for school in Roswell soon, Jorge," Ignacio said. The cantina owner nodded, still looking at Ian, but he said nothing. Then he got Ignacio a beer, and pointed to the young anglo.

"*Sí*," Ignacio said, "I think one would be all right."

While Jorge got another bottle from the chest behind the bar, Concepción came through the doorway at the back. She stopped short when she saw Ian, shook her head a little, then moved toward Ignacio, still looking at the boy. Yes, he thought, he has changed some since you saw him last.

"Are you staying in town tonight, Ignacio?" she said. The question was voiced in such an absent way it could have asked anything. She didn't even take her eyes from Ian when he answered.

"No, *cariña*, but I shall come back in for two or three days next week."

"*Bueno*." She looked at Ignacio then. There was a mist in her eyes of what, pain? Perhaps he did wrong to bring Ian here.

"He is a splendid-looking young man, Ignacio." She smiled, and the warmth of the smile told him that everything was fine.

Ian broke away from Josefina and settled himself at the bar. "*Gracias*, Mr. Martínez," he said as Jorge pushed the beer toward him. He turned to Concepción. "Miss Martínez, I haven't seen much of you since you were this stubborn old vaquero's nurse. Maybe you can get him to take care of himself again. I think he ought to see a doctor about that eye of his, but he won't listen to a kid like me."

Ignacio felt he should be angry about this interference—but he wasn't. He smiled. "Drink your *cerveza, muchacho*. We can't stay long."

Ignacio knew the D Cross A hadn't done well, but he had no idea of the losses of the past two years, nor of the amount of the overdue note.

Ben Hardy's bank, largely on the reputation of the ranch, and particularly that of Douglas MacAndrews, had advanced funds to Jamie without collateral. After two extensions of six months each, however, the directors called the loan. Ben was dead, Douglas was dead—business was business.

"Jamie," Ann said when the rancher broke the news, "don't you think we ought to contact Sarah? She's involved in this, you know—and so is Ignacio."

"Christ, no! She'd be on my back until the day I died. I'll work something out." He didn't sound confident, and the vaquero felt sick that he didn't know more about finances.

Without even telling Ignacio, Ann drove to town and put in a call to Taos.

The rider and Ann met Sarah at the train. Jamie had holed up at the D Cross A in the same kind of self-imposed seclusion which had been his habit after Douglas died, and Ignacio wondered if whatever woman or women he had been seeing were as understanding as Concepción.

Sarah, just past her thirtieth birthday now, had changed even more than on the previous visit. She wore her hair shorter, and there was a colorful look in her clothes which hadn't been there before. He could hardly remember her in Levis. It wasn't the bright dress or the heavy weight of turquoise and Indian silver which made the difference in her, though. The sureness he had seen in her the last time she was home seemed to have settled into a deeper course, and if she didn't laugh or talk as readily as before, still he knew he looked at a woman with whom contentment was an accepted fact of life.

At the meeting in the sitting room—so different from the reading of Douglas's will—she was patient with Jamie, and gentle to a degree which made it hard for him to remember the girl who had once flown at the rancher like a cougar.

"Well, Jamie. We've got to get you out of this some way. You can count on me."

"Ann never should have let you know," Jamie growled.

"Don't blame her, for God's sake," Sarah said. "After all, we're a family. Now—what's to be done?"

"Only one thing *can* be done." Jamie drew a breath. Still defiant, if guarded, it seemed he was intent on going down fighting. "We'll have to sell off part of the D Cross A!"

There was a silence.

"Jamie—" Ignacio was the first to break it. "There are the sixty sect—"

"No, Ignacio!" Ann cried.

"Forget it, *amigo*," Jamie said. "The old man didn't do you any favor with that rock pile. You couldn't get twenty cents an acre for that parcel from a greenhorn."

"Thanks, Nash," Sarah said. "Well then, Jamie—what?"

Jamie looked at the floor. "As I see it, the only thing we got that's salable, with most pastureland going a dime on the dollar around the county, is the stuff on the other side of the highway, up against Cuchillo."

"*The old Shelby place?*" Sarah said. Now she *was* holding back an explosion, and if Ann wasn't aware of it, Jamie was.

An hour's discussion brought them right back to where they started, and Sarah agreed it was the only course. Next day she drove to El Paso with Jamie to sign the necessary papers, and went straight back to Taos from there. In a week Jamie had a buyer. Ignacio never knew how much money was involved, and didn't care. Douglas MacAndrews never left his mind during the three weeks it took to rebuild the broken old fence which had marked the eastern boundary of the D Cross A when he first came to Chupadera County. He and Pepe herded the stock which had summered on Cuchillo into the pasture surrounding the foundation of the house which had never been completed. Jamie wasn't on hand to help. He had started going in to Black Springs once again.

The full extent of the danger the D Cross A had faced in the crisis over money didn't affect Ignacio until it had passed. He spent some sleepless nights in the shack, and burned a lot of kerosene, trying to read himself into oblivion.

For once, he worried about what might have become of him if Sarah had been stubborn and permitted Jamie and the D Cross A to sink. He was forty-five now; certainly not old, but not young if it meant looking for another job, particularly in the hard times which had gripped the rest of the country, and were even beginning to make themselves felt in Chupadera County. Besides, his name was Ortiz, and not Smith or Jones. That had made a considerable difference in the past, and certainly would these days, when the El Paso newspaper talked of little but the growing unemployment lines.

Well, for the moment that worry was behind him. There was something else of even greater importance. Ian was gone.

Thanksgiving came and went without the boy coming home. The vaquero knew before Ian went off to Roswell what a chasm it would create in his life, but even this knowledge hadn't prepared him for the depth of it. When he examined his longing for the dark youth closely, he told himself his feelings were absurd. From the time Ian was six years old and had moved into the Staffords's house on Estancia Street, he really hadn't been able to spend all that much time with his Tío Nash. Even when he was on the ranch the boy spent most of his free time shut up in his room painting, and *Dios* knew, when they were together on the range, working left little time for talk. Still, Ian had been there. Solitary and reserved as the boy was, his proximity had been a sort of talisman for the rider. He missed him now almost to the point of nausea sometimes, and even work, Concepción, and his books provided but a small part of the solace he felt he needed.

Worse, out of the secret reaches of his own loneliness, he could see the extent of Ann's. Hers must be far, far worse than his.

She now had nothing, less than nothing, for Jamie's behavior made him—in any hard assessment—such a minus quantity he must subtract something from whatever sum her life had been.

Angélica wanted to retire, not from any real desire to take advantage of the house and money Douglas left her, but simply because she was old and tired. Ignacio, feeling a little guilty, talked her into staying on at least until the range weathered in, and he could spend more time in the house with the señora. Through December, the lady of the D Cross A and the rider spent every evening together, alone in front of the fire in the sitting room. She would do needlework, and he would read, or sometimes they would just talk about the day. It was strange and wonderful how much they could find to say about the commonplace, ordinary events which filled their days. They never mentioned Jamie—or Ian, or Sarah, or Concepción. For Ignacio no other world existed until he said goodnight, and the December wind stripped the fire's warmth from him as he walked the pathway to the shack.

His feeling for this woman, who was more beautiful than ever at a few years past forty, had now become a quiet thing, but he knew it to be as strong as ever. He was proud he had been able to hide it from everyone around him—except Concepción, of course.

Once in a while he did permit himself to wonder why Ann had never left Jamie. That she loved him simply shouldn't have been enough. Nor should Ian have made the difference; the boy might be considerably better off in some other place. No one should have such blind loyalty and devotion to duty.

Then, one day a week or so before Christmas, she asked him to ride with her. They couldn't get as high on Cuchillo as they had once before, as there was too much early snow, but they did gain a vantage point from which they could look out over the expanse of the Ojos Negros. As he watched her face, he could see the traces of the years disappear completely. Whatever questions he had as to why she stayed disappeared as well. Her abiding love for the vast landscape at their feet seemed to play about her like St. Elmo's fire. She would never leave the D Cross A. In this regard she was as powerless as he.

As long as you and I, mi señora, can place our eyes on this— "all losses are restored, and sorrows end."

Then Christmas came and went, and with it, Ian. It seemed the boy was scarcely home before he was gone again.

In the spring, Jamie wrote Sarah for permission to sell another twenty sections. A long letter, it took the man several nights to write it, and neither Ignacio nor Ann was told exactly what he said. Sarah didn't come down from Taos this time. Papers for her signature flew back and forth between her and a highly nervous Jamie. When everything was done, Jamie told Ignacio he would have to let Pepe go.

Then the rancher was gone for almost an entire week. When he returned, it was in a brand new motor car, a dark green LaSalle the rider despised for its sumptuous elegance.

34

THE YEARS IAN MACANDREWS SPENT IN SCHOOL AT ROSWELL crept by haltingly for Ignacio Ortiz. Holidays and summers, when the boy was home, were joyous times of course, but they only deepened the loss the rider felt when they were over. Since the drought had ended, ranch work on the shrunken D Cross A wasn't as demanding as it had been, and they did a certain amount of traveling together. Often Ann went along with them. These were only day trips, but they opened the vaquero's eyes to how little he knew of the state he lived in, aside from the brooding Ojos Negros. He had a greater intimacy by far with Elsinore and Bosworth Field than with the ruins of Gran Quivira or the timbered archways of the highest Mescalero. The petroglyphs at Tres Ritos didn't excite him nearly as much as they did Ann and Ian, but he loved the wild fowl in the Bosque del Apache, and his heart was deeply stirred when they picnicked in the White Sands on a moonlit night.

Sometimes Jamie grudgingly allowed the use of the new LaSalle, as Ann's 1925 Buick couldn't be trusted at any altitude, and once in a while, if Ian took his easel and oils as well as the ever-present sketchbook, the three of them would attack some pretty sorry roads in the pickup truck. Those were times of unbearably sweet embarrassment for Ignacio. With the three of them crowded into the one seat, and with Ian driving, he would be pressed against Ann for hours.

If the vaquero ever wondered why he had such an abiding love for Ian—aside from the obvious fact that he was Ann's—a little thing which happened between the boy's junior and senior years provided the answer.

"Rustlers, Mr. MacAndrews?" Sheriff Ortega said. "You're not serious."

"I sure as hell am, God damn it!" Jamie shouted. Everyone in the county building must have heard him, Ignacio thought. Well, if he was embarrassed, Ian didn't seem to be. The boy was almost choking, holding back his laughter.

There were indeed a few cows missing. They wouldn't have missed them when Douglas was alive or during Jamie's big expansion just before the drought, but with the herd so small sometimes Ignacio thought he knew every animal by sight. Even so, he doubted that the rancher would have given the loss a second thought if he hadn't read the article in the *Chupadera County News.*

There was a sizeable rustling operation going on in the Texas Panhandle, the story said. The thieves didn't come whooping in on horseback as in the movies. They drove refrigerator trucks right onto the range, slaughtered twenty to a hundred head, dressed them out, and roared off into the night with meat, hides, everything, leaving only the bloody entrails for the buzzards to get at dawn.

Surely it wouldn't happen in the Ojos Negros. The most daring raider would want a good long highway to make his getaway, and the one east of the D Cross A would be too risky. Besides, a strange truck that size would be easy to pick out in Chupadera County.

"Mr. MacAndrews," the sheriff was saying, "if it was rustlers, wouldn't they have taken many more?"

"How the hell should I know? Maybe they're just trying us on for size!"

"Well," Ortega said, "I can't spare any men to patrol out your way, Mr. MacAndrews. I'm sorry."

"You mean you *won't*!" Jamie was steaming. "By Christ, if those sodbusters in the Río Concho missed a chicken, you'd be out there with an army. You greasers sure stick together!"

"I'm sorry, sir. There's nothing I can do." Ortega was still unruffled and Ignacio was proud of him. Jorge wouldn't be; he'd want Jamie tossed in jail for the slur.

"Okay, okay!" Jamie said, making no effort to control his anger, "We'll just have to take care of it ourselves. You better put out the word, though, Ortega—if anybody, and I mean *anybody*,

sets foot on the D Cross A without being asked, we'll be there
with guns!" The rancher turned and stamped out of the sheriff's
office, the limp so exaggerated it was comical.

Both Ortega and Ian were laughing as Jamie went, but he
was so beside himself, he wouldn't have heard a gunshot. Fifteen
minutes later, at the Florida, Ignacio laughed, too, when Ian told
the story to Jorge and Concepción—and Josefina.

"He is not like the father, that one," Jorge said, when Ian had
moved off with Jo. "Still, I will watch him for a while."

Then began the rides of the *"posole posse,"* as Ian dubbed
the operation. Jamie hired a pair of seedy youngsters to
patrol the highway, and got one of his cronies from the bar at the
Sacramento to ride with him. Ignacio was paired with Ian. "Just
for company," Jamie said, "on account of Nash ain't got the guts
to tote a gun."

For a week, the vaquero and the boy mounted up at sunset
and rode toward the eastern fence. They didn't find any rustlers, nor did they find the missing stock, but Ignacio knew there
were a hundred rocky gullies the cows could have stumbled into,
a thousand scrubwood thickets to hide them from view.

They were wondrous, haunting rides, so different from the
ones they had made together over the years. After an hour or two
of sweeping through the yucca near the highway they would lie
up in a draw or in the lee of the rocks if they found themselves on
higher ground—and talk. *Dios*, how they talked. Maybe it was
because it was dark (they never made a fire for fear of attracting
Jamie and his partner), but the talk ran freely, like a spring arroyo.
The only glimpses they got of each other's faces were when they
held matches to Ian's cigarette or the vaquero's stronger *cigarro*.

Books, art, politics—the terrible war in Spain, and its
consequences for the rest of the world, were much on Ian's
mind—there seemed to be no subject they didn't touch on.
Ignacio, realizing that until now he had taken this dark young
man on faith, was gratified to find him measure up in every way.
He liked as well as loved him.

Here in the darkness, too, he began to understand how Ian
had been shaped. As the boy talked, his voice surprisingly free of
complaint, the security of his mother's and Sarah's love ("And yours

too, Tío Nash," he said without a trace of embarrassment) made a
missed birthday party and his father's sneers at the very stuff of his
life seem all the more thoughtless and cruel. Any other young man,
the rider felt confident, would by now have turned hard and bitter.
Ian hadn't, and Ignacio hoped that the sorcery of the Ojos Negros
would heal his wounds without a surface scar. It was a healing process he had felt at work himself times without number. It was like the
black rock of the malpais, tortured and twisted by the inferno which
gave it birth, now yielding to the greater force of time, the softening
influence of the benign winds which moved steadily across its face.

Some of the rock, he admitted ruefully, resisted—or was
composed of elements so alien it couldn't change.

And he, Ignacio? Had he been shaped by this land? Or were
there forces from the time before his memory began which had
done all the work which could be done?

He guessed it really didn't matter. What did, and he retreated
into the comfort of the thought, was the fact that Ian and Ann
and he were linked together by a common love so great that all
the dislocations of their three lives faded into insignificance.
Of course the other two had no way of knowing how he felt, but
that was of no importance—none at all.

On the last night Ian said, "Doesn't Mr. Martínez like me,
Nash?"

Before these rides, Ignacio would have murmured "yes" or
"*sí*" or "certainly, Ian," but now that wasn't good enough. "He is
the father of a daughter, Ian. You could be a danger to her."

"Sure don't know what he's worried about. We've never been
alone—not once." Ignacio could see Ian's face quite clearly now,
the boy was drawing so fiercely on his cigarette.

"But you will sometime, Ian—and then?"

"I see what you mean, Nash. But he still wouldn't have a
care. I want more from Josefina than that."

They had been on high ground that night, above the piñon
line. Returning to the road they heard a movement in a small
dense grove—or did they see or feel it? Talking about it afterward,
neither of them was sure. They both agreed, though, that for some
reason neither of them could explain, their muscles had tensed
and become almost electrically alert. When they dismounted, and

went to have a closer look, the vaquero smelled something he was positive he recognized, a faint memory from the Sierra Madres on one of his flights from Ramos.

"Ian," he said, his whisper sounding loud and breathy, "I think we have just started up a lion!" Yes, the strong, hot odor was unmistakable now that they were closer.

"I didn't think there had been any here in more than fifty years," Ian said, whispering too.

In the blackness the rider could feel each individual hair at the back of his neck.

"There may be more things on the D Cross A than we know about."

In August Ann bubbled with a new idea. "Jamie," she said one night, "why don't you and I and Ian drive up to Taos, and visit Sarah?"

"Hell, no!" Jamie said, "I can't get away right now. Besides, I get my craw full enough of arty horseshit right here."

Ian went right on eating as if nothing had been said.

"Come on, Jamie," Ann said, "The change would do you good."

"Don't need no change. I'm fine the way I am."

That seemed to end it, but two days later the rancher insisted Ann and Ian make the trip—and take Ignacio along. He seemed to be making a kind of grim attempt to be affable about it, too. When the vaquero protested there was still some work to do before roundup, Jamie said he'd get one of Kincaid's hands from the Rocking T to help him while the three of them were gone. "You ain't had but three or four days off in the past two years, *amigo*," the rancher said. It was unlike Jamie to think of this, but Ignacio suddenly found himself excited by the prospect of the trip, and he gave it no further thought.

"Aunt Sarah, this place is great," Ian said. "I'd like to stay on here, instead of going back to Roswell. I know Max is a sculptor and I'm a painter, but I could learn a lot from him."

Never had Ignacio seen the boy's features so animated, except perhaps when he was with Josefina at the Florida. Well, Taos *was* a revelation. The sleepy look of the town itself contrasted sharply with the purposeful commotion of the villagers. While Ann spent time with Sarah, the rider and Ian wandered in and out of galleries until they were both intoxicated with color. Ian bought several strands of turquoise *heishi* for his mother, but it was Ignacio who couldn't wait to see it against her slender neck. The sky tone of the jewelry seemed made for her. A massive silver belt buckle caught Ian's eye, too, and he surprised the vaquero by getting it for Jamie.

They found a book store. Ignacio was too inundated by so many treasures to make a purchase—too shy as well—but he saw Ian watching him, reading the title of every book the rider lingered over. Without a doubt the boy would come back by himself.

The pueblo nestling under the blue mountains northeast of town affected Ignacio strangely. Even with twenty or more white-blanketed Taoseños in the plaza, the place breathed emptiness and sorrow. Smoke from cooking fires and from the curious, humped outdoor ovens which squatted like guards in front of every dwelling drifted up into the windless August air, blurring the ridges of the mountains and making them look more distant and unreal. The only thing that brought life to the plaza was the scant trickle of water in the stream that divided it.

Ian, on the advice of Max, had left his sketchbook in the car, but he carried Ann's camera. Standing on the earth-filled timber bridge above the little stream, he tried to take a picture of one of the Indian women doing a washing. She screamed at him for not asking permission first, and the rider was glad to use this as an excuse to leave. There was something about the blank walls on every hand which unsettled him.

Sarah gave a party for them, and Ignacio sat in a corner and watched the strangest group of people he had ever seen in one location. It didn't take very long to realize that these oddly assorted types had at least two things in common: they were all artists or craftsmen, and they all seemed to possess some wild kind of freedom. No few of them had money, too. He could smell it—great quantities of it.

Yes, Taos was a delirious experience, but for Ian Taos was Max Balutan. The sculptor was a rough bear of a man, with a beard which seemed made of barbed wire and a fierce scowl which dissolved into a smile of such warmth you couldn't believe it was the same face. No wonder Sarah was taken by him;

no wonder Ian was, too. The boy spent hours in the garage studio, watching silently while the sculptor worked, and Ignacio thought he should be a little jealous, but he wasn't. Max was as solid and honest as the stone he worked or the heavy welded pieces around the studio. It was impossible to feel less than love for him.

Sarah made no secret of the fact that Max shared her bed. "I had a scare three months ago," she said, in front of all three of them and Max. "Thought I was pregnant, sure as hell. Suppose I will be, someday."

Ignacio looked at Ann, wondering how she would take such frankness, but the señora didn't so much as blink or blush. It was Max Balutan who betrayed embarrassment, stuttering, "I've told Sarah we really should get married, Ann, but she thinks we might not last. Nonsense." At least *Max* was blushing.

"Damned well time!" was all Jamie said when they rolled to a stop in the yard of the D Cross A. Gone was any hint that he had given his blessing to the trip, had in fact insisted on it. He looked haggard, and even more out of sorts than usual.

They had taken the LaSalle to Taos, Jamie insisting the Buick would be fine for his one trip to town, but the old car was nowhere to be seen. When Ann asked about it, Jamie almost snarled. "Broke down in Orogrande—on my way back from El Paso." Ignacio was puzzled. Jamie had no business in El Paso that he knew about.

At supper their first night back, the rancher, who had been silent through the meal, suddenly turned to Ian, and with a voice charged with savagery, said, "I been hearing things in town I don't care to hear—not one bit!" Ian looked squarely at his father, waiting. "That Martínez girl at the cantina," Jamie went on, his voice rising, "what the hell you and her been up to?"

"Jamie!" Ann cried.

"Just keep out of this, Ann. Well, Ian?"

The boy continued looking at Jamie, but said nothing. "I don't want you," Jamie said, "fucking around with no Mex tramp."

Ian stood up and left the table. There was no hurried motion, he just walked quietly to the hall door, then turned around and looked at Jamie again. His face was totally without expression, blank, but the *eyes*—the eyes were two pinpoints of hate.

The vaquero didn't sleep well that night, but he didn't sleep at all five nights later, after what happened in the Black Springs depot. He had gone to town with Ian to send the youth's larger baggage off to Roswell for his senior year. Two men from town were lounging on the freight dock, and the rider and the boy were hidden from them by a pile of boxes.

"—and then, according to Clyde Perry," one of them was saying, "he roared up to the Gates house a week ago Tuesday in that old Buick. Practically hauled Millie bodily out of the house and took her to El Paso for an abortion. Well, I guess he's got *some* rights, at that. He sure spent a bundle on Millie's daddy over the past few years. No wonder he's had to start busting up that nice spread of his."

"He sure beats all, that big D Cross A stud," the other man said. "He's serviced half the mares in this town, but it used to be the Mexes when he was a kid, didn't it?"

Ignacio, for once, was glad to see Ian leave for school.

They never spoke to each other about the conversation they had overheard.

Ignacio declined Jamie's invitation to go to Roswell for Ian's commencement exercises. He didn't make any excuse or explanation, either; he just said, "No." He hoped Ian would recognize his refusal for what it was, a basic rejection of Jamie's insistence that his son attend the school in the first place. In a way, it was a completely quixotic gesture. Ian had actually grown fond of the military school in his four years there, but the vaquero knew it still rankled that he had been forced to go.

While the two MacAndrewses were gone, the rider made a little journey of his own. He went to town to have a talk with Dr. Sam. For the past four years, as regular as the seasons rolled around, Concepción had urged this visit, ever since Ian had enlisted her support. She hadn't nagged, but Ignacio knew she could—and would, someday.

"I honestly don't know, Mr. Ortiz. I'm a good enough man in general practice, but this is too delicate for me. You should see a specialist—El Paso, Albuquerque, or better still, back East.

Think I told you that years ago. I really don't know if they could do you much good now. There's damage to the optic nerve, that much I know. Should have been taken care of when it happened, but don't get the idea I'm apologizing. Had my hands full just keeping you alive back then. One thing—you've got to guard against any more shocks to that eye. Smoked glasses might help, if you'd wear them. But a blow of any kind, or too much exposure to intense light, especially suddenly, well . . ." Dr. Sam shrugged his helplessness.

The Ian MacAndrews who came home from Roswell in June of 1939 seemed to have acquired a wisdom almost as unearthly as it was surprising. He deferred to Jamie in every way he could, keeping most of his paintings carefully under wraps.

With Pepe gone, he moved his easel into the deserted bunkhouse, and did most of his work during the days and evenings when his father was away. Ignacio missed the smell of the oils in the ranch house, but he respected Ian's decision. He didn't intrude in the bunkhouse studio, and he wasn't asked into the building. No one was—not even Ann.

If Ian had, in most ways, trimmed his sails to Jamie's wind, there was one place where he made no change in course at all. If anything, he saw even more of Josefina Martínez than before. He did it without any help from Ignacio, and it was plain to the vaquero that Ian was trying to keep him blameless. He never went to the Florida with the rider; his visits were made exclusively when he went to Black Springs by himself. Often, though, Ignacio would chance across Ian in the cantina. The young couple would be sequestered in the alcove, while Jorge, watchful, did double duty waiting tables, unless Concepción was in the bar room, too.

If Jorge still sniffed the air for danger when Ian was there, Concepción had long since been won. "Jorge," she would say, "mind your own business. He is an honorable man—a woman can tell!"

"*Bueno!*" Jorge would retort, "And have you *always* had this second sight?"

With time, Jorge's voiced objections and piercing, suspicious looks grew weaker and more infrequent, and Ignacio smiled.

Sometimes, though, he wasn't entirely sure Ian's visits were the best thing in the world for Concepción. He would see her looking at the MacAndrews boy with eyes glazed with longing, and his heart ached for her.

"I'm going to marry Jo."

The vaquero was not surprised at the announcement—it was certain Ian would someday make it—but by the way it had come out of the blue, without warning or preparation. The two of them were stretching wire on the eastern fence when the younger man placed his hand on the rider's shoulder.

"Don't look so shocked, Nash." Ian smiled. "I don't mean now, or even soon. I'll spend a year at UNM to please the old man, maybe even two. Then I want to go to art school, and then to Taos. But I'm going to marry Jo. You can bet on that."

Five days later Ian came back from seeing Josefina in a rage. Jamie had gone to Socorro to dicker for some new dehorning gear he had read about in a stockman's magazine, and the rider was having supper alone with Ann.

"*Where is he?*" Ian demanded, his dark face drained to the white of cold, calculated anger. Both the señora and the vaquero were too shocked at his looks to speak. "You know what he's done now? He's ordered Sheriff Ortega to keep me out of the Florida on account of my being under age!"

Two weeks before Ian went off to the university in Albuquerque, war broke out in Europe. People in Black Springs said, "The U. S. of A. is too smart to get suckered into this one like we did in 1918," but Ignacio knew for a certainty that sooner or later the drums would roll for America, too.

At first, it was just a fifteen-minute war. Every night at five, he would switch on the radio in the sitting room, and hear a solemn voice say "This-is-London." Then, after the famous cracked bell chimed a dozen times, he would settle in to listen to the announcer tell about the small raids and the hunting of sea marauders which were the only incidents of the counterfeit war which followed the fall of Poland. Most evenings Ann would listen with him, but Jamie wasn't interested. "Let me know when they get down to some real fighting," he would say.

A letter he got from Ian showed the young man's excitement. It was only natural; if the vaquero was correct, this would be Ian's fight. After that, when the broadcasts came on the air, he didn't really hear the reports of bombings or the propaganda claims of the two sides. His mind would drift back to that hospital in Chicago.

No matter that the "phony war," the "*sitzkrieg,*" as he heard it called by someone in the post office one day, still fell far short of wholesale slaughter, he knew that someday the country would "cry havoc, and let slip the dogs. . . ." All he could do was pray Ian wasn't in their path.

Ian had much more time for himself at the university than he had at Roswell. On a few occasions, he went to Taos to see Max and Sarah, but most often he hitchhiked back to Chupadera County, seldom coming to the ranch until after he had gone first to Black Springs and Josefina. Sheriff Ortega had apparently lifted the ban on his going to the Florida, but if Jamie knew about it, he never mentioned it. Maybe, too, the rancher had an idea that the distance between the city and the town would take care of things. At any rate, there was peace of a sort that first year Ian was away.

When he came home for the summer, Jamie's attacks on Josefina began again in earnest. Ignacio marveled that the younger MacAndrews could be so stoic about the constant, unremitting sniping. He never answered his father, never so much as let his face twist when Jamie's remarks bordered on downright obscenity. "Surprised you ain't painted a picture of that Martínez slut," the rancher said one night. "She'd pose for you in the buff, wouldn't she, Ian? Kind of like to see that myself."

Ignacio was amazed to see that Ian was actually smiling at his father. When he looked closely at the smile, though, he was grateful Ann wasn't in the room. It was frightening. Apparently Jamie didn't see what the rider saw, for he was grinning back at Ian. *Dios*, didn't the man know he was looking straight into the barrel of a gun?

"You know, Dad," Ian said, "it just occurred to me that I've never painted anything especially for you. I'll have to take care of that." The smile was gone from Ian's face and something in the dead level voice told Ignacio that Jamie had forced his son to pull the trigger. The bullet hadn't reached its mark, but it would, it would.

A week later Ian walked into the ranch house with a painting. The vaquero, Ann, and Jamie were in the sitting room, and the young man marched past them without a word, leaning the canvas against the wall opposite the bookshelves and then going to work with a hammer and a nail. There was a cloth covering the picture, carefully stretched over the frame and tied in back with twine. Ignacio detected a faint odor of wet oil.

Ian lifted the painting to the wall and hung it on the nail. He had rigged the thing so the covering would come away in one pull. Looking straight at Jamie, he yanked a free end of the twine and the cloth floated to the floor without a sound.

It could have been an avalanche. There was Cuchillo, rising in blackness out of the rangeland, its flanks heaving under a sky which threatened to pour down molten lava. The nearby grass and the piñon marching away from the eye were wasted, seemed dead or dying.

Dios! What this painter had learned from Max! Every passage of brush or knife had a carved look, as if it had been gouged from solid rock. The deep cut in the shoulder of the mountain, where the road wound up to Las Sombras, had been slashed into the canvas with unbelievable intensity. Only one touch of grace appeared in the scene; the Shelby pasturage, gone now from the D Cross A, beckoned softly.

None of this, though, was what the picture was about. A cry from Ann told Ignacio she had seen it at the same moment he had. In the foreground, the stones as heavy as if they were holding down a grave, was the house Jamie had never finished. A lone figure stood in weeds reaching almost to the waist. It was Ann. It was the only picture of his mother Ian had ever painted.

Ian didn't come back to the D Cross A at all during his second year at the university in Albuquerque, despite the trip Ann made to plead with him. He came to Black Springs to see Josefina, and Ignacio learned from Concepción that her niece— over Jorge's not-too-strenuous objections—had spent a weekend on the campus.

He wanted Ian back at the D Cross A passionately, but there didn't seem to be a thing he, Ignacio, could do about it. He did write to Sarah, and had a difficult time trying to get his message across without seeming to interfere. Ian was spending a lot of time in Taos, and he hoped she would talk to him.

The rider wondered if he was being selfish, if he was thinking only of himself in this attempt to get the boy back to wade in the bad blood flooding the D Cross A. But when Ann asked him to go to Albuquerque to see Ian, he seized on her request as if it were a lifeline.

It was easier than he thought it would be. "You're right, of course, Tío Nash." It was good to hear the "Tío Nash" again, but it made him realize how much he wanted the boy to call him Ignacio—and without his asking. "You're right," Ian said. "Whenever I'm away from the D Cross A, I'm only half a man."

Ignacio looked at the paintings in Ian's room. They were mere daubs—even he could see it. As if he had read the vaquero's mind, Ian added, "And I can't paint worth a damn when I'm away from the Ojos Negros."

The day after the Imperial Japanese navy attacked Pearl Harbor, Ian MacAndrews left the University of New Mexico and returned to the D Cross A.

"Right away—soon as I can," he said when Ignacio asked him if he would enlist. This would be no romp for Ian, as Jamie intended his to be in 1917. The rider knew the youth felt strongly about the issues of this war, even if they hadn't talked of it much in the past two years.

It wasn't just a matter of pulling on a soldier suit and marching off. Ian had decided on the Air Corps, and it turned out that after enlistment there would be a time of waiting while the nation geared itself to take so many men. Ian had been too young to register under the selective service law, and he now needed Jamie's signature on his enlistment papers. This was no problem. The rancher, who hadn't paid a particle of attention to the war in Europe, turned jingoist with a passion after the Japanese attack. He couldn't wait to sign. Ann, moving about the ranch house like a sleepwalker, said very little. Ignacio knew she remembered the hospital in Chicago, too.

Ian spent a good deal of his time with his mother, and even some in the bunkhouse, painting, but, as the rider had expected, every chance the youth had, he raced to town to be with Josefina. Fortunately for the peace of the D Cross A, Jamie didn't notice— or pretended not to. He not only sanctioned Ian's unlimited use of the pickup truck or one of the cars, he encouraged it. "Have a good time, Ian. If you're old enough to fight you're old enough to raise a little hell!"

There certainly was enough "hell" being raised by the young men in Black Springs who were, like Ian, waiting. They crowded every bar in town. Aside from Patrick Kelly—old Michael's grandson—with whom Ian had been particular friends since grade school, young MacAndrews didn't see much of any of them. He deliberately avoided the farewell parties for the boys called up, reserving every available moment for the Florida and Josefina.

Jorge Martínez was a study in comedy. Watchful in the past, his eyes were very nearly lidless now as he glared at the pair seated in the alcove. "When she thinks a man might die, it is very easy for a girl to lose her honor," he said once. Ignacio shuddered at the "die" but couldn't suppress a smile at Jorge's use of the old fashioned "lose her honor." The smile widened when Jorge added, pensively, wistfully, "That is not to say I wouldn't understand. He isn't much of an *hombre* if he doesn't try."

One thing seemed clear. Of all the people at the Florida and the D Cross A, only three (if needed Ian had told Josefina) knew of the young man's intention to eventually marry the Martínez girl. Ignacio Ortiz was one of them. It pleased and flattered him. It frightened him.

Christmas came. It was a more joyous holiday than almost any the rider could remember. Ann outdid herself in decorating the sitting room, and the gifts they gave each other were more lavish and numerous than in most other years. The grim news of the reversals in the Philippines hadn't come as yet, and the vaquero, like the others, could almost forget that brave men were dying in unknown places—and that all too soon Ian might be one of them.

It was February before Ian's orders to report for induction in El Paso came. He had three weeks.

"Ignacio," Ann said to him the next day, "Ian told me last night he will marry Josefina Martínez before he leaves. He hasn't told his father yet. That comes tonight. If I'm to help, I'll need some preparation. What's she like? I scarcely know her."

There was fear in her eyes, but steel, too, and he told her all he knew of Josefina—and Jorge and Maria and Concepción. His own love for the cantina's people made him eloquent.

"None of this surprises me, Ignacio," Ann said when he stopped for breath. "Believe me, I didn't ask to see if she was 'good enough' but your opinion gives me everything I need. *Gracias.*"

Ignacio should have known it went too smoothly to be believed.

"—and the Martínezes are giving us an engagement party tomorrow night. I'd like you both to come, but if you'd rather not, I'll bring Jo out to meet you on Sunday afternoon."

"When will the wedding be, Ian?" Ann said.

"A week from Saturday, in Josefina's church."

"In Mex Town?" Jamie's voice was low, almost a whisper.

"Yes. Because of the war the padre didn't insist on the usual instruction or the other stuff. Will you come to the party?" He looked at all three of them.

"We'll see," Jamie said.

"Vaquero?"

"*Sí*, Ian. I will come."

James MacAndrews came to the party at the Cantina Florida. He didn't bring his wife. It was the only thing Ignacio Ortiz found to be grateful to him for. He came to the party late, but after all, a few hours made little difference when you considered that almost thirty years had slipped away since he had been there last.

35

"—AND IF I HAD SAID 'NO!' *NIÑA*," JORGE SAID, "WOULD IT HAVE MADE any difference?"

"Oh, *sí*, Papá!" Josefina said, smiling. "It would have made a lot of difference. We would have named the first one Pancho Villa MacAndrews!"

"The *first* one? It isn't on its way, is it?" Jorge opened his mouth in mock horror.

"*Quién sabe*, Papá?" The Martínez girl laughed as she danced off in Ian's arms.

Young Eloy, Jorge and María's son, was running the bar tonight, and two friends of Josefina were serving the tables. A *mariachi* band was playing from the alcove where Ian and Josefina usually sat. The tables had been pushed to the walls to make room for dancing.

"They are a good thing together, *amigo*," Jorge said, nodding toward the young couple. "Perhaps this will finally end the sickness in me all these years." He sighed. "You were more right than I, my friend. They are not all bad. Not this young *hombre*, anyway." Ignacio didn't feel the need to say a word. His heart was so full he could even forget, for this splendid evening anyway, that Ian would soon go off to war. He reached for Concepción's hand under the table, and she turned the pressure of his more strongly still. She didn't look at him, though. Her eyes hadn't left Ian MacAndrews since the party began.

The evening flew by like a song. There was a lot to drink, of course, but no amount the rider consumed did anything but fill him with wonderful elation. Once in a while, he wondered if Ann

271

and Jamie would come, and if they did, just how all this gaiety might strike them. They would have some catching up to do, and although the señora would take part quickly and readily, there was no telling how Jamie would behave. Well, the vaquero was confident that Concepción, and even Jorge now, would give him a decent welcome. The rest would be up to him.

Concepción pressed him to dance. It was something he had never done before, but no refusals prevented her from dragging him to the space in front of the long bar. It was a strange sensation, holding her like this, so different from their private embraces. He tried to follow her lead as best he could, just swaying to the music mostly, watching Ian and Josefina, María and Jorge, and the two or three other couples on the floor.

It was then, while the band was playing *"Aquellos ojos verdes,"* that he saw Jorge stop, release his wife, and look toward the door, an odd mixture of curiosity and apprehension in his face. The vaquero turned and saw that James MacAndrews had come to his son's engagement party. Ignacio's eyes searched beside and behind the rancher. No, the señora wasn't with him. Jamie had come alone.

Never had the rider seen the tall man look so big, so brutal and dominating, as he did standing there while the last measures of the song died away to nothing and one by one the dancing couples stopped.

"Cómo está, Señor MacAndrews," Jorge said. His voice was bright. *"Bienvenida!"* Surely the greeting was a little forced, but *Dios*, how the man meant it. Ignacio could have gone to his knees for the first time in forty years, praying Jamie would respond in kind.

Instead, Jamie ignored Jorge, ignored them all, even the vaquero. He lifted the heavy, ugly cane and pointed to the door behind him. His son was the only one he looked at. "Get your hat, Ian. It's time to go," he said. His voice was like a norther, and it turned Ignacio's heart to ice.

"But *señor*, the party is only starting"—there was a slight pleading in Jorge's voice—*"now that you are here!"* The rider blessed him for the attempt he made.

"IAN! Did you hear me?" Jamie still hadn't looked at any of the rest of them, much less Jorge. For the first time now,

Ignacio turned his eyes on Ian. If he expected to see the flare of anger he was wrong. Only stupefaction registered in the youthful face. He was holding Josefina's hand, and the pair looked so innocent and defenseless, Ignacio felt his eyes turn moist and stinging.

"Dad," Ian said, his voice so soft and gentle the vaquero knew he still hadn't heard the threat in Jamie's words. "You've never met Jo Martínez, Dad. I'd like—"

In the millionth of a second before Jamie's shout blasted through the cantina, Ignacio begged silently, Jamie, Jamie, take some notice of this girl before it costs you everything!

Jamie's bull-like roar blew away any hope he had. *"Get out of here, Ian! Get in your car and get back to the D Cross A!"*

Now the rider saw the meaning of it reach the MacAndrews boy, saw the pain, saw the dark features harden. Ian turned, first to Josefina and then to Jorge.

"I'm sorry, Mr. Martínez. I think I'd better leave, before there's any more of this." It wasn't a surrender, not in any way. Ian's voice was calm, his manner steady. He turned back to Josefina, took her in his arms. *"Cariña,* it would be foolish to tell you not to let this bother you, but I'll come back tomorrow, and we'll try to forget it all—together." Then he turned and faced Jamie. "I'll leave for now, but only because I don't want to put *my people* here through any more of you. I won't be coming back to the D Cross A, though. You can count on that." He crossed the floor and left the cantina, brushing by his father without so much as a glance.

There wasn't a sound in the cantina now, and later, when he could bring himself to put the pain aside and think about it, Ignacio would wonder—futilely, of course—why James MacAndrews hadn't had the decency, or the common sense, to let things be, stupid and tragic as they already were.

"Martínez!" he said, "It goes without saying there just ain't going to be any wedding!" If Ignacio could have guessed what would happen next, he most assuredly would have tried to stop it, but Jamie acted far too swiftly. The rancher suddenly plunged his hand in his pocket, brought out a wad of money, and flung it at the bar. Some of it fluttered to the floor. "There," he said, and to the rider's horror, the great, wide, dazzling smile lighted his features like a torch. "That ought to ease your feelings a little. Got a hunch the girl has earned it!" He turned and went through the door as though he would wrench it from its hinges.

Ignacio looked at Jorge. If Jorge moved as he had once before, he wouldn't lift a hand to stop him—not this time. *Jorge smiled.* "Don't look so terrified, *amigo,*" he said. "That *gringo* has nothing to fear from me. Help me pick up his money, so I can give it back to him." After they gathered the fallen bills—there must have been a thousand dollars—the vaquero and his friend went through the doorway to the porch. The two MacAndrews men were still there. Ian already in the Buick with the engine running, and Jamie, cane in hand, beside it.

Jorge, with Jamie's money in his hand, went down the steps and toward the car, while the rider watched from the porch. He didn't want to get too close to Jamie—not tonight.

"You'll damned well do as you're told, Ian!" Jamie was shouting. "Now get on home!"

"No, *sir*!" Ian said. "We're through—for good and all! You *can* tell Mom I'll be at the Sacramento until the wedding."

Jorge had stepped in front of the car, but even with the headlights on him there would have been no way of Ian seeing him, for at the word "wedding" Jamie raised the cane and brought it down on Ian's head. Blow followed angry blow, and at first Ian tried to take them without moving aside or flinching. The vaquero saw his hands whiten on the steering wheel.

Then, just as Ignacio left the porch himself, the car shot forward, the wheels spinning savagely, sending a shower of dirt and gravel high in the air.

Jorge never had a chance, as the big car ground him into the caliche and stone of Frontera Street.

36

IT WAS A YEAR BEFORE IAN RETURNED TO CHUPADERA COUNTY. Perhaps it should have surprised Ignacio that the young man, after the vow he had made that last night at the Cantina Florida, had come back at all—but it didn't. Ian, the rider felt certain, would always return to the Ojos Negros. His obsession, compulsion, blood magnetism—call it what you would—was as strong as that of Ignacio Ortiz himself. It transcended anything he would ever feel about his father.

It did surprise the vaquero a little, though, that the young man came back not only to the basin, but to the D Cross A. A few days' hard thought brought the answer to this puzzle. Josefina was gone. It had never been put in words by her or anybody else, but it was clear that she would never marry Ian. The blame for this, and for the terrible tragedy which precipitated it, should have been placed squarely on the shoulders of Ian's father, where it belonged; but the vaquero was convinced the boy felt some dark sense of guilt himself, no matter how undeserved. It was the absurd way Ignacio himself would have felt, although he couldn't have explained why. Ian could come back to the ranch, and be with Jamie, because he had shared in his father's transgression. It seemed of no account that his share had been unwitting and unwilling.

After training at half a dozen different bases, Ian had been assigned to a new bomber group in Mountain Home, Idaho, and was awarded leave to show his gold lieutenant's bars and silver wings to the folks at home. The allotted ten days stretched out to three full weeks with the "delays en route" granted in a string of official telegrams. Ian guessed a shortage of airplanes or bad flying weather was holding up formation of the unit with which he would train and fly in combat. At any rate, the extra time was welcomed by the rider—and the lieutenant's mother.

Ian and Jamie got along amazingly well. Perhaps they realized they both possessed weapons too terrible to wield. They talked little, but were civil to each other.

Ian only went in to Black Springs on two occasions. Once he did the shopping for his mother, and stopped at Kelly's to see how Patrick was doing in the navy. The other time was when he asked Ignacio to go with him to Jorge Martínez's grave.

As they drove through Mex Town to the cemetery by the adobe church, they passed the Florida. If Ian didn't flinch as they rolled by the old building, neither did he turn his head to look at it. At the cemetery, he was as silent as the stone above Jorge's head.

It must have been at Kelly's that Ian learned Josefina was getting married, sometime in June. All he could find out was that the man was a corpsman at the hospital at Fort Bliss, where she had gone to work a few months after her father's death. He told the vaquero, who had already heard it from Concepción, in a voice betraying no emotion whatsoever.

Two nights before his leave was up (late, it was well past ten), Ian kicked open the door of the shack.

Ignacio lowered the book he was reading, and stared at the young man, framed against the blackness of the doorway.

"Can I come in, Tío Nash?"

"*Sí*, Ian," the rider said, sitting up.

"If you've got a couple of glasses, we could have a drink or two." Ian held up a bottle. Ignacio nodded. He really didn't want to drink this late at night, but he reasoned his visit must hold some special importance for the dark youth. He struggled to his feet and motioned Ian to the chair at the table while he found a glass and an old tin cup.

Ian's first drink, a big one, was followed by another just as large before Ignacio was even halfway through his first.

"Don't worry," Ian said, following the rider's eyes to his glass. "I won't get drunk—not tonight. There's not enough in this bottle to do the trick." He went on, "I want you to do me a favor, Nash. If you don't know what Jo Martínez's married name will be, and where she'll live, find it out. When you do, send it to me at Mountain Home, or wherever I am. I'll keep you posted." He paused, and the dark eyes searched the vaquero's face. "Don't get alarmed, Nash. I won't bother her or try to see her. It's this. Kind of an odd thing, I'll admit, but—I want to make Jo the beneficiary of my G.I. insurance. Don't, for God's sake, say anything. It isn't likely she'll collect—and there's no need for her to have to explain me for nothing." Together they finished the bottle, and as he had predicted, Ian was sober when he left the shack.

It seemed Ian was overseas and back, through with his fighting, in no time at all. Perhaps it was some faculty Ignacio had developed in Jamie's war, some ability to shut the wearing passage of time away from him, but to the vaquero it was as if they had just tossed aside the bottle they shared in the shack before Ian was on the ranch again with another leave.

He was back even before the war in Europe was done; nervous, a trifle thinner, smoking more than Ignacio remembered, but otherwise unchanged. The war hadn't been as big an experience for Ian as those preceding it, that was plain, but the leave was far too short to tell. The rancher and his son were just as correct with each other as the first time, and if the rider might have wished for something warmer—for Ann's sake—still, it was no small thing to have something resembling peace again.

Ian managed to get home again at Christmas from the base in Florida where he was teaching navigation, and Ignacio could forget the news of the desperate counterattack the German army was mounting under the very skies Ian had left just months before. When the German push failed, and the good news from the Pacific poured across the country in a widening stream, Ignacio was happy. It would soon be over—and Ian would live.

Then, in that last year of the war, mid-July, something happened to the vaquero. It was something he never spoke of to another living soul. . . .

They had missed a dozen head of stock from the southwest pasture. Jamie and Ignacio thought they must have wandered into some unfamiliar mesquite near the malpais and would eventually turn up thirsty at one of the tanks. When the salt blocks and the seed cake Ignacio dumped from the back of the speeding pickup while Jamie leaned on the horn failed to bring them into view, the rancher and the vaquero became concerned. There hadn't been a sign of the cattle thieves in the Ojos Negros for twenty years or more, Jamie's hunt for "rustlers" notwithstanding (Ignacio still chuckled when he thought of it), but you never knew.

The rider packed a bedroll and a bag of grub. Refusing the rifle Jamie offered, he headed across the bridge on the big walking horse the señora sometimes rode. It was bigger than he liked, but ideal for this kind of work, covering a lot of ground with little effort, and strong enough to keep it up for hours. He struck out through the yuccas on the old ranch road, the south one. Setting an easy pace in the stifling heat, he moved steadily until he reached the gate he used to use on trips to town. From there, where the undergrowth thinned out and there was no shade at all, he turned toward the west.

It was half past noon when he left the buildings of the D Cross A; the afternoon was nearly gone by the time he checked the longest stretch of fence for breaks, and inspected all the low places where the flash flood runoffs had leveled out the land like some gigantic roadbed, horizon wide. He bent from the saddle, looking for tire tracks or hoofprints, until a nagging ache developed in his back, and his right eye burned like a ball of fire. For all of that, he enjoyed the afternoon. It was inferno hot in the alkali depressions, but when he reached the high ground near the malpais, it was cooler, even though the sun still hung high above him.

It didn't matter that he hadn't found his cattle yet. With every strand of wire secure and in its place, and with no sign of predators, animal or man, they had to be inside the fence. He would find them in the morning, if not tonight. He was moving through the farthest southwest corner of the ranch, but he still had time to turn about and make it home. *Sí*, he could work the draws which led back toward the butte, and be in the corral before darkness came.

On second thought, it would be pleasant to spend the night right here, or a little farther over, on some high vantage point of the blackcapped, rocky malpais. Maybe he could spot the wanderers with his one keen eye even before he saddled up at sunrise, and save himself the time and trouble of riding out again. He hadn't spent a night on the open range in years. Yes, he would do it—look the stars in the eye until it was time for sleep.

He made his camp. He picked a gently sloping slab of lava, high and open, but with a lip of stone curled against the north to give protection, if the wind should rise from there. A fire? *Sí,* he would build a fire; not so much for warmth or cooking, but because it seemed the thing to do. It would be a signal, a sign to all the things which squeaked or moved, to the land and the silent sky, that here was man, never quite defenseless or alone when his discovered magic glowed beside him.

The sun vanished under the western rim, and the dark came quickly from wherever it had lurked, splashing black on black as it reached the lava bed. He could hear the big horse shuffle restlessly on the patch of wiry grass where he had tethered him. The little fire winked its warm assurance. He was at peace.

It occurred to him that here, alone, with the stars almost dropping from the sky like silver rain, he could think big thoughts, ruminate on life and death, on love and conflict—and solve it all. He laughed into the desert silence. Thinking wouldn't bring one tenth the answers sleep would. He closed his eyes and let sleep claim him, and he didn't even dream big thoughts. . . .

How had he come so suddenly awake, with every nerve stretched tight, and all his muscles tensed and ready? There had been no sudden sound, and his sleep had been deep enough to keep him locked up tight. Above him he could see that the stars had shifted halfway across the sky. Most of the night was gone, and if it was still dark, the blackness had an air of impermanence. He peered into the desert shadows and set his ears to pick up any sound, but nothing showed its face or spoke to him. Closing his eyes, he tried for a few more moments' sleep, but it didn't work. Something wasn't right. He must be getting old. When the morning sun thundered out of the Capitans and dissolved the shadows, and when he stirred himself and went about his business, things would fall in place.

But there *was something*, no matter how he tried to shrug it off.

He packed his bedroll, deciding he wouldn't eat until he had been in the saddle for a while. His little fire had breathed its last hours earlier, but he found a dead ocotillo branch and scattered the lifeless ashes. In the quiet, the grating of the branch echoed from the curling lip of stone behind him and made him jump. A strange feeling moved along his spine, and all at once his skin tingled and became so sensitive he was sure it could pick up sound, movement, light, heat—anything—from many miles away.

He hurried now to strike his little camp, anxious to get away from this place which had been such a pleasant haven the night before. There was a touch of panic in his chest. Still, he paused to take one last look around; first to the Magdalenas in the west, north toward the black peak which hung above the malpais, then past the mighty double head of Sierra Blanca to the east, and finally—he felt his eyes pulled that way—almost directly south. From somewhere on the Jornada del Muerto, behind the Oscuras or the San Andres, it came—and when it did, he was looking straight into the heart of it.

He felt it before he saw it, a tremor so slight he wasn't certain it was real. Then it came again, and in earnest, a shock of unimagined fury, as if he stood in the center of converging forces which impacted in the marrow of his bones. For one brief terrifying moment he was sure his body would be shattered. How he stayed erect he would never know.

Later, when he thought of what had happened, he would realize it couldn't have been this way at all, but this was how he would always remember it: the shudder; the rippling shock, and the hot wind that rose behind it; and only then, the light.

Dios, the light! It was brilliant, awesome, horrifying. It tore the sky apart, made every rock and bush as far as he could see as incandescent as a bed of glowing coals. He felt as if he was staring into the mouth of hell.

Not until August did Ignacio learn the facts about what he had seen and felt. By the time the news of Hiroshima—and three days later Nagasaki—reached the D Cross A, the way it had seemed to happen had burned too deeply in him to be altered by any facts. *The light!* It was final, not (as some would have it) "in the beginning," but in the end. He never did put the thing in proper focus—and he never told a soul that he had seen it. There was only one fact he wanted to remember from that day. Ignacio Ortiz found his missing cows.

Still too stunned for thinking, he somehow saddled the horse and started out. Numbed, his hand uncertain on the reins, he never thought of abandoning the search. Finally, in an arroyo shaped like a miniature box canyon, all but lost to view behind some curious undergrowth, he found the truants, eleven of them, trapped by their own stupidity, as unmindful of what had happened as the horse he rode so poorly.

A week later, he faced the truth about another thing. The right eye which had pained him so terribly in the past was gone completely, dead and sightless as a chunk of stone. Ignacio never mentioned that fact, either.

Ian MacAndrews came home for good to find an even smaller D Cross A. With the herd still on the small side after the loss of so many during the dry time of the thirties, and depleted further by the demands of the war, Jamie had talked Sarah into letting him sell another fifty sections promising this would be the last. Ignacio wondered where the money went. There should, he reasoned, have been a swell of cash from the sale of stock over the last several years, but, of course, he didn't ask. Every year now, Jamie purchased another car, and that took money. He changed the one Ann drove almost as frequently, in spite of her protests that the old one was good enough. Maybe, too, Jamie was investing in the market again, but the rider had seldom been in the rancher's confidence, and he wasn't now.

If the diminution of the D Cross A disturbed Ian in any way he didn't speak of it. Never talkative, the young man who returned from the war was as mute as stone, not with a "modest stillness and humility," but more with a silence which loomed "as fearfully as doth a galled rock o'erhang and jutty his confounded base." When he wasn't working (and he did work, setting to the chores with a quiet will) he was either in the bunkhouse, painting, or bumping around the basin in the pickup, sometimes with only the familiar sketchbook, but more and more often with a full complement of paints, easel, and brushes. During his first year back he seldom went to Black Springs, and never, of course, to the Florida.

After that, the pattern changed. He didn't go to the Martínez place, but the vaquero learned from Concepción that Ian was a regular at the Hacienda Roja, the Mex Town saloon recently opened by a man from Tularosa. It was a different kind of tavern from the old Florida. The crowd was wilder, faster, heavier drinkers and more reckless gamblers by far than the staid regulars of Ignacio's haunt. "I know why he goes there!" Concepción blazed. "It is that *puta*!" Yes, Ignacio had heard there was a woman, and that there had already been several nasty brawls involving her. "If he is not careful," Concepción went on, "he will catch something from that—that—" Apparently she had no word strong enough. Well, if Ian was going to "catch something," the rider hoped it wouldn't be a knife blade between the ribs. "Tell him, Ignacio," Concepción said, "he is always welcome here at the Florida—no matter what happened." He did tell him, but Ian only turned away.

That was why he didn't relay the other thing Concepción told him—about Josefina. He would have, if Ian had asked about her. He never did, never mentioned the girl in the vaquero's hearing, nor anywhere else, Ignacio was sure of that. Josefina's marriage wasn't going well, even though there was a child, and another on the way. Concepción had gone down to El Paso for the first one, and would go again. "It will surprise you, Ignacio," she said. "The trouble is not with Horacio but with my niece. They have a nice little house, and he makes good money, but she is restless and they fight a lot. I know she still thinks of Ian." No, he didn't tell Ian. He didn't dream, either, that a day would come when he would wish he had.

The trips to town the two MacAndrews men and Ignacio made in those last years of the forties were strange affairs, each of them heading in his own particular silence for different destinations: Jamie to the Sacramento (and other places the rider made no attempt to learn), Ian to the Hacienda Roja, and Ignacio to the Florida and Concepción Martínez. Once or twice they were all in town at once, and the thought of the señora, alone and neglected at the D Cross A, weighed so heavily on Ignacio that he was no good to Concepción at all. From then on, he arranged his trips only when he was sure one of the other two would be staying at the ranch. Often this meant coming into town on horseback, no easy thing now that Kelly's was only selling gas and fixing cars.

Ian MacAndrews seemed like two people. If there was any truth in the rumors which came directly, or through Concepción, Ian was as wild as the others at the Hacienda Roja. There was talk of fights, and insane drinking, and more women than the first, and there was also a story about the wife of a colonel down at Holloman near Alamogordo. There had been a brawl, and the woman's husband had been hospitalized. The air force man thought of bringing charges but his base commander talked him out of it, and within weeks the flyer and his wife were reassigned to Germany.

This wasn't the Ian who worked and painted at the D Cross A. He was gentle with and tenderly solicitous of his mother. If he returned to the ranch after too wild a time with women and liquor, he spent the night in the bunkhouse. Ignacio was sure Ann never gave a thought to this, and if he hadn't heard the tales from town, Ignacio too, would have imagined that it was oils and canvas which occupied the man. Ian was decent to his father, too, but it was, at best, the kind of decency one gives to strangers. Ignacio concluded that Ian, wrongly, was taking the entire blame for Jorge's death, living so intensely with this guilt that all other feeling was small indeed.

It wasn't the best of worlds, but it could be lived with, and they all might have lived with it for a long, long time, if only Jamie had had the sense to leave well enough alone.

"If that crap you're up to in the bunkhouse is so hellfired important, when do we get to see it?" Jamie said one night at supper.

"I'm not ready to show my work just yet," Ian said.

"I still say there's something queer about a grown man smearing paint on a hunk of cloth."

The vaquero never saw Ian react to these sallies, but as time went by and they became more frequent, he was sure they must be having some effect. It would have been a good deal better, he thought, if Ian would respond to each of them a *little*. He was deathly afraid of the day when the cumulative results would blow it all wide open.

Fortunately, the father and son weren't together very much. The rancher was gone much of the time, especially in the summers, when the quarter horses were running at Ruidoso above the Mescalero. Ignacio wasn't sure, but he suspected this was where some of the money was going. He consoled himself that it had been a year since he heard talk in town of Jamie and other women.

But there was no denying that Jamie's neglect of the D Cross A was beginning to border on the criminal. All the vaquero could do was work and plan around him, setting schedules himself if he couldn't goad Jamie to a decision, using Ian and his willingness as judiciously as he could.

The younger MacAndrews could become a fine rancher. Mostly he followed Ignacio's lead, but from time to time he showed flashes of insight in his husbandry which brought Douglas or Angus quickly to mind. Then, and there was no guilt about it, only a strange, deep thump of the heart, Ignacio would think how magnificent it would be if only Ian MacAndrews could run the D Cross A.

He bought a pair of cheap reading glasses at the new Ben Franklin store on Stanton Street. The owner had moved in from Moriarty or someplace north, and wouldn't be likely to speak of the purchase to anyone Ignacio knew. It seemed foolish to keep his difficulty secret, but if he saw the doctor, or mentioned it to Ann or Ian, they would find out his eye was gone. That might lead to what had caused it, and he didn't want to speak of that with anyone.

He had read everything he could find about the thing he had seen light the desert, and when he exhausted the Black Springs library, he wrote away for more. It was the fine print in these books which alerted him to his need for glasses. His reading told him nothing of what he wanted to know. There was no *reality* in any of it. Shakespeare, for all that his slaves and peasants spoke like kings, was more real than all the technology responsible for the thing he had witnessed that dark morning. Nothing real ever happened in a formula—it took place on the reaches of the land, or in the recesses of the heart.

The man from Stratford knew that, and so, in his small way, did he.

The memory of the blast plagued him in the night and worried his days. He couldn't escape the feeling that man had somehow asked for this. The recollection was with him still of the ruined ranch he had visited with Douglas so long ago. Of course, he couldn't blame the forlorn and miserable rancher; it wasn't that man's fault that this destructive force had been unleashed. He looked at the D Cross A. Douglas MacAndrews's fence might not be quite enough.

When he had decided it was presumptuous of him to be considering such weighty matters, he got comfort from an unexpected source. A letter from Sarah—to all of them—said Max had been offered a commission to do a piece commemorating the first atomic bomb, to be erected at Trinity site. "He turned it down," Sarah said. "Max thinks it would be like memorializing original sin. He's gotten quite a bit of heat from the flag wavers, but some of the 'big think' types at Los Alamos have backed his stand."

Ian and Ann applauded the sculptor's decision. Jamie snorted his contempt. "What do you expect? God damned Jews ain't patriots!" Ignacio saw the look Ian gave his father. The uneasy peace was coming to an end.

37

"Hey! Have a drink and start smiling," Max Balutan said, holding the champagne bottle in a hand which looked strong enough to crush it. "This is a wedding—not a wake!"

As the sculptor filled their glasses and moved off to join the other guests in Sarah's house behind the gallery (*her* gallery now that Leila had gone back East) Ann, Ian, and the rider huddled together even more glumly than before.

"By God," Ian said, "you sure wouldn't know it to look at him." No, the vaquero thought, you wouldn't. Max, at sixty, was the picture of health, but Sarah had told them that Max, on this their wedding day, was a dying man. "Cancer!" she had said when they were just fifteen minutes inside the house. The letter announcing the marriage hadn't even hinted at it, and the three from the D Cross A had come to Taos like children on a picnic.

Jamie, of course, had pulled a face and refused to go. "Jesus!" he had exploded. "What the hell does she want to get married for now? People have pretty near forgot what she's been up to. Does she have to remind everybody she ain't nothing but a forty-five-year-old tramp?"

The wedding had indeed been something to speculate on, but now the answer came in the news of Max's illness. "How long, Sarah?" Ann had asked, and Sarah had given a helpless shrug.

"Don't really know, Ann," she said. "It's been two months since Max was willing to see the doctor, and he told us less than a year then."

"It must be terrifying," Ann said.

286

"To me, yes," Sarah said. "But Max? If it is, he doesn't let on. We don't talk a lot. He's too busy working, and when he isn't in the studio, he sleeps." There was an agony of silence until Ian spoke.

"No, Max hasn't any terror—not of dying, anyway."

The two women glanced at Ian for a moment, then turned to each other again. Only Ignacio continued to watch him. Something was happening inside that dark head. Even with the talk of death, there was a new vitality—missing since before the war, before Jorge.

"Sarah!" Ian said suddenly, "How *is* his work?"

"Oh, Ian, it's—magnificent!" There were tears in the blue-gray eyes for the first time since they arrived. "That's the worst of it. He doesn't realize it. Keeps trying for even more."

Ian nodded. There was a look of satisfaction on his face.

There was no pretense of a honeymoon, of course, and Ann, Ian, and the rider stayed on in Taos for a week. Max went to his workshop every morning (the "factory," he called it) and Ignacio and Ian, at his request, tagged along.

According to the sculptor, the decision to marry was made for business reasons. "I've got a storeroom in town full of stuff. Now I'm not Moore or Giacometti, or even in their class, but my junk's worth *something*. There's some greedy Balutans back in the Bronx who'd cart if off like pack rats when I—well, at any rate, it's easier to make Sarah my legal heir if she's my wife." He didn't fool Ignacio. The vaquero remembered the conversation when they first came to Taos. It probably would have pleased Sarah to be Max's "mistress" until she died, but there was a puritan heart in this bearded artist. Max must be chuckling behind the pain at having tricked Sarah into accepting his one last gift, respectability. It warmed Ignacio to think of it.

As they watched Max at work it amazed the vaquero that the dying man could show such strength in the way he used his tools. For some years he had worked exclusively in stone. The welding torch, the tanks, and other equipment which had fascinated the young Ian, now lay rusting in a corner. "It's more direct this way," Max said, "just me and the material, no middle man. But it beats hell out of me how complicated art gets, just when I thought I'd made it simple."

A great deal of good-natured banter passed between Ian and Max that last week, and Ignacio laughed with them. He could almost forget the thing Max was facing, and the sculptor seemed brightest when Ian teased him about his work.

"Look, Balutan," Ian would say, "I'll admit your whittling there has a certain charm, but—"

"CHARM?" Max would bellow, threatening the younger man with the hammer or the chisel.

"—as an art form it's light-years behind the work that's done in oil."

"Finger painting show-and-tell horseshit!" Max would roar, collapsing into laughter. Something echoed in Ignacio's memory; the words were like the ones Jamie used, but the tone was— Angus.

As the week wore on, Ian changed. Something Ignacio read when he studied the blast at Trinity came to mind, a physical law which governed the "conversation of energy." It was as if the strength now ebbing from Max Balutan were being distilled somehow, its essence stored in Ian.

Max turned deadly serious the day before they left. "Ian," he said, "isn't it time for you to have a show? Sarah would love to set it up." Ian shrugged, and Max went on, "Don't cop out on me, Ian. It's time."

"How do we know I'm any good?"

"Well, we'll find that out. Take a year, maybe a little longer, but not two. Work until you're sure it will kill you, and then let the world have a good look. I haven't the slightest notion if you're ready as an artist, Ian, but you're ready as a man."

38

As he grew older, Ignacio Ortiz noticed that time, the foot-dragging constant of his youth, was picking up pace, but the year that passed after Max and Sarah's wedding showed such an alarming burst of speed it left him gasping. The sculptor died just eleven months after the three of them had been in Taos. There wasn't any funeral; it was Max's last wish that no fuss be made, and Sarah honored it. She wrote to say that she was making it just fine, and had been busier than she dreamed administering her husband's artistic legacy.

Ian was working at such a pitch of energy and strength it seemed the bunkhouse emanated a field of force. The vaquero couldn't help thinking it an inheritance from Max. Not that Ian hadn't applied himself before; he was always industrious and serious, but this was more intense by far. Ignacio worked feverishly, too, partly because Ian's labors spurred him on, but mostly because he didn't want Jamie thinking the work in the bunkhouse caused any neglect of the D Cross A.

Ann and the rider still weren't permitted in the studio, but Ian's refusal now was a smiling one. "Don't worry," he told his mother and his friend. "You'll see it before anybody else. Be patient a few more months, please." He showed a new confidence. Ignacio didn't ask if the work was going well. He didn't have to.

There was an added bounty which seemed a direct result of this activity. There had been no friction of any consequence between Ian and his father. Of course, they rode separately working the ranch, and when Ian wasn't in the saddle he was at the easel. And Jamie was spending time away from the D Cross A again, lots of it. Ignacio was sure there was another woman.

Then the vaquero's thoughts were ripped away from the D Cross A. Concepción Martínez announced she was leaving the Cantina Florida, Black Springs, and the Ojos Negros.

"I will always love you, Ignacio, but I *must* do this."

"*Sí, cariña.* I understand." Yes, he did. That was the trouble.

"I won't even pretend it is unselfish, Ignacio. I *want* to do it."

"I pray you will be happy, Concepción, *verdad.*"

Josefina had left her husband, Horacio, and run off, to California, Concepción thought. It was a bad business, some time in coming, but Ignacio remembered the earlier report, that the young mother was "restless." Now, it seemed, there had been other men, a string of them. "It is a terrible thing to say," Concepción said, "but in a way I understand. Horacio was always just a substitute for Ian. But," her eyes flared, "how could she leave *los niños*, her children?" Concepción would go to El Paso and keep house for Horacio and raise Josefina's babies. Tears were brimming in her eyes, but there was joy mixed generously with the sorrow. "I will come back from time to time, Ignacio, and you can come to me."

"*Sí,* Concepción," he said. It would never happen.

All at once the enormity of his loss struck him and something twisted painfully inside. *Dios,* how could he give up this woman? For more than twenty years she had been his only refuge. When his poor body had been battered beyond belief she had nursed him back to life, and when his heart had been squeezed dry of blood, she had somehow filled it up again with hers. He still needed this, needed her.

"Ignacio," she said softly, looking down to her folded hands. "Although I want to do this as much as anything I can remember—if you want me to, I will stay with you, *mi corazón.*"

Yes! Why not? Why should he give her up? Why? Emotions he couldn't identify or separate washed over him in a terrible flood. His need and longing cried out from the farthest corner of his soul, and he felt deprived and frightened. All the rapes and robberies of his life demanded retribution. For once he would do something for Ignacio Ortiz. Yes, he would make her stay, her need was *not* as great as his.

What he said was, "No, Concepción. You must go to Josefina's children. *Vaya con Dios, mi amor.*"

He almost told Ian about Concepción and Josefina, but decided against it. When he thought of the work going on in the bunkhouse he knew he couldn't risk it. Ian had never once spoken of Josefina since that night in the shack, but the rider still feared that he might run off to find the girl. It would not be the worst thing in the world to happen, but it could wait. Ignacio had the strangest feeling the painting couldn't.

Later, when it was all over, and nothing could be done, he wondered whether, if he *had* told Ian, the affair with Vicki Hastings would ever have taken place.

"No, not yet!" This was an incredibly laughing Ian. "I'm going to take a horse and a bedroll and some fishing tackle and go up in the Whites for a few days. I just want to shake a few things out in my mind. When I get back," he told Ann and Ignacio, "the two of you can help me decide which ones go to the state fair, and which ones Sarah gets for the show in Taos. And you can help me get them crated and into town for shipment."

"Are *you* satisfied with what you've done, Ian?" Ann said.

"Yes. I am. I think I'm on my way at last."

Sarah came down from Taos to help. Jamie had gone up to Ruidoso for a week, but he wasn't even missed, so excited were the two women about the forthcoming shows. Sarah was beside herself at the thought of what was waiting for them in the padlocked bunkhouse, and once the vaquero found her in front of it with a crowbar in her hand. For a moment he really thought he might have to restrain her, but she finally walked away shaking her head. Well, it wasn't a great deal different for him. He couldn't work. He peered down the old road to the south and the new one to the highway, looking for Ian.

The first thing he saw was Jamie's Cadillac. The rancher was back on the D Cross A three days earlier than expected. He left the car in the middle of the yard and disappeared inside the house with a ravaged face. Jamie didn't show up at supper, or the next day, either. The enthusiasm and expectancy of the women was dampened momentarily by Jamie's sudden return, but it surged upward irrepressibly, and their conversation turned repeatedly to the "great unveiling" as Sarah called it.

Then, three days after his father returned, Ian came back, his horse loping across the plank bridge in the middle of a dark, moonless night. The stirring in the corral woke the rider, and he went to his window and saw Ian unsaddling. He was about to return to his bunk when he realized young MacAndrews was coming directly to the shack. He had the door open by the time Ian reached it. When Ignacio put a match to his oil lamp, he saw a face every bit as devastated as the one he'd seen on Jamie.

"I wouldn't tell you this if I had any hope you wouldn't find it out, anyway," Ian said, collapsing into the chair like a man who'd been beaten. "I guess I just want to make sure you know I didn't plan it. It just happened."

The story came in bits and pieces. After a day of no luck fishing the streams below Nogal Peak, Ian had moved over into the Mescalero, in the shadow of Sierra Blanca. He stopped for provisions at the general store at Alto, on the road between Capitan and Ruidoso. That was where he met Vicki Hastings.

"She had trouble with her car. Carburetor wasn't right for that altitude, and I fixed it for her. Well, nothing would do but that we have dinner together, and we wound up later at this cabin near the racetrack. Said she was renting it from some Texan—can't recall the name she mentioned—but when I went to the bathroom, I knew she wasn't there alone; a man's pajamas, shaving stuff, enough to tell me he was camped in solid." Ian lit a cigarette and stared at the smoke before going on. "I tried to leave, but she insisted her 'friend' wasn't coming up for another week.

"I'll admit I didn't *want* to leave. She was from someplace East, near Philadelphia, and as good to look at as she was bright. Divorced, no kids, a little older than I am, but not forty. So, I stayed." He was silent for a moment, and then he swallowed like a man taking medicine. "We were in bed together when her 'Texan' and another man and woman walked in on us.

"It would have been bad enough to see my father there, but with that blabbermouth Callaway and the broad he'd brought for the party they were going to have, I almost died." Ian looked straight at the vaquero. "I wasn't even mad or shocked, Nash. For the first time in my life I felt sorry for him. He must have aged twenty years in as many seconds."

The next day was awful. If he hadn't seen Ian the night before he would have fretted, as Ann and Sarah did, at the man's refusal to open the bunkhouse. It made it worse that he knew the reason. When Sarah asked him if he knew why and he shrugged his shoulders, he felt he had told her an outright lie.

He was amazed when Jamie showed up for supper. The rancher didn't flinch. He looked at Ian all through the meal, and the rider realized that Jamie thought his son would tell. It was an odd thought, but he couldn't help but admire the elder MacAndrews a little then. In his own crude way, he was actually facing up to something.

Neither Ian nor his father had to talk much while they ate. Sarah, her vexation growing by the minute, dominated what passed for conversation. "Look here, Ian," she finally said, "I'm going back to Taos tomorrow if I don't get to see your work tonight!"

Ian looked at his father, and said something which took the vaquero completely by surprise. "All right—provided Dad will come along and see it, too."

Ignacio's surprise turned to astonishment when Jamie nodded.

The rider knew he should be pleased, but all of a sudden he felt as if his heart had stopped completely. This was no good, no good at all, but he couldn't have said why to save his soul. If there were only some way to get Ian to withdraw the invitation—but, no, it was too late now.

39

"SARAH," IAN LAUGHED, "GET THE HELL OUT OF THE LIGHT, OR I'LL never get this lock open!"

Ignacio moved the lantern closer to where Ian fumbled with the key. He could see that the excitement and pleasure which had animated the young man's face since Jamie agreed to look at the paintings hadn't abated in the slightest. Maybe the misgivings he felt weren't justified, and he was being a weak and worried old woman.

"Hurry up!" Sarah barked. "I've waited more than twenty years for this, Ian!"

It came to the vaquero then that for the first time ever, he wasn't the one bringing up the rear. He couldn't see Jamie in the dark behind him, but he could feel him there—and the dread he had felt at the table assailed him with redoubled force.

When the lights came on, Sarah practically pushed Ian in ahead of her. When his one good eye adjusted to the light and Ignacio took his first look at Ian's world, he almost staggered.

The colors! They vibrated in the room like distinct and separate sounds. It was as if the far wall of the studio had been blasted out, as if they were looking straight to the outside, as if the range itself had moved in to overrun the five of them.

"My God!" Sarah said.

Ignacio's eyes raced from one canvas to another, coming back to the previous one when the afterimage told him he hadn't yet absorbed its impact. Ian stood stock still while Sarah, Ann, and Ignacio moved slowly around. The rider didn't look back, but he knew that Jamie had stopped just inside the door.

The three walls were hung solidly with canvases, and under them, in stacks, were more. Sarah, after her first shout, was silent, prowling in front of the hanging works like a cat, then falling to her knees to pull the stacks apart. Ann drifted about as if in a dream.

Most of the pictures, particularly those on the two side walls, were landscapes, and the vaquero looked at them first. For some reason, he saved the portraits on the facing wall for last. There were scenes from every part of the Ojos Negros; most of them, though, were places on the D Cross A itself. He recognized every stone, each great yucca; even the wiry strands of gramma grass seemed uniquely remembered from some special time when he had ridden over them. They were not pretty pictures. The painter, in his passionate honesty, had no illusions about this land, and would foster none. They were savage, but with a fearsome, anguished beauty almost more than the eye could stand—and more than the heart could bear. Ignacio choked back a sob.

Then, as he turned to the wall where the portraits hung, he heard Jamie breathing heavily behind him. *Dios!* If the landscapes showed how deeply the artist looked beneath the surface of the land, the people were more naked still. There they were, all of them, each one caught in a moment which would live far longer than the flesh experiencing it. The passage of the brush or painting knife had pinned them forever in time and form they each had chosen without knowing it.

There was Douglas, standing in the compound, massive, but with the hint of his ultimate collapse captured by tiny cracks in the granite face. Ann was pensive, a woman haunted by the strength she knew she had but could not put to work. Ian had painted Sarah in Agnes's old rocker by the fire. She looked defiant and yet defeated. There was one painting on the wall which contained no people. Bleak, forbidding, without one compromising stroke to relieve its grimness, it was the rockstrewn grave of Angus. To the side of it hung other portraits, two of them. Ignacio Ortiz was mounted on the back of Pavo, dressed as he had been the day he met Gibbon in the alley. And there was a full-length study of James MacAndrews.

The background was the D Cross A, a ruined D Cross A. Nothing was exaggerated or overdone. It was the way it was, the way even Ignacio Ortiz had refused to see it. Jamie, in the picture, was leaning on the cane. His face was bland, but as the rider looked at it, it seemed the man was smiling an inane and vacant smile.

"My God!" Sarah said again, and Ignacio realized she and the señora had seen it, too. Jamie left the bunkhouse.

Ann and Sarah were quiet as Ian talked about getting the "best of the stuff" ready for the fair in Albuquerque and the show at Sarah's place, La Galería Rincón in Taos. His bubbling excitement finally drew them out, and before they went to bed they were in such a soaring mood it almost captured Ignacio, too. Almost.

As he left the studio, with the other three coming out behind him, he saw, leaning by the door, one more of Ian's paintings. It was the one he had done as a boy, the one of Ann's unfinished house.

It was well past midnight. If he had been dreaming, the dream was shattered when he smelled the smoke, and heard the first shrill screams of the ponies in the corral. His one eye was barely open when he saw the orange light of the flames burst through the window of the shack, and he knew there was no time at all for thinking. He raced outside, and looked up the pathway to see the great tongues of flame licking at the rear of the bunkhouse. Somehow he made his legs work, and his heart pounding like the hoofbeats of a runaway, he ran wildly, his chest heaving.

When he reached the bunkhouse and kicked the door, he gave a small sigh of thanks Ian hadn't locked it. A blast of superheated air rushed out and almost sent him flying backward, but he managed to reach inside and grasp a painting in a hand which felt seared to the very bone. As he retreated to a safer distance he tried to think what, if anything, could be done. There was nothing. The fire had been set too carefully, and it was only minutes before the roof caved in.

By the time he took the one rescued painting to the shack, Ann, Ian, and Sarah were in the yard. He wouldn't go to them immediately. There were other things to do. It didn't look as if the stable or the tack room were in any danger, but he would check them just the same.

"I don't need to ask you to look after my mother, Nash," Ian MacAndrews said, as he dismounted. "I know you will."

The sun hadn't cleared the top of Cuchillo Peak by the time the two of them reached the highway. It had been a furious ride. Ian had beaten his poor mount until Ignacio feared the animal would quit on him. The brightest flames had died away, but the bunkhouse was still smoldering when they crossed the bridge and rounded the butte. He had nodded silently when Ian asked him to ride to the highway and bring back the horse he saddled. Ian's answer to Ann's suggestion that he stay the night had convinced him arguments wouldn't do.

"No," Ian said. "All I want from here is in that fire—and if I stay here half an hour more, *I'll kill him*!"

They rode off into the darkness, the image of the señora's face as she kissed her son so strongly in the rider's mind that he failed to notice the first sliver of dawn in the sky above Cuchillo until the ride was almost over.

"Thanks, Nash," Ian said. "I shouldn't have long to wait for a ride from here. And, Nash, don't stay with me. Forgive me, Tío, but I'd rather be alone."

The vaquero nodded. He made Ian's horse fast to his saddle horn, remounted, and turned his pony toward the D Cross A. When he reached the gate he reined in and looked back at Ian. The first rays of the sun had just reached the dark head, and he waved.

"Goodbye, my friend!" Ian shouted.

"No, no, Ian, *por favor*," he called back. "*Hasta la vista*—not goodbye, *please*!"

He saw Ian shake his head. "I'm sorry—no. It is *adiós*, Ignacio!"

It echoed in the dawn. "*Ignacio.*"

40

Now for Ignacio Ortiz began the desolate years, the long, lonely, truly wasted years. One, two, seven roundups slipped upon him and went their way. He worked them all, telling himself at first that he rode as well as ever, and perhaps he did, for the first day or so. Sooner or later, when his horse spotted a stray before he did, when the flies seemed more numerous than ever, or when sweat blinded his remaining eye, he faced the truth. He wasn't as young as he once had been. Just how young was that? Growing older was a relative thing; you had to know the starting point.

Sometimes the longing to remember the years before Ramos would sweep over him like a physical lust. Once or twice, after Ian left, the dreams almost opened the past to him, but when the curtain seemed about to part, he would awake. There would be the darkness of the shack, nothing more, and the full sense of his incompleteness would descend on him again.

For a long time none of them knew what had become of Ian. Ignacio, and Sarah, too, had expected he would turn up in Taos, but more than a year went by without a sign of him. In a way, the vaquero was encouraged by the lack of news. Since Ian hadn't been in touch, and hadn't gone to Sarah, he deluded himself that he might soon see him striding across the compound of the D Cross A—home for good.

It didn't happen. Two Christmases after he left Ian at the highway, a letter came for Ann. She showed it to the rider, but apparently not to Jamie. It was almost curt. He was in Chicago, had been for some months, working in the art department of an advertising agency. He was quite content, he said. There was no mention of coming back, but since it was not clear-cut that he wouldn't, Ignacio forced still more hope into a heart already badly strained by it.

When Sarah came to the ranch for the holiday, she read the letter, too. She had just sold an article on Max to a New York art review, and was leaving after New Year's to talk to a publisher who was thinking about a book on her husband's work. "I'll stop in Chicago and talk to him," she said. She didn't say she would try to bring him back, but Ignacio knew she would. When January came and went, and February, with no report from her, the rider knew he wouldn't be seeing Ian for another while.

These were the "funeral" years. There was one month when it seemed he spent as much time in his black suit as he did in Levis. Findlay Stafford gained a notoriety he didn't care a bit about by living past the century mark before he went. Carlos Sánchez passed away at harvest time, going to sleep quietly between the rows of beans on his little farm on the Río Concho. His nephew finished picking the biggest crop Carlos had in twenty years.

Dr. Sam Colvin died. At the services in the church Agnes and Douglas had been buried from, where Jamie and Ann had been married, where he had seen Ian and Sarah christened, Ignacio looked about him and saw middle-aged men and women whom Dr. Sam had delivered. In the front row, while the minister, who had taken the place not of Dr. Clifton but of the pastor who followed *him*, droned the familiar platitudes on life and death, he watched the back of the head of a woman sitting there. Her hair was silver, brilliant above the black dress she wore. He couldn't see her face, but there was something in the sag of the shoulders which told him she was old, very old.

When the service ended and she rose to leave, he saw, behind the lines in the forehead and around the mouth, the face of Sally Bannister. He didn't seek her out, sure that Sally wouldn't want to know he recognized her.

Once a month he got a letter from Concepción. They were poorly written, the penmanship crude and the wording execrable, her love for him stated in the same stilted phrase which ended each of them identically, but they were a regular and welcome source of joy. Here was one soul, at least, who had found a measure of fulfillment in this sorry life. *Los niños!* They were in their twenties now and taking care of *her*, but they were still *los niños*. The only sorrow he ever felt when he read her letters was that her happiness in the children made him think of Ian.

After the terrible events of Ian's leaving, he had tried to maintain the first, fine rapturous hatred for Jamie which had roared through his being like the flames of the bunkhouse fire. When he realized the rancher was becoming as wasted as the D Cross A, his hatred turned first to contempt, then pity, and at last—he could scarcely credit this himself—to something uneasily like the guarded affection he felt toward the man when they were boys.

There was still the vow to Douglas, but just as important in a way was the fact that they were still fellow riders—no small thing for Ignacio Ortiz. Beyond that, they were all that was left of the many men who had worked this range. If Jamie didn't share the passion Ignacio had for the rolling grasslands, the arroyos and yucca-studded pastures, he must care something for them. It was, indeed, the last hope the vaquero had.

Some of the grazing sections they had simply sealed off, as there was no need for the grass there to feed the diminished herd. Ignacio never rode to those places. He was sure the sight of all that good grass, with no cattle feeding, would be more than he could bear. He suggested they lease the meadows they were no longer using, but Jamie snapped, "I ain't giving it up yet, *amigo*. This is still the D Cross A!" Perhaps his hope was not misplaced.

Ann had become a mystery to him. He had expected some great change with Ian gone (for good now, presumably) but the dreamlike state which began to settle on her as far back as the years following the death of Douglas was now enhanced and magnified. Never once did she refer to the cause of Ian's flight, and he was certain she had never taken Jamie to task for it in private, either. It sometimes seemed she was listening to sounds he couldn't hear.

Sarah came to visit regularly. The gallery was doing a fantastic business, she reported, and she had any number of offers to lecture following the appearance of the book on Max. When she bumped across the bridge to spend a weekend, it was like a fresh breeze swept the old place—for a while. After a time Ignacio could see her become depressed. He wasn't sure whether it was the appearance of the ranch or Ian's absence.

On one trip he finally got her talking about Chicago. "You wouldn't know him, Nash. He's calm, and in a way as contented as a God damned milk cow! No spark, no fire. Dead. He isn't painting anymore except that crap he does to sell deodorant or ready-mades. Not a piece of real work. I think he knows he'll never do anything serious again—unless he comes back here. When I said as much he damned near threw me out." Here she laughed bitterly. "At that, it was the only life he showed the whole time I was there. You know," she was musing now, "he might listen to you—but no one else."

Ignacio was silent. He struggled against the wild hope which fluttered inside him.

Another dry summer cost them half a dozen head of stock. Jamie prevailed on Sarah to let him sell a little more of the D Cross A, but this time, at least, the money went right back into the ranch, and the vaquero actually began to feel hopeful. With fewer sections under his stewardship, new breeding stock, and a pair of years without major shipments, there was a chance their fortunes might be revived.

Sure enough, within two seasons they had enough work to do to hire a hand. A happy-go-lucky boy from town named Jacky Begley moved into a makeshift place in the tack room. They wouldn't need another bunkhouse for a long time yet.

If Ignacio thought this slight upward trend in the affairs of the D Cross A would lift his spirits, he was mistaken. First, he had another dream about the wall which was a good deal worse than any in recent years. Then, he found that the new hand irritated him beyond endurance. It wasn't young Begley who was at fault; he was a decent enough youth. It was Ignacio. He caught himself apologizing for the D Cross A to Jacky and could have bitten his tongue. At any rate, the boy didn't seem to care.

To make matters worse, Jamie wasn't any help at all. The limp he had cultivated for so many years was real enough at last. The rancher couldn't ride, could hardly work some days. He couldn't move without the cane, and although the rider thought about the boy who cried "wolf," he knew the pain was genuine.

Then, Ignacio Ortiz, *vaquero*, was thrown from a not-very-difficult horse.

It was October, after a rare and wonderful wet summer. The cows at the eastern tank, the one near the highway, were fat as slugs. He was watching from the back of Taracea, the spotted pony who looked so much like Pavo and even more like Calico, while Jacky climbed the rocks above the tank with the .22 rifle in his hand. Every time they rode this way Jacky packed the slim gun along to pepper the little black ducks bobbing like toys on the surface of the tank. Ignacio never saw him hit one. Shooting into the reflection-filled water must be harder than it looked; Jacky never missed the cans and bottles he set up as targets in the yard of the D Cross A.

While the boy moved into position, Ignacio let his eye wander to the cows again. Maybe that was why he wasn't ready when the shot was fired. Without a warning toss of the head, the pony reared. The vaquero tried to snap the reins down in the old, sure, easy way that always came to him as naturally as breath itself, but as he did the left arm became a streak of flame, and his chest felt as if a rockslide had settled on it. Taracea spun into a lurching, four-footed buck—and what couldn't happen, happened. Ignacio fell. He sat in the dust while Taracea danced away. Sweat bathed his face like liquid fire, and he couldn't breathe at all.

He didn't want to talk of it to anyone, but there was no way to silence Jacky Begley. Three days later he yielded to Ann's arguments and let her take him in to see the doctor. Jamie even went with him inside the new clinic which was so different from Dr. Sam's old office. He had to wait in a small, cold room while the doctor took care of someone else, and he persuaded Jamie to leave him alone.

The doctor peered closely at the long strip of paper, while the nurse cleaned the jelly off his naked chest where she had taped the wires down a few moments earlier. "Well, Mr. Ortiz," the doctor said, "you've had one." A heart attack. Ignacio nodded.

"Not much I can tell you. We should run this through again after a decent length of time. Meanwhile, there's not a lot I can do for you. Don't see any danger at the moment, but, to be truthful, your age is against you. You can help yourself, though. Take life easy—no smoking—but, *this is most important*, don't get too tired or emotional. Live life on as even a keel as you can manage."

As Ignacio put his shirt on, he looked at the doctor squarely. "*Señor*," he said, "is it necessary to tell anyone else of this?"

"No, but remember what I said about your emotional balance."

As he left the clinic, he set to work on a plausible lie for Ann and Jamie.

Jamie hadn't spoken for a week. It wasn't the usual sulk Ignacio had grown accustomed to over the years, and he wondered if the man was actually sick. He hobbled about the compound, stopping every fifteen feet or so to lean on his cane as if he could never take another step. He kept at it, though, morning and afternoon, once going as far as the rock outcropping, a struggle which took the better part of an hour. He sat up there a long time. It made the rider think of the time Jamie had perched on the high lip of the arroyo while he had buried Angus; but there was a difference. This Jamie wasn't avoiding anything.

Rather, the man was exposing himself, Ignacio thought, gazing over the buildings of the D Cross A, the corral and holding pens, with a look which seemed to shout *mea culpa* into the bright air.

That night, after supper, when Jacky Begley had gone back to the tack room and the three of them were having coffee in front of the fire, he watched the rancher intently, no longer trying to disguise the look as he might have once. Several times Jamie seemed about to speak, but each time his mouth opened, he closed it again and shook his head. Ann was watching him, too, with the same tender look of the first days, the one the rider realized he had once begrudged the man.

Finally, Jamie sighed—a hollow sound with a weight of something. Sadness? Submission? "Jacky tells me he'll be drafted in another month."

"*Sí*, Jamie," Ignacio said.

"Have you looked for another hand?"

"Not yet."

"Well, Nash, I'd hold off on that for a bit."

"We will need someone, Jamie."

A peculiar shadow passed over Jamie's face. "Yeah," he said at last, "I guess we will, but hold off all the same."

Ignacio saw that the señora was as mystified as he was.

He tried to "take life easy" as the doctor ordered, but Jacky looked a little put upon, as if the rider were taking advantage of his last month, and he found himself in his old routine. Well, he felt good, and he *had* cut down on his smoking. As for the other, the "emotional balance," there was little to worry him on that score.

Life, which used to run as giddily as an arroyo torrent in the spring, had now dried up like a stream choked with ages of debris; it was unlikely any storm of passion would fill it to overflowing from here on out. The towering joys, the strong, corrosive sorrows he used to know, would never come again. All was mildness now, a quiet progress of days. There were echoes of the past, and they sounded back and forth faster then they ever had—but fainter.

Time was oddly dislocated, too. His thinking mind seemed to have one clock, his heart another. It was only yesterday the boy Ignacio had ridden wide-eyed into the Ojos Negros with Terry and the trail herd. Long before that, it seemed, he had been a man, known pain and suffering—and desire and its never-quite-complete satisfaction. He knew better, but his memory didn't work the way it should. Sometimes he was certain the sight on the malpais, the burning of Mex Town, and the destruction of the bunkhouse were all parts of the same occurrence. He laughed at himself when he thought like this, but the notion kept returning and it sobered him. Assuredly, the "time was out of joint." Well, unlike the tragic prince, he needn't curse. He, Ignacio, wasn't "born to set it right."

All that was left for him was to drift idly through what remained of life, taking what small enjoyment came his way. It wasn't a completely unpromising prospect. He could still ride the great reaches of the D Cross A.

Once, when he dismounted to rest his pony near the top of a rise in the north pasture, he looked toward big Cuchillo and the notch on its left which led to Las Sombras. A strange, small thought moved through his head with shuddering violence, as he thought of Douglas and the old señora up there, silent under their granite marker. "In a way, I have lied to you these many years, *señor*." He said it aloud, and the sound of it made him shake. Well, it was true. The unspoken vow made in the Black Springs plaza over fifty years before had been a useless one, unnecessary. *Without* such a promise he never would have left this land. The real, binding, crushing vow, the one which counted, was the one he had made himself, day by day, since first he came here.

His one eye looked freshly at the D Cross A after that. He never thought his love for the place could deepen, but it did. Without flinching, he faced the fact that Ian was never coming back. This was all he would ever have. It was enough.

When Jacky Begley left, the small, sealed world he had been unwittingly constructing suddenly came apart.

He went to Jamie for permission to look for another hand.

"No, Nash. I'm sorry," Jamie said. "I've decided to ask Sarah to let me sell the place, before it goes under by itself—and takes us with it."

He felt no anger toward James MacAndrews now. After the first shock had worn away, he told himself the new young doctor would be pleased with him, the way he had kept his emotions fully checked. Jamie talked of a house he had seen for sale in town, "just big enough for the three of us, walking distance from anything we'd want to do," and he felt real warmth toward the rancher for including him.

Somehow, he convinced himself, the sale and the move were all for the best—or thought he had. Then, on one last ride along the north side fence with Jacky before the youngster left, he suddenly broke away form the puzzled boy and rode pell-mell to the arroyo where Angus lay. He looked down at the cairn for a long, long time. It needed work. He was too tired to fix it now—he would come back up in another week.

He rode back to the main fence over land he suddenly remembered belonged to him, Ignacio Ortiz.

When Jacky left the next morning, the vaquero went along to bring back the horse he rode, as he had done for Ian.

"Well, old-timer," Jacky said, as they shook hands, "take care of yourself. I'll come out and see you when I'm home on furlough—if you're still here."

Ignacio Ortiz thought this over carefully before he said a word. *"I will be here,"* he said, finally. *"Verdad!"*

He didn't sleep that night. Near dawn, his throat dry and raw from too many cigarettes, eyes aching from staring into the darkness, he dressed and went outside. He paced up and down until exhaustion seized him and dropped him into the discarded truck seat in front of the shack, just as the sun leaped above the rimrock of Cuchillo. There was still an hour to wait before Ann was up and fixing breakfast.

Oh, how the doctor would take him to task for the night he had spent. The impatience he felt now as he prepared himself to talk with Jamie wasn't good for him, either, he supposed, but it didn't matter now. Ignacio Ortiz was going to bring the wasted years to a long overdue conclusion.

41

"IT'S NO USE, NASH!" JAMIE SAID. "I'LL ADMIT THAT EVERYTHING you've said—up to a point—makes sense, but it don't change the facts. We're just plain too damned old!" The despair in Jamie's voice, deep and final, didn't even dull the edge of the excitement which sustained the vaquero all through the argument. He resisted smiling at how shrewdly he had worked Jamie to this point, and it wasn't easy not to smile, watching Ann at the stove behind Jamie's back. He knew that the señora had seen where his talk was leading, and the look on her face made his worry at the way his heart beat worth every erratic flutter.

Yes, Jamie had agreed, the beef market was rising, and, yes, the grass was good, but—and his refusal stuck at just this one place—*they needed at least one good man*, not just for the heavy riding, but to take charge. Neither of them could do it anymore, and the kind of man they needed came too dear—if you could find him.

Ignacio looked at Ann. Yes, she understood. He held her eyes with his one good one until he saw her tiny nod. Then he drew a breath and plunged ahead.

"What if—" he said. He had to fight back the fear which rose. "What if—*Ian came back to the D Cross A?*"

For a fleeting second, when he saw the wounded look in James MacAndrews's eyes, he felt like a murderer. Nothing the man had ever done deserved this kind of punishment; but it had to be, and he pressed on. "Well, Jamie?"

The rancher closed his eyes, squeezed them shut. Tears rolled down cheeks which trembled. "He wouldn't come," Jamie said. The voice was so low the vaquero barely caught the words.

"But if he did, Jamie, if he did?"

"He—wouldn't come," Jamie said again.

As he packed the few things he needed, he came across the painting he had rescued from the fire in the bunkhouse. The frame was charred black, and even one corner of the canvas had suffered burns, but it was still worth saving. Well, as long as he was going to see Sarah before he went on to Chicago, he could have her fix it in her gallery. He sharpened his knife on the old whetstone Douglas had given him; the stone had a deep dish in it now from all the years he had wiped different blades across it. Carefully cutting the painting from the frame, he rolled it up and packed it in the suitcase Ann had lent him.

Sarah drove down from Taos to Albuquerque and met him there. From the bus station they went to the airport to see about his tickets. When he had telephoned her from Black Springs three days earlier (to make sure she didn't let Jamie sell the D Cross A before he returned), she had been horrified to learn he planned to make the trip by train.

"That is the way we went before, *muchachita*."

"My God, Nash! That was more than fifty years ago."

As it turned out, there was no time to go to Taos. The only space available for a week was on the next day's flight. They took rooms in a motel on Central Avenue, and the next morning Sarah took him to his plane.

Just before he boarded, she looked at him. "Don't count on this too much, vaquero."

"I cannot fail, *niña*."

Even with so much on his mind the flight was a marvel. Below him, as they climbed away from Albuquerque and over the Sandias, the arid land stretched away to a horizon lost in haze. Within the curve of the earth, the country was unbelievably flat, even the great mountains to the north and south were ripples on its surface. There seemed no texture to the land, and little color. As high as he had been on the side of Sierra Blanca or Cuchillo, the flat basin showed more character, more ruggedness than this.

If only he could sail high enough above the troubles which were besetting the D Cross A and its few remaining people, perhaps they, too, would roll out as featureless as the mosaic beneath him. Now, miles above the globe which turned below the airplane, he suddenly wondered what in the name of God he was doing on this journey. He put his hand on his chest, over the place where the faulty heart was said to be. This trip was, very likely, the worst thing he could have done, but he had really had no choice. And if he had, would he have chosen differently?

He was in Chicago two full days before Ian found him. Sarah had wanted to place a call to Ian, after the rider refused her offer to go along, but, for the same reason he wanted to make the trip alone, he insisted there would be value in surprise. The decision had been an error. In the office where Ian worked he found he was out of town, not expected for another day.

He thought of going to the Palmer House, but panicked at the memory of the huge hotel, and the prospect of how alone he would feel there now. A policeman sent him to a seedy looking place at the south end of the Loop. There were elevated train tracks just outside his window this time, too, and the noise and flashing sparks seemed even wilder than before.

It was a full day before he thought to call Ian's company and tell them where he was, a day of agonizing loneliness. Then, Ian called, concern and affection in his voice, and the vaquero was positive everything would be all right. He didn't remain in the room even five minutes after Ian's call. His things had never really been unpacked, and he grabbed the suitcase and walked down the four flights, of stairs rather than take the elevator he didn't understand. He paid his bill, and sat like a rock on a hard bench in the musty smelling, dirty lobby.

42

"WHAT SAY, *VIEJO*?" IAN MACANDREWS SAID, AS HE OPENED THE DRAPES of the apartment windows. "Where shall we eat tonight?"

"It makes no difference, Ian," Ignacio said, wearily. He had been in Chicago for a week, and they hadn't sat still for an hour. "We have been so many places, my poor head can't keep them straight."

"Well," Ian said, "you don't come to the big city every day, *amigo*. Don't know when I'll see you here in Chicago again."

Never, Ian, never, the rider thought.

Every beginning he had made with Ian had ended in frustration. The man knew why he was here, but each time he approached the issue, Ian shied from it like a calf from a cutting horse. There hadn't been the blink of an eye when the rider blurted out Jamie's terrible decision. He couldn't let it be the same way now.

"Ian—" He despised the pleading he heard in his voice. "Ian, could we not stay in tonight? I have still not said the things I came to say—about the ranch, the señora—and your father." Ian had that look again. He would twist, and dodge, and flee—if the vaquero let him. "Does it mean nothing at all to you that the D Cross A must soon be sold?"

"Get your hat, Ignacio. Let's go to supper," Ian said.

They ate at a Mexican restaurant near Ian's lakefront high-rise. "The *gringos* here think they're getting the real thing, Tío." The place was almost a caricature of the old Florida. Perhaps that was why Ian rushed through his meal. Suddenly Ignacio reached a decision.

"I think I will leave for home tomorrow, Ian."

"No, no, vaquero. Not quite yet. Stay a little longer."

"No, Ian. Tomorrow it must be *adiós*."

Ian was silent. Ignacio tried to meet his eyes, but couldn't find them. Finally the anglo spoke. "Well, if you must. But make it *hasta la vista*."

"No, Ian. As *you* said once, it has to be *adiós*."

It began to drizzle as they walked back to the apartment, the crowded, dirty streets shimmering a little under the lights of the heavy traffic. Neither of them said a word. As they walked, the vaquero sought store windows where he could see Ian's face reflected. He didn't want Ian to see him studying him directly. Perhaps he had already done too much of that this week.

He had been prepared for the sight of an Ian who was no longer young, but the dead eyes were still a shock to him. The face, pale under this weak northern sun, was as passive as a frozen pond. Sarah was right. This journey had been a waste of time.

When they entered Ian's hallway, the telephone was ringing. While Ian answered it, Ignacio walked to the big window which overlooked the lake. Down below him he could see the Outer Drive, diamond-studded in the dark. It was still raining. From here he couldn't hear the cars which moved so slowly. Somewhere on the lake itself a red light winked. Another time he might have enjoyed all this. All he felt now was an aching tiredness.

"No, I'm sorry, not tonight. Look, I said I'm sorry. Hell, Laurie, you knew it would be like this. A day or two, I guess. No, I won't rush him. Look, I'll call tomorrow. Good night. Yes—me too—good night." Ignacio heard the phone lowered none too gently to the cradle.

"Tío," Ian said. There was something more somber in the voice now.

"*Sí*, Ian?"

"Sit down, *viejo*—please."

The vaquero crossed from the window and sank into the couch which faced Ian's chair by the phone.

"I guess—since you're set on leaving—we'll have to have that talk you wanted. You aren't going to like my end of it, you know." Hope had fluttered up and crashed again.

"I know how much you want me to say I'll come back to the D Cross A," Ian said. "But I have to tell you straight out

I just can't do it." He looked up at the ceiling for a second, then back to the rider's face. "Can you honestly tell me my father's changed?"

Ignacio shook his head. "No, Ian," he said, "—but he is old. Maybe that will do as well."

"He'll never get old in any way that will make a difference."

"Maybe then *you* have changed, Ian. That would make a difference."

Ian stood up and walked to the window. "I guess I do owe you an explanation," he said, "—if you want to hear it."

"*Sí*, Ian. I want to hear anything you have to say."

"All right. Do you remember how I was when I left the ranch? Well, here there isn't any violence working in me. *Now*. It took me years to leave the D Cross A behind me—and the terror of what I might have done." He looked out the window again. "The life I have here isn't bad at all. I do my work, I see a woman from time to time—and I'm at peace. Not exciting, but it works. And, by Christ, I don't suffer, or see others suffer!"

"Ian." The man in front of Ignacio would never know how much it cost to say this. "You don't suffer—but you don't *live*." Ian turned and looked at him as the rider went on, "I do not see in this apartment one sign that you are painting."

Ian's face became a mask. "I think," he said, "we've now said all there is to say."

"*Sí*, Ian." Ignacio stood up. "I will pack tonight."

In the closet he found the battered suitcase of Jamie's that Ann had lent him. He laid it on the bed and tried to open it. Something was caught, jamming it, and he struggled with it before the bag swung wide. Wedged against one side was the painting of the unfinished house he meant to leave with Sarah. Well, it was not surprising he had forgotten it in all the haste and confusion.

He took it from the bag and unrolled it on the pillow. As he looked at it, his one eye blinking, he heard Ian's voice and realized the man was behind him, at the bedroom door. "One thing, vaquero," Ian was saying, "one thing that might make you feel better. Dad won't—" Ignacio turned and saw him staring at the painting.

"My God," Ian said. The words were soft enough to make a prayer, but when they came again, they were softer still,

"My God." Ignacio watched his face, saw the mask soften and fall away, saw the mouth work for breath.

The rider could hear the raindrops beat against the window in the other room, fully twenty feet away, lightly, to be sure, but each one a hammer blow to ears alerted for sounds as hidden as the beating of a heart.

"*Sí*, vaquero—Ignacio," Ian MacAndrews said, "I *will* come home."

43

SLEEP PADDED TOWARD IGNACIO ORTIZ LIKE A LION IN THE ROCKS, but he sniffed it out, and forced his good eye open even wider. It was imperative he see the headlights of the Cadillac the very first second they appeared. After that it might be too late. In the old days it would not have been so critical; he could have spotted them more than three miles down the south road. Nowadays anyone approaching the D Cross A came from the east, from the highway, and a rise shut off vision in that direction except for a stretch a quarter of a mile in length. When the car, *the car with Ian in it*, raced across that short span, the headlights would only be in sight for twenty or thirty seconds. Then they would drop into the low plain on the far side of the arroyo, completely hidden until they came around the butte. He must be ready with the generator at that very instant.

Ignacio lit another cigarette. If Ian's plane was on time in Albuquerque, they should have crossed the Chupadera County line an hour ago. At any second now, the lights should appear through the yucca and seek him out. They would be tired, Jamie in particular. By now his leg would be stiffening badly, and he would need the new crutches he had insisted on leaving by the kitchen door.

In the afternoon Ignacio had rushed through his chores so carelessly that at another time he would have blushed for shame. It had been like that to some degree ever since the letter arrived from Sarah, telling Ann and Jamie she would pick them up this morning and drive them to Albuquerque to meet their son.

It was right after the letter came that he dreamed up the surprise for Ian. It was a small, worthless thing and the others

314

would think it childish, but Ian would understand. He always did. With everybody gone, and the house, the stable, and the tack room in the best order he could manage and still leave time, he had worked feverishly to make everything ready. He had gone through all the buildings on the place, everywhere there was a light or motor, everywhere the wiring system reached. Anything which drew power not for light he had turned off or disconnected, but he made sure every source of illumination— every light in the house and the outbuildings—would burn with welcome when the gasoline-powered generator came to life.

He tested it once to see if the sudden heavy load would kick the system out. It worked, worked beautifully. He chuckled to himself then, as he pictured what he planned for Ian's eyes—the D Cross A ablaze with light. He debated whether he should work this foolish magic when the car was still behind the butte, or wait until he glimpsed the headlights a second time. The latter was the better choice, *sí*. From behind the butte they might see the glow against the sky, ruining the effect. This way, after driving through the blackness above the rangeland, it would be a revelation. He chuckled again, thinking about how whoever was at the wheel would have to stop, and wait until his eyes adjusted to the flood of light. *Dios!* He must be quick! He must pull the starter cord the instant they made the turn. It wouldn't do to have them blinded as they crossed the bridge.

Ignacio Ortiz was an incredibly happy man. But in the name of something, how he wished they would come! How long this week had been since Sarah's letter. In the past few years time had accelerated its already headlong rush, and he had been sure he would never again have the capacity for impatience, but this week had dragged in an agony of delay. Well, it was almost over, but the minutes crept by like ages. It seemed years since he left Chicago.

What an evening the last one had turned out to be. He and Ian had talked until four in the morning, first about things needing to be done at the D Cross A, and then about the best way to arrange Ian's return. They decided to continue the deception about Ignacio's trip. Ian still had fears about Jamie's attitude. So they called Sarah.

When she picked up the rider in Albuquerque, she had driven him to the ranch and stayed on a few days, and it was during this time she talked with Jamie. Finally, she came to the shack and said, "It's all right with Jamie, Nash. I'm convinced. I'll leave in the morning, call Ian from the first phone I reach, and then I'll write and let you all know the details." The vaquero hadn't seen her so happy since before Max died.

When Ann tore the letter open and read it, first to herself, and then to Jamie and Ignacio, her hands trembled. The rider watched Jamie, and felt that worst fear of all—the kind that always comes with hope. It only lasted for the briefest moment, before the look on the rancher's face banished it. It would be all right. If Ignacio had any doubts at all about the wisdom of his interfering, the sight of the señora all week had dispelled them without a trace. He could almost allow himself to think the fence was tight.

A star fell right in that section of the sky about the east road where he had fixed his eye, and it startled him. When he pulled his mind back to where he was and why he was waiting there he realized it had suddenly, and without warning, become quite cold. The wind had shifted to the north. He thought of going inside the shack for a moment, and decided against it. He couldn't leave this post even for a second.

It was good there was no moon. The surprise would be that much better, and it would keep his eye from wandering as it did on moonlit nights. If his eye didn't wander up toward Las Sombras his mind wouldn't either. There was no time now to think of anything except the future.

Why had he thought of Las Sombras? Douglas, of course, but Agnes and the others, too; Angus in his arroyo, and Jorge under the caliche of the Mex Town cemetery—they would have to rest quietly and let Ian go about rebuilding the D Cross A. It would be difficult enough without anyone remembering how things used to be. When the good work was well under way, maybe Ian and Ignacio could ride together to where all these shadows were, maybe there would then be time to seek the answers, and—

Wait! Was that something on the road, or were more stars playing tricks? Was it possible he had really seen them? *Sí!*

It well could be. There *was* that one high spot on the road where the lights might have been visible for just a moment before they reached the longer open space which would lead them to the butte. He strained his eye into the uneven desert darkness, his blood surged in a torrent, and he could hear the stepped up, insistent pounding of his heart. But had he really seen anything? Yes, yes! There they were again, the lights, unmistakable this time.

Ian MacAndrews was on the D Cross A.

Ahora, vaquero—it is time to move. He watched just until the lights disappeared behind the butte, willing the car to greater speed while a splendid turmoil raged inside his head. Then, he turned, breaking into a shuffling run as he moved toward the pumphouse door. *Dios!* Could the latch be stuck? Had he not checked even that small detail as he made his rounds this afternoon? Panic lent him extra strength as he wrenched the stubborn door open and propped it wide with the crowbar he had planted there. He moved inside, stumbling, his breath coming even faster. When he reached the engine he pulled the choke out full and grasped the handle of the starter cord, then turned back to look through the doorway to where the butte loomed dark against the sky. Nervous, he wrapped the starter cord several times around his wrist. There, it couldn't slip no matter what excitement seized him.

Ian is back! It could only be seconds now. The first faint glow at the edge of the butte was already hinting at the brighter light behind it. *Sí*, only seconds! *Ian is almost home.*

Then—the pain took charge. From the center of his chest it ran down his left arm in searing jumps to the very ends of his rigid fingers, and he felt the heart within him as it expanded like a thunderhead. Nausea tried to double him over, but he forced himself even more erect, and kept his eyes at the corner of the butte. His right hand, unaware of what was happening on the left, tightened its grip on the starter cord. The pain racked him more, and the swelling feeling in his chest grew stronger, and—

The headlights! IAN! He whipped the cord out swiftly to its entire length, and heard the engine wheeze—and cough—and start. The lights of the D Cross A came on like sunrise!

And Ignacio Ortiz began to fall. The pain was gone before he struck the floor and he didn't feel the impact. As he fell the light came brighter, whiteness everywhere—and a wall.

Now he was falling again, through a great bottomless well of light. It was a slow floating fall he knew would never end, taking him through a crowd of faces hovering just beyond the edge of recognition, but they drifted downward with him, and he knew he would know them soon. He knew where he was going.

Back, way back, past Ramos and the mission, to the village. . . .

DESTINOS

It was too small to have a name; some called it "*aldea* Aguilar," because of the great hacienda surrounding it, or, simply, "*las casas.*" It was just a cluster of adobe houses at the crossing of the main road to Casas Grandes and the *camino* which ran from Don Sebastian's *estancia* to the fields.

Not many were in the fields that summer day in 1897 when El Sapo and his mounted band rode into the *plazuela*. It was still a month until the harvest, and even Alejandro Ortiz, *mozo de caballos* for Don Sebastian, was taking a *siesta* in his house.

Ignacio and the other boys who sat on the rim of the village well had known the bandit chieftain's name as long as any of them could remember, but none of them had seen El Sapo until that day. It was easy to see how the name had come about. He looked like a toad. The squat body was jammed into a dirty, high-cantled saddle, and above his thick neck a darkly mottled, warty face held a pair of bulging eyes which blinked. Ignacio stared at the *jefe* while the other boys leaped to hold the horses.

A few of the villagers and their women came out of their houses, and in the time it took for the horses to fill their bellies at the trough, the tiny square filled with people.

"*Usted! Señora!*" El Sapo croaked, pointing a finger at the mother of Juan Guerra, Ignacio's special friend, "My men and I need food—and wine. Bring it, *pronto!*" He added, "*Por favor,*" but in spite of the grotesque, almost comic smile, Ignacio doubted if he meant it.

319

Señora Guerra didn't hesitate. She ran to her house, calling to some of the other women, who disappeared as quickly. Within minutes a feast was spread before El Sapo and his men, and the armed riders sat in the dust and ate and drank. The sun glinted from the bandoliers crossed on their sweaty shirts. The village boys held the horses quiet while the bandits gorged themselves.

When the meal was finished El Sapo belched and smiled at the gathered crowd. "We have provided fine entertainment, have we not, *amigos*?" He patted his bulging stomach. "Now it is time to pay the actors. *Dinero, por favor*—some from every *casa*."

It was more like play than violence. Making jokes and smiling, the raiders moved through the crowd, their high-crowned sombreros doffed and held in front of them to take the money and trinkets which fell like contributions, not like loot. Some of the villagers had stayed inside, and when the collectors reached a door which had not been opened, they crashed their rifle butts against it until the frightened householder showed his face. It went a bit harder on these reluctant ones, but it still seemed more like holiday than terror. Then, Ignacio realized he hadn't seen his father in the crowd. His eyes went to the door of the whitewashed adobe only seconds before El Sapo's henchmen reached it. He knew when the door was shut that tightly it was bolted fast inside. A movement at the window told him his mother was pulling the kitchen curtain shut, and he knew the men approaching had seen the movement, too. He might have known that the father who feared neither horse nor man wouldn't surrender his pittance easily.

It was a sturdy door, and it took three of the bandits a full ten minutes to knock it from its hinges. Then, Alejandro Ortiz, his wife, Ana, and the twin girls younger than Ignacio by a year, were in the street, blinking against the sun which beat the white adobe wall until it shrieked with light. Two of the riders held Ortiz, a third struck him hard across the mouth, and another pair went inside the house. It didn't take them long to find the few things of value it contained. He could hear the thieves cry out when they found the bit of money his mother kept in the water *olla* in the kitchen.

Then, El Sapo, still smiling, was in the saddle once again. He called to his men to mount, and in seconds they were on their horses, circling the *plazuela*, waving their sombreros in salute. A sigh rose from the crowd as the band headed away from the well, toward the *camino* which led to the fields and the hills beyond.

They still had to pass Ignacio's house once more, and as they reached it, El Sapo raised his hand and the horses stopped.

The firing of the rifles, furious as it was, took far less time than it took the echoes to die away.

Ignacio found himself running, running hard, seeming never to close the gap between himself and the plunging, snorting horses. Smoke and dust hid things from him as he ran. He couldn't breathe, it was so thick and choking. It was an age before he reached El Sapo. He leaped, clawing at the gross body atop the horse, not seeing the rider next to the *jefe* swing his rifle by the barrel—scarcely feeling the impact on his head. Then he was falling, falling freely through a great, bottomless well of light, and the mounted men were gone, galloping away to the hills, sucking the dust behind them, pulling it in their wake as if a curtain had been jerked aside.

He lay in the dirt and dust. When he lifted his battered head he could see everything quite clearly. He could see the wall. He could see the awful wall and the bodies beneath it.

Ignacio's mother, Ana, was stretched out beside her husband and the little girls. Under the brown flesh which curved from neck to breast, a swamp of blood was rising. Before the rifles had stilled the pulse, she must have clapped her hand across her throat, and raked the wall with bloody fingers. Five streaks ran burning to her body where it lay.

White unconsciousness took possession of the boy Ignacio.

* * *

The man Ignacio, vaquero of the D Cross A, knows the fall is coming to an end. *Bueno!* His life is now his own—in its entirety.

Sarah MacAndrews Balutan stopped the car at the shack. When there was no answer to her call, she got out and looked for the vaquero. Seeing the pumphouse door standing open, she went to it immediately.

Ignacio Ortiz lay on his back, mouth and eyes wide open. His right hand, which had gripped the reins of scores of forgotten and remembered ponies, was twisted in the starter cord of the engine which ran the generator. Vibrations from the engine twitched the arm in a counterfeit of life.

Sarah looked at the vaquero for a long moment, then turned and walked slowly back to where the car was idling in front of the rider's shack. She leaned inside and spoke to the aged man and woman sitting there.

"Well, one thing is taken care of." Her voice was very low, and they had to bend forward to catch her words. "We won't have to tell him that Ian didn't come."

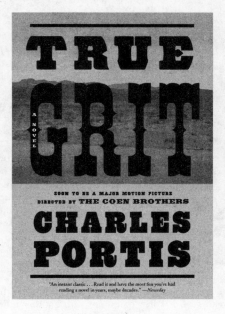
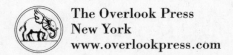

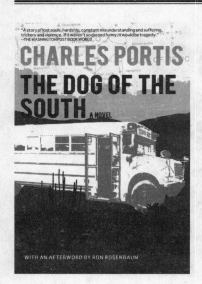

"A story of lost souls, hardship, constant misunderstanding and suffering, trickery and violence. If it weren't so darned funny, it would be tragedy."
—THE WASHINGTON POST BOOK WORLD

CHARLES PORTIS
THE DOG OF THE SOUTH A NOVEL

WITH AN AFTERWORD BY RON ROSENBAUM

The Dog of the South
978-1-58567-931-7

"Charles Portis is the greatest writer you've never head of."
—*The Boston Herald*

'Charles Portis is perhaps the most original, indescribable sui generis talent overlooked by literary culture in America' Esquire 'Hilarious and heart breakingly odd you find yourself laughing so hard in sections that tears run down your face' Baltimore Sun 'The funniest novel in decades'
—GQ

Hapless, rhetorically challenged Ray Midge would more than fulfill any novel's quota for comic creation. But Portis pairs him with another indelible nutter, Dr. Reo Symes. A font of dubious financial schemes, Symes attaches himself to Ray like a peevish, passive-aggressive Pancho Sanza, and his non-sequitur-studded riffs must be heard to be believed:

> I always tried to help Leon and you see the thanks I got. I hired him to drive for me right after his rat died. He was with the Murrell Brothers Shows at that time, exhibiting a fifty-pound rat from the sewers of Paris, France. Of course it didn't really weigh fifty pounds and it wasn't your true rat and it wasn't from Paris, France, either. It was some kind of animal from South America. Anyway, the thing died and I hired Leon to drive for me. I was selling birthstone rings and vibrating jowl straps from door to door and he would let me out at one end of the block and wait on me at the other end.

The vibrating jowl straps are the kicker here, of course. But it's the overall futility of the enterprise that gives Symes his comic potency, and makes him Ray's natural companion in arms. Neither of these guys is going to accomplish anything: they're Beckett clowns in Sansabelt trousers, too enervated by the heat even to agonize. Still, you won't find a more delicious (or less reliable) narrator in contemporary fiction, and Charles Portis's genius for inventing all-American eccentrics is anything but futile.

—James Marcus

The Overlook Press
New York
www.overlookpress.com